His
Not-So-Blushing
Bride

KAT CANTRELL

ANNA DEPALO

FIONA BRAND

MILLS & BOON

First Published in Great Britain 2016
By Mills & Boon, an imprint of HarperCollins*Publishers*
1 London Bridge Street, London, SE1 9GF

HIS NOT-SO-BLUSHING BRIDE © 2016 Harlequin Books S. A.

Marriage With Benefits, *Improperly Wed* and *A Breathless Bride* were first published in Great Britain by Harlequin (UK) Limited.

Marriage With Benefits © 2013 Katrina Williams
Improperly Wed © 2011 Anna DePalo
A Breathless Bride © 2012 Fiona Gillibrand

ISBN: 978-0-263-92081-9

05-0916

Our policy is to use papers that are natural, renewable and recyclable products and made from wood grown in sustainable forests. The logging and manufacturing processes conform to the legal environmental regulations of the country of origin.

Printed and bound in Spain
by CPI, Barcelona

MARRIAGE WITH BENEFITS

BY
KAT CANTRELL

Kat Cantrell read her first Mills & Boon novel in primary school and has been scribbling in notebooks since she learned to spell. What else would she write but romance? She majored in literature, officially with the intent to teach, but somehow ended up buried in middle management at Corporate America, until she became a stay-at-home mum and full-time writer.

Kat, her husband and their two boys live in north Texas. When she's not writing about characters on the journey to happily-ever-after, she can be found at a football game, watching the TV show *Friends* or listening to eighties music.

Kat was the 2011 So You Think You Can Write winner and a 2012 RWA Golden Heart finalist for best unpublished series contemporary manuscript.

This one is for you, Mom.
Thanks for sharing your love of books with me.

One

Other single, twenty-five-year-old women dreamed of marriageable men and fairy-tale weddings, but Dulciana Allende dreamed of a divorce.

And Lucas Wheeler was exactly the man to give it to her.

Cia eyed her very male, very blond and very broad-shouldered target across the crowded reception hall. The display of wealth adorning the crush between her and Lucas bordered on garish. A doddering matron on her left wore a ring expensive enough to buy a year's worth of groceries for the women's shelter where Cia volunteered.

But then, if Cia had the natural ability to coax that kind of cash out of donors, she wouldn't be here in the middle of a Dallas society party, where she clearly did not belong, about to put plan B into action.

There was no plan C.

She knocked back the last swallow of the froufrou drink some clueless waiter had shoved into her hand. After she'd put considerable effort into securing a last-minute invitation to Mrs. Wheeler's birthday party, the least she could do was play along and drink whatever lame beverage the Black Gold Club pretended had alcohol in it. If she pulled off this negotiation, Mrs. Wheeler would be her future mother-in-law, and Cia did want to make a favorable impression.

Well, Mrs. Wheeler was also her future ex-mother-in-law, so perhaps the impression didn't matter overly much.

A guy near the bar tried to catch her eye, but she kept walking. Tonight, she cared about only one man and, conveniently, he stood next to his mother greeting guests. Cia's unfamiliar heels and knee-binding slim dress slowed her trek across the room. Frustrating but fortunate, since a giraffe on roller blades had her beat in the grace department.

"Happy birthday, Mrs. Wheeler." Cia shook the hand of the stylish, fifty-something woman and smiled. "This is a lovely party. Dulciana Allende. Pleased to meet you."

Mrs. Wheeler returned the smile. "Cia Allende. My, where has the time gone? I knew your parents socially. Such a tragedy to lose them at the same time." She clucked maternally.

Cia's smile faltered before she could catch it. Of course Mrs. Wheeler had known her parents. She just didn't know Cia's stomach lurched every time someone mentioned them in passing.

"Lucas, have you met Cia?" Mrs. Wheeler drew him forward. "Her grandfather owns Manzanares Communications."

Cia made eye contact with the man she planned to marry and fell headfirst into the riptide of Lucas Wheeler in the flesh. He was so…everything. Beautiful. Dynamic. Legendary. Qualities the internet couldn't possibly convey via fiber-optic lines.

"Miz Allende." Lucas raised her hand to his lips in an old-fashioned—and effective—gesture. And set off a whole different sort of lurch, this time someplace lower. *No, no, no.* Attraction was not acceptable. Attraction unsettled her, and when she was unsettled, she came out with swords drawn.

"Wheeler." She snatched her hand from his in a hurry. "I don't believe I've ever met anyone who so closely resembles a Ken doll."

His mother, bless her, chatted with someone else and thankfully didn't hear Cia's mouth working faster than her brain. Social niceties weren't her forte, especially when it came to men. How had she fooled herself into believing she could do this?

Lucas didn't blink. Instead, he swept her from head to toe with a slow, searching glance that teased a hot flush along her skin. With an amused arch to one brow, he said, "Lucky for me I've got one up on Ken. I bend all sorts of ways."

Her breath gushed out in a flustered half laugh. She did not want to like him. Or to find him even remotely attractive. She'd picked him precisely because she assumed she wouldn't. As best as she could tell from the articles she'd read, he was like the Casanovas she'd dated in college, pretty and shallow.

Lucas was nothing but a good-time guy who happened to be the answer to saving hundreds of women's lives. This marriage would help so many people, and just in case that wasn't enough of a reason for him to agree to her deal, she'd come armed with extra incentives.

That reassuring thought smoothed out the ragged hitch to her exhale. Refocusing, she pasted on a smile. His return smile bolstered her confidence. Her business with Lucas Wheeler was exactly that—business. And if she knew anything, it was business. If only her hands would stop shaking. "To be fair, you do look better in a suit than Ken."

"Now, I'd swear that sounded like a compliment." He leaned in a little and cocked his head. "If our parents knew each other, how is it we've never met?"

His whiskey-drenched voice stroked every word with a lazy Texas drawl that brought to mind cowboys, long, hard rides in the saddle and heat. She met his smoky blue eyes squarely and locked her knees. "I don't get out much."

"Do you dance?" He nodded to the crowded square of teak hardwood, where guests swayed and flowed to the beat of the jazz ensemble playing on a raised stage.

"Not in public."

Something flittered across his face, and she had the impression he'd spun a private-dance scenario through his head. Lips pursed, he asked, "Are you sure we haven't met before?"

"Positive."

And Cia wished circumstances had conspired differently to continue their mutual lack of acquaintance. Men like Lucas—expert at getting under a woman's skin right before they called it quits—were hazardous to someone who couldn't keep her heart out of it, no matter what she promised herself.

But she'd make any sacrifice necessary to open a new women's shelter and see her mother's vision realized. Even marrying this man who radiated sensuality like a vodka commercial laced with an aphrodisiac. "We're only meeting now because I have a proposition for you."

A slow, lethal smile spilled across his face. "I like propositions."

Her spine tingled, and that smile instantly became the thing she liked least about Lucas Wheeler. It was too dangerous, and he didn't hesitate to wield it. *Dios,* did she detest being disconcerted. Especially by a man she hoped to marry platonically. "It's not that kind of proposition. Not even close. I cannot stress enough how far removed it is from what that look in your eye says you assume."

"Now I'm either really interested or really not interested." Smoothly, he tapped his lips with a square-cut nail and sidled closer, invading her space and enveloping her with his woodsy, masculine scent. "I can't decide which."

The man had the full package, no question. Women didn't throw themselves at his feet on a regular basis because he played a mean hand of Texas hold 'em.

"You're interested," she told him and stepped back a healthy foot. He couldn't afford not to be, according to her meticulous research. She'd sifted through dozens of potential marriage candidates and vetted them all through her best friend, Courtney, before settling on this one.

Of course, she hadn't counted on him somehow hitting spin cycle on her brain.

"So," she continued, "I'll get right to it. Hundreds of women suffer daily from domestic abuse, and my goal is to help them escape to a place where they can build new lives apart from the men using them for punching bags. The shelters in this area are packed to the brim, and we need another one. A big one. An expensive one. That's where you come in."

They'd already taken in more bodies than the existing shelter could hold, and it was only a matter of time before the occupancy violation became known. Lucas Wheeler was going to change the future.

A shutter dropped over Lucas's expression, and he shook his head. "My money is not subject to discussion. You're barking up the wrong sugar daddy."

"I don't want your money. I have my own. I just have to get my hands on it so I can build the shelter my way, without any benefactors, investors or loans."

She flinched a little at her tone. *What* about this man brought out her claws?

"Well, darlin'. Sounds like I'm unnecessary, then. If you decide to go in the other direction with your proposition, feel free to look me up." Lucas edged away, right into the sights of a svelte socialite in a glittery, painted-on dress, who'd clearly been waiting for the most eligible male in the place to reject her competition.

"I'm not finished." Cia crossed her arms and followed him, shooting a well-placed glare at Ms. Socialite. She wisely retreated to the bar. "The money is tied up in my trust fund. In order to untie it, I have to turn thirty-five, which is nearly a decade away. Or get married. If my husband files for divorce, as long as the marriage lasts at least six months, the money's mine. You're necessary since I'd like you to be that husband."

Lucas chuckled darkly and, to his credit, didn't flinch. "Why is every woman obsessed with money and marriage? I'm actually disappointed you're exactly like everyone else."

"I'm nothing like everyone else." Other women tried to keep husbands. She wanted to get rid of one as soon as possible, guaranteeing she controlled the situation, not the other way around. Getting rid of things before they sank barbs into her heart was the only way to fly. "The difference here is you need me as much as I need you. The question is can you admit it?"

He rolled his eyes, turning them a hundred different shades of blue. "That's a new angle. I'm dying to hear this one."

"Sold any big-ticket properties lately, Wheeler?"

Instantly, he stiffened underneath his custom-made suit, stretching it across his shoulders, and she hated that she noticed. He was well built. So what? She had absolute control of her hormones, unlike his usual female companions. His full package wasn't going to work on her.

"What's real estate got to do with your trust fund?"

She shrugged. "You're in a bit of a fix. You need to shore up your reputation. I need a divorce. We can help each other, and I'll make it well worth your while."

No other single male in the entire state fit her qualifications, and, honestly, she didn't have the nerve to approach another stranger. She scared off men pretty quickly, which saved her a lot of heartache, but left her with zero experience in working her feminine wiles. That meant she had to offer something her future husband couldn't refuse.

"Hold up, sweetheart." Lucas signaled a waiter, snagged two drinks from the gilded tray and jerked his head. "You've got my attention. For about another minute. Let's take this outside. I have a sudden desire for fresh air. And double-plated armor for that shotgun you just stuck between my ribs."

Lucas could almost feel the bite of that shotgun as he turned and deftly sidestepped through the crowd.

His brother, Matthew, worked a couple of local businessmen, no doubt on the lookout for a possible new client, and glanced up as Lucas passed. The smarmy grin on Matthew's face said volumes about Lucas's direction and the woman with him.

Lucas grinned back. Had to keep up appearances, after all. A hard and fast quickie on the shadowed balcony did smack of his usual style, but it was the furthest thing from his mind.

The gorgeous—and nutty—crusader with the intriguing curtain of dark hair followed him to the terrace at the back of the club. By the time he'd set down the pair of drinks, she'd already sailed through the door without waiting for him to open it.

Lucas sighed and retrieved the glasses, seriously considering downing both before joining the Spanish curveball on the balcony. But his mama had raised him better than that.

"Drink?" He offered one to Cia, and surprise, surprise, she took it.

Twenty-five stories below, a siren cut through the muted sounds of downtown Dallas, and cool March air kissed the back of his hot neck. If nothing else, he'd escaped the stuffy ballroom. But he had a hunch he'd left behind the piranhas in favor of something with much sharper teeth.

"Thanks. Much better than the frilly concoction I got last round." She sipped the bourbon and earned a couple of points with him. "So. Now that I have your attention, listen carefully. This is strictly a business deal I'm offering. We get married in name only, and in six months, you file for divorce. That's it. Six months is plenty of time to rebuild your reputation, and I get access to my trust fund afterward."

Reputation. If only he could laugh and say he didn't care what other people thought of him.

But he was a Wheeler. His great-great-grandfather had founded Wheeler Family Partners over a century ago and almost single-handedly shaped the early north Texas landscape. Tradition, family and commerce were synonymous with the Wheeler name. Nothing else mattered.

"You're joking, right?" He snorted as a bead of sweat slid between his shoulder blades. "My reputation is fine. I'm not hard up for a magic wand, thanks."

The little bundle of contradictions in the unrevealing, yet oddly compelling, dress peered up steadily through sooty lashes. "Really, Wheeler? You're gonna play that card? If this fake marriage is going to work, know this. I don't kowtow to the Y chromosome. I won't hesitate to tell you how it is or how it's going to be. Last, and not least, I do my research. You lost the contract on the Rose building yesterday, so don't pretend your clients aren't quietly choosing to do business with another firm where the partners keep their pants zipped. Pick a different card."

"I didn't know she was married."

Brilliant, Wheeler. Astound her with some more excuses. Better yet, tell her how great Lana had been because she only called occasionally, suggested low-key, out-of-the-way places to eat and never angled to stay overnight. In hindsight, he'd been a class A idiot to miss the signs.

"But she was. I'm offering you some breathing room. A chance to put distance and time between you and the scandal, with a nice, stable wife who will go away in six months. I insist on a prenup. I'm not asking you to sleep with me. I'm not even asking you to like me. Just sign a piece of paper and sign another one in six months."

Breathing room. Funny. He'd never been less able to breathe than right now. His temple started throbbing to the muted beat of the music playing on the other side of the glass.

Even a fake marriage would have ripples, and no way could it be as easy as a couple of signatures. Mama would have a coronary if he so much as breathed the word *divorce* after giving her a daughter-in-law. She'd dang near landed in the hospital after her first daughter-in-law died, even though Amber and Matthew had barely been married a year.

A divorce would set his gray-sheep status in stone, and he'd been killing himself to reverse the effects of his monumental lapse in judgment with Lana. Why eliminate what little progress he'd achieved so far?

The other temple throbbed. "Darlin', you're not my type. Conquistador Barbie just doesn't do it for me."

The withering scowl she leveled at him almost pared back his skin. "That's the beauty of this deal. There's no chance of being tempted to turn this physical. No messy ties. It's a business agreement between respected associates with a finite term. I can't believe you're balking at this opportunity."

Because it was *marriage*. Marriage was a "someday" thing, a commitment he'd make way, way, way in the future, once he found the right woman. He'd be giving this stranger his name, sharing his daily life with her.

And of course, he'd be married, the opposite of single. "For the record, I'm wounded to learn my temptation factor is zero. It can't be as simple as you're making it out to be. What if someone finds out it's not real? Will you still get the money?"

"No one will find out. I'm not going to tell anyone. You're not going to tell anyone. We only have to fake being madly in love once or twice around other people so my grandfather buys it. Behind closed doors, we can do our own thing."

Madly in love. Faking that would be a seriously tall order when he'd never been so much as a tiny bit in love. "Why can't you have the money unless you get divorced? That's the weirdest trust clause I've ever heard."

"Nosy, aren't you?"

He raised a brow. "Well, now, darlin', you just proposed to me. I'm entitled to a few questions."

"My grandfather is old-fashioned. When my parents died…" Her lips firmed into a flat line. "He wants me to be taken care of, and in his mind, that means a husband. I'm supposed to fall in love and get married and have babies,

not get a divorce. The money is a safety net in case the husband bails, one I put considerable effort into convincing my
grandfather to include."

"Your grandfather has met you, right?" He grinned. "Five
minutes into our acquaintance, and I would never make the
mistake of thinking you can't look after yourself. Why thirty-
five? You don't strike me as one to blow your trust fund on
cocaine and roulette."

"I donated all the money I inherited from my parents to
the shelter where I work," she snapped, as if daring him to
say something—anything—about it. "And don't go thinking
I'm looking for handouts. My grandfather set up the trust and
deposits the considerable interest directly into my bank account. I have more than enough to live on, but not enough to
build a shelter. He's hoping I'll lose enthusiasm for battered
women by thirty-five."

"Well, that's obviously not going to happen."

"No. And I don't enjoy being manipulated into marriage."
She tightened the lock of her crossed arms. "Look, it's not
like I'm asking you to hurt puppies or put your money into
a pyramid scheme. This is going to save lives. Women who
suffer domestic abuse have nowhere to go. Most of them don't
have much education and have to work to feed their kids.
Consider it charity. Or are you too selfish?"

"Hey now. I'm on the Habitat for Humanity board. I tithe
my ten percent. Give me a break."

Good button to push, though, because against his will,
wheels started turning.

Six months wasn't too much of a sacrifice for the greater
good, was it? Abuse was a terrible evil, and a charity that
helped abuse victims was well worth supporting. He took in
Cia's fierce little form and couldn't help but wonder what had
sparked all that passion. Did she reserve it for crusading or
did she burn this brightly in other one-on-one situations, too?

Through the glass separating the balcony from the ballroom, he watched his grandparents slow dance in the midst of

his parents' friends. Could he make this fake marriage work and protect his family from divorce fallout at the same time? He couldn't deny how far a nice, stable wife might go toward combating his problems with Lana's husband. Probably not a bad idea to swear off women for a while anyway. Maybe if he kept Cia away from his family as much as possible, Mama would eventually forget about the absentee daughter-in-law.

No. No way. This whole setup gave him hives.

Mama would never let him keep a wife squirreled away, no matter what he intended. Cia could find someone else to marry, and together he and Matthew would straighten out the kinks in Wheeler Family Partners' client list. "As...interesting as all this sounds, afraid I'll have to pass."

"Not so fast." Her gaze pierced him with a prickly, no-nonsense librarian thing. "I'm trusting you with this information. Don't disappoint me or you'll spend the next six months tied up in court. My grandfather is selling the cell phone division of Manzanares and moving the remainder of the business to a smaller facility. I'm sure you're familiar with his current location?"

Four buildings surrounding a treed park, centrally located and less than ten years old. Designed by Brown & Worthington in an innovative, award-winning Mediterranean/modern architectural mix. Approximately three million square feet with access to the DART light-rail.

"Slightly."

"My grandfather would be thrilled to give the exclusive sales contract for the complex to my husband."

She waited, but calculations had already scrolled through his head.

The commission on Manzanares beat the Rose building by quadruple. And the prestige—it could lead to other clients for Wheeler Family Partners, and instead of being the Wheeler who'd screwed up, he'd be the family's savior.

Out of nowhere, the fifty-pound weight sitting on his chest

rolled off. "If I went so far as to entertain this insane idea, can I call you Dulciana?"

"Not if you expect me to answer. My name is Cia, which, incidentally, sounds nothing like *darling,* so take note. Are you in or out?"

He had to tell her *now?* Evidently Cia did not subscribe to the Lucas Wheeler Philosophy of Life—anything worth doing was worth taking the time to do right. "Why me?"

"You may play the field well and often, but research shows you treat women with respect. That's important to me. Also, everything I've read says you'll keep your word, a rare commodity. I can't be the one to file for divorce so I have to trust you will."

Oddly, her faith touched him. But the feeling didn't sit well. "Don't you have a boyfriend or some other hapless male in your life you can railroad into this?"

"There's no one else. In my experience, men have one primary use." She let her gaze rove over him suggestively, and the atmosphere shifted from tense to provocative. Hidden terrace lighting played over her features, softening them, and that unrevealing dress dangled the promise of what she'd hidden under it.

Then she finished the sentiment. "To move furniture."

That's why this exotically beautiful woman didn't have a boyfriend stashed somewhere. Any guy sniffing around Miz Allende had to want it bad enough to work for it. Nobody was worth that much effort, not even this ferocious little crusader with the mismatched earrings who'd waltzed into the Black Gold Club and walked across the room with a deliberate, slow gait he'd thoroughly enjoyed watching. "You win. I'll call you Cia."

Her brows snapped together. "Throw down your hand, Wheeler. You've got nothing to lose and everything to gain by marrying me. Yes or no?"

She was all fire and passion, and it was a dirty shame she seemed hell-bent on keeping their liaison on paper. But he usually liked his women uncomplicated and easygoing, so treating this deal as business might be the better way to go.

He groaned. At what point had he started to buy into this lunatic idea of a fake-but-pretend-it's-real marriage to a woman he'd just met? Call him crazy, but he'd always imagined having lots of sex with the woman he eventually married…way, way, way in the future.

If he pursued her, he'd have to work hard to get Miz Allende into bed, which didn't sound appealing in the least, and the deal would be difficult enough.

Business only, then, in exchange for a heap of benefits.

The Manzanares contract lay within his grasp. He couldn't pass up the chance to revitalize his family's business. Yeah, Matthew would be right there, fighting alongside Lucas no matter what, but he shouldn't have to be. The mess belonged to Lucas alone, and a way to fix it had miraculously appeared.

"No," he said.

"No?" Cia did a fair impression of a big-mouth bass. "As in you're turning me down?"

"As in I don't kowtow to the X chromosome. You want to do business, we'll do it in my office tomorrow morning. Nine sharp." Giving him plenty of time to do a little reconnaissance so he could meet his future wife-slash-business-partner toe-to-toe. Wheelers knew how to broker a deal. "With lawyers, without alcohol, and darlin', don't be late."

Her face went blank, and the temperature dropped at least five degrees. She nodded once. "Done."

Hurricane Cia swept toward the door, and he had no doubt the reprieve meant he stood in the eye of the storm. No problem. He'd load up on storm-proof, double-plated armor in a heartbeat if it meant solving all his problems in one shot.

Looked like he was going to make an effort after all.

Two

Cia had been cooling her heels a full twenty minutes when Lucas strolled into the offices of Wheeler Family Partners LLC at 9:08 a.m. the next morning. Renewed anger ate through another layer of her stomach lining. She'd had to ask Courtney to cover her responsibilities at the shelter to attend this meeting, and the man didn't have the courtesy to be on time. He'd pay for that. Especially after he'd ordered her not to be late in that high-handed, deceptively lazy drawl.

"Miz Allende." Lucas nodded as if he often found women perched on the edge of the leather couch in the waiting area. He leaned on the granite slab covering the receptionist's desk. "Helena, can you please reschedule the nine-thirty appraisal and send Kramer the revised offer I emailed you? Give me five minutes to find some coffee, and then show Miz Allende to my office."

The receptionist smiled and murmured her agreement. Her eyes widened as Cia stalked up behind Lucas. The other women often found on Lucas's couch must bow to the master's bidding.

Cia cleared her throat, loudly, until he faced her. "I've got other activities on my agenda today, Wheeler. Skip the coffee, and I'll follow *you* to your office."

Inwardly, she cringed. Not only were her feminine wiles out of practice, she'd let Lucas get to her. She couldn't keep being so witchy or he'd run screaming in the other direction long before realizing the benefits of marrying her.

If only he'd stop being so…Lucas for five minutes, maybe she'd be able to bite her tongue.

Lucas didn't call her on it, though. He just stared at her, evaluating. Shadows under his lower lashes deepened the blue of his irises, and fatigue pulled at the sculpted lines of his face. Her chin came up. Carousing till all hours, likely. He probably always looked like that after rolling out of some socialite's bed, where he'd done everything but sleep.

Not her problem. Not yet anyway.

Without a blink, he said, "Sure thing, darlin'. Helena, would you mind?"

He smiled gratefully at the receptionist's nod and ushered Cia down a hall lined with a lush Turkish rug over espresso hardwood. Pricey artwork hung on the sage walls and lent to the moneyed ambience of the office. Wheeler Family Partners had prestige and stature among the elite property companies in Texas, and she prayed Lucas cared as much as she assumed he did about preserving his heritage, or her divorce deal would be dead on arrival.

She had to convince him to say yes. Her mother's tireless efforts on behalf of abused women must reach fruition.

They passed two closed doors, each with name plaques reading Robert Wheeler and Andrew Wheeler, respectively. The next door was open. Lucas's office reflected the style of the exterior. Except he filled his space with a raw, masculine vibe the second he crossed the threshold behind her, crowding her and forcing her to retreat.

Flustered, she dropped into the wingback chair closest to

the desk. She had to find her footing here. But how did one go about bloodlessly discussing marriage with a man who collected beautiful women the way the shore amassed seashells?

Like it's a business arrangement, she reminded herself. Nothing to get worked up over. "My lawyer wasn't able to clear her morning schedule. I trust we can involve her once we come to a suitable understanding."

Actually, she hadn't called her lawyer, who was neck-deep in a custody case for one of the women at the shelter. There was no way she could've bothered Gretchen with a proposal Lucas hadn't even agreed to yet.

"Lawyers are busy people," Lucas acknowledged and slid into the matching chair next to Cia instead of manning the larger, more imposing one behind the desk.

She set her back teeth together. What kind of reverse power tactic was that supposed to be?

He fished a leather bag from the floor and pulled a sheaf of papers from the center pocket, which he then handed to her. The receptionist silently entered with steaming coffee, filling the room with its rich, roasted smell. She passed it off and exited.

With a look of pure rapture stealing over his face, Lucas cupped the mug and inhaled, then drank deeply with a small moan. "Perfect. Do you think I could pay her to come live with me and make my coffee every morning?"

Cia snorted to clear the weird little tremor in her throat. Did he do everything with abandon, as if the simplest things could evoke such pleasure? "She'd probably do it for free. You know, if there were other benefits."

Shut up. Why did the mere presence of this man turn her stupid?

"You think?" Lucas swept Cia with a once-over. "Would you?"

"Ha. The other benefits couldn't possibly be good enough

to warrant making coffee. You're on your own." Her eyes trailed over the sheaf of papers in her hand. "What's all this?"

"A draft of a prenuptial agreement. Also, a contract laying out the terms of our marriage and divorce agreement." Lucas scrutinized her over the rim of his mug as he took a sip. He swallowed, clearly savoring the sensation of coffee sliding down his throat. "And one for the sale of Manzanares."

Taken aback, she laughed and thumbed through the papers. "No, really. What is it?"

He sat back in his chair without a word as she skimmed through the documents. He wasn't kidding—legalese covered page after page.

Now completely off balance, she cocked a brow. "Are you sleeping with your lawyer? Is that how you got all this put together so fast?"

"Sure enough," he said, easily. "Can't put nothing past you."

Great. So he'd no doubt ensured all the terms favored him. Why hadn't she had her own documents drawn up last week? She'd had plenty of time, and it threw her for a loop to be so unprepared. Business was supposed to be her niche. It was the only real skill she brought to the equation when continuing her mother's work. If passion was all it took, her mother would have single-handedly saved every woman in danger.

"Run down the highlights for me, Wheeler. What sort of lovely surprises do you have buried in here?"

It dawned on her then. He was on board. She'd talked Lucas Wheeler into marrying her. Elation flooded her stomach so hard, it cramped. *Take that, Abuelo.* Her grandfather thought he was so smart, locking up the money, and she'd figured out a way to get it after all.

"No surprises. We each retain ownership of our assets. It's all there in black and white." His phone beeped, but he ignored it in favor of giving her his full attention. "You were up front with me, and I appreciate that. No better way to start a partnership than with honesty. So I'll direct your attention to page fifteen."

He waited until she found the page, which took longer than it should have, but she had this spiky, keen awareness of him watching her, and it stiffened her fingers. "Fifteen. Got it."

"I want you to change your name to Wheeler. It's my only stipulation. And it's nonnegotiable."

"No." She spit out the word, eyes still stumbling over the lines of his unreasonable demand. "That's ridiculous. We're going to be married for a short time, in name only."

"Exactly. That means you have to do the name part."

The logic settled into her gut and needled. Hard. She couldn't do it, couldn't give up the link with her parents and declare herself tied to this man every time she gave her name. It was completely irrational. Completely old-fashioned. *Cia Wheeler.* And appalling. "I can't even hyphenate? No deal. You have to take out that stipulation."

Instead of arguing, he unfolded his long frame from the chair and held out his hand. "Come with me. I'd like to show you something."

Nothing short of a masked man with an Uzi could make her touch him. She stood without the offered hand and scouted around his pristine, well-organized office for something worth noting. "Show me what?"

"It's not here. I have to drive you."

"I don't have all day to cruise around with you, Wheeler." If his overwhelming masculinity disturbed her this much in a spacious office, how much more potent would it be in a tiny car?

"Then we should go."

Without waiting for further argument, he led her out a back entrance to a sleek, winter-white, four-door Mercedes and opened the passenger door before she could do it. To make a point, obviously, that he called the shots.

She sank into the creamy leather and fumed. Lucas Wheeler

was proving surprisingly difficult to maneuver, and a husband she couldn't run rings around had not been part of the plan. According to all the society articles she'd read, he only cared about the next gorgeous, sophisticated woman and the next party, presumably because he wasn't overly ambitious or even very bright.

Okay, the articles hadn't said that. *She'd* made presumptions, perhaps without all the facts.

He started the car and pulled out of the lot. Once on the street, he gradually sped up to a snail's pace. She sat on her hands so she couldn't fiddle with a hem. When that failed, she bit alternate cheeks and breathed in new-car smell mixed with leather conditioner and whatever Lucas wore that evoked a sharp, clean pine forest.

She couldn't stand it a second longer. "*Madre de Dios,* Wheeler. You drive like my grandfather. Are we going to get there before midnight?"

That drawn-out, dangerous smile flashed into place. "Well, now, darlin', what's your hurry? Half the fun is getting there and the pleasures to be had along the way, don't you think?"

The vibe spilling off him said they weren't talking about driving at all. The car shrank, and it had already been too small for both her and the sex machine in the driver's seat.

Slouching down, she crossed her arms over the slow burn kicking up in her abdomen. Totally against her will, she pictured Lucas doing all sorts of things excruciatingly slowly.

How did he do that? She'd have sworn her man repellant was foolproof. It had worked often enough in the past to keep her out of trouble. "No. I don't think. The fun is all in the end goal. Can't get to the next step unless you complete the one before. Taking your time holds that up."

Lucas shook his head. "No wonder you're so uptight. You don't relax enough."

"I relax, women suffer. Where are we going? And what does all this have to do with me changing my name? Which

I am not going to do, by the way, regardless of whatever it is we're going to see."

He fell quiet for a long moment, and she suspected it wasn't the last time she'd squirm with impatience until he made his move. Their whole relationship was going to be an unending chess match, and she'd left her pawns at home.

"Why don't we listen to the radio?" he said out of nowhere. "Pick a station."

"I don't want to listen to the radio." And if she kept snapping at him, he'd know exactly how far under her skin he'd gotten. She had to do better than this.

"I'll pick one, then," he said in that amiable tone designed to fool everyone into thinking he couldn't pour water out of a boot with instructions printed on the heel. Not her, though. She was catching on quick.

George Strait wailed from the high-end speakers and smothered her with a big ol' down-home layer of twangy guitars. "Are you trying to put me to sleep?"

With a fingertip, she hit the button on the radio until she found a station playing Christina Aguilera.

"Oh, much better," Lucas said sarcastically and flipped off the music to drop them into blessed silence. Then he ruined it by talking. "Forget I mentioned the radio. So we'll have a quiet household. We're here."

"We are?" Cia glanced out the window. Lucas had parked in the long, curving driveway of an impressive house on a more impressive plot of painstakingly landscaped property. The French design of the house fit the exclusive neighborhood but managed to be unique, as well. "Where is here?"

"Highland Park. More specifically, our house in Highland Park," he said.

"You picked out a house? Already? Why do we need a house? What's wrong with you moving in with me?" A house was too real, too…homey.

Worse, the two-story brick house was beautiful, with elegant stone accents and gas coach lights flanking the arched entryway. Not only did Lucas have more than a couple of working brain cells, he also had amazing taste.

"This place is available now, it's close to the office and I like it. If this fake marriage is going to work, we can't act like it's fake. Everyone would wonder why we didn't want to start our lives together someplace new."

"No one is going to wonder that." Is that what normal married people did? Why hadn't she thought longer and harder about what it might take to make everyone believe she and Lucas were in love? Maybe because she knew nothing about love, except that when it went away, it took unrecoverable pieces with it. "You're not planning on sharing a bedroom, are you?"

"You tell me. This is all for your grandfather's benefit. Is he going to come over and inspect the house to be sure this is real?"

Oh, God. He wouldn't. Would he? "No, he trusts me."

And she intended to lie right to his face. Her stomach twisted.

"Then we'll do separate bedrooms." Lucas shrugged and crinkled up the corners of his eyes with a totally different sort of dangerous smile, and this one, she had no defenses against. "Check out the house. If you hate it, we'll find another one."

Mollified, she heaved a deep breath. Lucas could be reasonable. Good to know. She'd need a huge dollop of reasonable to talk him out of the Cia Wheeler madness. *Dios,* it didn't even sound right. The syllables clacked together like a hundred cymbals flung against concrete.

She almost got the car door open before Lucas materialized at her side to open it the rest of the way. At least he had the wisdom not to try to help her out. With a steel-straight spine, she swung out of the car and followed him to the front door, which he opened with a flourish, then pocketed the key.

With its soaring ceilings and open floor plan, the house

was breathtaking. No other word would do. Her brain wasn't quick on the draw anyway with a solid mass of Lucas hot at her back as she stopped short in the marble, glass and dark wood foyer.

He skirted around her and walked into the main living area off the foyer.

Heavy dustcovers were draped over furniture, and heavier silence added to the empty atmosphere. People had lived here once and fled, leaving behind fragments of themselves in their haste. Why? And why did she want to fling off the covers and recapture some of the happiness someone had surely experienced here once upon a time?

"Well?" Lucas asked, his voice low in the stillness. "Do you want to keep looking? Or will it do?"

The quirk of his mouth said he already knew the answer. She didn't like being predictable. Especially not to him. "How did you find this place?"

He studied her, and, inexplicably, she wished he'd flash that predatory smile she hated. At least then his thoughts would be obvious and she'd easily deflect his charm. This seriousness freaked her out a little.

"Vacant properties are my specialty," he said. "Hazard of the job. The owner was willing to rent for six months, so it's a no-brainer. Would you like to see the kitchen? It's this way."

He gestured to the back of the house, but she didn't budge.

"I don't have to see the kitchen to recognize a setup. You're in commercial real estate, not residential. Why did you bring me here?"

"I'm throwing down my hand." He lifted his chin. In the dim light, his eyes glinted, opening up a whole other dimension to his appeal, and it stalled her breath. What was wrong with her? Maybe she needed to eat.

"Great," she squeaked and sucked in a lungful of air. "What's in it?"

In a move worthy of a professional magician, he twirled

his hand and produced a small black box. "Your engagement ring."

Her heart fluttered.

Romance didn't play a part in her life. Reality did. Before this moment, marrying Lucas had only been an idea, a nebulous concept invented to help them reach their individual goals. Now it was a fact.

And the sight of a man like Lucas with a ring box gripped in his strong fingers shouldn't make her throat ache because this was the one and only proposal she'd ever get.

"We haven't talked about any of this." She hadn't been expecting a ring. Or a house. She hadn't thought that far ahead. "Do you want me to pay half?"

"Nah." He waved away several thousand dollars with a flick of his hand. "Consider the ring a gift. Give it back at the end if it makes you feel better."

"It's not even noon, Wheeler. So far, you've presented me with contracts, a house and a ring. Either you already planned to ask someone else to marry you or you have a heck of a personal assistant." She crossed her arms as she again took in the fatigue around his eyes.

Oh. That's why he was tired. He'd spent the hours since she'd sprung this divorce deal on him getting all this arranged, yet he still managed to look delicious in a freshly pressed suit.

She refused to be impressed. Refused to reorganize her assumptions about the slick pretty boy standing in the middle of the house he'd picked out for them.

So he hadn't been tearing up the sheets with his lawyer all night. So he'd rearranged his appointments to bring her here. So what?

"Last night, you proposed a partnership," he said. "That means we both bring our strengths to the table, and that's what I'm doing. Fact of the matter is you need me and for more than a signature on a piece of paper. You want everyone to believe this marriage is real, but you don't seem to have any concept of how to go about it."

"Oh, and you do?" she shot back and cursed the quaver in her voice.

Of course she didn't know how to be married, for real or otherwise. How could she? Every day, she helped women leave their husbands and boyfriends, then taught them to build new, independent lives.

Every day, she reminded herself that love was for other people, for those who could figure out how to do it without glomming on to a man, expecting him to fix all those emotionally bereft places inside, like she'd done in college right after her parents' deaths.

"Yeah. I've been around my parents for thirty years. My brother was married. My grandfather is married. The name of the company isn't Wheeler Family Partners because we like the sound of it. I work with married men every day."

Somehow he'd moved back into the foyer, where she'd remained. He was close. Too close. When he reached out to sweep hair from her cheek, she jumped.

"Whoa there, darlin'. See, that's not how married people act. They touch each other. A lot." There was that killer smile, and it communicated all the scandalous images doubtlessly swimming through his head. "And, honey, they like to touch each other. You're going to have to get used to it."

Right. She unclenched her fists.

They'd have to pretend to be lovey-dovey in public, and they'd have to practice in private. But she didn't have to start this very minute.

She stepped back, away from the electricity sparking between her and this man she'd deny to her grave being attracted to. The second she gave in, it was all over. *Feelings* would start to creep in and heartbreak would follow. "The house will do. I'll split the rent with you."

With a raised eyebrow, he said, "What about the ring? You haven't even looked at it."

"As long as it's round, it's fine, too."

"I might have to get it sized. Here, try it." He flipped open the lid and plucked out a whole lot of sparkle. When he slid it on her finger, she nearly bit her tongue to keep a stupid female noise of appreciation from slipping out. The ring fit perfectly and caught the sunlight from the open front door, igniting a blaze in the center of the marble-size diamond.

"Flashy. Exactly what I would have picked out." She tilted her hand in the other direction to set off the fiery rainbow again.

"Is that your subtle way of demonstrating yet again how much you need me?" He chuckled. "Women don't pick out their own engagement rings. Men do. This one says Lucas Wheeler in big letters."

No, it said Lucas Wheeler's Woman in big letters.

For better or worse, that's what she'd asked to be for the next six months, and the ring would serve as a hefty reminder to her and everyone else. She *had* proposed a partnership; she just hadn't expected it to be fifty-fifty. Furthermore, she'd royally screwed up by not thinking through how to present a fake marriage as real to the rest of the world.

Lucas had been right there, filling in the gaps, picking up the slack and doing his part. She should embrace what he brought to the table instead of fighting him, which meant she had to go all the way.

"I'll take the contracts to my lawyer this afternoon. As is."

Cia Wheeler. It made her skin crawl.

But she was perfectly capable of maintaining her independence, no matter what else Lucas threw at her. It was only a name, and with the trust money in her bank account, the shelter her mother never had a chance to build would become a reality. That was the true link to her parents, and she'd change her name back the second the divorce was final. "When can we move in?"

Three

Cia eased into her grandfather's study, tiptoeing in deference to his bowed head and scribbling hand, but his seventy-year-old faculties hadn't dimmed in the slightest. He glanced up from the desk, waved her in and scratched out another couple of sentences on his yellow legal pad. Paper and pen, same as he'd used for decades. Benicio Allende owned one of the premier technology companies in the world, yet remained firmly entrenched in the past.

A tiny bit of guilt over the lie she was about to tell him curled her toes.

Abuelo folded his hands and regarded her with his formidable deep-set gaze. "What brings you by today?"

Of course he cut right to the purpose of her unusual visit, and she appreciated it. A dislike of extraneous decorum was the only thing they had in common. When she'd come to live with him after her parents' accident, the adjustment had been steep on both sides. Prior to that, he'd been just as much her dad's boss as her dad's father. She'd long since stopped wishing for a grandfather with mints in his pocket and a twinkly smile.

Instead, she'd gleaned everything she could from him about how to succeed.

"Hello, Abuelo. I have some news. I'm getting married." Better leave it at that. He'd ask questions to get the pertinent information.

Their stiff holiday dinners and occasional phone calls had taught her not to indulge in idle chatter, especially not about her personal life. Nothing made him more uncomfortable than the subject of his granddaughter dating.

"To whom?"

"Lucas Wheeler." Whose diamond glittered from her third finger, weighing down her hand. She'd almost forgotten the ring that morning and had had to dash back to slip it on. A happily engaged woman wouldn't even have taken it off. "Of Wheeler Family Partners."

"Fine family. Very good choice." He nodded once, and she let out a breath. He hadn't heard the rumors about Lucas and his affair with the married woman. Usually Abuelo didn't pay attention to gossip. But nothing about this fake marriage was usual.

"I'm glad you approve."

The antique desk clock ticked as Abuelo leaned back in his chair, his shock of white hair a stark contrast to black leather. "I'm surprised he didn't come with you for a proper introduction."

Lucas had insisted he should do exactly that, but she'd talked him out of it in case Abuelo didn't buy the story she and Lucas had concocted. Everything hinged on getting over this hurdle, and she needed to handle it on her own. She owed Lucas that much.

"I wanted to tell you myself first. We're getting married so quickly...I knew it could be viewed as impulsive, but I actually dated Lucas previously. When I started focusing on other things, we drifted apart. He never forgot me. We reunited by chance at an event last week, and it was as if we'd never been separated."

Dios. When she and Lucas had discussed the story, it hadn't sounded so ridiculously romantic. Since she'd never talked to Abuelo about her love life, hopefully he wouldn't clue in on the implausibility of his granddaughter being swept off her feet.

"Other things? You mean the shelter." Abuelo's brows drew into a hawklike line. He didn't like the way she'd buried herself in her mother's passion and never missed an opportunity to harp on it, usually by telling her what her life should look like instead. "I expect you'll now focus on your husband, as a wife should."

Yeah, that was going to happen.

Abuelo was convinced a husband would make her forget all about the shelter and help her move past the loss of her parents. He grieved for his son and daughter-in-law by banishing them from his mind and couldn't accept that she grieved by tirelessly pursuing her mother's goal—a fully funded shelter with no danger of being closed due to lack of money.

Her grandfather refused to understand that the shelter provided more lasting satisfaction than a husband ever could.

"I know what's expected of me in this marriage."

Did she ever. She had to pretend to be in love with a man who turned her brain into a sea sponge. Still, it was worth it.

"Excellent. I'm very pleased with this union. The Wheeler fortune is well established."

Translation—she'd managed to snag someone who wasn't a fortune hunter, the precise reason Abuelo hadn't tied the trust to marriage. The reminder eliminated the last trace of her guilt. If he'd shown faith in her judgment, a fake marriage could have been avoided.

"I'm pleased that you're pleased."

"Dulciana, I want you to be happy. I hope you under-stand this."

"I do." Abuelo, though fearsome at times, loved her in his way. They just had different definitions of *happy*. "I'm grate-ful for your guidance."

He evaluated her for a moment, his wrinkles deepening as he frowned. "I don't pretend to understand your avid in-terest in hands-on charity work, but perhaps after you've es-tablished your household, you may volunteer a few hours a week. If your husband is supportive."

She almost laughed. "Lucas and I have already come to an agreement about that. Thanks, though, for the suggestion. By the way, we're going to have a small civil ceremony with no guests. It's what we both want."

"You're not marrying in the church?"

The sting in his tone hit its mark with whipping force. She'd known this part couldn't be avoided but had left it for last on purpose. "Lucas is Protestant."

And divorce was not easily navigated after a Catholic cer-emony. The plan was sticky enough without adding to it.

"Sit," he commanded, and with a sigh, she settled into the creaky leather chair opposite the desk.

Now she was in for it—Abuelo would have to be con-vinced she'd made these decisions wisely. In his mind, she was clearly still a seventeen-year-old orphan in need of pro-tection from the big, bad world. She put her game face on and waded into battle with her hardheaded grandfather, de-termined to win his approval.

After all, everything she knew about holding her ground she'd learned from him.

Four days, two phone calls and one trip to notarize the con-tracts and apply for a marriage license later, Lucas leaned on the doorjamb of Matthew's old house—correction, his and

Cia's house, for now anyway—and watched Cia pull into the driveway. In a red Porsche.

What an excellent distraction from the text message his brother had just sent—We lost Schumacher Industrial. Lucas appreciated the omission of "thanks to you."

Matthew never passed around blame, which of course heightened Lucas's guilt. If Wheeler Family Partners folded, he'd have destroyed the only thing his brother had left.

As Cia leaped out of the car, he hooked a thumb in the pocket of his cargos and whistled. "That's a mighty fine point-A-to-point-B ride, darlin'. Lots of starving children in Africa could be fed with those dollars."

"Don't trip over your jaw, Wheeler," she called and slammed the door, swinging her dark ponytail in an arc. "My grandfather gave me this car when I graduated from college, and I have to drive something."

"Doesn't suck that it goes zero to sixty in four-point-two seconds, either. Right, my always-in-a-hurry fiancée?" His grin widened as she stepped up on the porch, glare firmly in place. "Come on, honey. Lighten up. The next six months are going to be long and tedious if you don't."

"The next six months are going to be long and tedious no matter what. My grandfather is giving us a villa in Mallorca as a wedding present. A *villa,* Wheeler. What do I say to that? 'No, thanks, we'd prefer china,'" she mimicked in a high voice and wobbled her head. That dark ponytail flipped over her shoulder.

The times he'd been around her previously, she'd always had her hair down. And had been wearing some nondescript outfit.

Today, in honor of moving day no doubt, she'd pulled on a hot-pink T-shirt and jeans. Both hugged her very nice curves, and the ponytail revealed an intriguing expanse of neck, which might be the only vulnerable place on Cia's body.

Every day should be moving day.

"Tell your grandfather to make a donation, like I told my parents. How come my family has to follow the rules but yours doesn't?"

"I did. You try telling my grandfather what to do. *Es imposible.*" She threw up her hands, and he bit back a two-bulldozers-one-hole comment, which she would not have appreciated and wouldn't have heard anyway because she rushed on. "He's thrilled to pieces about me marrying you, God knows why, and bought the reunion story, hook, line and sinker."

"Hey now," Lucas protested. "I'm an upstanding member of the community and come from a long line of well-respected businessmen. Why wouldn't he be thrilled?"

"Because you're—" she flipped a hand in his direction, and her engagement ring flashed "—you. Falling in and out of bimbos' beds with alarming frequency and entirely too cocky for your own good. Are we going inside? I'd like to put the house in some kind of order."

Enough was enough. He tolerated slurs—some deserved, some not—from a lot of people. Either way, his wife wasn't going to be one of them.

"Honey?" He squashed the urge to reach out and lift her chin. Determined to get her to meet him halfway, he instead waited until she looked at him. "Listen up. What you see is what you get. I'm not going to apologize for rubbing you the wrong way. I like women, and I won't apologize for that, either. But I haven't dated anyone since Lana, and you're pushing my considerable patience to the limit if you're suggesting I'd sleep with another woman while my ring is on your finger. Even if the ring is for show."

A slight breeze separated a few strands of hair from the rest of her ponytail as she stared up at him, frozen, with a hint of confusion flitting across her face. "No. I didn't mean that. It was, uh… I'm sorry. Don't be mad. I'll keep my big mouth shut from now on."

He laughed. "Darlin', I don't get mad. I get even."

With that, he swept her off her feet and carried her over the threshold. She weighed less than cotton candy, and her skin was fresh with the scent of coconut and lime. Did she smell like that all the time or only on moving day?

Her curled fist whacked him in the shoulder, but he ignored it, too entranced by the feel of previously undiscovered soft spots hidden amid all her hard edges.

"What is this?" she sputtered. "Some caveman show of dominance?"

Gently, he set down the bundle of bristling woman on the marble floor in the foyer.

"Neighbors were watching," he said, deadpan.

They hadn't been. Matthew had carried Amber over the threshold and had told the story a bunch of times about nicking the door frame when he whacked it with his new bride's heel.

Lucas had always envisioned doing that with his way, way, way in the future wife, too—minus the door frame whacking—and wasn't about to let the Queen of Contrary tell him no. Even if they weren't technically married yet. Close enough, and it was practice for the eventual real deal, where his wife would gaze at him adoringly as he carried her.

He couldn't get a clear picture of this fictitious future wife. In his imagination, Cia reappeared in his arms instead.

"We have an agreement." She jammed her hands down onto her hips. "No division of property. No messiness. And *no* physical relationship. What happened to that?"

He smirked. "That wasn't even close to physical, darlin'. Now, if I was to do this—" he snaked an arm around her waist and hauled her up against him, fitting her into the niches of his body "—I'd be getting warmer."

She wiggled a little in protest and managed to slide right into a spot that stabbed a hot poker through his groin. He sucked in a cleansing breath.

This was *Cia,* the most beautiful and least arousing female he'd ever met. Why did his skin feel as if it was about to combust? "That's right. Snuggle right in, honey. Now that's so close to physical, it's scorching hot."

"What are you doing, Wheeler?" She choked on the last syllable as he leaned in, a hairbreadth from tasting that high-speed mouth, and trailed a finger down her tight jaw.

"Practicing."

If he moved one tiny neck muscle the right way, they'd be kissing. Soon, this firecracker in his arms would be Mrs. Lucas Wheeler, and he hadn't kissed her once. Maybe he should. Might shut her up for a minute.

"Practicing for what?"

"To be a happy couple. My parents invited us over for dinner tonight. Engagement celebration." Instantly she stopped wiggling, and the light hit her upturned face and her wide, frightened eyes. "Well, I'll be hog-tied and spoon-fed to vultures for breakfast. Your eyes are blue. Not brown."

"My grandparents came from northern Spain. It's not that unusual."

"A man should know the color of his wife's eyes. Marriage 101." Disconcerted, he released her. He had to get her scent out of his nose.

He shoved a hand through his hair, but it didn't release a bit of the sudden pressure against his skull.

He'd wanted to kiss her. It had taken a whole lot of willpower not to. What had he gotten himself into?

He barely knew her, knew nothing about how to handle her, nothing about her past or even her present. He had to learn. Fast.

The Manzanares contract represented more than a vital shot in the arm for his livelihood. It was a chance to fix his problems on his own, without his big brother's help, and prove to everyone that Lucas Wheeler wasn't the screw-up womanizer people assumed.

"What else don't I know?" he asked.

"That I have to work tonight. I can't go to your parents' for dinner. You have to check with me about this kind of stuff."

Yeah. He should have. It hadn't occurred to him. Most women of his acquaintance would have stood up the president in order to have dinner with his parents. He'd just never invited any of them. "Call in. Someone else can cover it. This is important to my mother."

"The shelter is important to me. Someone else has been covering my responsibilities all week." Her hands clenched and went rigid by her sides. "It's not like I'm canceling a round of golf with a potential client, Wheeler."

Golf. Yeah. His workday consisted of eye-crossing, closed-door sessions with Matthew, poring over his brother's newest strategies to improve business. "What is it like, then? Tell me."

"The women who come to the shelter are terrified their husbands or boyfriends will find them, even though we go to extreme lengths to keep the location secret. Their kids have been uprooted, jammed into a crowded, foreign new home and have lost a father, all at the same time. They're desperate for someone they know and trust. Me."

Bright, shiny moisture gathered in the pockets of her eyes as she spoke, and that caught him in the throat as much as her heartfelt speech. No one could fake that kind of passion for a job. Or anything else. "Dinner tomorrow night, then."

Mama would have to understand. God Almighty, what a balancing act. The ripples were starting already, and it was going to be hell to undo the effects after the divorce.

He had to believe it would be worth it. He had to believe he could somehow ensure his family didn't get attached to Cia without vilifying her in the process. He needed a nice, stable wife to combat the Lana Effect nearly as much as he needed Manzanares.

She nodded, and a tear broke loose to spill down her cheek. "Thanks."

All of a sudden, he felt strangely honored to be part of something so meaningful to her. Sure, his own stake meant a lot, too, but it was nice that his investment in this fake marriage would benefit others.

"Come on." He slung an arm around her slim shoulders. Such a small frame to hold so much inside. "Better. You didn't even flinch that time."

"I'm trying." As if to prove it, she didn't shrug off his arm.

"We'll get there."

Legs bumping, he guided her toward the kitchen, where he'd left every single box intact because God forbid he accidentally put the blender in the wrong spot.

Most of Amber's touches had been removed, thrown haphazardly into the trash by a blank-faced Matthew, but a few remained, like the empty fruit bowl his sister-in-law had picked up at the farmers' market.

Must have missed that one. During those weeks following the funeral, even he had been numb over Amber's sudden death, and neither he nor Matthew had put a whole lot of effort into clearing the house.

Maybe, in some ways, his marriage to Cia would be a lot easier than one built on the promise of forever. At least he knew ahead of time it was ending and there would be no emotional investment to reconcile.

"Look how far we've come already," he told her. "You're not going to make cracks about my past relationships, and I'm not going to make plans for dinner without checking first. The rest will be a snap. You just have to pretend you love me as much as you love being a crusader. Easy, right?"

She snorted and some color returned to her cheeks.

Good. Hell's bells, was she ever a difficult woman, but without him, she'd be lost. She had no idea how to fake a relationship. Her fire and compassion could only go so far, though he liked both more than he would have thought. If she ditched that prickly pear personality, she'd be something else. Thank the good Lord she hadn't.

Otherwise, he'd be chomping at the bit to break the no-physical-relationship rule and that would be plain stupid. Like kissing her would have been stupid.

No complications. That was the best way to ensure he put Wheeler Family Partners back on the map. He and Cia were business partners, and her proposal challenged him to be something he'd never been before—the hero. She deserved his undivided attention to this deal.

But he had to admit he liked that she wasn't all that comfortable having a man's hands on her. Maybe he had some caveman in him after all.

Cia spent a few hours arranging the kitchen but had to get to the shelter before finishing. Okay, so she took off earlier than planned because there was too much Lucas in the house.

How could she sleep there tonight? Or the next night or the next?

This was it, the real thing.

She'd taken her bedroom furniture, clothes and a few other necessary items, then locked up her condo. She and Lucas now lived together. They'd attend Mr. and Mrs. Wheeler's engagement dinner tomorrow night, and a blink after making the man's acquaintance, she'd marry Lucas at the courthouse Monday afternoon.

Cia Wheeler. It wasn't as if Lucas had made forty-seven other unreasonable demands. It was petty to keep being freaked about it.

So she spent a lot of her shift trying to get used to the name, practicing it aloud and writing it out several hundred times while she manned the check-in desk.

Dios, she'd turned into a love-struck teenager, covering an entire blank page with loopy script. *Mrs. Lucas Wheeler.*

Cia Wheeler. Dulciana Alejandra de Coronado y Allende Wheeler. Like her full name hadn't already been pretentious enough. Well, she wouldn't be writing that anywhere except on the marriage certificate.

The evening vaporized, and the next set of volunteers arrived. Cia took her time saying goodbye to everyone and checked on Pamela Gonzalez twice to be sure she was getting along okay as her broken arm healed.

A couple of weeks ago, Cia had taken the E.R. nurse's call and met Pamela at the hospital to counsel her on options; then she'd driven Pamela to the shelter personally.

Victims often arrived still bloodstained and broken, but Cia considered it a win to get them to a safe place they likely wouldn't have known about without her assistance. It wasn't as if the shelter could advertise an address or every abuser would be at the door, howling for his woman to be returned.

Pamela smiled and shooed Cia out of the room, insisting she liked her three roommates and would be fine. With nothing left to do, Cia headed for the new house she shared with her soon-to-be husband, braced for whatever he tossed out this time.

She found Lucas's bedroom door shut as she passed the master suite on the way to her smaller bedroom.

She let out a rush of pent-up air. A glorious, blessed reprieve from "practicing" and that smile and those broad shoulders, which filled a T-shirt as if Lucas had those custom-made along with his suits. A reprieve by design or by default she didn't know, and she didn't care. Gratefully, she sank into bed and slept until morning.

By the time she emerged from her room, Lucas was already gone. She ate a quick breakfast in the quiet kitchen someone had lovingly appointed with warm colors, top-of-the-line appliances and rich tile.

The house came equipped with a central music hub tied to the entertainment system in the living room, and after a few minutes of poking at the touch-screen remote, she blasted an electronica number through the speakers. Then she went to work unpacking the remainder of her boxes.

Sometime later, Lucas found her sitting on the floor in the living room, straightening books. She hit the volume on the remote, painfully aware that compromise and consideration, the components of a shared life, were now her highest priority.

"You're up," he said and flopped onto the couch. His hair was damp, turning the sunny blond to a deep gold, and he wore what she assumed were his workout clothes, shorts and a Southern Methodist University football T-shirt. "I didn't know how late you'd sleep. I tried to be quiet. Did I wake you?"

"You didn't. I always sleep in when I work the evening shift at the shelter. I hope I didn't make too much noise when I came in."

"Nah." He shrugged. "We'll learn each other's schedules soon enough I guess."

"About that."

She rose, shook the cramps out of her knees—how long had she been sitting there?—and crossed to the matching leather couch at a right angle to the one cradling entirely too much of Lucas's long, tanned and well-toned legs. "I appreciate the effort you put into making all this possible. I want to do my part, so I found a questionnaire online that the immigration office uses to validate green card marriages. Here's a copy for you, to help us learn more about each other." He was staring at her as if she'd turned into a bug splattered on his windshield. "You know, so we can make everyone believe we're in love."

"That's how you plan to pretend we're a real couple? Memorize the brand of shaving cream I use?"

"It's good enough for the immigration department," she countered. "There are lots of other questions in here besides brand names. Like, which side of the bed does your spouse sleep on? Where did you meet? You're the one who pointed out I haven't got a clue how to be married. This is my contribution. How did you think we would go about it?"

His eyes roamed over the list and narrowed. "A long conversation over dinner, along with a good bottle of wine. The way people do when they're dating."

"We're not dating, Wheeler." *Dating.* Something else she had no idea how to do. If she'd had a normal high school experience, maybe that wouldn't be the case. "And we don't have that kind of time. Your parents' party is tonight."

"Yeah, but they're not going to ask questions like which side of the bed you sleep on."

"No. They'll ask questions like how we met." She stabbed the paper. "Or what made us decide to get married so quickly. Or where we plan to go on our honeymoon. Look at the questionnaire. It's all there."

"This is too much like school," he grumbled and swept a lock of hair off his forehead. "Is there going to be a written exam with an essay question? What happens if I don't pass?"

"My grandfather gets suspicious. Then I don't get my money. Women don't get a place to escape from the evil they live with. You don't get the Manzanares contract." She rattled the printed pages. "Pick a question."

"Can I at least take a shower before spilling my guts?"

"Only if you answer number eighteen."

He glanced at the paper and stood, clearly about to scram as soon as he recited the response. "'What do the two of you have in common?'" Eyebrows raised, he met her gaze. Then he sat back down. "This is going to take hours."

"I tried to tell you."

For the rest of the day, in between Lucas's shower, lunch, grocery shopping and an unfinished argument over what Cia proposed to wear to dinner, they shot questions back and forth. He even followed her to her room, refusing to give her a minute alone.

Exhausted, Cia dropped onto her bed and flung a hand over her eyes. "This is a disaster."

Lucas rooted around in her closet, looking for an un-frumpy dress. So far, he'd discarded her three best dresses from Macy's, which he refused to acknowledge were practical, and was working up to insulting the more casual ones in the back.

"I agree. Your wardrobe is a cardigan away from an episode of Grandmas Gone Mild." Lucas emerged from her closet, shaking his head. "We gotta fix that."

"Nowhere in our agreement did it say I was required to dress like a bimbo. You are not allowed to buy me clothes. Period." Knowing him, he'd burn her old outfits, and then what would she wear to the shelter? BCBG and Prada to work with poverty-stricken women? "That's not the disaster."

"You dressing like something other than a matronly librarian is for my benefit, not yours. What could possibly be more of a disaster than your closet?"

It was disconcerting to have that much Lucas in her bedroom, amid her familiar mission-style furniture, which was decorating an unfamiliar house. An unfamiliar house they would share for a long six months. "Do you realize we have nothing in common other than both being born in Texas and both holding a business degree from SMU?"

He leaned his jean-clad rear on her dresser, and *Dios en las alturas,* the things acid-washed denim did to his thighs. *Not noticing,* she chanted silently. *Not noticing at all.*

But therein lay the problem. It was impossible not to notice Lucas. He lit up the room—a golden searchlight stabbing the black sky, drawing her eye and piquing her curiosity.

"What about bourbon?" he asked. "You drink that."

"Three things in common, then. *Three.* Why didn't I look for someone who at least knows how to spell hip-hop?"

His nose wrinkled. "Because. That's not important. Marriages aren't built on what you have in common. It's about not being able to live without each other."

First clothes. Then declarations à la Romeo and Juliet. "Are you sure you're not gay?"

"Would you like to come over here and test me? Now, darlin', that's the kind of exam I can get on board with." His electric gaze traveled over her body sprawled out on the bed, and she resisted the intense urge to dive under the covers. To hide from that sexy grin.

"Save it for tonight, Wheeler. Go away so I can get dressed."

"No can do. You've maligned my orientation, and I'm not having it." He advanced on her, and a dangerous edge sprang into his expression. "There must be a suitable way to convince you. Shall I make your ears bleed with a range of baseball statistics? Rattle off a bunch of technical specs for the home theater system in the media room down the hall? Hmm. No, none of that stuff is specific to straight men. Only one way to go on this one."

In an effortless move, he tumbled onto the bed, wrapped her up in his arms and rolled, tangling their legs and binding her to his hard body. Heat engulfed her, and that unique, woodsy Lucas scent swirled through her head in a drugging vortex.

When his lips grazed the hollow beneath her ear, she gasped for air as the world ignited around her.

Lucas's fingers threaded through her hair, and his mouth burned down her throat. The impressive evidence of his orientation pressed against her thigh, and she went liquid.

The plan to ignore her feminine parts for the next six months melted faster than ice in the blazing sun.

This wasn't supposed to be happening, this flood of need for a man who did this for sport. She was smarter than that.

He hadn't even kissed her yet.

"Stop," she choked out before surrender became inevitable.

No doubt he could make her body sing like a soprano with little effort. But intimacy at that level was never going to happen for her. Not with anybody. She'd learned her lesson the hard way in college, and it still stung.

He took one look at her face and swore, then rolled away to stare at the ceiling. "I'm sorry. That was juvenile, even for me. Please, let's pretend I'm not such a jerk."

She jumped off the bed and backed away from the slightly rumpled and wholly inviting male lying in it. "It's not a big deal. I know you were only messing around."

"It is a big deal. You're skittish enough already." He glanced up at her, and darkness dawned in his eyes. "Oh, man, I'm slow, I'll admit, but I shouldn't be *that* slow. Some guy beat up on you, didn't he? That's why you're so passionate about the shelter."

"What? No way. I teach self-defense. Any creep who laid a hand on me would find his balls in his back pocket. If I was in a good enough mood to return them."

"Then why are you so scared of men touching you?"

"I'm not scared of men touching me." *Just you.* History proved she couldn't trust herself, and she didn't plan to test it.

She shrugged and prayed her expression conveyed boredom or nonchalance or anything other than what she was feeling. "I'm just not interested in you that way. And that little interlude was four exits past practicing. We'll never have a public occasion to be lying in bed together."

Her tone could have frosted glass, and he didn't overlook it. In his typical fashion, he grinned and said, "I might have missed the exit for practicing, but the one I took had some great scenery. Meet me downstairs at six?"

She tried to be irritated but couldn't. He'd apologized and put them back on even ground effortlessly. No point in sulking about it. "I'll be downstairs at six. I'll expect you about ten after."

Chuckling, he left and shut the door behind him, sucking

all the vibrancy out of the room. She took a not-so-hot shower and washed her hair twice but couldn't erase the feeling of Lucas's fingers laced through it. The towel scraped across her still-sensitized flesh, and she cursed. She couldn't give him any more openings. It was too hard to fake a nonreaction.

In deference to Lucas's parents, she spent an extra couple of minutes on her hair and makeup. Lucas would likely complain about her lack of style regardless, so it certainly wasn't for his sake. The less she encouraged the trigger on his libido, the better.

With a small sigh, she twisted Lucas's diamond ring onto her finger, the only jewelry a man had ever bought her, and pretended she hated it.

Four

After firing off at least half a dozen emails and scheduling a couple of walk-throughs for early Monday afternoon, Lucas descended the hardwood and wrought-iron stairs at six sharp. Dinner was important to Mama, which meant being on time, plus he'd already done enough to provoke Cia today. Though she should be apologizing to him for the solid fifteen minutes it had taken to scrub the coconut and lime from his skin.

Why did that combination linger, like a big, fruity, tropical tattoo etched into his brain? Couldn't she wear plain old Chanel like normal women? Then the slight hard-on he'd endured since being in Cia's bed, her luscious little body twisted around his, would be easy to dismiss. Easy, because a blatant, calculated turn-on he understood.

This, he didn't.

He shouldn't be attracted to her. Keeping his hands to himself should be easy. Besides, he scared the mess out of her every time he touched her. That was reason enough to back off, and there were plenty more reasons where that one came from. He'd have to try harder to remember them.

Cia had beaten him to the living room, where she paced around the sofa in a busy circle. The demons drove her relentlessly tonight. There must be a way to still them for a little while.

"Ready?" he asked, and caught her hand to slow her down. It was shaking. "Hey. It's just dinner with some old people. It's not like barging into a birthday party and proposing to a man you've never met."

"My hands were shaking then, too." She actually cracked a tiny smile. "It's not just dinner. It's a performance. Our first one, and we have to get it right. There's no backup parachute on this ride."

"That's where you're wrong, darlin'. I always have a backup parachute in my wallet."

"Only you could twist an innocent comment into an innuendo." Her eyes flashed deep blue with an unexpected hint of humor. How had he ever thought they were brown?

"If you don't like it, stop giving me ammo."

Her bottom lip poked out in mock annoyance, but he could see she was fighting a laugh. "You really are juvenile half the time, aren't you?"

And there she was, back in the fray. *Good.* Those shadows flitting through her eyes needed to go. Permanently. He'd enjoy helping that happen.

"Half the time? Nah. I give it my all 24/7." He winked and kissed her now-steady hand. A hand heavy with her engagement ring. Why did that flash on her finger please him so much? "But you're not nervous about dinner anymore, so mission accomplished. Before we go, can we find you some matching earrings?"

Fingers flew to her ears. "What? How did that happen?"

"Slow down once in a while maybe. Unless of course you

want my parents to think we rolled straight out of bed and got dressed in a big hurry."

She made a face and went back upstairs. The plain black dress she wore, the same one from the other night, did her figure no favors. Of course, only someone who had recently pressed up against every inch of those hidden curves would know they were there.

He groaned. All night long he'd be thinking about peeling off that dress. Which, on second thought, might not be bad. If she was his real fiancée, he'd be anticipating getting her undressed *and* the other choice activities to follow. No harm in visualizing both, to up the authenticity factor.

Imagining Cia naked was definitely not a chore.

When she returned, he tucked her against his side and herded her toward the garage before she could bolt. Once he'd settled her into the passenger seat of his car, he slid into the driver's seat and backed out.

Spring had fully sprung, stretching out the daylight, and the Bradford pears burst with white blooms, turning the trees into giant Q-tips. Likely Cia had no interest in discussing the weather, the Texas Rangers or the Dow, and he refused to sit in silence.

"You know, I've been curious." He glanced at the tight clamp of her jaw. Nerves. She needed a big-time distraction. "So you're not personally a victim of abuse, but something had to light that fire under you. What was it?"

"My aunt." She shut her eyes for a blink and bounced her knee. Repeatedly. "The time she showed up at our house with a two-inch-long split down her cheek is burned into my brain. I was six and the ghastly sight of raw flesh…"

With a shudder, she went on, "She needed stitches but refused to go to the emergency room because they have to file a report if they suspect abuse. She didn't want her husband to be arrested. So my mom fixed her up with Neosporin and

Band-Aids and tried to talk some sense into her. Leave that SOB, she says. You deserve better."

What a thing for a kid to witness. His sharpest memory from that age was scaring the maid with geckos. "She didn't listen, did she?"

"No." Cia stared out the window at the passing neighborhood.

When he looked at a house or a structure, he assessed the architectural details, evaluated the location and estimated the resale value. What did she see—the pain and cruelty the people inside its walls were capable of? "What happened?"

"He knocked her down, and she hit her head. After a two-month coma, they finally pulled the plug." Her voice cracked. "He claimed it was an accident, but fortunately the judge didn't see it that way. My mom was devastated. She poured all her grief into volunteer work at a shelter, determined to save as many other women as she could."

"So you're following in your mom's footsteps?"

"Much more than that. I went with her. For years, I watched these shattered women gain the skills and the emotional stability to break free of a monstrous cycle. That's an amazing thing, to know you helped someone get there. My mom was dedicated to it, and now she's gone." The bleak proclamation stole his attention from the road, and the staccato tap of her fingernail against the door kept it. "I have to make sure what happened to my aunt doesn't happen to anyone else. Earlier, you said marriage is about not being able to live without someone. I've seen the dark side of that, where women can't leave their abusers for all sorts of emotional reasons, and it gives me nightmares."

Oh, man. The shadows inside her solidified.

No wonder she couldn't be still, with all that going on inside. His chest pinched. She'd been surrounded by misery for far too long. No one had taken the time to teach her how to have fun. How to ditch the clouds for a while and play in the sun.

Wheeler to the rescue. "Next time you have a nightmare, you feel free to crawl in bed with me."

Her dark blue eyes fixed on him for a moment. "I'll keep that in mind. I'd prefer never to be dependent on a man in the first place, which is why I'll never get married."

"Yet that looks suspiciously like an engagement ring on your left hand, darlin'."

She rolled her eyes. "Married for real, I mean. Fake marriages are different."

"Marriage isn't about creating a dependency between two people, you know. It can be about much more."

Which meant much more to lose. Like what happened to Matthew, who'd been happy with Amber, goofy in love. They'd had all these plans. Then it was gone. Poof.

Some days, Lucas didn't know how Matthew held it together, which was reason enough to keep a relationship simple. Fun, yes. Emotional and heavy? No.

Lucas had done Matthew a favor by taking over his monument of a house, not that his brother would agree. If Matthew had his way, he'd mope around in that shrine forever. Cia had already begun dissolving Amber's ghost, exactly as Lucas had hoped.

"Looks suspiciously like a bare finger on your left hand, Wheeler. You had an affair with a married woman. Sounds like you deliberately avoid eligible women."

At what point had this conversation turned into an examination of the Lucas Wheeler Philosophy of Marriage? He hadn't realized he had one until now.

"Marrying you, aren't I?" he muttered. Lana had been an eligible woman, at least in his mind.

"Boy, *that* proves your point. I'm the woman who made you agree to divorce me before we got near an altar," she said sweetly and then jabbed the needle in further. "Gotta wonder what *your* hang-up is about marriage."

"Nagging wife with a sharp tongue would be hang-up number one," he said. "I'll get married one day. I haven't found the right woman yet."

"Not for lack of trying. What was wrong with all of your previous candidates?"

"Too needy," he said, and Cia chortled.

He should have blown off the question, or at least picked something less cliché. But cliché or not, that's what had made Lana so disappointing—she'd been the opposite of clingy and suffocating. For once, he'd envisioned a future with a woman. Instead, she'd been lying.

Had he seen the signs but chosen to ignore them?

"Exactly," she said. "Needy women depend on a man to fill holes inside."

"Who are you, Freud?"

"Business major, psych minor. I don't have any holes. Guess I must be the perfect date, then, huh, Wheeler?" She elbowed his ribs and drew a smile from him.

"Can't argue with that."

Now he understood her persistent prickliness toward men. Understood it, but didn't accept it.

Not all men were violent losers bent on dominating someone weaker. Some men appreciated a strong, independent woman. Some men might relish the challenge of a woman who went out of her way to make it clear how not interested she was five seconds after melting into a hot mess in a guy's arms.

The stronger she was, the harder she'd fall, and he could think of nothing better than rising to the challenge of catching her. Cia wasn't scared like he'd assumed, but she nursed some serious hang-ups about marriage *and* men.

Nothing about this marriage was real. None of it counted. They had the ultimate no-strings-attached arrangement, and he knew the perfect remedy for chasing away those shadows—

not-real-doesn't-count sex with her new husband. Nothing emotional to trip over later, just lots of fun. They both knew where their relationship was going. There was no danger of Cia becoming dependent on him since he wasn't going to be around after six months and she presented no danger to his family's business.

Everyone won.

Instead of only visualizing Cia out of that boring dress, he'd seduce her out of it. And out of her hang-ups. A lot rode on successfully scamming everyone. What better way to make everyone think they were a real couple than to be one?

Temporarily, of course.

Lucas's parents lived at the other end of Highland Park, in a stately colonial two-story edging a large side lot bursting with tulips, hyacinth and sage. A silver-haired older version of Lucas answered the door at the Wheelers' house, giving Cia an excellent glimpse of how Lucas might age. She hadn't met Mr. Wheeler at the birthday party.

"Hi, I'm Andy," Mr. Wheeler said and swung the door wide.

Lucas shook his dad's hand and then ushered Cia into the Wheelers' foyer with a palm at the small of her back. The casual but reassuring touch warmed her spine, serving as a reminder that they were in this together.

Through sheer providence, she'd gained a real partner, one who didn't hesitate to solve problems she didn't know existed. One who calmed her and who paid enough attention to notice she wore different earrings. She'd never expected, never dreamed, she'd need or want any of that when concocting this scheme.

Thanks to Lucas everything was on track, and soon they could get on with their separate lives. Or as separate as possible while living under the same roof.

Lucas introduced Cia to his brother, Matthew, and Mrs.

Wheeler steered everyone into the plush living area off the main foyer.

"Cia, I'm happy to have you here. Please, call me Fran. Have a seat." Fran motioned to the cushion next to her on the beige couch, and Cia complied by easing onto it. "I must tell you, I'm quite surprised to learn you and Lucas renewed a previous relationship at my birthday party. I don't recall the two of you dating the first time."

"I don't tell you everything, Mama," Lucas interrupted, proceeding to wedge in next to Cia on the couch, thigh to thigh, his heavy arm drawing her against his torso. "You should thank me."

Fran shot her son a glance, which couldn't be interpreted as anything other than a warning, while Cia scrambled to respond.

Her entire body blipped into high alert. She stiffened and had to force each individual muscle in her back to relax, allowing her to sag against Lucas's sky-blue button-down shirt as if they snuggled on the couch five times a day. "It was a while back. A couple of years."

Matthew Wheeler, the less beautiful, less blond and less vibrant brother, cleared his throat from his position near the fireplace. "Lucas said four or five years ago."

Cia's heart fell off a cliff. Such a stupid, obvious thing to miss when they'd discussed it. Why hadn't Lucas mentioned he'd put a time frame to their fictitious previous relationship?

"Uh...well, it might have been four years," Cia mumbled. In a flash of inspiration, she told mostly the truth. "I was still pretty messed up about my parents. All through college. I barely remember dating Lucas."

His lips found her hairline and pressed against it in a simple kiss. An act of wordless sympathy but with the full force of Lucas behind those lips, it singed her skin, drawing heat into her cheeks, enflaming them. She was very aware of his fingertips trailing absently along her bare arm and very aware an engaged man had every reason to do it.

Except he'd never done it to her before and the little sparks his fingers generated panged through her abdomen.

"Oh, no, of course," Fran said. "I'm so sorry to bring up bad memories. Let's talk about something fun. Tell me about your wedding dress."

In a desperate attempt to reorient, Cia zeroed in on Fran's animated face. Lucas had not inherited his magnetism from his father, as she'd assumed, but from his mother. They shared a charisma that made it impossible to look away.

Lucas groaned, "Mama. That's not fun—that's worse than water torture. Daddy and Matthew don't want to hear about a dress. I don't even want to hear about that."

"Well, forgive me for trying to get to know my new daughter," Fran scolded and smiled at Cia conspiratorially. "I love my sons, but sometimes just because the good Lord said I have to. You I can love because I want to. The daughter of my heart instead of my blood. We'll have lunch next week and leave the party poopers at home, won't we?"

Cia nodded because her throat seized up and speaking wasn't an option.

Fran already thought of her as a daughter.

Never had she envisioned them liking each other or that Lucas's mother might want to become family by choice instead of only by law. The women at the shelter described their husbands' mothers as difficult, interfering. Quick to take their sons' sides. She'd assumed all new wives struggled to coexist. *Must have horrible mother* should have been on her criteria list.

And as long as she was redoing the list, *Zero sex appeal* was numero uno.

"Isn't it time for dinner?" Lucas said brightly, and everyone's gaze slid off her as Fran agreed.

The yeasty scent of baked bread had permeated the air a

few minutes ago and must have jump-started Lucas's appetite. She smiled at him, grateful for the diversion, and took a minute to settle her stomach.

Andy and Matthew followed Fran's lead into the dining room adjacent to the living area, where a middle-aged woman in a black-and-white uniform bustled around the twelve-seat formal dining table. A whole roasted chicken held court in the center, flanked by white serving dishes containing more wonderful food.

Lucas didn't move. He should move. Plenty of couch on the other side of his thigh.

"Be there in a minute," he called to his family and took Cia's hand in his, casually running a thumb over her knuckles. "You okay? You don't have to have lunch with my mother. She means well, but she can be overbearing."

"No." She shook her head, barely able to form words around the sudden pounding of her pulse. "Your mother is lovely. I'm…well—we're lying to her. To your whole family. Lying to my grandfather is one thing because he's the one who came up with those ridiculous trust provisions. But this…"

"Is necessary," he finished for her. "It would be weird if I never introduced you to my parents. For now it's important to play it like a real couple. I'll handle them later. Make something up."

He didn't understand. Because he'd had a mother his whole life.

"More lies. It's clear you're all close. How many other grown sons go to their mother's birthday party and then to dinner at her house in the same week?" Cia vaulted off the couch, and Lucas rose a split second later. "I'm sorry I put you in this position. How do we do this? How do I go in there and eat dinner like we're a happy, desperately in love couple?"

"Well, when I'm in an impossible situation, and I have no idea how to do it, I think to myself, 'What would Scooby do?'"

In spite of the ache behind her eyes, a shuddery laugh

slipped out. A laugh, when she could hardly breathe around the fierce longing swimming through her heart to belong to such a family unit for real.

"Scooby would eat."

"Yep." Lucas flashed an approval-laden smile. "So here's a crazy idea. Don't take this so seriously. Let's have fun tonight. Eat a good meal with some people I happen to be related to. Once it's over, you'll be one step closer to your money and I'll be one step closer to Manzanares, which will make both of us happy. Voilà. Now we're a happy couple. Okay?"

"We're still lying to them."

"I told my parents we're engaged to be married, and that's true."

"But there's an assumption there about us—"

He cut her off with a grunt. "Stop being so black-and-white. If anyone asks, don't lie. Change the subject. My parents are waiting on us to eat dinner. You've got to figure it out."

She took a deep breath. One dinner. One short ceremony. Then it would be over. "I'm working on it."

"Maybe you need something else to think about during dinner."

In a completely natural move, Lucas curved her into his arms, giving her plenty of time to see him coming. Plenty of time to anticipate. The crackle in the air and the intent in his eyes told her precisely what he'd give her to think about.

And still, when he kissed her, the contact of Lucas's mouth against hers swept shock waves down her throat, into her abdomen, spreading with long, liquid pulls.

She'd been kissed before. She had. Not like this, by a master who transformed the innocent touching of mouths into a carnal slide toward the depths of sinful pleasure.

He cupped her jaw with a feathery caress. When her knees buckled, he squeezed her tighter against him and deepened the kiss slowly, sending the burn of a thousand torches down the length of her body.

Her brain drained out through her soles to puddle on the Wheelers' handmade rug.

Then it was over. He drew his head back a bit, and she nearly lost her balance as she took in the dark hunger darting through his expression.

He murmured, "Now, darlin'. You think about how we'll finish that later on. I know I will be."

Later?

Lucas tugged at their clasped hands, and she followed him on rubbery legs into the dining room, still raw from being kissed breathless. Raw and confused.

It didn't mean anything. It couldn't mean anything. That kiss had been window dressing. It had been a diversion to get her to lay off. She wasn't stupid. Lucas had a crackerjack gift for distraction when necessary, and this had been one of those times. There was no later.

No one asked about the relationship between her and Lucas during dinner.

It might have had to do with the scorching heat in his eyes every time he looked at her. Or the way he sat two inches from her chair and whispered in her ear every so often. The comments were silly, designed to make her laugh, but every time he leaned in, with his lips close to her ear, laughing didn't happen.

She was consumed with *later* and the lingering taste of him on her lips.

Clearly, she'd underestimated his talent when it came to women. Oh, she wasn't surprised at his ability to kiss a fake fiancée senseless, or how the wickedness of his mouth caused her to forget her own name. No. The surprise lay in how genuine he'd made it feel. Like he'd enjoyed kissing her. Like the audience hadn't mattered.

He'd been doing his job—faking it around other people.

And despite the unqualified awareness that it wasn't real, that it never, ever could be, he'd made her *want* it to be real.

A man who could spin that kind of straw into gold was dangerous.

After dinner, Fran shooed everyone to the huge screened-in porch for coffee. Andy, Matthew and Lucas small talked about work a few feet away, so Cia perched on the wicker love seat overlooking the pool, sipping a cup of coffee to ward off the slight chill darkness had brought. Decaf, because she'd have a hard enough time sleeping tonight as it was. Her body still ached with the unfulfilled promise of Lucas's kiss.

After a conspicuous absence, Fran appeared and joined her.

"This is for you," Fran said, and handed Cia a long, velvet jewelry box. "Open it."

Cia set her coffee aside and sprung the lid, gasping as an eighteen-inch gray pearl and diamond necklace spilled into her hands. "Oh, Fran, I couldn't."

Fran closed Cia's hand over the smooth, cool pearls. "It belonged to my mother and my grandmother before that. My mother's wedding ring went to Ambe—" She cut herself off with a pained glance at Matthew. "My oldest son, but I saved this for Lucas's wife. I want you to have it. It's your something old."

Madre de Dios, how did she refuse?

This was way worse than a villa—it was an heirloom. A beautiful expression of lineage and family and her eyes stung as Fran clasped it around Cia's neck. It hung heavy against her skin, and she couldn't speak.

"It's stunning with your dark hair. Oh, I know it's not the height of fashion," Fran said with a half laugh. "It's old-lady jewelry. So humor me, please, and wear it at the ceremony, then put it away. I'll let Lucas buy you pretty baubles more to your taste."

Cia touched the necklace with the tips of her fingers.

"Thank you." A paltry sentiment compared to the emotion churning through her.

Fran smiled. "You're welcome. At the risk of being tactless, I was crushed you didn't want any family at the wedding. I'm more than happy to pitch in as mother of the bride, if that's part of the issue. You must be missing yours."

Before Cia's face crumpled fully, Lucas materialized at her side and pulled her to her feet. "Mama. I told you Cia doesn't want a big ceremony or any fuss. She doesn't even like jewelry."

Obviously he'd been listening to the conversation. As Fran sputtered, Cia retreated a few mortified steps and tried to be grateful for the intervention.

Her dry eyes burned. No big church wedding for her. No flower girls, chamber music or a delicate sleeveless ecru dress with a princess waist, trimmed in lace. All that signified the real deal, an ability to gift someone with her love and then trust the fates not to rip her happiness away with no warning.

Neither could she in good conscience develop any sort of relationship with Mrs. Wheeler. Better to hurt her now, rather than later.

With her heart in shredded little pieces, Cia unclasped the necklace. "Thank you, but I can't wear this. It doesn't go with a simple civil ceremony. I'm pretty busy at work for the foreseeable future, so lunch is out of the question."

Fran's expression smoothed out as she accepted the return of her box and necklace. "I overstepped. You have my apologies."

"It's fine, Mama. We should go," Lucas said and nodded to the rest of his family, who watched her coolly.

Excellent. Now they all hated her. That's what she should have been going for all night. Then when she and Lucas divorced, he could blame it all on her, and his family would welcome him back into the fold with sympathy and condolences. His mother would say she knew Cia wasn't the right girl for him the moment she'd thrown his great-grandmother's pearls back in her face.

Cia murmured her goodbyes and followed Lucas through the house and out into the starless night.

Once they were settled in their seats, he drove away, as slow as Christmas. But she didn't care so much this time and burrowed into the soft leather, oddly reassured by the scent of pine trees curling around her.

"Thanks, Lucas," she said, and her voice cracked. "For giving me the out with your mother. It was…"

"No problem," he said, jumping in to fill the silence when she couldn't go on. "It takes two to make marriage work, fake or otherwise. I'll do damage control with Mama in the morning. And, darlin', I must confess a real fondness to you calling me Lucas."

His gaze connected with hers, arcing with heat, and the current zinged through the semidark, close quarters of the car. Goose bumps erupted across her skin and her pulse skittered.

All of a sudden, it was later.

Five

Lucas spent the silent, tense ride home revamping his strategy.

Fragileness deepened Cia's shadows, and it was enough to cool his jets. Nothing would have pleased him more than to walk into the house, back her up against the door and start that kiss over again, but this time, his hands would stroke over the hot curves of her body and she'd be naked in short order.

But she wasn't like other women. She wasn't in touch with her sexuality, and he had to live with her—and himself—for the next six months. While he'd like to sink straight into a simple seduction, he had to treat her differently, with no idea what that looked like.

Once they cleared the detached garage, he slid his hand into hers. "Thanks for going to dinner."

Her fingers stiffened. She glanced at him, surprise evident. "You say that like I had a choice."

"You did. With me, you always have a choice. We're partners, not master and slave. So, I'm saying thank you for choosing to spend the evening with my family. It was difficult for you, and I appreciate it."

Her gaze flitted over him, clearly looking for the punch line. "You're welcome, then."

He let go of her hand to open the door. "Now, I don't know about you, but my parents' house always makes me want to let loose a little. I'm half-afraid to move, in case I accidentally knock over one of Mama's precious knickknacks."

Cia smiled, just a little, but it was encouraging all the same. "It is easier to breathe in our house."

Our house. She'd never called it that before, and he liked the sound of it. They were settling in with each other, finding a groove.

He followed her into the living room. "Let's do something fun."

"Like what?"

Instead of answering, he crossed to the entertainment center and punched up the music she'd been playing earlier, when he'd returned home from playing basketball. A mess of electronic noise blasted through the speakers, thumping in his chest. "Dance with me," he yelled over the pulsing music.

"To this?" Disbelief crinkled her forehead. "You haven't even been drinking, white boy."

"Come on." He held out a hand. "You won't dance in public. No one is watching except me, and I can't dance well enough to warrant making fun of you."

He almost fell over when she shrugged and joined him. "I don't like people watching me, but I never said I couldn't dance."

To prove it, she cut her torso in a zigzag and whirled in an intricate move worthy of a music video, hair flying, hands framing her head.

He grinned and crossed his arms, content to be still and watch Cia abandon herself to the beat. His hunch had been right—anyone with her energy would have to be a semicompetent dancer.

After a minute or so of the solo performance, she froze and threw him a look. "You're not dancing."

"Too hard to keep up with that, honey. I'm having a great time. Really. Keep going."

"Not if you're just going to stand there. You asked me to dance *with you*."

Only because he hadn't actually thought she'd say yes. "So I did."

He could be a good sport. But he could not, under any circumstances, dance to anything faster than Brooks & Dunn.

So, he let her make fun of him instead, as he flapped his arms and stomped his feet in what could easily be mistaken for an epileptic seizure. When she laughed so hard she had to hold her sides, nothing but pure Cia floated through her eyes.

The shadows—and the fragileness—had been banished. Score one for Wheeler.

"All right, darlin'. Unless you want to tend to me as I'm laid out flat on my back with a pulled muscle, we gotta dial it down a notch."

She snickered. "What are you, sixty? Shall I run and collect your social security check from the mailbox?"

Before she could protest, he grabbed her hand and twirled her into his arms, body to body. "No, thanks. I've got another idea."

Her arms came up around his waist and she clung to him. Progress. It was sweet.

"Slow dancing?" she asked.

"Slow something, that's for sure." He threaded fingers through her amazing hair and brushed a thumb across her cheek. Her skin was damp from dancing.

As he imagined the glow she'd take on when he got her good and sweaty between the sheets, he went hard. She noticed.

Her eyes widened, and all the color drained from her face as she let go of him faster than a hot frying pan. "It's late. I have a shift in the morning, so I'm about danced out."

All his hard work crumbled to dust under the avalanche of her hang-ups. He let her go with regret. Should have gone with slow dancing, and, as a bonus, she'd still be in his arms. "Sure thing. Big day tomorrow."

The wedding. Realization crept over her expression. "Oh. Yeah. Well, good night."

She fled.

He stalked off to bed and stared at the news for a good couple of hours, unsuccessfully attempting to will away his raging hard-on, before finally drifting off into a restless sleep laced with dreams of Cia wearing his ring and nothing else.

In the morning, he awoke bleary eyed but determined to make some progress in at least one area sorely requiring his attention—work.

The muted hum of the shower in Cia's bathroom traveled through the walls as he passed by.

Cia, wet and naked. Exactly as he'd dreamed.

He skipped breakfast, too frustrated to stay in the house any longer. An early arrival at work wasn't out of line anyway, as Mondays were usually killers. A welcome distraction from the slew of erotic images parading around in his head.

At red lights, he fired off emails to potential clients with the details of new listings. His schedule was insane this week. He had overlapping showings, appraisals and social events he'd attend to drum up new business.

An annoying buzz at the edge of his consciousness kept reminding him of all the balls he had in the air. He'd been juggling the unexpected addition of a full-time personal life and the strain was starting to wear. As long as he didn't drop any balls or clients, everything was cool.

Four o'clock arrived way too fast.

As anticipated, Cia waited for him outside the courthouse,

wearing one of her Sunday-go-to-meeting dresses a grand-mother would envy and low heels.

With her just-right curves and slender legs, put her in a pair of stilettos and a gauzy hot-pink number revealing a nice slice of cleavage…well, there'd be no use for stoplights on the street—traffic would screech to a halt spontaneously. But that wasn't her style. Shame.

Her gaze zeroed in on the bouquet of lilies in his fist. "You just come from a funeral, Wheeler?"

So they were back to *Wheeler* in that high-brow, back-off tone. One tasty kiss-slash-step-forward and forty steps back.

"For you." Lucas offered Cia the flowers. Dang it, he should not have picked them out. If he'd asked Helena to do it, like he should have, when Cia sneered at the blooms, as she surely would, he wouldn't be tempted to throw them down and forget this whole idea. Even a man with infinite patience could only take so much.

But she didn't sneer. Gently, she closed her fingers around the flowers and held them up to inhale the scent.

After a long minute of people rushing by and the two of them standing there frozen, she said, "If you'd asked, I would have said no. But it's kind of nice after all. So you get a pass."

He clutched his chest in a mock heart attack and grinned. "That's why I didn't ask. All brides should have flowers."

"This isn't a real wedding."

She tossed her head and strands of her inky hair fanned out in a shiny mass before falling back to frame her exotic features. This woman he was about to make his wife was such a weird blend of stunning beauty and barbed personality, with hidden recesses of warmth and passion.

What was wrong with him that he was so flippin' attracted to that mix? This marriage would be so much easier if he let it go and worried about stuff he could control, like scaring up new clients.

But he couldn't. He wanted her in his bed, hot and enthusiastic, hang-ups tossed out the window for good.

"Sure it is. We're going to be legally married. Just because it's not traditional doesn't make it less real."

She flipped her free hand. "You know what I mean. A church wedding, with family and friends and cake."

"Is that what you wanted? I would have suffered through a real wedding for you." His skin itched already to think of wearing a tux and memorizing vows. God Almighty…the rehearsal, the interminable ceremony, the toasts. Matthew had undergone it all with a besotted half smile, claiming it was all worth it. Maybe it was if you were in love. "But, darlin', I would have insisted on a real honeymoon."

He waggled his brows, and she laughed nervously, which almost gave him a real heart attack.

A hint of a smile still played around her lips. "A real wedding would have made both of us suffer. That's not what I wanted. I don't have a perfect wedding dress already picked out in hopes my Prince Charming will come along, like other women do. I'm okay with being single for the rest of my life."

"Hold up, honey. You're not a romantic? All my illusions about you have been thoroughly crushed."

Romantic gestures put a happy, glowy expression on a woman's face, and he liked being the one responsible. It was the only sight on this earth anywhere near as pleasurable as watching a woman in the throes of an orgasm he'd given her.

He had his work cut out for him if he wanted to get Cia there.

He put an arm around her waist to guide her inside the courthouse because it was starting to seem as if she wanted to avoid going inside.

The ceremony was quick, and when he slid the slender wedding band of diamonds channel-set in platinum onto her finger, Cia didn't curl her lip. He'd deliberately picked something low-key that she could wear without the glitzy engagement ring. The set had cost more than his car, but he viewed both as an investment. Successful real estate brokers didn't cheap out, and especially now, with Lana's husband on the warpath, every last detail of his life was for show.

With a fast and unsexy kiss, it was over. They were Mr. and Mrs. Wheeler.

The cool, hard metal encircling his finger was impossible to ignore, and he spun it with his pinkie, trying to get used to the weight. Uncomfortable silence fell as they left the courthouse and neither of them broke it. Cia had asked a friend to drop her off, so she rode home with him.

Half-surprised Mama hadn't crashed the event, he called her with the update before he pulled out of the courthouse parking lot. By the time the wheels hit the driveway of the house, Mama had apparently posted the news to Facebook, which then took on a life of its own.

Text messages started rolling in, and he glanced at them as he shifted into Park.

Pete: Dude. Are we still on for bball Sunday? Or do you have to check with the missus?

Justine: REALLY Lucas???? Married???? REALLY????

Melinda: **&^$%. Missed it by that much. Call me the second you get tired of her.

Lucas rolled his eyes. He hadn't spoken to either woman in months. Pete yanked his chain twice a day and had since college.

When Lucas went to shut off his phone, a message came in from Lana: Congrats. Nothing else. The simple half a word spoke volumes and it said, *Poor Lucas, marrying that woman on the rebound.*

"You're popular all of a sudden," Cia said after the fourth beep in a row, and her tone tried and convicted him for a crime he'd not been aware of committing.

"It's just people congratulating us."

And he was done with that. Lana's name popping up on

the screen, after all this time, had unburied disillusionment he'd rather not dwell on.

He hit the phone's off button and dropped it in his pocket, then left the car in the driveway instead of pulling into the garage so it would be easier for Cia to get out.

His efforts to untangle Cia's hang-ups last night had failed. Tonight, he'd try a different approach. "Have dinner with me. To celebrate."

Before he could move, she popped the door and got out. He followed her up the drive and plowed through Amber's fancy flowerbed to beat her to the porch.

"Celebrate what?" she asked, annoyance leaking from her pores. "I was thinking about soaking for an hour or two in a hot bath and going to bed early, actually."

Before she could storm through the entryway, Lucas stopped her with a firm hand on her prickly little shoulder. "Wait."

With an impatient sigh, she turned. "What?"

"Just because you've got your marriage license doesn't mean we're going to walk through this door and never speak again. You realize this, don't you?" He searched her face, determined to find some glimmer of agreement. "This is the beginning, not the end. We've been faking being a happily engaged couple. Now we have to fake being a happily married couple. No, we don't have to put on a performance right now, when no one's around. But to do it in public, trust me, darlin', when I say it will be miles easier if you're not at my throat in private."

Her tight face flashed through a dozen different emotions and finally picked resignation. "Yeah. I know. I owe you an apology. It's been a rough day."

For both of them. "Because you didn't want to get married?"

She shrank a little, as if she couldn't support the heavy weight settling across her shoulders. As if she might shatter

into a million shards of razor-sharp glass if he touched her.
So he didn't.

But he wanted to, to see if he could soften her up, like during the five seconds he'd had her pliant and breathless in his arms and so off guard she'd actually kissed him back.

"I've been prepared to be married ever since I came up with the idea." Misery pulled at her full mouth. "It's just…I didn't have any idea how hard it would be to get married without my father walking me down the aisle. Me. Who was never going to get married in the first place. Isn't that ridiculous?"

One tear burst loose, trailing down her delicate cheekbone, and he had to do something.

"Hey now," he said, and wrapped his arms around her quivering shoulders, drawing her in close. She let him, which meant she must be really upset. Prickly Cia usually made an appearance when she was uncomfortable about whatever was going on inside her. "That's okay to cry about. Cry all you want. Then I'll get you drunk and take advantage of you, so you forget all about it."

She snorted out a half laugh, and it rumbled pleasantly against his chest. There was something amazing about being able to comfort a woman so insistent on not needing it. He'd grown really fond of soothing away that prickliness.

"I could use a glass of wine," she admitted.

"I have exactly the thing. Come inside." He drew back and smiled when some snap crept back into her watery eyes. "You can drink it while you watch me cook."

"You cook?" That dried up her waterworks in a hurry. "With an oven?"

"Sure enough. I can even turn it on by myself." As he led the way into the kitchen, a squawk cut him off. "Oh, good. Your wedding present is here."

Cia raised her brows at the large cage sitting on the island in the middle of the kitchen. "That's a bird."

"Yep. An African gray parrot." He shed his suit jacket and draped it over a chair in the breakfast nook.

"You're giving me a bird? As a wedding present?"

"Not any bird. African grays live up to fifty years, so you'll have company as you live all by your lonesome the rest of your life. And they talk. I figure anyone who likes to argue as much as you do needed a pet who can argue back. I named her Fergie." He shrugged. "Because you like hip-hop."

Speechless, Cia stared at the man she had married, whom she clearly did not know at all, and tried to make some sort of sound.

"I didn't get you anything," she managed to say.

"That's okay." He unbuttoned his sleeves and rolled them deftly halfway up his tanned forearms, then started pulling covered plates out of the stainless steel refrigerator. "I wasn't expecting anything."

"Neither was I," she mumbled. "Doesn't seem like that matters either way."

She'd never owned a bird and would have to take a crash course on its recommended care. As she peered into the cage, the feathered creature blinked and peered back with intelligent eyes, unafraid and curious. She fell instantly in love.

The psychology of the gift wasn't lost on her. Instead of showering her with expensive, useless presents designed to charm her panties off, he'd opted for a well-thought-out gift. An extremely well-thought-out gift designed for...what?

Every time she thought he was done, Lucas Wheeler peeled back another one of his layers, and every time, it freaked her out a little more.

Regardless, she couldn't lie. "It's the best present I've ever gotten." And she'd remember forever not that her father hadn't been there to give her away, but that her fake husband had given her something genuine on their wedding day. "Thanks, Lucas."

The sentiment stopped him in his tracks, between the

stove and the dishwasher, pan dangling, forgotten, from his hand. That indefinable energy crackled through the air as he treated her to a scorching once-over. "Darlin', you are most welcome."

"Didn't you mention wine?" she asked, to change the subject, and slid onto a barstool edging the granite island.

There was a weird vibe going on tonight, and she couldn't put her finger on it. Alcohol probably wouldn't help.

Lucas retrieved a bottle from the refrigerator. "Sauvignon blanc okay?"

When she nodded, he pulled a corkscrew from a wall hanger, then expertly twisted and wiggled the cork out in one smooth motion. The man did everything with care and attention, and she had a feeling he meant for her to notice. She did. So what?

Yes, his amazing hands would glide over her bare body in a slow seduction and turn her into his sex-starved lover. No question about it.

The real question was why she was envisioning Lucas touching her after simply watching him open wine. Okay. It had nothing to do with wine and everything to do with being in his arms last night. With being kissed and watching him dance like a spastic chicken, draining away all her misery over hurting his mother.

Lucas skirted the barstools and handed her a glass of pale yellow wine. His fingers grazed hers for a shocky second, but it was over so fast, she didn't have time to jerk away. Good thing, or she would have sloshed her drink.

He picked up his own glass and, with his smoky blue-eyed gaze locked with hers, dinged the rims together. "To partnership," he said. "May it be a pleasurable union."

"Successful, you mean. I'll drink to a successful union." As soon as the words came out, she realized her mistake. She and Lucas did not view the world through the same lens.

He took his time swallowing a mouthful of wine, and she

was so busy watching his throat muscles ripple that when his forefinger tipped up her chin, she almost squealed in surprise. His thumb brushed her lips, catching on the lower one, and her breath stuttered when he tilted his head toward hers.

"Darlin'," he said, halting way too close. His whiskey-smooth voice flowed over her. "If you find our union as pleasurable as I intend, I'll consider that a success. Dinner will be ready in forty-five minutes."

A hot flush stole over her cheeks and flooded the places he'd touched. He went back to cooking.

As she watched him chop and sauté and whatever, she had to instruct her stomach to unknot. He'd been messing around, like always. That's all. For Lucas, flirting was a reflex so ingrained he probably didn't realize he was doing it, especially when directing it at his fake wife in whom he had no real interest.

She bristled over his insincerity until Fergie squawked. A fitting distraction from obsessing about the feel of Lucas's thumb on her mouth. She retrieved her laptop from the bedroom and researched what parrots ate while Lucas finished preparing the people food.

"The guy at the pet store said to feed her papaya. They like fruit," Lucas said and refilled her wineglass. "There's one in the refrigerator if you want to cut it up."

She sighed. He'd even bought a papaya. Did the man ever sleep? "Thanks, I will."

Silence fell as she chopped alongside her husband, and it wasn't so bad. She shouldn't be hard on him because he dripped sexiness and made her ache when he looked at her, as if he knew the taste of her and it was delicious. Might as well be ticked over his blue eyes.

The simple celebratory dinner turned into a lavish poolside spread. Lucas led her outside, where a covered flagstone patio edged the elegant infinity pool and palm trees rustled overhead in the slight breeze. Dust coated the closed grill in the top-of-the-line outdoor kitchen, but the landscaping appeared freshly maintained, absent of weeds and overgrown limbs.

Lucas set the iron bistro table with green Fiestaware and served as she took a seat.

"What kind of chicken is this?" she asked and popped a bite into her mouth. A mix of spices and a hint of lime burst onto her tongue.

He shrugged. "I don't know, I made it up. The kitchen is one of the places where I let my creativity roll."

Gee. She just bet she could guess the other place where he rolled out the creativity.

"Oh. I see." She nodded sagely. "Part of your date-night repertoire. Do women take one bite and fall into a swoon?"

"I've never made it for anyone else." His eyes glowed in the dusky light as he stared at her, daring her to draw significance from the statement.

When he stuck a forkful of couscous in his mouth and withdrew it, she pretended like she hadn't been watching his lips.

This was frighteningly close to a conversation over a good bottle of wine, the idea he'd thrown out as the way to get to know each other. But they still weren't dating. Perhaps he should be reminded. "Really? What do you normally make when you have a hot date you want to impress?"

He stopped eating. As he sat back in his chair, he cupped his wineglass and dangled it between two fingers, contemplating her with a reckless smile. "I've never cooked for anyone, either."

She dropped her fork. Now he was being ridiculous. "What, exactly, am I supposed to take from that?"

"Well, you could deduce that I cooked you dinner because I wanted to."

"Why? What's with the parrot and dinner and this—" she waved at the gas torches flaming in a circle around the patio and pool "—romantic setting? Are you trying to get lucky or something?"

"Depends." His half-lidded gaze crawled up inside her and speared her tummy. "How close am I?"

Why couldn't he answer the question instead of talking in his endless, flirty Lucas-circles?

Oh, no.

His interest in her was real. As real as the hunger in his expression after kissing her. As real as the evidence of his arousal while dancing last night. Clues she'd dismissed as... what? She didn't even know; she'd just ignored them all so she didn't have to deal with them. Now she did.

Firmly, she said, "We can't have that kind of relationship." The kind where she gave him a chunk of her heart and he took it with him when he left. The kind where she'd surrender her hard-won self-reliance, which would happen over her dead body. "We have an agreement."

"Agreements can be altered." That dangling wineglass between his fingers raked up her nerves and back down again. He couldn't even be serious about holding stemware.

"This one can't. What if I got pregnant?"

Dios. With fingers trembling so hard she could scarcely grip the glass, she drained the remainder of her wine and scouted around for the bottle. There'd be no children in her future. Life was too uncertain to bring another generation into it.

"Well, now that's just insulting. What about me suggests I might be so careless?"

"Arrogance is your preferred method of birth control?"

They were discussing *sex.* She and Lucas were talking *about having sex.* Sitting by the pool, eating dinner and talking about sex with her fake-in-name-only-going-away-soon husband.

"I'm not worried, darlin'. It's never happened before."

She stood so fast the backs of her knees screeched the chair

backward until it tipped over. "Well, that's a relief. Please stand back as I become putty in your hands."

He followed her to his feet without fanfare, no more bothered than if they were discussing what color to paint the bathroom.

In one step, he was an inch away, and then he reached out and placed a fingertip on her temple. Lazily, he slid the fingertip down her face, traced the line of her throat and rested it at the base of her collarbone with a tap. "What's going on in there? You're not afraid of getting pregnant."

"Stop touching me." She cocked a brow and refused to move away from the inferno roiling between Lucas's body and hers. He was the one who should back down, not her. Last night, she'd run from this confrontation and look where that had gotten her. "Nothing is going on other than the fact that I'm not attracted to you."

Liar. The hot press of his fingertips against her skin set off an explosion way down low. But wanting someone and being willing to surrender to the feeling were poles apart.

"I don't believe you," he murmured.

He wasn't backing down. His hands eased through her hair, and unmistakable heat edged into his eye.

"What, you think you're going to prove something by kissing me?"

"Yep," he said and dipped his head before she could protest.

For a sixteenth of a second, she considered all possible options, and then his lips covered hers and she went with dissolving into his arms. It was all she could do when Lucas kissed her, his mouth hot and the taste of his tongue sudden and shocking.

His fingers trailed sparklers through her hair and down her spine, molding her against the potent hardness of his body. Clicking them together like nesting spoons, foretelling how sweetly they would fit without clothes.

He angled his head and took her deeper, yanking a long, hard pull from her abdomen. A burst of need uncoiled from a hidden place inside to burn in all the right places. It was real, and it was good. He was good.

So good, she could feel her resistance melting away under the onslaught of his wicked mouth. But she couldn't give in, and, *Dios,* it made her want to weep.

If only he'd kept a couple of those layers hidden. If only she had a way to insulate herself from someone like him. The intensity between them frightened her to the bone, because he had the unique ability to burrow under her defenses and take whatever he wanted.

Then he'd leave her empty, and she'd worked too hard to put herself back together after the last disastrous attempt at a relationship.

She broke away, wrenched out of his arms and rasped, "All that proves is you've practiced getting women naked."

His face was implacable and his shoulders rigid beneath the fabric of his slate-gray button-down. He cleared his throat. "Darlin', why are you fighting this so hard? At first I thought it was because you've been around so much misery, but there's something else going on here."

"Yeah. Something else, like I don't want to. Is your ego so inflated you can't fathom a woman not being interested in you?"

He laughed. "Hon, if that's how you kiss a guy you're not interested in, I'll lick a sardine. Pick a different card."

How dare he throw her own phrase back in her face.

"This is funny to you? How's this for a reason? You might very well be the hottest male on the planet, but I am not willing to be your latest conquest, Wheeler." Her hands clenched into fists and socked against his chest. For emphasis. And maybe to unleash some frustration. He didn't move an iota.

For who knew what ill-advised reason, he reached out, but then he wisely stopped shy of her face. "Is it so difficult

to believe you intrigue me and I simply want to unwrap the rest of you?"

"Yeah. It is." She crossed her arms to prevent any more unloading of frustration. His chest was as hard as his head. And other places. "You're feeling deprived. Go find one of the women who text messaged you earlier in the car and scratch your itch with her, because I'm not sleeping with you."

A smile curved his mouth, but the opposite of humor flashed through his steely gaze. "In case it's slipped your mind, I'm married. The only person I'll be sleeping with for the next six months is my wife."

Panic spurted at the back of her throat. Upon meeting her for the first time, he'd kissed her hand—how had she not considered that his old-fashioned streak didn't end there?

Of course, he'd also flat-out told her he wouldn't sleep with another woman while she wore his ring. "Your wife just turned you down flat."

"For tonight anyway."

His supreme confidence pricked at her temper. So he thought he could seduce away her resistance?

"For forever. Honestly, I don't care if you sleep with someone else. It's not really cheating."

The sudden image sprang to mind of Lucas twined with another woman, the way he'd been with her on the bed, his mouth open and heated against the tramp's throat, then kissing her senseless and dipping a clever hand under her clothes.

Her stomach pitched. Ridiculous. She didn't care what he did. She really didn't.

"I care," he said, his silky voice low.

"Why? This isn't a real marriage. You aren't in love with me. You barely like me."

"We're legally married. That makes it really cheating, whether I've had you naked and quivering in my arms or not. Have I made my position clear enough?" Fierceness tightened his mouth and scrunched his eyes and had her faltering.

Anger. It was so foreign, so wrong on Lucas, she didn't know what to do with it.

"I think so." She swallowed against a weird catch in her throat. So, maybe he wasn't quite the horn dog she'd assumed. "Are you clear on my position?"

"Crystal."

Relieved he wasn't going to push some macho, possessive sexual agenda on her, she nodded. "Great. I'm glad we talked this out. It's incredibly important that we handle this fake marriage like rational adults. Now we can go forward as we've discussed, as pure business associates, without any additional complications. Agreed?"

Reflected torchlight danced in his eyes, obscuring his true thoughts. He leaned in and motioned her closer.

With his lips almost touching her earlobe, he said succinctly, "Sweetheart, the only thing I plan to do going forward is regroup. And then, my darlin' Mrs. Wheeler, all bets are off."

He turned on his heel and left her on the patio. She had the distinct impression he was both mad *and* plotting how to get even.

Six

Lucas waited almost a week before cornering the lioness in her den, partially because he'd been hustling his tail off eighteen hours a day to secure at least one elusive client—which had failed miserably—and partially because Cia needed the distance. Pushing her was not the right strategy. She required delicacy and finesse. And patience. God Almighty, did she ever require patience. But when her thorny barriers came tumbling down...well, experience told him she'd be something else once she felt safe enough to let loose. He'd gladly spent a good chunk of unrecoverable work hours dreaming up ways to provide that security.

He did appreciate a challenge. No woman he'd ever romanced had forced him to up his game like she did. He'd have sworn on a stack of Bibles that kind of effort would have him bowing out before sunset. Not this time.

Cia's routine hadn't varied over the past week, so she'd be home from the shelter around four. Usually, he was mired in paperwork in the study or on a conference call or stuffing food in his mouth while doing research as he prepared for a late meeting with a potential client—all activities he could have done at the office.

But he'd developed the habit of listening for her, to be sure she and her zero-to-sixty-in-four-point-two-seconds car made it home in one piece.

Today, he waited in the kitchen and talked to Fergie, who so far only said "hello," "goodbye" and imitated the microwave timer beep so perfectly he almost always turned to open it before realizing she'd duped him. He'd been trying to get her to say "Lucas," but Fergie might be more stubborn than her owner.

When Cia walked in the door, hair caught up in a sassy ponytail, he grinned but kept his hands by his sides instead of nestling her into his arms to explore that exposed neck.

A woman named Dulciana had to have a sweet, gooey center, and he itched to taste it.

"Hey," she said in wary surprise. They hadn't spoken since she'd laid down the law during his aborted celebratory poolside dinner. "What's up?"

"I have a favor to ask," he said. It was better to get to the point since she'd already figured out he wanted something. Being married to Mrs. Psych Minor kept him honest. When the woman at the heart of the challenge was onto him, it made things so much more interesting.

Guarded unease snapped her shoulders back. "Sure. What is it?"

"WFP sold a building to Walrich Enterprises a few months ago, and they're having a ribbon cutting tonight. I'd like to take you."

"Really?" Her forehead bunched in confusion. "Why?"

He swallowed a laugh. "You're my wife. That's who you take to social stuff for work. Plus, people would speculate why I attended solo after just getting married."

"Tell them I had to work." She cocked her head, swinging that ponytail in a wide pendulum, taunting him. So she wanted to play, did she?

"I used that excuse at the last thing I went to. If everyone was curious before, they're rabid now. You don't have much of a social presence as it is, and you're going to get labeled a recluse if you keep hiding out."

"You didn't ask me to go to the last thing." She smiled sweetly enough, but he suspected it was a warning for what would be an excellent comeback. "If I get a reclusive reputation, seems like we might revisit who's to blame."

Yep. She got the first point in this match. But he was getting the next one. "The last thing was boring. I did you a favor by letting you skip it, so you owe me. Come to the ribbon cutting tonight."

"Wow. That was so slick, I didn't see it coming." She crossed her arms, tightening her T-shirt—sunny yellow today—over her chest. "I'd really prefer to skip it, if it's all the same."

With a couple of drunken ballerina sidesteps, she tried to skirt him.

"Cia." He easily stepped in front of her, halting her progress and preventing her from slamming the door on the conversation.

Her irises transformed into deep pools of blue. "You called me 'Cia.' Are you feeling okay?"

His brow quirked involuntarily as he filed away how mesmerizing her eyes became when he called her Cia. It was worth a repeat. "This is important or I wouldn't have asked. You proposed this marriage as a way to rebuild my reputation. That's not going to happen by taking a picture of our marriage license and posting it on the internet. With my nice, stable wife at my side during this event tonight, people will start to forget about Lana."

With a sigh, she closed her lids for a beat. "Why did you have to go and make the one logical point I can't argue with?

Let's pretend I say yes. Are you going to complain about my outfit all night?"

Here came the really tricky part. "Not if you wear the dress I bought you."

Fire swept through her expression, and she snapped, "I specifically asked you not to buy me clothes."

"No, you ordered me not to, and I ignored you. Wear the dress. The guests are the cream of society."

"And you don't want to be ashamed to be seen with me." Hurricane force winds of fury whipped through her frame, leaving him no doubt she'd gladly impale him with a tree limb or two if her path happened to cross them.

"Darlin', come on." He shook his head. "You'd be gorgeous in pink-and-teal sofa fabric, and I'd stand next to you all night with pride. But I want you to be comfortable alongside all those well-dressed people. Appearance is everything to them."

"To them. What about you? Are you that shallow, too?" Her keen gaze flitted over him.

"Appearances aren't everything, but they are important. That's what a reputation is. Other people's view of how you appear to them, which may or may not reflect reality, and that's what makes the world go round. All you can do is present yourself in the best possible light."

Her ire drained away, and a spark of understanding softened her mouth. "That's why you got so angry when I said I didn't care if you slept with other women. Because of how it would look."

And here he thought he'd covered up that unexpected temper flare. Must need more practice. He rarely let much rile him, and it was rarer still to let it show. A temporary, in-name-only wife shouldn't have that kind of effect. He shrugged. "People talk and it hurts, no matter how you slice it. I would never allow that to happen to you because of me."

If Lana had been of the same mind, he'd never have met

this fierce little conquistador now called Mrs. Lucas Wheeler. A blessing or a curse?

"I'm sorry I suggested it. It was insensitive." With a measured exhale, she met his gaze. "I'll go. But I want to see the dress before I agree to wear it. It's probably too big."

Well, then. She'd conceded not just the point but the whole match. A strange tightness in his chest loosened. "It's hanging in your closet. Try it on. Wear it if you like it. Throw it in the trash if you hate it. We should leave around seven, and I'll take you to dinner afterward." He risked squeezing her hand, and the cool band of her wedding ring impressed his palm. "Thanks. I promise you'll have fun tonight."

She rolled her eyes. "I don't even want to know how you plan to guarantee that." She let their hands slip apart and successfully navigated around him to leave the kitchen. Over her shoulder, she shot the parting volley. "See you at seven-ten."

Later that night, Lucas hit the ground floor of their house at six fifty-five. When Cia descended the stairs at seven on the dot, his pulse stumbled. Actually *stumbled*. He'd known the floor-length red sheath would look amazing on her as soon as he'd seen it in the window.

Amazing didn't cover it. She'd swept her hair up in a sexy mess of pins and dark locks and slipped black stockings over legs that peeped through the skirt's modest slit.

"Darlin', you take my breath away," he called up with a grin contrived to hide the fact that he was dead serious. His lungs hurt. Or at least something in his chest did.

Compared to his vivacious wife, Lana was a pale, lackluster phantom flitting along the edges of his memory.

"Yeah, well, I have a feeling when I trip over this long dress, I'll take *my* breath away, too," she said as she reached the ground floor. "Did you seriously tell me to throw Versace in the trash?"

The distinctive scent of coconut and lime wafted over him.

"Not seriously." His mouth was dry. He needed a drink. Lots of drinks. "I knew you wouldn't hate it."

"Don't pat yourself on the back too hard. I'm only wearing it because the price tag is equal to the GDP of some small countries. It would be wrong to throw it away." Sincerity oozed from her mouth. But he was onto her.

He stared her down. Even in heels, she only came up to his nose. "I still have the receipt. Pretty sure the store would take it back. Run upstairs and change. I'll wait."

"All right, all right." She spit out a bunch of Spanish, and danged if it wasn't sexy to watch her mouth form the foreign words. Then she sighed, and it was long-suffering. "It's beautiful and fits like a dream. Because your ego isn't big enough already, I will also admit you have an excellent eye for style. If you undress a girl as well as you dress one, your popularity with the ladies is well deserved."

A purifying laugh burst out of him. He'd missed sparring with her this past week and the mental gymnastics required. When she engaged him brain to brain, it thoroughly turned him on.

Something was definitely wrong with him.

"Well, now. As it happens, I believe I'm pretty proficient at both. Anytime you care to form your own opinion, let me know. Ready?"

She laughed and nodded. Obviously, something was wrong with both of them, because he'd bet every last dollar that she enjoyed their heated exchanges as much as he did, though she'd likely bite off her tongue before saying so. Which would be a shame since he had a very specific use in mind for that razor-sharp tongue of his wife's.

The ribbon-cutting ceremony at Walrich's new facility was packed. People talked to Lucas, and he talked back, but he couldn't for the life of him recall the conversations because he spent the evening entranced by his wife's bare neck.

Since they were in public, he had every reason to touch

her whenever the inclination hit, which happened often. The torch-red dress encased her slim body with elegance, and the sight of her very nice curves knifed him in the groin.

Sure he'd bought women clothes before, but not for a woman who lived under his roof and shared his last name. Everything felt bigger and more significant with Cia, even buying her an age-appropriate dress. Even bringing her to a social event with the strict intent of jump-starting his reputation rebuild.

Even casually resting his hand on the back of her neck as they navigated the room. The silk of her skin against his fingers bled through him with startling warmth. Startling because the response wasn't only sexual.

And that just wasn't possible.

"Let's go," he told Cia. Matthew could work potential clients, which was his strength anyway. "We've done enough mingling."

"Already?" She did a double take at the expression on his face. "Okay. Where are we going for dinner?"

He swore. Dinner put a huge crimp in his intent to distance himself immediately from the smell of coconut and lime.

But if he bailed, whatever had just happened when he touched Cia would stick in his mind, nagging at him. Not cool. That fruity blend was messing with his head something fierce.

What was he thinking? He couldn't leave the schmoozing to Matthew like he used to. Cia hadn't balked at attending the ribbon cutting. What kind of coward let his wife do all the hard work?

The best way to handle this divorce deal, and his disturbing attraction to the woman on his arm, was obviously to remember the Lucas Wheeler Philosophy of Relationships—have a lot of sex and have a lot of fun, preferably at the same time.

This was a temporary liaison with a guaranteed outcome, and besides, he was with an inarguably beautiful woman. What other kind of response was there except sexual?

Shake it off, Wheeler.

"A place with food," he finally said.

Cia eyed her decadently beautiful husband, who should be required by law to wear black tie every waking hour, and waited a beat for the rest of the joke. It never came.

She hadn't seen Lucas in a week and had started to wonder exactly how mad she'd made him by the pool. Then he'd appeared and asked her pretty please to attend this boring adult prom, which she couldn't legitimately refuse, so she hadn't. For her trouble, he'd spent the evening on edge and not himself. "Great. Places with food are my favorite."

Matthew Wheeler materialized in front of them before they could head for the exit.

Lucas glanced at his brother. "What's the climate with Moore?"

Since Matthew was pretending she was invisible, Cia openly studied her authoritative, remote brother-in-law. A widower, Lucas had said, and often dateless, as he was tonight. Clearly by choice, since any breathing woman would find Matthew attractive—as long as he didn't stand next to Lucas. When he did, he was invisible, too.

"Better than I expected." Matthew signaled a waiter and deposited his empty champagne flute on the tray. "He's on the hook. I booked reservations in your name at the Mansion for four. Take Moore and his wife to dinner on me. Since closing the deal is your forte, I'll bow out. Bring it home."

As if they'd practiced it a dozen times, Lucas kissed Cia's temple, and she managed to lean into it like his lips weren't hotter than a cattle brand. Nothing like a spark of Lucas to liven up the prom.

Not that she'd know anything about prom. She'd missed that and the last half of senior year, thanks to the accident that had taken her parents.

"Do me a favor," Lucas said, "and hang out with Matthew

for a minute. Looks like we might have different plans for the evening."

Then he strode off through the crowd to go work his magic on some unsuspecting guy named Moore.

Matthew watched her coolly through eyes a remarkably close shade to Lucas's. "Having a good time, Cia?"

Oh, so she'd miraculously reappeared. But she didn't mistake the question as friendly. "Yes, thank you. Your clients are impressive."

"What few we have, I suppose." His shrewd gaze narrowed. "I'll be honest. I have no idea what got into Lucas by marrying you, but I see the way he looks at you and I hope there's at least a chance you're making him happy."

What way did Lucas look at her—like a spider contemplating a particularly delectable fly? His brother should find a pair of glasses. She narrowed her gaze right back. "So, you'll hunt me down if I hurt him?"

He laughed, and the derisive note reminded her again of Lucas. They didn't look so much alike but they did have a similar warped sense of humor, apparently.

"I highly doubt you have the capacity to hurt Lucas. He's pretty good at staying emotionally removed from women. For example, he didn't blink when he found out about Lana. Just moved right along to the next one."

As warnings went, it was effective—if she'd been harboring some romantic illusion about Lucas's feelings toward her. "How many of the next ones did Lucas marry?"

"Touché." Her brother-in-law eyed her and then nodded to an older couple who'd swept past them on the way to the bar. "I know you're not after Lucas's money. I checked out you and your trust fund. I'm curious, though, why didn't you stay at Manzanares?"

The loaded question—and Matthew's bold and unapologetic prying—stomped on her defenses. "I worked there for a year to appease my grandfather. I'm probably the only one he'd trust to take over." Shrugging, she wrapped it up. She didn't owe him any explanations. "It's not my passion, so he plans to live forever, I guess."

Matthew didn't smile. Thank goodness Lucas had been the one in need of a wife and not his brother. There was a brittleness to Matthew Wheeler, born of losing someone who meant everything, and she recognized it all too well.

In contrast, Lucas played at life, turning the mundane fun, and he smiled constantly in a sexy, self-assured way, which sometimes caught her with a lovely twist in the abdomen. That was the thing she liked most about him.

Dios. When had that happened?

"Family may not mean much to you, Cia. But it's everything to us." Matthew's expression hardened, and she revised her opinion. The frozen cerulean of his irises scarcely resembled the stunning smoky blue of Lucas's. "Lana punched a hole in Lucas's pride, which is easily dismissed, but in the process, she nearly destroyed a century of my family's hard work. That's not so easily overcome. Be an asset to him. That's all I'll say."

Matthew clammed up as Lucas rejoined them with a deceptively casual hand to the place where her neck and shoulder met. The dress she wore nearly covered her from head to foot and yet her husband managed to find the one bare spot on her body to brush with his electric fingertips.

She'd missed him. And no way would she ever admit it.

"Dinner's on," he told Matthew. "I'll call you later."

Matthew's advice echoed in her head as she let Lucas lead her to his car. Well, she was here, wasn't she? There was also a contract somewhere in Lucas's possession granting him the sales rights to the Manzanares complex, which Abuelo had gladly signed.

Her relationship with Lucas was as equitable as possible. How much more of an asset could she be?

Regardless, all through dinner she thought about Fergie.

And the house. She wore the Versace and the diamond rings her husband had selected. The scales in her mind unbalanced, and she was ashamed Matthew had to be the one to point out how little she'd given Lucas in return for throwing his strengths on the table.

She'd been so focused on making sure she didn't fall for his seduce-and-conquer routine, she'd forgotten they had an agreement.

Their partnership wasn't equitable at all, not with her shrewish behavior and giving him a hard time about attending a social event. She should have been glad to attend, but she wasn't because her husband was too much of a temptation to be around.

Lucas didn't try to kiss her or anything at the end of the evening, and she reminded herself four times how pleased she was the back-off messages were sinking in.

She slept fitfully that night and woke in the morning to dreary storm clouds, which she should have taken as a warning to stay in bed.

A young Hispanic woman in a crisp uniform was scrubbing the sink when Cia walked into the kitchen.

The girl smiled. *"Buenos días, señora."*

Cia looked over her shoulder automatically and then cursed. *She* was the *señora,* at least for the next few months. "Good morning," she responded in Spanish. "I'm sorry, I didn't realize Mr. Wheeler hired a maid."

Of course if he'd bothered to tell her, she would have. Men.

"I'm to come three days a week, with strict instructions you must be happy with my work." The girl bobbed her head and peeled yellow latex gloves from her hands, which she dropped into the sink. "I've already cleaned the master suite. With your permission, I'd like to show you what I've done."

"Sure." Cia was halfway to the stairs before the raucous clang of a big, fat warning bell went off in her head. "You, um, cleaned the master suite? The bathroom, too?" Where there was a noticeable lack of cosmetics, hair dryer or conditioner.

Her heart flipped into overtime.

Satanás en un palo. The maid had cleaned Lucas's bedroom while Cia slept in her room down the hall. They might as well have put out a full-page ad in the *Dallas Morning News*—Mr. and Mrs. Lucas Wheeler Don't Share a Bedroom.

While the maid politely pointed out the sparkling tile and polished granite vanity in the master bathroom, Cia listened with about a quarter of her attention and spent the other three-quarters focusing on how to fix it.

Lucas had royally screwed up. Not on purpose. But still.

"So you'll be back on Wednesday?" Cia asked when the maid finished spouting about the cleaning process.

"Tomorrow, if acceptable. This week, I have Wednesday off. And then back again on Friday."

Of course she'd be back tomorrow. "Fine. That's fine. Your work is exceptional, and I'm very pleased with it. Please let me know when you've finished for the day."

The maid nodded and went off to clean, oblivious to Cia's ruined day. Cia called the shelter to let them know she'd be unavoidably late and sent Lucas a text message: Come home before eight. I have to talk to you.

The second the maid's compact car backed out of the driveway, Cia started transferring her clothes into Lucas's bedroom. Fortunately, there was a separate, empty walk-in closet inside the bathroom. It took twelve trips, fourteen deep breaths and eight minutes against the wall in a fetal position, forehead clamped between her fingers, to get all her clothes moved.

Toiletries she moved quickly with a clamped jaw, and then had to stop as soon as she opened the first dresser drawer, which contained tank tops and drawstring shorts. Sleepwear.

She'd have to sleep in the same room with Lucas. On the floor. Because there was no way she'd sleep in the same bed.

No way she'd sleep in it even if he wasn't in it. No doubt the sheets smelled all pine-tree-like and outdoorsy and Lucas-y.

And, boy, wouldn't the floor be comfortable? Especially with Lucas breathing and rustling and throwing the covers off his hard, tanned body as he slept a few feet away.

God, he better be several feet away. What if he pounced on the opportunity to try to sweet-talk her into bed?

What if? Like there was a snowball's chance he'd pass up the opportunity. And after last night, with the dress and the warm hand on her shoulder all evening and the way he kept knocking down her preconceptions of him, there was a tiny little corner of her mind afraid she'd let herself be swept away by the man she'd married.

Her feminine parts had been ignored for far too long—but not long enough to forget how much of a mess she'd been after the last time she'd jumped into bed, sure that *this* was finally the right man to heal the pain from losing her parents, only to scare yet another one away with colossal emotional neediness.

She was pretty passionate about whatever she touched, and there weren't many men who could handle it, especially not when it was coupled with an inadvertent drive to compensate for the gaping wound in her soul. Until she figured out how to be in a relationship without exposing all the easy-to-lose parts of herself, the best policy was never to get involved— or to get out as quickly as possible.

There had to be another way to solve this problem with the maid besides sleeping in the same room with Lucas. What if she moved her stuff to Lucas's room and got ready for bed there but slept in her room? She could get up early the days the maid came and make up the bed like she'd never been there. Or maybe she could pretend the maid hadn't met her standards and dismiss her. Maybe moving her stuff was a total overreaction.

Her phone beeped. She pulled it from her back pocket. Incoming text from Lucas: What's wrong? What do you need to talk about?

She texted him back: It's an in-person conversation. BTW, how did you find the maid?

In thirty seconds, the message alert beeped again. Lucas: She just started working for my mother and came highly recommended by your grandfather. Why?

Abuelo. She moaned and sank to the floor, resting her forehead on the open drawer full of sleepwear.

Well, if anything, she'd underreacted. The maid was her grandfather's spy, commissioned to spill her guts about Cia's activities at the shelter, no doubt. Abuelo probably didn't even anticipate the coup of information coming his way about the living arrangements.

It was too late to dismiss her. Imagine the conversation where she said a maid who was good enough for Lucas's mother wasn't good enough for Cia. And was she really going to fire a maid who probably sent at least fifty percent of her take-home pay back to extended family in Mexico?

Not only did she and Lucas need to be roommates by tomorrow, she'd have to come up with a plausible reason why they hadn't been thus far and a way to tell the maid casually.

With a grimace, she weaved to her feet and started yanking tank tops out of the drawer, studiously avoiding thoughts about bedrooms, Lucas, beds and later.

Beep. Lucas: Still there? What's up?

Quickly, she tapped out a response: Yeah. No prob with the maid. Late for work. Talk 2U tonight. Have a good day.

She cringed. Wait until he found out his wife telling him to have a good day was the least of the surprises in store.

Seven

Lucas rescheduled three showings he could not afford to put off and pulled into the garage at home by five, thanks to no small effort and a white-knuckle drive at ten over the speed limit. Suspense gnawed at his gut. Something was wrong, and Cia being so closemouthed about it made it ten times worse. Most women considered it worthy of a hysterical phone call if the toilet overflowed or if they backed the car into the fence. With his wife, the problem could range from serious, like the shelter closing down, to dire, like her grandfather dying.

Cia's car wasn't in the garage or the driveway, so he waited in the kitchen. And waited. After forty-five minutes, it was clear she must be working late. More than a little irritated, he went upstairs to change. As he yanked a T-shirt over his head, he caught sight of the vanity through the open bathroom door.

The counter had been empty when he left this morning. Now it wasn't.

A mirrored tray sat between the twin sinks, loaded with

lotion and other feminine stuff. He picked up the lotion and opened it to inhale the contents. Yep. Coconut and lime.

In four seconds, he put the cryptic text messages from Cia together with the addition of this tray, a pink razor, shaving cream and at least six bottles of who knew what lining the stone shelf in the shower.

The maid had spooked Cia into moving into the master bedroom. Rightly so, if the maid had come recommended by Cia's grandfather, a detail he hadn't even considered a problem at the time.

Man, he should have thought of that angle long ago. In a few hours, Cia might very well be sleeping in his bed.

He whistled a nameless tune as he meandered back to the kitchen. No wonder Cia was avoiding home as long as possible, because she guessed—correctly—he'd be all over this new development like white on rice. Her resistance to the true benefit of marriage was weakening. Slowly. Tonight might be the push over the edge she needed.

At seven o'clock, he sent her a text message to find out what time she'd be home. And got no answer.

At eight o'clock he called, but she didn't pick up. In one of her texts, she'd mentioned being late for work. Maybe she'd stayed late to make up for it. He ate a roast beef sandwich and drank a dark beer. Every few bites, he coaxed Fergie to say his name.

But every time he said, "Lucas. Looo-kaaaas," she squawked and ruffled her feathers. Sometimes she imitated Cia's ringtone. But mostly the parrot waited for him to shove a piece of fruit through the bars, then took it immediately in her sharp claws.

At nine-thirty, Lucas realized he didn't know the names of Cia's friends and, therefore, couldn't start calling to see if they'd heard from her. There was avoidance, and then there was late.

Besides, Cia met everything head-on, especially him. Radio silence wasn't like her.

At eleven o'clock, as he stared at the TV while contemplating a call to the police to ask about accidents involving a red Porsche, the automatic garage door opener whirred.

A beat later, Cia trudged into the kitchen, shoulders hunched and messy hair falling in her face.

"Hey," he said.

"Hey," she repeated, her voice thinner than tissue paper. "Sorry. I got your messages."

"I was kind of worried."

"I know." The shadows were back in full force, and there was a deep furrow between her eyes he immediately wanted to soothe away.

"I'm sorry," she repeated. "It was unavoidable. I'm sure you saw my stuff in your room."

None of this seemed like the right lead-up to a night of blistering passion. "I did. So we're sharing a bedroom now?"

She squeezed her temples between a thumb and her middle finger, so hard the nail beds turned white. "Only because it's necessary. Give me fifteen minutes, and then you can come in."

Necessary. Like it was some big imposition to sleep in his bed. He knew a woman or two who'd be there in a heartbeat to take her place. Why couldn't he be interested in one of them instead of his no-show wife, who did everything in her power to avoid the best benefit of marriage?

Fearful of what he might say if he tried to argue, he let her go without another word and gave her twenty minutes, exactly long enough for his temper to flare.

He was married, mad and celibate, and the woman responsible for all three lay in his bed.

When he strode into the bedroom, it was dark, so he felt his way into the bathroom, got ready for bed and opted to sleep naked, like normal. This was his room and since she'd moved into it without asking, she could deal with all that entailed.

He hit the button on the TV remote. She better be a heavy sleeper, because he always watched TV in bed, and he wasn't changing his habits to suit anyone, least of all a prickly wife who couldn't follow her own mandate to be home by eight.

The soft light of the flat screen mounted on the wall spilled over the empty bed. He glanced over at it. Yep, empty. Where was she?

A pile of sheets on the floor by the bay windows answered that question. "Cia, what are you doing over there?"

"Sleeping," came the muffled reply from the mass of dark hair half-buried under the pile.

Since she still faced the wall, he turned the volume down on the TV. "You can't sleep on the floor."

"Yes, I can."

"This bed is a California king. Two people could easily sleep in it without touching the entire night." Could. But that didn't necessarily mean he'd guarantee it. Although, given his mood, he was pretty sure he'd have no problem ignoring the unwilling woman in his bed.

After a lengthy pause, she mumbled, "It's your bed. I'm imposing on you. The floor is fine."

The martyr card. Great. A strangled sigh pushed out through his clamped teeth. "Get in the bed. I'll sleep on the floor."

"No. That's not fair. Besides, I like the floor. This carpet is very soft."

"Well, then." Two could play that game. "Since it's so comfortable, I'll sleep on the floor, too."

With a hard yank, he pulled the top sheet out from under the comforter, wrapped it around his waist and threw a pillow on the floor a foot from hers. As he reclined on the scratchy carpet, she rolled over and glared at him.

"Stop being so stubborn, Wheeler. The bed is yours. Sleep in it."

Coconut and lime hit his nose, and the resulting pang to the abdomen put a spike in his temper. "Darlin', you go right ahead and blow every gasket in that pretty little head of yours. I'm not sleeping in the bed when you're on the floor. It's not right."

She made a frustrated noise in her throat. "Why do you always have to be such a gentleman about *everything?*"

"'Cause I like to irritate you," he said easily.

She flipped back to face the wall. As he was about to snap out more witticisms, her shoulders started shaking.

"Hey," he called. "Are you crying?"

"No," she hissed, followed by a wrenching sob.

"Aw, honey, please don't cry. If it'll make you feel better, you can call my mother and yell at her for teaching me manners. Either way, I'm not sleeping in the bed unless you do."

This pronouncement was greeted with a flurry of sobbing. Every ounce of temper drained away.

Obviously, his manners weren't as well practiced as he'd bragged, and he'd been too worked up to remember arguing and prickliness were Cia's way of deflecting the comfort she sorely needed but refused to ask for.

He scuttled forward and cursed the binding sheet and sandpaper carpet impeding his progress, but finally he wormed close enough to gather her in his arms. "Shh. It's okay."

She stiffened as the war going on inside her spread out to encompass her whole body. Then, all at once, she surrendered, melting into a puddle of soft, sexy woman against him, nestling her head on his shoulder and settling her very nice backside tight against his instantly firm front side.

Hell on a horse. He'd only been trying to get her to stop crying. He honestly expected her to kick him away. The sheet chafed against his bare erection, spearing his lower half with white-hot splinters. He sucked in a breath and let it out slowly. It didn't help.

Prickly Cia he could resist all day long. Vulnerable Cia got under his skin.

Her trim body was racked with sobs against his, yet he was busy trying to figure out what she had on under that pile of sheets. *Moron.*

He shut his eyes and pulled her tighter into his arms, where she could sob to her heart's content for as long as it took. His arousal ached every time he moved, but he stroked her hair and kept stroking until she fell still a million excruciating years later.

"Sorry." She sniffed into the sudden silence. "I'm just so tired."

He kept stroking her hair in case the torrent wasn't over. And because he liked the feel of its dark glossiness. "That wasn't tired. That was distraught."

"Yeah." A long sigh pushed her chest against his forearm. "But I'm tired, too. So tired I can't pretend I hate it when you calm me down. I don't know what's worse, the day I had or having to admit you've got the touch."

His hand froze, dark strands of her hair still threaded through his fingers. "What's so bad about letting me make you feel better?"

She twisted out of his arms and impaled him with the evil eye. "I hate being weak. I hate you seeing my weaknesses. I hate—"

"Not being able to do everything all by yourself," he finished and propped his head up with a hand since she was no longer curled in his arms. "You hate not being a superhero. I get it. Lie down now and take a deep breath. Tell me what tall building you weren't able to leap today, the one that made you cry."

Her constant inner battle played out over her face. She fought everything, even herself. No wonder she was tired.

With a shuddery sigh, she lay on the pillow, facing him, and light from the TV highlighted her delicate cheekbones. Such a paradox, the delicacy outside veiling the core of steel inside. Something hitched in his chest.

Oh, yeah. This strong woman hated falling. But he liked being the only one she would let catch her.

"One of the women at the shelter…" she began and then faltered. Threading their fingers together, he silently encouraged her to go on. A couple of breaths later, she did. "Pamela. She went back to her husband. That bastard broke her arm when he shoved her against a wall. And she went back to him. I tried to talk her out of it. For hours. Courtney talked to her, too. Nothing we said mattered."

He vaguely recalled Courtney was Cia's friend and also her partner in the new shelter. A psychologist. "You can't save everyone."

She pulled their fingers apart. "I'm not trying to save everyone. Just Pamela. I work with these women every day, instilling confidence. Helping them see they can be self-sufficient…" Her voice cracked.

She looked at this as failure—as her failure. Because these women, and what she hoped to accomplish with them, meant something, and she believed in both. It went way past fulfilling her mother's wishes. Her commitment was awe inspiring.

The line between her eyes reappeared. "She threw it all out to go back to a man who abused her. He might kill her next time. What could possibly be worth that?"

"Hope," he said, knowing his little psych minor couldn't see past her hang-ups. "Hope people can change. Hope it might be different this time."

"But why? She has to know it's got a one hundred percent certainty of ending badly."

"Honey, I hate to rain on your parade, but people naturally seek companionship. We aren't meant to be alone, despite all your insistence to the contrary. This Pamela needs to hope the person she chose to marry is redeemable so they can get on with their lives together. Without hope, she has nothing."

Hair spilled into her face when she shook her head. "That's not true. She has herself, the only person she can truly rely on. The only person who can make sure she's taken care of."

"Are you talking about Pamela or Cia?"

"Don't go thinking you're smart for shoving a mirror in my face. It's true for both of us, and I've never had any illusions about my beliefs, particularly in relation to men."

"Illusions, no. Blind spots, yes." He ventured a little closer. "You're so black-and-white. You saw the trust clause and assumed your grandfather intended to manipulate you into a marriage where you'd be dominated by a man. You said it yourself. He wants you to be taken care of. Allowing someone to take care of you isn't weakness."

Her mouth tightened. "I can take care of myself. I have money, I have the ability to—"

"Darlin', there's more to being cared for than money." He swept a lock of hair off her shoulder and used the proximity as an excuse to run his hand across her silky skin again. "You have physical needs, too."

"Oh, my God. You do indeed have a gift. How in the world did you manage to drop sex into this conversation?"

He grinned in spite of the somber tone of their illuminating conversation. "Hey, I didn't say anything about sex. That was you. I was talking about holding you while you cry. But if you want to talk about sex, I could find some room in my schedule. Maybe start with telling me the most sensitive place on your body. Keep in mind, I'll want to test it, so be honest."

She smacked him on the arm without any real heat. "You're unbelievable. I'm not having sex with you simply because we've been forced into sharing a room."

Touching him on purpose. Would wonders never cease? He caught her gaze. "Then do it because you want to."

Her frame bristled from crown to toe, and the sheet slipped

down a few tantalizing inches. "I don't want to, Wheeler! You think you're God's gift to women and it never occurs to you some of us are immune to all your charm and…and—" her hungry gaze skittered over his chest, which he had not hidden under a sheet mummy-style, like she had "—sexiness. Stop trying to add another notch to your bedpost."

Could she have protested any more passionately? "Okay."

"Okay?" One eye narrowed and skewered him. "Just like that, you're giving up?"

"That was not an okay of concession. It was an okay, it's time to change the subject. Roll over."

"What? Why?"

A growl rumbled through his chest. "Because I said so. You need to relax or you'll never go to sleep. If you don't go to sleep, you'll keep arguing with me, and then I won't sleep. I'm just going to massage your shoulders. So shut up and do it."

Warily, she rolled, and he peeled the sheet from her as she spun, resettling it at her waist. Tank top with spaghetti straps. Not the sexiest of nightclothes, but when he lifted the dark curtain of hair away from her neck, the wide swath of bare skin from the middle of her back up to her hairline pleaded for his touch.

So he indulged.

First, he traced the ridges of her spine with his fingertips, imprinting the textures against his skin. Once he reached her neck, he went for her collarbone, following it around to the front and back again.

She felt amazing.

He wanted more of her naked flesh under his fingers. Under his body. Shifting against his skin, surrounding him with a hot paradox of hard and soft.

The stupid floor blocked his reach, so he settled for running his fingers over her exposed arm, trying to gauge whether she'd notice if he slipped the tank top strap off her shoulder.

"What, exactly, are you doing?" She half rolled to face him. "This is the least relaxing massage I've ever had."

"Really?" he asked nonchalantly and guided her back into place. No way was he missing a second of unchecked access to Cia. "Someone who's immune to my charms should have no problem relaxing while I'm impersonally rubbing her shoulders."

"Hmpf." She flipped back to face the wall. Must not hate it too much.

He let the grin spread wide and kneaded her neck muscles. "Darlin', there's no sin in enjoying it when someone touches you."

She snorted but choked on it as his hand slid up the inside of her arm again and a stray finger stroked her breast. He needed the tank top gone and that breast cupped in his palm.

"There is the way you do it," she rasped.

"You know," he said, closing the gap between them, spooning her heated back to murmur in her ear, a millimeter from taking the smooth lobe into his mouth. "I don't for a moment believe I'm God's gift to women. Women are God's gift to man. The female form is the most wonderful sight on earth. The beautiful design of your throat, for example."

He dragged his mouth away from her ear and ran his lips down the column of her neck. "I could live here for a decade and never completely discover all the things I love about it," he said, mouthing the words against her skin.

He was so hard and so ready to sink into her, his teeth hurt

Her head fell back onto his shoulder, her eyes closed and her lashes fluttered, fully exposing the area under discussion. Her sweet little body arched in wanton invitation, spreading against his. He wanted to dive in, find Dulciana's gorgeous, gooey center and feast on it.

This visceral attraction would be satisfied, here and now.

"Lucas," she breathed, and his erection pulsed. "Lucas, we can't. You have to stop."

"Why?" He slid a hand under her tank top, fanning his palm out on her flat stomach and working it north. Slowly. Familiarizing his fingertips with velvety skin. "And if you use that smart mouth to lie to me again about your lack of interest, I will find something better to do with it."

"I doubt even I could pull off that lie anymore," she said wryly.

The admission was so sweet, he couldn't help it.

He found her lips and consumed them, kissing her with every bit of frustrated, pent-up longing. And God Almighty, her lips parted just enough, and he pushed his tongue into her mouth, tasting her, reveling in the hot slide of flesh.

For a few magnificent seconds she tasted him back, triggering a hard coil of lust.

But then she ripped her lips away, mumbling, "No more," as his thumb brushed the underside of her breast.

She bowed up with a gasp, and his erection tingled. She was so responsive, like it had been ages since she'd... He pulled his hand free and gripped her chin to peer into her eyes. "Hold up a sec. You're not a virgin, are you?"

That would explain a few things.

He let his fingers fall away as she sat up. "My past experience is not the issue. We agreed to keep this business only."

No. No more of this endless circling. *Business only* disappeared eons ago, and she knew it as well as he did.

"Why are you here, in my bedroom? You could have easily moved your stuff and still slept in your room. But you didn't. Your signals are so mixed up, you've even confused yourself. Talk to me, honey. No more pretending. Why the roadblocks, when it's obvious we both want this?"

She crossed her arms and clamped her mouth shut. But then she said, "I don't like being some big challenge. If I give in, you win. Then off you go to your cave to beat your chest and crow over your prize."

"Give in?" He shook his head to clear it. They should both

be naked and using their mouths on each other. Not talking. "You better believe you challenge me. Something fierce, too, I'll admit. You challenge me to be better than I ever thought I could be, to rise to the occasion and go deep so I can keep up. I dig that seven ways to Sunday. Feel what you do to me, Cia."

Her eyes went liquid as he flattened her hand over his thundering heart, and when the muscle under her cool palm flexed, she curled her fingers as if trying to capture his response. She weaved closer, drawn by invisible threads into his space.

"You're so incredibly intelligent," he continued, fighting to keep from dragging her against him and sinking in like he ached to do. She had to choose this on her own. "How have you not figured out that gives you all the power? I'm just a poor, pathetic man who wants to worship at the altar of the goddess."

She hesitated, indecision and longing stamped all over her face. Whatever stopped her from jumping in—and it wasn't dislike of being a challenge—drove the battle inside of her to a fever pitch. She spent way too much energy thinking instead of feeling and way too much time buried in shadows.

And here he was trying to help her fix that, if she'd lay down that stubborn for a minute.

"You're the strongest woman I've ever met, and I like that about you," he said. "We both know strings aren't part of the deal. This is about one thing only. Sex. Fantastic, feel-good, uncomplicated sex. Nobody gets hurt. Everyone has fun. Sounds perfect for an independent woman with a divorce on the horizon, doesn't it?"

"Seducing me with logic. Devious."

"But effective."

The curve of her lips set off a tremor in his gut. "It's getting there."

Hallelujah. He threw his last-ditch inside straight on the table. "Then listen close. Let me take care of you. Physically. You give to your women till it hurts. Take for once. Let me make you feel good. Let me help you forget the rest of the world for a while. Use me, I insist. Do I benefit from it, too? Absolutely. That's what makes for a great partnership."

He'd laid the foundation for a new, mutually beneficial agreement. The next move had to be hers. She needed to be in control of her fate, and he needed to know she could never accuse him of talking her into it.

"Now, darlin', the floor sucks. I'm going to get in that nice, comfortable bed over there and if you want to spend the next few hours being thoroughly pleasured, join me. If not, don't. You make the choice."

Eight

Choice.

Instead of seducing her, Lucas had given her a choice. And with that single empowering act, Cia's uncertainty disappeared.

They were partners—equals—and he'd done nothing but respect that, and respect her, from the very beginning. He got her in ways she'd only begun to realize. Domination was not part of his makeup, and all he wanted from her was to join him in taking pleasure from sex, the way he took pleasure from every aspect of life.

She longed to indulge in the foreign concept, to seize what she wanted—Lucas.

To let his talents wash away all the doubt and frustration and disappointment about Pamela and help Cia forget everything except how he made her feel. He'd stripped the complexity from the equation and, suddenly, sex didn't mean she'd lose something.

The only way Lucas Wheeler could take a chunk of her

soul when he left was if she gave it to him. She wouldn't. Simple as making a choice. Who knew the secret to avoiding emotional evisceration was to lay out divorce terms first?

She stood and crossed the carpet with sure steps until her knees hit the side of the bed. Lucas lounged against a pillow, watching her, sheet pulled up to midtorso, bisecting the trio of intriguing tribal circles tattooed along the left edge of his ribs.

His eyes were on fire.

He was so gorgeous, and he was all hers for the night. As many nights as she chose, apparently. A shiver shimmied up her back, part anticipation and part nerves.

"You want to know what tipped the scales?" she asked, arms crossed so it wasn't obvious her hands were shaking.

"More than I want to take my next breath."

She eyed the length of his body stretched out in the bed. "Ironically, that you were willing to sleep on the floor."

He laughed, and the vibration thrummed through her abdomen. "So you're saying I had you at hello?"

"No. I'm pretty sure you had me at Versace. It's painful to admit I was so easily bought with a designer gown." She said it flippantly, so he'd know she was kidding.

Except she wasn't, exactly. It was difficult to swallow how much she liked his gifts. What did that say about her?

"I'm glad one of us thinks this was easy. I've never worked so hard to get a woman into bed in my life."

"An unrecoverable blow to your ego, no doubt." She cocked her hip and jammed a hand down on it. Had she been so exhausted less than an hour ago that she could barely stand? Adrenaline and a hefty craving for Lucas coursed through her. "And it's so funny, but I'd swear I'm not actually in bed yet. Perhaps your work isn't done after all."

With a growl, he flung off the sheet, sprang up from the mattress and crawled toward her, completely, beautifully naked. Her mouth went dry.

Wickedness flashed through his expression, and the shiver

it unleashed in her this time was all anticipation. She absolutely could not mistake how much she turned him on.

This was all for her. Not for him. He'd said so, and she intended to hold him to it.

He rose up on his knees in front of her and extended a hand. She took it and braced to be yanked onto the bed. Instead, he held each finger to his lips and kissed them individually. By the time he reached the pinkie, he'd added licking and sucking and the rough texture of his tongue burned across her flesh.

He pressed her palm to his chest and left it there. Then, he cupped her face reverently. "Beautiful. So beautiful."

Before she could squawk out a lame "Thank you," he captured her mouth with his and held the kiss, lips suspended in time, and a tornado of need whirled through her womb.

Slowly, he angled his head and parted her mouth with his lips, and heat poured into her body. His tongue found hers, gliding forward and back in a sensuous dance.

Her nails dug into his rock-hard chest, scrabbling for purchase to keep her off the carpet. The kiss went on and on and stoked the flame of desire higher and higher in her belly.

Slow. It was all about slow with Lucas, and it was exquisite torture. She needed more, needed him now.

She broke away and reached for him, but he shook his head. His hands skimmed up her arms and down her back, came around to the front again, and both thumbs hooked the hem of her tank top. Gradually, he drew it skyward as he watched her from below half-closed lids.

"You're, um, not going to make me get in the bed?" she asked hoarsely.

"Nope." He pulled her top free from her raised arms and tossed it over his shoulder, and then he encircled her waist with an arm to draw her closer, his gaze ravenous as it traveled over her bare breasts. "You chose not to get in bed. I choose to take care of you right where you're at."

Her nipples rubbed his naked torso and beaded instantly and fire erupted in her womb, drawing a moan from deep in her throat. If he kept whispering that whiskey-smooth voice across her bare skin, it wouldn't take long to rip a verbally induced climax out of her. But she hoped for a hands-on approach.

He obliged her. One hand glided to the small of her back and pushed, jutting her breasts up and allowing him to capture a nipple with his tongue in a searing, swirling lasso.

She gripped his shoulders, lost in a slow spiral toward brainlessness as he sucked and laved at her sensitive flesh.

He switched sides and treated the other nipple to his magically delicious mouth. When he skated hard teeth across the peak, her legs buckled. Why hadn't she gotten in bed?

His hand delved inside her shorts, along her bare bottom. His fingers slipped into the crevice, lifting her and crushing her to his torso, supporting her.

The shock of Lucas touching her *there* had her gasping, but a solid pang of want swallowed the shock. *"Madre de Dios."*

Lucas groaned against her breast. With it still in his mouth, he mumbled, "I love it when you talk dirty."

A throaty laugh burst out of her. "It means mother of God, dingbat."

"I don't care. Anything you say in Spanish sounds dirty. Say something else." He licked his way down her stomach and bit the tie on her shorts, pulling the strings loose with his mouth.

"Quiero que ahora—"

And then her brain shut off when he yanked down her shorts and panties. He turned her and pressed her spine to his torso, settling her rear against his hard length. His firm arm snaked between her breasts, locking her in place, and his clever fingers slid down her stomach to find her center.

He mouthed her throat and rubbed the hard button between

her folds until she squirmed against the restraining band of steel disguised as his arm.

One finger slid inside and then two, in and out, and her head rolled against his shoulder in a mindless thrash. So good, so hot. So everything.

His heavy arousal burned into the soft flesh of her bottom, thrilling her. His thumb worked her nub in a circle and the sensuous onslaught swirled into one bright gathering point against his fingers. She came so hard she cried out.

The ripples tightened her inner walls around his fingers, and he plunged his fingers in again and again to draw out the climax to impossible lengths until, finally, it ended in a spectacular burst.

Lucas had just ruined her for any other man.

Too spent to stand on her own, she slumped in his arms and her knees gave out. The additional weight must have caught him off guard, and she pulled him down with her. In a tangle of limbs, they hit the carpet, and Lucas laughed as he rolled her back into his arms.

"There you have it," he said into her hair. "Now we don't have to lie. Next time someone asks why we got married, you can truthfully say we fell for each other."

A giggle slipped out and cleared the fog in her head, along with any lingering tension from being with Lucas, naked and exposed. His ability to bring the fun was unparalleled.

He picked her up and laid her gently on the bed.

"The first one is for you," he said, eyes crystal clear blue and dazzling. "The next one is for me."

"That's fair." She cleared her throat. He deserved more than she knew how to give him. "Lucas? I'm nowhere near as um…practiced at this as you are. However, I promise to give it my best shot."

She dragged an elbow under her to sit up but he knocked it away. She flopped back on the tangle of sheets and watched as he straddled her, powerful thighs preventing his gorgeous body from crushing her.

All of him was beautiful, but in this position, the really good stuff lay at eye level. She didn't hesitate to look her fill and reached out to run her palms along his legs. So hard and so delectable.

"No." He shook his head. "*Your* next orgasm is for me. The first one doesn't count. It's only to take the edge off, and, honey, you were wound tight. I barely touched you and you went off like a Roman candle."

She moaned. "That was a demonstration of 'barely'?"

With a wicked smile, he laced their fingers together and drew her arms up above her head, manacled her wrists together with one hand and slid the other hand down the length of her side from shoulder to hip. "Oh, yeah. There's much, much more. But this time, I get to pick where you'll be, and it'll be right here, where I can watch you."

He began to touch her, watching her as he did, and his heavy-lidded stare unnerved her, even as it heightened the sensations of his hands and mouth on her bare skin. He did something sinful to every inch of her body until she couldn't breathe with the need for him to fill her.

Why had she resisted a man with Lucas's skill for so long? There wasn't a whole lot of taking pleasure necessary when he gave it so freely. How selfish was she that she stingily lapped it up?

After what felt like hours of lovely agony, he settled between her legs and his talented mouth dipped to the place he'd pleasured with his fingers. With his lips and teeth and, oh, yes, his tongue working her flesh, he drove her into the heavens a second time.

His eyes never left her, and her shuddering release intensified with the knowledge that he was watching her, taking his own pleasure in hers. The manifestation of the power he spoke of, the power she held, was exhilarating.

"Enough," she gasped. "I admit it. You were right. I could have slept in my room, but I guess part of me wanted you to force the issue. So I could keep pretending I'm not attracted to you. No more pretending. I want you. Now."

"That might be the sweetest confession I've ever heard." He rose up over her and captured her mouth in way-too-short, musky kiss. "But we have all night. And tomorrow night. So, slow down, darlin'. Half the fun is getting there."

"How is it not making you insane to keep waiting your turn?"

He laughed and threaded his hands through her hair in a long caress. "Good things come to those who wait. Besides, I'm dead center in the middle of my turn. Every nuance of desire flashing through your eyes turns me on. Every moan from your mouth is like music. I could watch you shatter for hours."

Hours? *Dios*. She should have read between the lines a little better when he blew off the pregnancy issue back by the pool. "You, um, do plan to eventually get around to a more traditional version of sex. Right?"

"Oh, you better believe it, honey. Later."

Later. She loved later.

Sacrifice and selflessness had ruled her for so long, it felt incredible to let go. To let Lucas take care of her. To be greedy for once and wallow in pure sensation and pleasure instead of shoving aside her needs for fear everything she depended on would be taken away in an instant.

How freeing to have it all on the table and be given permission to just have fun.

For all his talk, Lucas almost lost it—again—during Cia's third climax.

She was beautiful, like Mozart at sunrise, and she was so sensitive, he set off the third one accidentally by blowing on her. She cried out his name and exploded, bowing up with that awesome arch to her back, and an answering pulse grew stronger in his gut.

He clamped his teeth down hard to keep his own release under control. His muscles strained, aching with the effort it took not to plow into her sweet, sweet center right then and there, no condom, just her and unbelievable satisfaction.

The battle stretched out for an eternity and, for a moment, he feared he'd do it. He rolled away and fixated on the oscillating ceiling fan above the bed, willing back the crush of lust.

This little fireball he'd married was not going to break his self-control. Never mind that he'd invented this game of multiple orgasms to demonstrate this was nothing but sex between two people who were hot for each other. To confirm that this insane attraction wasn't as strong as he'd imagined and that there was nothing special about this particular woman.

Somewhere along the way, the scent of Cia's arousal and the total surrender in her responses eliminated his intentions.

She fell back onto the pillow with a sexy sigh, lifting her breasts and making his mouth water. "You melted my bones that time. As soon as I can walk, I'm going to make you the best cup of coffee you've ever had in your life."

That pulled a chuckle out of him, though it hurt clear to his knees to laugh. "The benefits are good enough to reverse your stance on making a man coffee, huh?"

"I cannot believe there wasn't a picket line of your ex-lovers at the courthouse the day we got married."

Yeah, he knew a trick or two about pleasuring a woman, and his genuine enjoyment of it helped, but this was a far cry from how he normally went about it. Nothing about this affair with Cia remotely resembled how he normally interacted with a woman.

How did he explain that to her when he didn't get it, either?

"You're funny. There are more women who would be happy to read my obituary notice than would be upset I married you."

She snorted. "I doubt that. But as your wife, I believe I have the right to claim a few privileges."

If he breathed through his mouth, he couldn't smell her lotion anymore, and the lack eased the pain a tiny bit. "Yeah? Like what?"

"Like the right to say it's later."

Without another word, she flipped and crawled on top of him, sliding up the length of his body, hot as a lava flow, and whipping his crushing need into a frenetic firestorm.

Her eyes were so dark, they were almost black. They met his with thirst in their depths. The evidence of her desire lanced through his gut.

Her mouth fit to his, pulling on his lips and sucking his tongue forward. A guttural moan wrenched free from his throat, and she absorbed it into the heat of her kiss. He flung his arms around her and bound her to his chest, desperate to keep her in place.

The things this woman did to him. It defied description. Thankfully, she'd agreed to exorcise this wicked draw between them by acting on it instead of pretending it didn't exist.

Long dark hair fell into his face, trailing along his fevered skin, sensitizing it and begging for attention. He wound it up in a fist and guided her head to the side, lips following the line of her neck with fierce suction, laving her skin with his tongue, crazy with the craving to taste her.

Lime and coconut invaded his senses, both curse and cure, snaking through his head like a narcotic, heightening the wild lust.

Her body covered his, scalding breasts flat against his chest, her hands shoved in his hair, fingers sparking where she touched his scalp. One leg straddled him, opening her up. Her hips gyrated and tilted her center against his throbbing tip. Damp heat flared out, enveloping him, and his eyes glazed.

Now. The keening scream exploded in his head as she dragged her slick center up the length of his erection.

"Wait," he bit out, with no idea whether he was talking to her or his questing hips, which had a mind of their own.

He stretched out a hand to fumble with the drawer knob on the bedside table, shifting her center. Should have already had a foil packet under the pillow, top torn off. Fingers closed over the box and an eternity later, he unrolled the condom.

The second he was sheathed, Cia wiggled back into place atop him, nudged him once and impaled herself to the hilt with a feminine gasp.

His eyelids snapped shut as he filled her. His body shrieked to start pumping, but he forced himself to give her a minute to adjust.

Amazing. So tight. He pulsed as she stretched to accommodate him. Stretched perfectly, just enough, just right. Experimentally, she slid up and back down, rolling her pelvis, driving him home.

Home. A place for him. Only him.

He echoed her hip thrusts and heaviness built upon itself, spiraling higher and energizing him to move faster and faster.

"Lucas," she breathed. "I… Will you, um, look at me? I like it when you watch me."

He worked his lids open and greedily soaked in the visual perfection of the female form astride him. Why had his eyes been closed this whole time? The empowerment, the sheer magnificence, plastered across her face forced all the air from his lungs in a hard whoosh.

He'd done that for her. Unleashed her desire from its boundaries and allowed her free rein to take pleasure from his body, exactly as he'd insisted.

And she was taking it. Acknowledging it. Returning it tenfold. It was unbelievably hot.

Her torso undulated in a primal dance, nipples peaked and

firm atop alabaster breasts. She threw her head back, plunging him deeper, and long hair brushed his thighs.

Sparkling pressure radiated from his groin. Willing it back, he clamped a hand on her thigh, trying to slow her wanton thrusts, but she bucked against him and the tightness shoved him to the very edge.

He couldn't stop. He couldn't wait for her.

But then she came apart and the shock waves blasted down his length, triggering his release. Their simultaneous climaxes fed each other, like oxygen to a flame, dragging out the sensations and flooding his whole body with warmth.

Flooding his body with something else, something nameless and heavy and powerful.

With a sated moan, she collapsed against him, nestling into the hollow of his shoulder, and he gripped her close, absorbing every last bit of warmth, too lost in the lush, thick haze of Cia to move. They were still joined, and he basked in a thrilling sense of triumph.

Only with him could Cia be like this.

Now would be an excellent time to put distance between them. But he couldn't find the energy. Couldn't figure out why he wasn't all that interested in distance when he knew he should be. Never had sex been like that, a frantic and mindless rush toward completion.

Completion, not release. Even this—*especially* this—was bigger, stronger and more meaningful with Cia.

He'd proven something to himself, all right. Something earthshaking. Something fearsome. This wasn't casual sex between two people. He'd been making love to his wife.

Nine

In the morning, Cia woke half-buried under Lucas, and it made her smile. One heavy arm pinned her to his chest and his legs tangled with hers, trapping her bottom against his abdomen. His heat at predawn was delicious, warming her sore and stretched body.

It had been a while. Since college, back when she'd still been convinced the right man's love would heal her. All she'd done was prove sex didn't equal love, and both were ingredients in the recipe to misery.

If her high school days had resembled most red-blooded Americans', she might have figured out how to handle relationships then, instead of lumbering into her mid-twenties without a clue. Now she finally got it.

As long as she divorced sex from emotion and commitment, no problem. Divorce rocked.

She unscrambled their limbs without waking him and slipped out of bed to head for a much-needed hot shower. It probably wouldn't have taken any effort at all to nudge

Lucas into semiawareness and then take shameless advantage of him, but she was anxious to get to the shelter. A part of her hoped Pamela would still be there, but in her heart, she knew better. Regardless, the other women would need someone to talk to.

In no time, she dressed and tiptoed out of the bedroom she now shared with the sexy, slumbering man sprawled out across the bed. *Later,* she promised. No-strings-attached sex was the most awesome thing ever invented.

Pamela was indeed gone for good when Cia arrived at the shelter. The other women seemed dejected and upset. How self-centered was she for being in such a good mood, for shutting her eyes and savoring memories of the previous night? But she couldn't help it and had to force herself to stop humming three times while handling the most unexciting tasks.

Since she'd stayed so late the night before and arrived at seven that morning, Cia elected to leave at three.

She should be wiped out, but as she drove home, her mind got busy with one topic only—seeing Lucas again as soon as possible. She couldn't stop fantasizing about him. About the beyond-sexy trio of tattoos down the length of his torso and how she'd like to experiment on him a little to see how many times she could make him explode in a night.

Was it cool to call him and ask about his schedule? She'd almost sent him a text at least once every ten minutes, just to check in. Or say thanks for an awesome time last night. Or something else not so lame, but she had no idea about the rules when the person she was sleeping with was also her fake husband.

They'd done a lot of talking last night. But not once had Lucas mentioned what their relationship would look like going forward.

So frustrating. And ridiculous. It wasn't as if she could casually ask Courtney the requisite number of days to wait before calling when the guy involved was Cia's husband. As far as her friend knew, the marriage was still business only, and Cia wanted to get used to the change before admitting anything to anyone.

Besides, she and Lucas *still* weren't dating. Maybe it was okay to let her spouse know she was into him. In a strictly hot for his body kind of way.

Once at home, she stopped in the kitchen to get a glass of water and drank it while standing at the sink. Before she could swallow the second mouthful, said spouse blew through the door, startling her into dropping the glass into the sink.

"What are you doing home?" she asked.

Lucas strode toward her in a dark suit, which encased his shoulders with perfection, and a dark, impossible-to-misread expression on his face. Raw masculinity whipped through the kitchen to engulf her a moment before the man did.

He caught her in his arms and kissed her, openmouthed, hungrily, working her backward until her butt hit the countertop's edge.

She was trapped between hard granite and hard Lucas, and he was devouring her whole with his mouth. A whirlwind of desire kicked up in her center.

Dull thunks registered, and Lucas's hands delved inside her shirt, yanking down her bra and palming her breasts. Buttons. He'd popped all the buttons on her shirt and they'd thunked to the floor.

Four seconds later, he stripped her. Then he tore off his jacket, ripped the rest of his clothes half off and boosted her onto the counter. Cold stone cooled her bare bottom and sizzled against her fevered core.

Less than five minutes after he'd walked in the door, he spread her legs wide and plunged in with a heavy groan.

She dropped into the spiral of need and hooked her legs behind him, urging him on. His mouth was everywhere, hot and insatiable. His thrusts were hard, fast. She met him each time, already eager for the next one. Pinpoints of sensation swirled and then burst as she came, milking his climax.

What happened to *slow down?*

They slumped together, chests heaving, her head on his shoulder and his head on hers. She put her arms around him for support since her spine had been replaced with Jell-O.

"Um, hi," she said, without a trace of irony. If this was what their relationship would look like going forward, the view agreed with her quite well.

"Hi," he repeated, and she heard the smile in his voice.

"How was your day?"

He laughed and it rumbled against her abdomen. "Unproductive except for the last ten minutes. You distracted me all day. Don't disappear tomorrow morning. I'd like to wake up with you."

The explosive countertop sex had been hot, but the simplicity, the normalcy, of his request warmed her. "It's not my fault you're such a heavy sleeper. Set an alarm."

"Maybe I will." Carefully, he separated from her and trashed the condom. He helped her to the floor and gathered up her clothes, which he handed off, then began pulling on his own clothes with casual nonchalance. "I have another favor. I swear I was going to ask first but, darlin', you have to stop looking at me like that when I come in."

When his muscled, inked torso disappeared behind his ruined shirt, she sighed. Those tribal tattoos symbolized Lucas to a T—untamed, unexpected and thoroughly hidden beneath the surface. One of his many layers few people were aware existed, let alone privileged enough to experience. How lucky was she?

"You looked at me first." Of course, he always looked at her like a chocoholic with unlimited credit at the door of a sweetshop. "What's the favor? Do I get another dress out of the deal?"

He grinned and kissed her hand. "Of course. Except this time, I intend to take it off of you afterward."

"Or during." She shrugged and opted to toss her irreparable blouse in the trash. Lucas might end up buying her a new wardrobe after all, by default. "You know, if it's boring and you happen to spy a coat closet or whatever."

His irises flared with heat and zinged her right in the abdomen. "Why, Mrs. Wheeler, that is indeed a fine offer. I will surely keep it under advisement. Come with me and let's see about your dress."

Mrs. Wheeler. He'd called her that before, and it was her official title, so it shouldn't lodge in her windpipe, cutting off her air supply.

But it did. Maybe because she'd just been the recipient of a mind-blowing climax courtesy of Mr. Wheeler.

He took her hand and led her upstairs, where the couture fairies had left a garment bag hanging over her closet door. Her fake husband was a man of many, many talents, and she appreciated every last one.

"By the way," Lucas said. "When I ran into the maid earlier, I told her we'd had a little misunderstanding about a former girlfriend, but you were noble enough to get past it. I hope that's okay. Any excuse for why we weren't sharing a bedroom is better than nothing, right?"

"More than okay. Perfect." And not just the excuse. While she still basked in the afterglow of amazing sex, everything about Lucas was perfect.

The deep blue dress matched her eyes and eclipsed the red one in style and fit. Lucas leaned against the doorjamb of the bathroom, watching her dress with a crystalline focus and making complimentary noises. His attention made her feel beautiful and desired, two things she'd never expected to like.

Lucas Wheeler was a master of filling gaps, not creating them. Of giving, not taking. Ironic how she'd accused him of being selfish when trying to convince him to marry her.

As they entered the Calliope Foundation Charity Ball, a cluster of Wheelers surrounded them. Lucas's parents, she already knew, but she met his grandparents for the first time and couldn't help but contrast the open, smiling couple to Abuelo's tendency to be remote.

Matthew joined them amid the hellos, and his cool smile reminded her she owed Lucas one asset of a wife. It was the very least she could do in return for his selflessness over the entire course of their acquaintance.

A room full of society folk and money and lots of opportunities to put her foot in her mouth were nearly last on her list of fun activities, right after cleaning toilets and oral surgery. But she kept her hand in Lucas's as they worked the room; she laughed at his jokes, smiled at the men he spoke to and complimented their wives' jewelry or dress.

There had to be more, a way to do something more tangible than tittering over lame golf stories and smiling through a fifteen-minute discourse on the Rangers' bull pen.

"Are these clients or potential clients?" she asked Lucas after several rounds of social niceties and a very short dance with Grandfather Wheeler because she couldn't say *no* when he asked so nicely.

"Mostly potential. As I'm sure you're aware, our client list is rather sparse at the moment."

"Is there someone you're targeting?"

"Moore. He still hasn't signed. Matthew invited another potential, who's up here from Houston. George Walsh. He's looking to expand, and if I'm not mistaken, he just walked in."

If Walsh lived elsewhere, the Lana fiasco probably factored little in his decision process. "Industry?"

"Concrete. Pipes, foundations, that sort of thing. He's looking for an existing facility with the potential to convert but wouldn't be opposed to build-to-suit." He laughed and shook his head. "You can't be interested in all this."

"But I am. Or I wouldn't have asked. Introduce me to this Walsh."

With an assessing once-over, he nodded, then led her to where Matthew conversed with a fortyish man in an ill-fitting suit.

Matthew performed the introductions, and Cia automatically evaluated George Walsh. A working man with calluses, who ran his company personally and preferred to get his hands dirty in the day to day. Now what?

Schmoozing felt so fake, and she'd never been good at it. Lucas managed to be genuine, so maybe her attitude was the problem. How could she get better?

Though it sliced through her with a serrated edge, she shut her eyes for a brief second and channeled her mother in a social setting. What would she have done? Drinks. Graciousness. Smiles. Then business.

Cia asked Walsh his drink preference and signaled a waiter as she chatted about his family, his hobbies and his last vacation. Smiling brightly, she called up every shred of business acumen in her brain. "So, Mr. Walsh, talk to me about the concrete business. This is certainly a booming area. Every new building needs a concrete foundation, right?"

He lit up and talked for a solid ten minutes about the weather, the economy and a hundred other reasons to set up shop in north Texas. Periodically, she threw in comments about Lucas and his commitment to clients—which in no way counted as fabrication since she had firsthand experience with his thoughtful consideration and careful attention to details.

Somehow, the conversation became more than acting as an asset to Lucas and enhancing his reputation, more than reciprocation for upholding his end of the bargain. She'd failed at drumming up donations for the shelter, despite believing in it so deeply. Here, she was a part of a partnership, one half of Mr. and Mrs. Wheeler, and that profoundly changed her ability to succeed.

It reiterated that this marriage was her best shot at fulfilling her mother's wishes.

"Did I do okay?" she whispered to Lucas after Matthew took Walsh off to meet some other people.

Instead of answering, he backed her into a secluded corner, behind a potted palm, and pulled her into his arms. Then he kissed her with shameless heat.

Helplessly, she clung to his strong shoulders as he explored every corner of her mouth. His strength and solid build gave him the means to do the only thing he claimed to want—to take care of her. It wasn't as horrible or overbearing as she might have anticipated.

It was…nice. He understood her, what she wanted. Her dreams. Her fears. And they were partners. Who had amazing sex.

When he pulled back, the smile on his face took her breath.

"More than okay," he said. "Are you angling to join the firm?"

"Well, my name *is* Wheeler," she said in jest, but it didn't seem as funny out loud. That was a whole different kind of partnership. Permanent. Real. Not part of the plan.

"Yes. It is." He lifted her chin to pierce her with a charged look. The ballroom's lighting refracted inside his eyes, brightening them. He leaned in, and the world shrank down to encompass only the two of them as he laid his lips on hers in a tender kiss. A kiss with none of the heat and none of the carnal passion sizzling between them like the first time.

It was a lover's kiss. Her limp hands hung at her sides as her heart squeezed.

Oh, no. No, no, no.

"We have to find that coat closet. Now," she hissed against his mouth. Sex. That's all there was between them, all she'd allow. No tenderness, no affection, no stupid, girlie heart quivers.

His eyebrows flew up. "Now? We just got he— Why am I arguing about this?"

Linking hands, he pulled her along at a brisk trot, and she almost laughed at the intensity of his search for a private room. Around a corner of the hotel's long hallway, they found an empty storage room.

Lucas held the door and shooed her in, slammed it shut and backed her against the wood, his ravenous mouth on hers.

The world righted itself as the hard press of his body heated hers through the deep blue dress. This, she accepted. Two people slaking a mutual wild thirst and nothing more.

"Condom," she whispered.

He had about four seconds to produce it. An accidental pregnancy would tie her to this man for life, and, besides, she didn't want children. Well, she didn't want to cause herself heartache, which was practically the same thing.

"Right here. I was warned I'd need it."

Fabric bunched around her waist an instant later, and her panties hit the ground. He lifted her effortlessly, squashing her against the door and spreading her legs, wrapping them around him.

The second he entered her—buried so deep, every pulse of his hard length nudging her womb—she threw her head back and rode the wave to a mind-draining climax.

Yes. Brainless and blistering. Perfect.

When she came down and met the glowing eyes of her husband, a charged, momentous crackle passed between them.

She'd keep right on pretending she hadn't noticed.

Warm sunlight poured through the window of Lucas's office. He swiveled his chair away from it and forced his attention back to the sales contract on his laptop screen. Property—dirt, buildings, concrete or any combination—lived in his DNA and he'd dedicated his entire adulthood to it. It shouldn't be so difficult to concentrate on his lifeblood.

It was.

His imagination seemed bent on inventing ways to get out of the office and go home. In the past few weeks, he'd met a sprinkler repairman, an attic radiant barrier consultant and a decorator. A *decorator.* Flimsy, he had to admit.

A couple of times after showings, he'd swung by the house, which was mostly on the way back to the office. Through absolutely no fault of his own, Cia had been home all those times, as well, and it would have been a crime against nature not to take advantage of the totally coincidental timing.

Ironic how a marriage created to rescue his business was the very thing stealing his attention from business.

Moore had signed. Walsh had signed. Both men were enthusiastic about the purchases they'd committed to, and Lucas intended to ensure they stayed that way. Cia's interactions with them had been the clincher; he was convinced.

His dad had gone out of his way to tell Lucas how good this marriage was for him, how happy he seemed. And why wouldn't he be? Cia was amazing, and he got to wake up with her long hair tangled in his fingers every morning.

The past few weeks had been the best of his life. The next few could be even better as long as he kept ignoring how Cia had bled into his everyday existence. Every time they made love, the hooks dug in a little deeper. Her shadows rarely appeared now, and he enjoyed keeping them away for her. He liked that she needed him.

If he ignored it all, it wasn't really happening.

Matthew knocked on the open door, his frame taut and face blank. "Dad called. Grandpa's in the hospital," he said. "Heart attack. It's not good. Dad wants us to come and sit with Mama."

Heart attack? Not Grandpa. That heavy weight settled back into place on his chest, a weight that hadn't been there since the night he met Cia.

Lucas rose on unsteady legs. "What? No way. Grandpa's

healthier than you and me put together. He beat me at golf a month ago."

Protesting. Like it would change facts. His grandfather was a vibrant man. Seventy-five years old, sure, but he kept his finger on the pulse of Texas real estate and still acted as a full partner in the firm.

When Lucas had graduated from college, Grandpa had handed him an envelope with the papers granting Lucas a quarter ownership in Wheeler Family Partners. A careworn copy lined the inner pocket of his workbag and always would.

"I'll drive." Matthew turned and stalked away without waiting for Lucas.

Lucas threw his laptop in his bag and shouldered it, then texted Helena to reschedule his appointments for the day as he walked out. Once seated in Matthew's SUV, he texted Cia. His wife would be expected at the hospital.

The Cityplace building loomed on the right as Matthew drove north out of downtown. They didn't talk. They never talked anymore except about work or baseball. But nothing of substance, by Matthew's choice.

They'd been indivisible before Amber. She'd come along, and Matthew had happily become half of a couple. Lucas observed from a distance with respect and maybe a small amount of envy. Of course his relationship with Matthew had shifted, as it should, but then Amber died and his brother disappeared entirely.

Lucas sat with his family in the waiting room, tapped out a few emails on his phone and exchanged strained small talk with Mama. His dad paced and barked at hospital personnel until a dour doctor appeared with the bad news.

Lucas watched his dad embrace Mama, and she sobbed on his shirt. In that moment, they were not his parents, but two people who turned to each other, for richer or poorer, in sickness and in health.

Apart from everyone, Matthew haunted the window, stoic

and unyielding as always, refusing to engage or share his misery with anyone. Not even Lucas.

The scene unfolded in surreal, grinding slow motion. He couldn't process the idea of his grandfather, the Wheeler patriarch, being gone.

Cia, her long, shiny hair flying, barreled into the waiting room and straight into Lucas. He flung his arms around her small body in a fierce clinch.

The premise that she'd come solely for the sake of appearances vanished. She was here. His wife was in his arms, right where she should be. The world settled. He clutched her tight, and coconut and lime wafted into his senses, breaking open the weight on his chest.

Now it was real. Now it was final. Grandpa was gone, and he hadn't gotten to say goodbye.

"I'm glad you came," Lucas said, and his voice hitched. "He didn't make it."

"I'm sorry, so sorry. He was a great man," she murmured into his shirt, warm hands sliding along his back, and they stood there for forever while he fought for control over the devastating grief.

When he tilted his head to rest a cheek on top of Cia's hair, he caught Matthew watching them, arms crossed, with an odd expression on his face. Missing his own wife most likely.

Finally, Lucas let Cia slip from his embrace. She gripped his hand and followed silently as he spoke to his dad, then she drove him to his parents' house with careful attention to the speed limit.

Mama talked about funeral arrangements with his father and grandmother, and through it all Cia never left his side, offering quiet support and an occasional comforting squeeze. Surely she had other commitments, other things she'd rather be doing than hanging out in a place where everyone spoke in hushed tones about death.

Her keys remained in her purse, untouched, and she didn't leave.

It meant a lot that she cared enough to stay. It said a lot, too—they'd become friends as well as lovers. He hadn't expected that. He'd never had that.

For the first time, he considered what might happen after the divorce. Would they still have contact? Could they maintain some kind of relationship, maybe a friends-with-benefits deal?

He pondered the sudden idea until Matthew motioned him outside. Cia buzzed around the kitchen fixing Mama a drink, so he followed his brother out to the screened-in porch.

Matthew retrieved a longneck from a small refrigerator tucked into the corner, popped the top with the tail of his button-down in a practiced twist and flopped into a wicker chair, swigging heartily from the bottle.

Lucas started to comment about the hour, but a beer with his brother on the afternoon of his grandfather's death didn't sound half-bad. Might cure his dry throat.

Bottle in hand, Lucas took the opposite chair and swung one leg over the arm. "Long day."

Matthew swallowed. "Long life. Gets longer every day."

"That's depressing." His life got better every day, and considering the disaster it had been, that was saying something. Lucas hesitated but plunged ahead. "Do you want to talk about it?"

"No. But I have to." He sighed. "First Amber. Now Grandpa. I'm done. It's the last straw. I can't take it anymore."

That sounded serious. Suicidal even. Lucas looked at his normally solid and secure brother. "Do you need a vacation?"

"Yeah." Matthew laughed sarcastically. "From myself. Problem is they don't offer that with an all-inclusive resort package. I don't know what it's going to take to get me back on track, but whatever it is, it's not here."

"Where is it?"

Shrugging, Matthew drained his beer in record time. "I

have no idea. But I have to look for it. So I'm leaving. Not just for a few days. Permanently."

"Permanently?" Lucas shook his head. Matthew was a Wheeler. Wheelers didn't take off and let the chips fall. Everything Lucas knew about being a Wheeler he'd learned from watching his brother succeed at whatever he attempted. Obviously Matthew was overtired. "You can't leave. Take some time away. You've been working too much, which is my fault. Let me handle clients for a week or two. Backpack through the Himalayas or drink margaritas in Belize. But you have to come back."

"No, I don't. I can't." Stubborn to the core. That was one Wheeler trait they shared.

"Wheeler Family Partners isn't a one-man show. We just lost Grandpa. Dad's been taking a backseat for a couple of years, and now he's going to be the executor for Grandpa's estate. We're it."

And Matthew was more it than Lucas-the-gray-sheep could ever be.

Matthew's sharp gaze roved over Lucas in assessment. "You can do it without me. You've changed in the past year. Maybe Lana snapped some sense into you, or maybe it started happening long before and I didn't see it. Regardless, you've turned into me."

"Turned into you? What does that mean?"

"Responsible. Married. Committed. I always thought I'd be the one to settle down, have a family. Raise the next generation of Wheelers to carry on WFP. But lo and behold, it's not going to be me. It's going to be you."

The beer bottle slipped out of Lucas's hand and broke in two against the concrete patterned patio. The sharp yeasty scent of the last third of a beer split the air. "What are you talking about? I'm not settling down. There's no family in my future."

"Right." His brother snorted. "If Cia's not pregnant within a month, I'll fall over in a dead shock."

Oh, man. They'd done a spectacular job of fooling everyone into believing this was the real thing, and now Matthew felt safe leaving the firm in Lucas's hands. "Uh, we're being careful. She's not interested in having children."

"Yeah, well, accidents happen. Especially as many times as I'd bet you're doing it. You're not quite as subtle as you must think when you dash off during an event and sneak back in later, without giving Cia a chance to comb her hair. You two are so smoking hot for each other, I can't believe you haven't set something on fire."

So now he was supposed to apologize for enjoying sex with his wife? "Sorry if that bothers you," Lucas retorted. "We have a normal, healthy relationship. What's the problem?"

Matthew raised his brows. "No problem. Why so defensive? I'm pointing out that you landed on your feet. That's great. I'm happy for you. I admit, I thought you rushed into this marriage because of Lana or, at the very least, because you'd screwed up and gotten a one-night stand pregnant. Clearly, I was wrong. Cia's good for you. You obviously love each other very much."

He and Cia surely deserved Oscars if Matthew, who missed nothing, believed that. "Thanks."

"Although," Matthew continued in his big-brother tone, "you probably should have thought twice about marrying someone who doesn't want kids. Isn't family important to you?"

If the marriage had been intended to last, he definitely would have thought more about it back on that terrace. Now Matthew's words crowded his mind, shoving everything else out. "Isn't it important to *you?* You're the one talking about abandoning everyone."

"Only because you can take my place. You can be me and

I can be you. I'll go find fun and meaningless experiences, without worrying about anything other than myself."

"Hey now." Was that how his brother saw him? "Lay off the cheap shots."

"Sorry." Matthew gave him an assessing once-over. "Six months ago, you wouldn't have blinked at such a comment. It's an interesting transposition we have going on. You have no idea how hard it is for me to think about marrying again. Having a baby with someone who isn't Amber. Something is busted inside, which can't be repaired. Ever."

Quiet desperation filled Matthew's voice, the kind Lucas would never have associated with his older brother, who had always looked out for him. Whom Lucas had always looked up to, ever since the first time Matthew had stood shoulder to shoulder with his little brother against bullies. As Matthew took full responsibility for a broken flowerpot because he hadn't taught Lucas the proper way to hold a bat. As Matthew passed off the first client to his newly graduated brother and whispered the steps to Lucas behind the scenes.

A long surge unsettled Lucas's stomach. His brother had never been so open, so broken.

Matthew needed him. The firm, his family, his heritage all needed him. Lucas had to step up and prove his brother's faith in him wasn't misplaced. To show everyone Lucas knew what it meant to be a Wheeler, once and for all.

It would be hard, and parts of it would suck. But he had to.

Of course, he lacked a wife who wanted all the ties of a permanent marriage or who looked forward to filling a nursery with blankets and diapers. Where in the world would he find someone he liked as much as Cia, who excited him like she did even when they were nowhere near a bed? It would take a miracle to tick off all the points on his future-wife mental checklist. A miracle to find a wife as good as Cia.

Matthew clamped his mouth into a thin line and shifted his attention as Cia's hand slid across Lucas's shoulder.

"I didn't mean to interrupt," she said. "I just wanted to check on you. Doing okay?"

Concern carved a furrow between her brows, and he didn't like being the cause of that line. "Fine, darlin'. Thanks."

"Okay. I'm going to sit with your mom for a little while longer. She's pretty upset." She smiled and bent to kiss the top of his head, as if they were a real married couple in the middle of for better or worse.

His vision tunneled as future and present collided, and a radical idea popped fully formed into his head. An idea as provocative and intriguing as it was dangerous. One that would pose the greatest challenge thus far in his relationship with Cia.

What if they didn't get divorced?

Ten

A noise woke Cia in the middle of the night. No, not a noise, but a sixth sense of the atmosphere changing. Lucas. He'd finally pried himself loose from his laptop and paperwork. His study might be in the same house, but it might as well have been in Timbuktu for all she'd seen of him lately.

She glanced at the clock—1:00 a.m.—as he slid into bed and gathered her up against his warm, scrumptious body, spooning them together.

"Sorry," he whispered. "Time got away from me."

"It's okay. You're earlier than last night." And the night before that and the night before that. In the weeks since his grandfather's death and Matthew's disappearance, he'd been tense and preoccupied, but closemouthed about it other than to say he'd been working a lot.

She rolled in his arms and glued her body to his, silently offering whatever he wanted to take, because he'd done the same when she'd needed it. Sometimes he held her close and dropped into a dead sleep. Sometimes he was keyed up and wanted to talk. Sometimes he watched TV, which she always left on for him despite her hatred of the pulsing lights.

Tonight, he flipped off the TV and covered her mouth in a searing kiss. His hands skimmed down her back to cup her bottom, sliding into the places craving his careful attention.

Oh, yes. Her favorite of the late-night options—slow, achingly sensual and delicious. The kind of night where they whispered to each other in the dark and pleasured by touch, lost inside a world where nothing else existed.

In the dark, she didn't have to worry about what hidden depths of the heart might spring into her eyes. No agonizing over whether something similar crept through his eyes, as well. Or didn't. It was better to leave certain aspects of their relationship unexamined.

Of course, ignoring the facts didn't magically rearrange them into a new version of truth.

The truth was still the truth.

This was more than just sex.

Sex could be fun, but it didn't erase the significance of doing it with Lucas. Not some random, fun guy. *Lucas,* who got out of the way and let her make her own choices. Lucas, who'd proven over and over he was more than enough man to handle whatever she threw at him.

When the earth stopped quaking, Lucas bound her to him in a tight tangle of limbs. He murmured, *"Mi amante,"* and fell asleep with his lips against her temple.

When had he managed to squeeze in a Spanish lesson? His layers were endless and each one weighed a little more, sinking a little deeper into her soul.

This thing with Lucas was spiraling out of control. They were still getting a divorce, and all this *significance*—and how much she wanted it—freaked her out. It would be smart to back off now, so it wouldn't be so hard later.

In the morning, she woke sinfully late, still nestled in Lucas's arms for the first time in a long time, and she didn't hesitate to test how heavily he slept. The exact opposite of backing off. *Stupid* was her middle name lately.

"Mmm. Darlin', that is indeed a nice way to wake up," he murmured, after she'd sated them both.

"Stay in bed tomorrow morning, and you might get a repeat." She flipped on the TV and settled in to watch the weather while contemplating breakfast. "Can you eat or are you going to go drown yourself in listings right away?"

"I'm taking a little personal time this morning. I deserve it, don't you think?"

"Yeah. Does that mean I'm breakfast?"

He laughed. "Yep. Then I want to take you somewhere."

But he wouldn't tell her where until after they'd eaten, showered and dressed, and he'd driven to a run-down building miles off the freeway in an older part of town full of senior centers and assisted-living facilities.

"This just came up for sale," he told her as he helped her out of the car and led her to the edge of the parking lot. "It's an old hotel."

She glanced at him and back at the building. "I'm sorry. I'm not following why we're here or what the implication of this is."

"For the shelter," Lucas said quietly. "It can be retrofitted, and I checked on the zoning. No problems."

"The shelter." It took another thirty seconds for his meaning to sink in. "You mean my shelter? I'm planning to have it built."

"I know. This is another option. A less expensive option. Thirty-five percent down and I know a few people we can talk to about the financing."

"Financing?" If he'd started speaking Swahili, she'd have been equally as challenged to keep up. "I'm not getting a loan. That's the whole point of accessing my trust fund, so I can pay cash and the shelter will never be threatened with closure. We went over this. Without the trust money, I don't have thirty-five percent, let alone enough to purchase."

He clasped her hand with painstaking care. "I'll give you the money for the down payment."

The air grew heavy and ominous, tightening her chest. Their agreement specifically called for their assets to remain separate, and that might prove to be a touchier subject than sex. "You didn't get a terminal cancer diagnosis or something, did you? What's this all about?"

"You inspire me. Your commitment to victims of abuse is amazing. If I help you do this, you could start the shelter now instead of waiting until you get your money when the divorce is final. Save a few more women in the meantime."

"Oh, Lucas."

And that was it. Her heart did a pirouette and splattered somewhere in the vicinity of her stomach.

She rushed on, determined not to dwell on how many king's horses and how many king's men it would take to put everything back together again. "I appreciate what you're saying—I really do. But I can't get a loan, not for the kind of money we're talking about. I told you, Courtney and I tried. Our business plan wasn't viable, and venture capitalists want profits. Asking you to marry me was the absolute last resort, but it turned out for the best. If we have a loan, there's always a possibility of foreclosure if donations dry up, and I can't have that hanging over our heads."

No bank would ever own her shelter. Nothing would have the power to rip it from her fingers. It was far, far better to do it all on her own and never depend on anyone else. Much less painful that way.

"Okay. So, no loan." A strange light appeared in his eyes. "At least think about the possibility of this place. The owner is motivated to sell. Adding in the renovations, the purchase price is around a third of the cost to build. You could save millions."

Yes, she could. The savings could be rolled forward into operating costs, and it would be years and years before she needed to worry about additional funds beyond the trust money. The idea had merit. She could run the shelter without donations, a huge plus in her mind.

Maybe Lucas could talk the owner into waiting to sell until the divorce came through and she had access to the trust.

She surveyed the site again. The hotel was tucked away in a heavily treed area, off the beaten path. Bad for a hotel and good for a shelter the victims didn't want their abusers to find. "I do like the location. It's important for women who've taken the step to leave their abusers to feel safe. An out-of-the-way place is ideal. Tell me more about your thoughts."

Lucas started talking, his voice wandering along her spine, the same way his hands did when he reached for her at night. He threw around real estate terms and an impressive amount of research. When he was all professional and authoritative about his area of expertise, it pulled at her and bobbled her focus, which wasn't so sharp right now anyway.

Her brain was too busy arguing with her heart about whether she'd actually been stupid enough to fall for her all-too-real husband.

No question about it. She'd put herself in exactly the position she'd sworn never to be in again—reliant on a man to make her complete and happy. All her internal assurances to the contrary and all the pretending had been lies.

This was where brainless had gotten her: harboring impossible feelings for Lucas.

It hardly mattered if Lucas freed her to jump in and enjoy life alongside him. It hardly mattered if she'd accidentally married a man who understood her and everything she was about. It hardly mattered if she wished her soul had room for a mate and that such fairy tales existed.

They didn't.

Life didn't allow for such simplicity. Anything she valued

was subject to being taken away, and the tighter she held on, the greater the hurt when it was gone. The only way to stay whole was to beat fate to the punch by getting rid of it first.

She'd married Lucas Wheeler because he wasn't capable of more than short-term. She could trust him to keep his word and grant her a divorce, the sole outcome she could accept.

They had a deal, not a future.

Midway through an email, Lucas realized it had been four days since he'd spent time with his wife outside of bed. Their time together in bed had been less than leisurely and far from ideal. It was criminal.

He picked up the phone. "Helena. Can you reschedule everything after five today?"

"I can," she said. "But your five-thirty is with Mr. Moore and it's the only day this week he can meet. The counteroffer was a mess, remember?"

He remembered. Once upon a time, he would have passed it off to Matthew and dashed for the door. The deficiency created by his brother's vanishing act multiplied every day, demanding one hundred percent of his energy and motivation, leaving none for Cia.

He missed her. "Reschedule everything else, then. Thanks—you're the best."

If he put aside a potential new client's proposal, skipped lunch and called in a couple of favors, he'd have an infallible amended contract ready to go by five-thirty and a happy Moore out the door by six. Dinner with Cia by seven.

The challenge got his blood pumping. The tightrope grew thinner and the balancing act more delicate, but without his brother to fall back on, new strengths appeared daily.

He was thriving, like Matthew had predicted, because every night Lucas went to bed with the ultimate example of sacrifice and commitment. He and Cia were partners. How could he look in the mirror if he didn't step up?

He texted Cia with the dinner invitation, and her response put a smile on his face for the rest of the day: It's a date.

A date with his wife. The wife he secretly contemplated keeping. *Forever* didn't fill him with dread or have him looking for the exit. Yet. He'd been nursing the idea in the back of his mind, weighing it out. Testing it for feasibility. Working the angles. If he didn't file for divorce, he'd have to give up Manzanares because he hadn't fulfilled his end of the bargain.

There was a lot to consider, especially the effort required to convince Cia to look at their agreement in a different light.

It was time to take the next step and see how difficult Cia would be about staying married. The six months were more than half over, and he had a suspicion it would take a while to bring her around, even with the added incentive of his idea of using the hotel for the shelter.

Moore agreed to the amended contract and walked out the door at five forty-five, giving Lucas plenty of time to cook a spectacular dinner for Cia. The poolside venue beat a restaurant by a country mile, and the summer heat wasn't unbearable yet.

They sat at the patio table and exchanged light stories about their day as a breeze teased Cia's hair. He waited until dessert to broach the main topic on his mind. "Have you thought any further about the hotel site?"

Her eyes lit up. "That's all I've thought about. Courtney and I have been redoing the numbers, and she's excited about it. I'm pretty sure I'm going to buy it. It was a great idea, and I appreciate all the work you put into it." She hesitated for a beat and met his gaze. "Would it be weird to ask you to be my broker if we're in the middle of a divorce?"

Perfect segue. "About that. You can't wait until you get your trust fund to buy. There are other interested parties already. A bank loan is out, I realize, but I can scrape up the money. Would you accept it?"

She stared at him. "The entire purchase price, plus renovation costs? Not just the thirty-five percent down? Lucas, that's millions of dollars. You'd be willing to do that for me?"

Yeah, he knew the offer was substantial. What he hadn't realized until this moment was that his high level of motivation at work hadn't been solely to prove something to himself and to Matthew. The more successful he could make WFP now, the less of a blow it would be to lose Manzanares, which was a given if he convinced her to forget about the divorce.

"Not as a loan. In trade."

"Trade? I don't have anything worth that much except my trust fund."

"You do. You."

"We're already married. It's not like you have a shot at some sort of indecent proposal," she said with a half laugh.

What he had in mind was a thoroughly decent proposal. "I'm curious. What do you think of this house?"

"Could you veer between subjects any faster?" Her eyes widened. "Oh, you were seriously asking? I love this house. It'll be hard to go back home to my tiny Uptown condo after living here. Why, are we about to be kicked out?"

"Before Matthew left, he sold it to me."

"This is *Matthew's* house? Shocking how that hasn't come up before." She waved it away before he could formulate a response. "But I'm not shocked you bought it. It's beautiful, and I'm sure you'll be happy here for a long time."

It hadn't come up before because it hadn't been important. When she'd first proposed this deal, the house represented a place to live, which he had been able to access quickly and easily, and it had provided a good foundation for their fake relationship.

Now, as he sat at the patio table with his wife, eating dinner in a house he owned, it represented a potential future. A real future. One where he could fulfill the expectations that came with being a Wheeler.

"Actually…" He traced a line across the back of Cia's hand

and then threw every last card and a whole second deck on the table. "I'd like for you to be happy here, too. Married to me. Long-term."

The sip of wine she'd taken sprayed all over the flagstone patio. "That wasn't funny."

"It wasn't a joke. We're partners, and we're amazing together. Why ruin a good thing with a divorce?"

"Why?" Fire shot from her expression and singed the atmosphere. "Why? Because we *agreed*. If you don't file for divorce, I can't access my trust fund and I'll tear up the Manzanares contract. We both have a huge stake in this."

Interesting how her argument summarized the deal instead of listing the evils of marriage. He shrugged. "But the divorce isn't necessary if I give you the money for the shelter."

She sprang to her feet and both palms slammed the table, rattling the dishes. "Are you sure you have a business degree, Wheeler? You're forgetting about a minor detail called operating expenses. Without the trust fund, I won't have a dime once we open the doors. The residents have to eat. There are administrative costs. Utilities."

Like that, they were back to *Wheeler* and insults. And logic. No, he hadn't considered the operating expenses because his involvement in any deal ended the moment papers were signed. Poor excuse, regardless, and a huge miss. It had been much easier to coax her into his bed.

He blew out a frustrated breath. "What if we could get donations for operating expenses? Would you still want a divorce?"

Her eyes flared wide, deepening the blue. "What have you been drinking, Wheeler? Our whole agreement centers on the divorce."

Okay. He'd botched this up. Clearly. He'd opted to go with money as his negotiation instrument and had ignored what he'd learned about Cia over the past few months.

Figure it out, or lose everything.

Pulse tripping with a rush of sudden alarm, he rose and cornered her against the table. The heat between them, the absolute beauty and inexpressible pleasure of making love—that was his best bargaining tool, his best shot at getting her to stay.

Her arms came up and latched into a knot across her chest. She was not budging an inch.

"Darlin'," he said and slid a hand through her curtain of hair to cup the back of her silky neck. "I've been drunk on you since the moment you said I look like a Ken doll. Loosen up a little. We're just talking."

The rigid set of her shoulders and the corded neck muscles under his fingers were the opposite of loose and getting tighter by the moment. "Talking about how you're second-guessing our divorce."

He leaned in and set his lips on her forehead, mouthing his way down to her ear. "Not second-guessing. Presenting a possible alternative. Can you blame me? Honey, the things you do to me are indeed mind-blowing. I'd be a few cows shy of a herd if I was willing to give that up so easily."

His hands found her breasts, and she moaned. "Animal analogies. That's sexy, Wheeler. Talk to me some more like that." Her arms unknotted and fell to her sides, melting into pliancy as he sucked on her throat. She didn't move away.

"You like that? How about this?" He backhanded the dishes to the ground, and amid the crash of breaking pottery, set her on the table, splaying her legs wide to accommodate his hips. Her dress bunched at her thighs and hot pink flashed from the vicinity of her center. "You make me crazier than a monkey on fermented melons. Hotter than a rattler on asphalt. Shall I go on?"

"No. No more animals."

She was laughing, and he captured it in his mouth, then parted her lips and tasted the wine lingering inside with firm strokes of his tongue. She arched against him, rubbing her heat against his blistering erection.

He worked a hand under her bottom and pushed, grinding that heat hard against his length. "You feel that?" he growled. "That's what you do to me. I want to be inside you every minute of every day. I want your gorgeous naked body under me, thrashing with climax, and my name on your lips. I cannot get enough of you."

Her body spasmed, and she moaned again, her chest vibrating against his. He pulled her dress over her head and feasted on the sight of one very sexy hot-pink bra and panty combo.

It needed to come off now. He needed to touch her.

With one finger, he hooked her bra and dragged it down across her taut nipples, popping them free. He took one in his mouth, rolling it across his tongue, nibbling and sucking, and she pushed against his teeth, begging him to take her deeper.

He sucked harder. Her nails bit into the back of his head, urging him on. His erection pulsed, aching to be free of the confines of his clothes.

Not yet.

He dragged his tongue down the length of her abdomen and fingered off her panties, then knelt between her legs to pleasure her there.

"Do you like this?" he asked. "Do you like the way I make you feel?" He treated her to a thorough openmouthed French kiss square in the heart of her wet heat. She bucked against his lips, seeking more.

"Yes. *Yes.*"

She was so responsive, so hot. Fingers deep inside her, he flicked her sweet nub with his tongue. "What do you need?"

She whimpered, writhing as he held back from granting her the release she sought. "You, Lucas," she said on a long sob. "I need you."

The syllables uncurled inside him, settling with heavy, warm weight, and only then did he realize how much he'd burned to hear them. He vaulted to his feet. His clothes hit the patio, and he had a condom in his hand in record time.

His luscious wife watched him with dark, stormy eyes, one leg dangling over the edge and one leg bent up, opening her secrets wide. A wanton gift, spread out on the table, just for him.

He kissed her, covering her mouth and her body simultaneously, then entered her with a groan, filling her, and squeezed his eyes shut to savor the hot, slick pressure.

They were awesome together. How could she deny it? How could she walk away? No other man could fulfill her like he could.

She needed him.

She only thought she wasn't in the market for a long-term marriage, like she'd once insisted she didn't want him like this. She was wrong, so wrong, about both, and he had to convince her of it.

Relentlessly, he drove her off the edge and followed her down a brilliant slide toward the light.

Later, when Cia lay snuggled in his arms in their bed, she blasted him with the last word. "The divorce is happening, no matter how hot the sex is. I asked you to marry me because you're a close-the-deal-and-move-on guy. Stop talking crazy and do what you're good at."

Yeah, he excelled at moving on. Always on the lookout for the next deal, the next woman, the next indulgence. Matthew was the solid, responsible one.

Was. Not anymore.

Lucas pulled Cia tighter into his arms without responding. Matthew was gone. Lucas had assumed his place at the helm of Wheeler Family Partners. Lucas owned a house constructed for marriage. With these shifts, life could be whatever he wanted.

He wanted what Matthew had lost. With Cia. For the first time in his life, Lucas wasn't interested in moving on. But how did he convince Cia to stick around? Maybe she was right and he wasn't cut out for long-term. Gray sheep didn't spontaneously turn white overnight.

But the shifts had already occurred, and he didn't have to stay on the same path. This was it, right here, right now. If he wanted to change the future, he had to figure out how to make it happen.

Eleven

When the doorbell chimed, Fran Wheeler was the very last person Cia expected to view through the peephole. She yanked open the door and summoned a smile for her mother-in-law. "Mrs. Wheeler. Please come in."

"I'm sorry to drop by unexpectedly." Fran stepped into the foyer, murmuring appreciatively at the way Cia had decorated the living room. "And please, call me Fran. Formality makes me feel old, and if I wanted to be reminded of my age, I'd look in a mirror."

"Of course. Fran, then. Lucas isn't home, I'm afraid." Cia waved at the couch. "Would you like a seat? I'd be happy to get you a drink while you wait, if you'd like."

Coolly, as only a pillar of Dallas society could, Fran cocked her head, and the chic style of her blond hair stayed firmly in place. "I'm here to see you. Lucas is with his father at a boring real estate seminar, so I took a chance you'd be home alone."

Uh-oh. Well, she was way overdue for the tongue-lashing Fran likely wanted to give her for refusing the pearls. "Your timing is good, then. I took the day off from work. The offer of a drink still stands."

A squawk cut her off. Fergie couldn't stand it when someone had a conversation without her.

Fran glanced toward the back of the house. "Was that a bird?"

"A parrot." Another squawk, louder and more insistent. "Fergie. She was a wedding present from Lucas."

"Oh." Fran's raised brows indicated her clear interest, but she appeared reluctant to ask any further questions.

Cia's fault, no doubt, as she had no idea how to break the awkward tension. The divorce loomed on the horizon. She was sleeping with this woman's son. The mechanics of a relationship with a mother figure escaped her. The odds of successfully navigating this surprise visit were about the same as winning the lottery without buying a ticket.

Squawk.

"Fergie probably wants to meet you." Cia shook her head. "I mean, she's a little temperamental and likes people around. If you're not opposed to it, we can sit in the kitchen. She'll quiet down if we do."

"That's fine." Fran followed Cia into the kitchen and immediately crossed to Fergie's cage. "Oh, she's precious. Does she talk?"

"When she feels like it. Say hello to her. Sometimes that works."

Cia poured two glasses of iced tea.

Fran and Fergie exchanged hellos several times, and Fergie went off on a tangent, first singing the national anthem and then squawking, "Play ball!" to the older woman's delight. Fran laughed and praised the bird for a good five minutes. Cia wasn't about to interrupt.

Finally, Fran joined Cia at the breakfast table and sipped her tea. "The last few weeks have been difficult, and I wanted to thank you for the shoulder. It meant a lot to me that you stayed with us the afternoon Andy's father died and then all through the funeral and..." She took a deep breath. "Well, you know, you were there. So thanks."

"Oh, um, you're welcome." Cia's tongue felt too big for her mouth, swollen by the sincerity of Fran's tremulous smile. "I know how it feels to lose a parent. I was glad to do what I could."

"You're very good for Lucas—did you know that? Andy says you're all he talks about at work. My boys are everything to me, and I'm grateful Lucas has found someone who makes him happy." The older woman reached out and clasped Cia's hand. "We got off on the wrong foot when I pushed too soon for a relationship with you, but I'm hopeful we can start over now."

Cia shut her eyes for a blink. What was she supposed to do? She wasn't just sleeping with Lucas; they were married. And it wasn't over yet. Abuelo could still get suspicious if Fran happened to mention Cia's aloof brush-offs. Dallas was a small town in all the worst ways.

"Fran, you aren't to blame. It's me." Might as well lay it all out there. "I just don't know how to be around a mother-in-law. Or a mother, for that matter."

Okay, she hadn't meant to lay it *all* out there. Tears stabbed at her eyelids, and Fran's expression softened.

"There aren't any rules, honey. Let's just sit here, drink tea and talk. That's all I want."

Yeah, she could pretend all day long this was about keeping the heat off and guarding against her grandfather's suspicions. It wasn't. Fran was offering something she couldn't refuse—friendship.

Cia nodded and cleared her throat. "That sounds nice. What would you like to talk about?"

"Tell me about the shelter. I've been looking for a volunteer opportunity. Can I help?"

And for the second time in less than a week, Cia's heart

splattered into a big, mushy mess. A man she could get over in time. A mother? Not so much. And now it was too late to back away.

With her nerves screaming in protest, Cia told Fran every detail about the shelter and how she'd picked up where her mother left off. Silently, she bargained with herself, insisting the cause could use a good champion like Fran Wheeler and evaluating the possibility of still working with her after the divorce.

But she knew Fran wouldn't speak to her again after Lucas divorced her. That was better anyway. A clean break from both mother and son would be easier.

Way back in the far corner of Cia's mind, a worm of suspicion gained some teeth. What if Lucas had put his mother up to coming by in some weird, twisted ploy to get her to reconsider the divorce?

No, he wouldn't do that. She pushed the doubt away.

Lucas was honest about everything, and he hadn't mentioned staying married again anyway, thank goodness. For a second after he'd casually thrown out *long-term,* her pulse had shuddered to a halt and her suddenly active imagination had come up with all sorts of reasons why it could work. All pure fiction.

His suggestion had been nothing but an off-the-cuff idea, which he hadn't been serious about in the first place. Exactly why she was ignoring all the feelings Lucas had churned up when they'd stood outside the old hotel—she'd be gutted if she gave him the slightest opening.

Besides, there was no *alternative* to divorce. The trust clause stated she couldn't file for divorce. He had to.

As she ushered Fran to the door with the promise of meeting her for lunch next Monday, Cia had herself convinced she and Lucas were on the same page about the divorce.

* * *

The green dress Lucas bought Cia for the Friends of the Dallas Museum of Art benefit gala was her favorite. Sheer silk brushed her skin like a cloud, and the neckline transformed her small breasts, giving her a bit of cleavage. She'd twisted her hair into an updo and a few rebel tendrils fell around her face. Sexy, if she did say so herself.

Lucas, criminally stunning in an Armani tux, came into the bathroom as she stepped into her black sandals. He swept her hand to his lips and zapped heat straight through her tummy.

The man had touched her as intimately as possible, in more ways than she'd imagined existed. Yet a simple kiss on the back of her hand turned her knees to jelly.

"Mrs. Wheeler, you are indeed ravishing." He pulled a flat box from the pocket of his jacket. Without taking his eyes off her, he opened the lid and offered her the box.

Cia glanced inside and her already weak knees almost pitched her to the travertine tile.

"Lucas," she squeaked, and that was the extent of her throat's ability to make sound.

He extracted the necklace and guided her to the mirror, then stood behind her to clasp the choker around her neck. Emeralds set in delicate filigreed platinum spilled over her collarbone, flashing fire and ice against her skin. Every eye would be drawn to the dazzling piece of art around her neck, and no one would even notice her cleavage.

"It reminds me of you," he murmured in her ear, not touching her at all, but his heat, a signature she recognized the moment he walked into a room, raced up her bare back. "An inferno captured inside a beautiful shell. All those hard edges polished away to reveal a treasure. Do you like it?"

Did she *like* it? That was akin to asking if she liked the sun or breathing. The necklace wasn't jewelry, the way every other man on earth gave women jewelry. It was a metaphor for how well he understood her.

Lucas had an uncanny ability to peer into her soul and pluck out her essential desires, then present them to her.

Similar to his mother's pearls, this necklace represented all the frightening, unexamined things in her heart, which Lucas never let her forget. Neither could she forget he'd very pointedly failed to mention the things in *his* heart.

"I can't keep it." Her hand flew to the clasp, only to be stilled by his.

"Yes. You can. I insist."

"It's too…" Personal. Meaningful. Complicated. "Expensive. I'm sure you still have the receipt. Take it back."

"The artist custom-made it for you. All sales are final."

She shut her eyes for a beat. "That's not the kind of thing you do for a woman you're about to divorce. How are we going to make it look like we're on the outs if you're buying me custom-made jewelry?"

They had time, but they'd done such a bang-up job of making a fake marriage look real, reversing it presented a whole new set of difficulties. She wished she'd considered that before hopping into Lucas's bed.

"Maybe I'm trying to earn your forgiveness," he suggested, and in the mirror, his gaze locked on hers, a blue firestorm winding around her, daring her to ask what he'd done that required forgiveness.

Was this an apology for bringing up an *alternative* to divorce? "Forgiveness for an affair, maybe? You wouldn't do that."

His forehead tightened. "How do you know what I'm capable of?"

She spun away from the mirror, about to remind him that he'd been the one to convince her he'd never cheat. His black expression changed her mind. "Because I do. Only someone with a huge ego and a heaping spoonful of selfish has an affair. You don't have the qualifications."

They stared at each other for the longest time, and, finally, Lucas blinked, clearing his expression, and gave her a slow smile. "So maybe I'm trying to earn your forgiveness for slaving away at the office. Leaving you alone for days on end, crying into your pillow about how your husband never pays attention to you anymore."

"That could work," she said, then squealed as he backed her up against the vanity and slid magic fingertips up her leg, gathering green silk against his wrist.

"It's been so long, hasn't it, darlin'? Are you desperate for my hands on you? Like this?" His palm flattened against her bottom and inched under her panties, stealing her breath as he dipped into her instantly wet center.

Yes, exactly like that.

"We have to leave or we'll be late," she choked out and squirmed against his wicked fingers. "Rain check. You and me and a coat closet. Nine o'clock. We'll pretend it's the first time we've been able to connect in weeks."

With his eyes blazing, he hooked the edge of her panties and drew them off to puddle on the floor. "How about we connect right now *and* I meet you in the coat closet? But only if you make it eight-thirty and leave your underwear at home."

As if she could resist him. Within moments, he'd sheathed himself and they joined, beautifully and completely.

She clung to him, wrapped her legs around him and plunged into pleasure. Pleasure with an edge because her brain had left the building, and he'd ended up with a piece of her heart after all. She couldn't find the courage to shut off what she was feeling.

When Lucas made love to her, she forgot all the reasons why the *alternative* wasn't plausible. Lucas glided home slowly, watching her with a searing, heavy expression, and her heart asked, "What if it could be?"

The question echoed with no answer.

No answer, because Lucas was *not* presenting an alternative to divorce so they could continue having spectacular sex, no matter what he claimed.

Sex wasn't the basis for a relationship. Sex wasn't guaranteed to stay good, let alone spectacular. He hadn't miraculously fallen in love with her. So why had he really brought up long-term?

And why was she so sad? Because his alternative hadn't included a declaration from his heart or because it felt as though she didn't know the whole truth?

It didn't matter. This time she wouldn't end up brokenhearted and disillusioned because she wasn't giving Lucas the chance to do either.

They arrived at the benefit twenty minutes late, and it would have been thirty if Lucas hadn't tipped the driver to speed. Regardless, heads swiveled as they entered the ballroom, and Cia struggled not to duck behind Lucas.

"What are they looking at?" she whispered. "I told you there was no such thing as fashionably late."

"Maybe they know you're not wearing any panties," he said, a lot more loudly than she would have liked, and made her skin sizzle with a sinful leer.

She smacked his arm with her clutch. "Maybe they know you stuffed them in your pocket."

The swish of fabric alerted her to someone else's presence. Lucas's mother. She stood right in front of them, and as far as Cia knew, still possessed working ears. Cia's smile died as heat climbed across her face.

"Lovely to see you, Mrs. Wheeler," Cia croaked. The fire in her face sparked higher. "I'm sorry, I mean Fran. You'd think it would be easy to remember. I don't like being called Mrs. Wheeler, either. Makes me feel like an impostor."

Where had that come from? She sealed her lips together before more stupid comments fell out, though dragging her son's sex life into public had probably already killed any warm feelings her mother-in-law might have developed over afternoon tea.

The older woman's cheeks were a little pink, but she cleared her throat and said, "No problem. I couldn't answer to it for at least a year after Andy and I married. Such a big change in identity. Wait until you have kids and they start calling you 'Mama.' That one's worse, yet so much more wonderful."

Another couple joined them, and Cia was caught up in introductions instead of being forced to come up with a neutral response to Fran's casually thrown out comment. It didn't stop the notion from ricocheting through her head.

Kids. No, thank you.

Lucas's warm hand settled at the small of her back as he talked shop to the couple who had asked Fran for an introduction. The wife needed larger office space for her CPA business. Cia smiled and nodded and pretended as though she wasn't imagining how Lucas would approach fatherhood.

But she was.

He'd kiss her pregnant belly while peering up at her through those clear blue eyes. He'd treat her reverently, fetching her drinks and rubbing her feet.

When the baby cried at night, he'd smooth Cia's hair back and tell her to stay in bed while he handled it. Later, he'd throw a ball for hours with a little dark-haired toddler. Lucas would label it fun and insist work could wait, even if it couldn't.

As quickly as those wispy images materialized, they vanished in favor of much clearer images of flashing lights atop black-and-white squad cars and grim-faced policemen who knocked on the door in the middle of the night to utter the words, "I'm sorry. The accident was fatal. Your parents are gone."

The only way she could guarantee that no child of hers

would ever go through that was not to have any children. She tucked away the sudden, jagged longing for a life that would never be.

Fran's friends wandered toward the dance floor, the wife clutching the business card Lucas had retrieved from a hard, silver case, and another well-dressed couple looking for a real estate broker promptly replaced them.

"This is my wife, Cia Wheeler," Lucas said.

"Robert Graves," the male half of the couple said and shook Cia's hand. "Formerly Allende, right?"

"Right. Benicio Allende is my grandfather."

Robert's eyes grew a touch warmer. "I thought so. My company does the advertising for Manzanares. It keeps us hopping."

"Oh?" Cia asked politely.

It never ceased to amaze her how people loved to name-drop and rub elbows because of her last name. *Former* last name. Robert Graves was no exception, prattling on about Abuelo's shrewd negotiations and then switching gears to announce right then and there that he'd like to do business with Lucas. It wasn't said, but it was clearly implied that he'd decided because of her.

She made Lucas stable. Connected. Exactly as they'd hoped this marriage would do.

The room spun. Was that why Lucas wanted to blow off the divorce? Because he didn't need the Manzanares contract to save his business anymore but he did need her?

Not possible. A few paltry clients couldn't compare to the coup of Manzanares. She'd done exhaustive research. She'd considered all the angles.

Except for the one where she worked hard to be an asset to her husband and succeeded.

No. He'd keep his word. He had a high ethical standard. Surely he'd return to form before too long. Lucas excelled at racing off to the next woman—his brother had even warned her of it.

Lucas didn't want to give up sex. Fine. Neither did she, and *compromise* wasn't a foreign word in her vocabulary. They could keep seeing each other on the sly after the divorce.

The idea loosened the clench of her stomach. She didn't have to quit Lucas cold turkey, and, as a bonus, she would gain a little extra time to shut off all these unwelcome feelings she'd been fighting.

As soon as the Graves couple coasted out of earshot, Fran signaled a waiter, and Andy Wheeler joined the group in time to take a champagne flute from the gilded tray.

"A toast," Lucas's dad suggested with a raised glass. "To all the new developments and those yet to be born."

Cia raised her glass and took a healthy swallow.

"Oh, you're drinking," Fran said with obvious disappointment. "I guess there's no news yet."

Lucas flashed a wolfish smile in Cia's direction. "You'll be the second to know, Mama."

"Why do I feel like you're talking in code?" Cia whispered to Lucas.

"I might have casually mentioned we're trying to get pregnant," Lucas whispered back. "Don't worry. It's just window dressing."

"Window dressing?" Cia said at normal volume, too startled to rein in her voice. "What kind of window dressing is that?"

"Excuse us for a moment, please." Lucas nodded at his parents and dragged Cia away by the waist to an unpopulated corner of the room.

"Pregnant? Really?" she hissed and blinked against the scarlet haze over her vision. "No wonder your mom stopped by for tea and chatted me up about identity and being called 'Mama.'"

"Well, now. I guess I don't have to ask you how you feel

about the idea." Lucas tucked a tendril of hair behind her ear, and it took supreme will not to slap his hand away.

"It doesn't matter. We don't have a 'trying to get pregnant' marriage and never will. Should I say it again? In Spanish, maybe?" She stuck a finger deep into his ribs. "Why did you tell your parents something so ridiculous? We don't need any more window dressing. In fact, we should be taking the dressing *off* the window."

"Since several people are at this very moment watching us argue, I believe dressing is peeling away rapidly with every finger jab," Lucas responded. "Simmer down, darlin'. Matthew's gone. I'm the only Wheeler who has a reasonable shot at producing the next generation. It's Wheeler Family Partners. Remember?"

She swallowed, hard, and it scraped down her throat as if she'd gargled with razor blades. "So I'm supposed to be the factory for the Wheeler baby production? Is that the idea?"

"Shocking how people leap to cast my wife in that role. One might wonder why you're having a meltdown about the mere contemplation of bearing my children, when you've been so clear about how our marriage is fake and we're divorcing, period, end of story." He stared her down with raised eyebrows. "Mama was upset when Matthew left, and I told her we were trying for a baby to soften the blow. Not because I have some evil scheme to start poking holes in the condoms. Okay?"

Oh, God. All part of the show.

She filled her lungs for what felt like the first time in an hour and let the breath out slowly, along with all the blistering anger at Lucas for…whatever offenses she'd imagined. It was a lot to balance, with the sudden presentation of *alternatives* and being an asset and baby talk.

Evil scheme aside, Lucas still had a serious obligation to start a family, and he'd never shun it. Her lungs constricted again. They'd have to be extremely careful about birth control going forward.

Going forward? There wasn't much forward left in their relationship, and she stood in the way of his obligations. It would be selfish to keep seeing him after the divorce.

She grimaced at the thought of another woman falling all over herself to be the new Mrs. Wheeler. Cooing over his babies. Sleeping in his bed. Wearing his ring.

Soon, she'd be Señorita Allende again. That should have cheered her up. It didn't. "We could have easily coordinated stories. Why didn't you tell me earlier?"

Lucas lifted one shoulder and glanced at his Rolex. "Slipped my mind. It's almost eight-thirty. I'll race you to the coat closet."

She crossed her arms over another pang in her chest. "It's seven-fifteen, Wheeler. What is going on with you? As slippery as your mind is, you did not forget casually mentioning we're trying to get pregnant. You wanted to see my reaction in a place where I couldn't claw your skin off. Didn't you?"

A smear of guilt flashed through his eyes. He covered it, but not quickly enough to keep her stomach from turning over.

She was right. Oh, God, she was *right*.

Long-term marriage suddenly didn't seem like an off-the-cuff, not-really-serious suggestion. The anger she'd worked so hard to dismiss swept through her cheeks again, enflaming them.

"Not at all," he said smoothly. "I have a lot of balls in the air. Bound to drop one occasionally."

"Learn to juggle better or a couple of those balls will hit the ground so hard, I guarantee you'll never have children with anyone." She whirled to put some distance between them before she got started on that guarantee right this minute.

Lucas followed her back into the mix of people, wisely opting to let her stew instead of trying to offer some lame apology or, worse, throwing out an additional denial. Matthew's exodus had triggered more changes than the obvious ones.

Lucas's commitment phobia had withered up and died and now he'd started hacking away at hers with a dull machete. How could this night be any more of a disaster?

Fifteen minutes later, she found out exactly how much more of a disaster it could become when she overheard a conversation between four middle-aged men with the distinct smell of money wafting off them. They were blithely discussing her shelter.

She listened in horror, frozen in place behind them, as they loaded up plates at the buffet with shrimp and caviar, oblivious to the fact that they were discussing *her shelter*.

"Excellent visibility for the donors," one said, and another nodded.

Donors? Maybe she'd misheard the first part of the conversation. Maybe they weren't talking about the hotel site or her new shelter. They couldn't be. She'd made it very clear to Lucas she didn't want to depend on donations to run the shelter. Hadn't she?

"Any venture tied to Allende is a gold mine," the third declared. "How could you not be in after Wheeler's fantastic sales pitch? The property's in great shape. Most of the updating will be cosmetic, and the renovation contract is already on my lawyer's desk."

The property? Lucas had taken people to the site? How many people?

"Domestic violence is a little, shall we say, uncouth?" the fourth one suggested with a laugh. "But the Hispanic community is a worthwhile demographic to tap from a charitable perspective. It'll cinch my bid for mayor. That's the kind of thing voters want on your résumé."

Acid scalded her stomach. No. She hadn't misheard. Lucas had charged ahead without her—without her permission or even her knowledge. He'd made the proposed shelter site public, rendering it useless.

What more had Lucas done? Had he been presenting an *alternative* to divorce or a done deal?

What exactly had the necklace been an apology for?

Twelve

Lucas and Cia had been home a good twenty minutes and she hadn't spoken yet. In the car, she'd blasted him with a tirade about an overheard conversation, which she'd taken out of context, and then went mute. That alone chilled his skin, but coupled with the frosty set of her expression, even a stiff drink didn't melt the ice forming along his spine. So he had another.

Then he went looking for her.

The little ball in the center of the mattress was quiet, so he eased onto the edge of the bed. "I didn't know they were going to make such a big deal out of it."

Nothing.

He tried again. "Talk to me, honey. Scream at me. I don't care, as long as you don't keep up this deep freeze. This is all a big misunderstanding. I can fix it."

"Fix it?" The lethal whip of her tone sank into his skull, which was already sloshy with alcohol and the beginnings of a headache. She sat up, and the light from the bedside lamp cast half of her scrubbed face in shadow. "You've done enough fixing for today, Machiavelli. I'm tired. Go away and sleep somewhere else."

"Ouch. I'm in that much trouble?" He grinned, and she didn't return it. So, jokes weren't the way to go. Noted. "Come on, darlin'. I messed up. I shouldn't have taken people to the site. I'll find another hotel for your shelter if that site's compromised. It's not worth getting so upset over."

"Do I seem upset?" She stared at him, and her dry eyes bothered him more than the silent treatment. Unease snaked through his gut.

"No." He'd wandered into the middle of uncharted territory full of quicksand. This had all the trappings of their first official fight as a couple. Except they weren't really a couple—yet—and, technically, they argued all the time. "Does that mean you've already forgiven me?"

She palmed her forehead and squeezed. "You really don't get any of this, do you?"

"Yeah, I get it." Somehow, his plan to come up with the operating expenses for the shelter hadn't happened as envisioned. "You're ticked because I tried to tap sponsors for the shelter site, and now the location is compromised. I'm in real estate, darlin'. I'll find another one. A better one."

"I'm sure you will. Eventually." She lay back down and covered her head with an arm, blocking his view of her face. His firecracker's fuse was noticeably fizzled. How could they get past this if she wouldn't yell at him?

"Cia." He waited until she peeked out from below the crook of her elbow. "I should have talked to you before talking to the money. I'm sorry. Let's kiss and make up now, okay?"

"No. No more kissing. This isn't only about the shelter." Her voice was steady, a monotone with no hint of the fire or passion she normally directed at him. "It's about you running the show. You say I have a choice, but only if it's a choice you agree with. I'm not doing this anymore. In the morning, I'm moving back into my condo."

"What? You can't." This situation was unraveling faster than he could put it back together. But whatever happened, he couldn't let her leave. He wiped damp palms on the comforter and went with reason. "We have a deal. Six months."

The arm came off her face, and bitter laughter cut through the quiet bedroom. "A deal, Wheeler? We have a *deal?* Oh, that's rich. We have a deal when it's convenient for you to remember it. Every other waking moment, you're trying to alter the deal. Presenting alternatives. Trying to give me money. Talking about babies with your mother and seducing me into believing you really understand me. It's all about the deal, isn't it? As long as it's the best deal for *you*. What about what I want?"

He swore. Some of her points could be considered valid when viewed from a slightly different perspective. But her perspective was wrong—the tweaks to the deal were good for everyone. "What do you want?"

"A divorce! The same thing I've wanted since day one. I fail to understand how or when that fact became confusing to you."

"It's not confusing." He refused to lose control of the conversation. She needed him, and his job was to help her realize it. "I know that's what you think you want. But it's not."

"Oh, well, everything is so clear now. Are you aware of the fact that you talk in circles most of the time? Or is it deliberate, to bewilder your opponent into giving up?"

"Here's some straight talk for you. We're good together. We have fun, and I like being with you. You're fascinating, compelling, inspiring and all of that is out of bed. In bed…" He whistled. "Amazing. Beyond compare. I've told you this. No circles then. No circles now. Why can't you see a divorce is not what you need?"

"Do you hear yourself?" she asked so softly he strained

to pick up the words. "Your whole argument was about why a divorce is not what *you* need. My needs are foreign to you. And you've spent the last few months fooling me into believing the opposite, with the dresses and taking care of me and pretending you were interested in the shelter because you wanted to help me."

"I *do* want to help you," he snapped. God Almighty, she pushed his limits. Stubborn as a stripped screw. He forced his tone back into the realm of agreeable before he gave away the fact that she'd gotten to him. "You're mad because it was mutually beneficial? That's what made the original deal so attractive. We both got value out of it. Why is it so bad to continue the tradition?"

"All lies! Matthew left and now you're hot for a wife who'll give you a baby. You're too lazy to go find one, so you thought, 'Hey, I already have a wife. I'll hang on to her.'"

Lazy? She was more work than a roomful of spoiled debutantes and jaded supermodels. Yet there was not one woman he'd want long-term besides Cia. They were compatible on every level, and the thought of living his life without her—well, it wasn't a picture he liked. Why else would he be talking about it? "I get the feeling anything I say at this point would be wrong."

"Now you're onto something. There's no defense for any of it, least of all compromising the shelter site. If a woman's abuser finds the shelter, he might kill her. Do you understand how horrible your cavalier attitude is? Do you have any clue how it made me feel when I realized what those men were talking about?"

"I'm sorry. I do understand how important discretion is. It was a mistake. But I stand by my offer to find another site."

"How magnanimous of you," she said with a sneer. "I'm not stupid, Wheeler. You got me all excited about it, then oh, no. Bring in the entire upper crust of Dallas, so everyone knows where the shelter is. Oops. You sabotaged that site, hoping to buy time to talk me out of the divorce. Maybe *accidentally* get pregnant in the meantime."

Was she listening to anything he had said? He'd apologized twice already. "Compromising the site might have been the result but that was not my inten—"

"Betrayed. That's how I felt when I stood there listening to my entire world crumble around me."

Everything with Cia was a hundred times more effort than it needed to be, which he knew good and well she did on purpose to keep everyone at bay. But why was she still doing it with him? Hadn't they gotten past this point already? "That's a little melodramatic, don't you think?"

There came a tear, finally, sliding down her cheek. "Melodramatic? You broke my heart, Lucas!"

"What?" Every organ in his chest ground to a halt, and he couldn't tear his eyes away from the lone tear laden with despair and hurt.

No. No way. This marriage was about the benefits, both physically and business-wise. She needed his unique contribution to the relationship. Period.

He'd been one hundred percent certain she was on board with that. Hurt and feelings and messiness weren't part of the deal. And when the deal fell apart, he walked away. Usually.

But he was still here.

She dashed away the teardrop, but several more replaced it. "Surprised me, too."

All of this was too fast. Too much to process. "Whoa. What are you saying?"

"Same thing I've been saying. Since you have to file for the divorce, I have no power here. Therefore, I'm leaving, and I have to trust you'll eventually find another potential mother for your next generation, at which point I'll get my divorce. Clear enough for you?"

"No." He shook his head. "Back up, honey. Now *you're*

talking in circles. I didn't make you mad—I hurt you. How did that happen?"

"Because I'm an idiot." Her eyes shone with more unshed tears. "I had expectations of you that you couldn't fulfill. You're not the man I thought you were."

"Wait a minute. What did you expect?" He was still reeling from the discovery she'd developed *feelings* for him and hadn't bothered to say anything.

What would he have done with such information? Run in the other direction? Run faster toward her?

Actually, he didn't know what to do with it now.

"I expected you to be honest, not hide your real agenda." She snorted. "*Dios,* how naive am I? I walked right into it, eyes wide open, certain I could hang on to my soul since you weren't asking for it. You gave and gave, and I never saw it for what it was. An exchange. You slipped under my guard, and the whole time, you were planning to exact payment. You betrayed me, not once but twice, with alternatives and then with sponsors. You don't get a third chance to screw me over."

When thunderclouds gathered across Lucas's face, Cia was too tired to care that she'd finally cracked his composure.

"That's enough," Lucas declared. "I listened to your mental origami, and let me tell you, I am impressed with your ability to fold facts into a brand-new shape. But it's my turn to talk. Are you in love with me?"

She almost groaned. Why did he have to go there? "That's irrelevant."

He tipped her chin up and pierced her with those blue laser beams. Scared of what he'd see, she jerked away and buried her face in the pillow.

Great. The entire bed smelled of pine trees mixed with her lotion.

"It's not irrelevant to me," he countered quietly. "I'd like to know what's going on inside you."

So would she. Thoughts of babies and long-term should not be so hard to shove away. The hurt shouldn't be so sharp.

"Why?" she mumbled, her face still in the pillow.

He growled in obvious frustration, "Because I care about you."

She rolled over and said, "You have a funny way of showing it."

"Really? I'd argue the exact opposite."

"You can argue about it all day long. But you'd be wrong. You like to take care of me. That's different than caring about me."

He snapped out a derisive laugh. "Maybe we should start this whole conversation over. We suck at communicating unless it's 'more,' 'faster' or 'again,' don't we?"

No, they didn't have any communication problems when they were naked, which was exactly what had gotten her into this mess. Intimacy with Lucas could never be divorced from emotion. Why had she pretended it could be? "Which is why we're done with that part of our relationship."

He sighed. "Look, honey. I messed up. But I'm here, talking to you, trying to fix it. And you still never answered the question. Are you in love with me?"

"Stop asking me!" she burst out, determined to cut off his earnestness and dogged determination to uncover the secret longings of her heart that she didn't understand and did not want to share. He had enough power over her already. "It's just warm feelings for the man I'm sleeping with because he's superawesome in bed, okay? It doesn't change anything. You're not in love with me. You're still on the lookout for a baby factory. And I need a divorce, not all of these complications."

"Complications are challenges you haven't conquered yet," he said, and the tension in his face and shoulders visibly eased.

Her tension went through the roof.

Of course he hadn't fallen all over himself to declare his undying love. Not that she had expected him to after she'd backtracked about her broken heart.

In matters of the heart, they were cut from the same cloth—excellent at emotional distance and not much else. The divorce deal was perfect for them both.

"I'm not up for any more complications *or* challenges, thanks. Can we cut to the chase?" She sat up and faced him. "Are you going to file for divorce or not?"

He held her gaze without blinking, without giving away his thoughts. "No."

Her eyelids snapped closed. He'd finally made his move. *Checkmate.* "You can't do this to me, Lucas. Please."

"I can't do what? Give you what you really need instead of a divorce you'll regret? You're a vibrant, beautiful woman, yet you aim to shrivel up alone for the rest of your life. That's not right."

He ran a hand through her hair, letting it waterfall off his fingers, and his touch, so familiar, nearly caved in her stomach.

Being alone had never been her goal. Avoidance of suffering had been the intent, but she'd done a shoddy job of it, hadn't she? The tsunami of agony hadn't just drowned her; it had broken through every solid barrier inside, allowing sharp-edged secret dreams to flow out, drawing blood as they went.

"Cia, I'm offering a long-term partnership, with advantages for both of us. We already know we like each other. The sex is great. We'll figure out how to do your shelter without the trust fund. Together, we're unstoppable. Why can't you consider it?"

"Because it's not enough. There's a reason why I'll be alone for the rest of my life. I don't know how to do long-term." He started to respond, but she cut him off. "And neither do you. Sex isn't enough. Liking each other isn't enough."

He hurled out a curse. "What is enough?"

Love.

Oh, God. She wanted something he couldn't give her. Something she didn't know how to give him. No wonder she couldn't answer his questions.

She shied away from relationships because she had no idea how to love a man when living in constant fear of the pain and loss sure to follow. She had no idea how to love without becoming dangerously dependent on it.

Her parents had been in love. Until Lucas, she hadn't remembered all the long glances and hand-holding. The accident had overshadowed the history of their lives before that one shattering, defining moment. If they had lived, would she be having an entirely different conversation about the magic ingredients of a long-term relationship?

Would she better understand her own heart and demand Lucas know his?

"I can't tell you," she said. "You have to figure it out on your own."

He pressed the back of his neck with stiff fingers. "Fantastic. An impossible puzzle with no correct answer. Why can't this be about what looks good on paper?"

Sacar los ojos a uno. He was bleeding her white.

"It's all about how things look with you." She should have seen that before. Appearances were everything because skin-deep was all he permitted. Nothing could penetrate the armor he kept over his heart. "As long as it looks like fun, you're on board, right?"

"That's not fair. I never said a long-term marriage would be a big party. I don't know what it'll look like, but I do know I don't want what we have to be over." Gently he gripped her shoulders, and for a moment raw tenderness welled in his eyes. It made her pulse stutter and wrenched a tendril of hope from inside her. But then he said, "And I know you need what I bring to this relationship. You need me."

"No." She looked straight at him as her heart broke anew.

His entire offer hinged on dependency, the certainty that she was willing to be dependent. Not because he wanted to be with her. "Need is dangerous. It creates reliance. Addiction. Suddenly, you can't survive without the thing you crave. What happens when it's gone? I don't need selfishness disguised as partnership. I don't need someone who doesn't understand me. I don't need you, Lucas. Let me go."

Pain flashed across his face. Finally. This conversation had gone on for far too long. She'd run out of arguments, ways to get him out of the room before she went completely insane and begged him to figure out how to give her what she wanted.

"Yeah," he said and cleared his throat. "Okay. It's for the best."

As he slid off the bed and gathered some clothes from the dresser, she twisted off her rings and set them on the bedside table. The light scorched her eyes. She reached out and snapped it off, staring at the now-invisible rings until she had to blink.

At the door of their bedroom, he stopped. Without turning around, he said, "I'll help you pack in the morning. It'll work in our favor to separate now so it won't be such a surprise when I file for divorce."

Then he did turn, and his gaze sought hers. The hall light created a shadow of his broad shoulders against the carpet and obscured his face. "Is there anything I could have offered you that would have been worth reconsidering the divorce?"

Her throat cramped with grief. If she tried to talk, she'd break down, and every time she cried, he held her and made her feel things she shouldn't. Feelings he couldn't return.

When she didn't answer, he nodded and left.

In the darkness, she whispered, "You could have offered to love me."

Thirteen

The divorce papers sat on the edge of Lucas's desk, where they'd sat for a week now, without moving. Cia's loopy script was buried on the last page, where he couldn't see it. The papers lacked only his signature, but he couldn't sign. It didn't feel right. Nothing did. Certainly not his big, empty house, where he'd aimed to remove all traces of the previous couple who'd lived there and had succeeded beyond his wildest dreams.

Cia was everywhere. Sitting on the counter in the kitchen, eyes black with passion as he drove her to a brilliant climax. Walking down the stairs with careful steps, wearing a dress that had taken him an hour to find because none of the others would put appreciation on her face the way this exact one would.

Cia sleeping in his bed, hair tousled and flung across two pillows as she nestled right at the mattress's halfway mark, ripe for him to join her, to fold her against his body and sink in.

He groaned and slammed his head into his hands, ignoring the document filling the laptop screen before him.

That was the worst, trying to sleep alone after having Cia there, night after night. A blink in time, compared to how long he'd slept without her. But no matter how many times the maid washed the sheets, lime and coconut lingered in the creases, lying in wait to spring from hiding and invade his nose with the memory of what he'd lost.

No, not lost—what he'd never had in the first place.

He'd been wrong. Cia didn't need him. What could he say, what could he do, to counter that? If she didn't need him, he had no place in her life, as hard as that was to accept. She'd probably already whisked away whatever feelings she'd had for him, warm or otherwise.

At least he could bury himself in eighteen-hour days with no distractions and no one waiting at home.

All those closed-door sessions with Matthew had taken root. New clients vied for his attention. Contracts spilled from his workbag. Wheeler Family Partners for-sale signs dotted properties all across the city. The National Commercial Development Association had nominated WFP for an award—the highest percentage increase in listings for the year. Manzanares was icing on the cake.

Success and acknowledgment of his efforts. That's what he should be focusing on. Not on how every contract reminded him he should be closing the deal on his divorce and moving on. Every contract mocked him, silently asking why he couldn't just pick up a pen, for crying out loud.

He had to get out of here. Take a walk or a drive to clear his head. When he got back, he'd sign the papers and send them to his lawyer to be filed with the court. In no time, he'd be rid of this ache behind his ribs and free to pursue…something. Anything. The world was his for the taking.

But nothing interested him. At all.

He fingered the box in his pocket, which held Cia's rings.

It was time—past time—to stop carrying them around, but whenever he dug out the box and held it on his palm, his lungs cramped. The same cramp happened when he tried to remove his ring.

Maybe he should see a doctor. His throat hurt all the time. Some bug had probably wormed its way into his system.

When he rounded the corner to the reception area, Helena gave him her you-have-company-and-it's-not-a-client smile and said, "I was about to buzz you. You have a visitor."

Cia. His stomach flipped and a cold sweat broke out across his forehead. Maybe she'd thought it through and had recognized the excellent logic he'd so clearly laid out for why they belonged together.

Maybe she was pregnant. The image of her belly rounded with his child materialized in his head and pricked the backs of his eyes.

Or—he dragged his imagination back to the real world—she intended to flay him alive for not filing the papers yet. He pasted a smile on his face and pivoted to face the wrath of Hurricane Cia in full category-five mode.

He could never have prepared enough to greet the woman seated on the leather couch.

"Lana." *Not Cia.* Of course not. She'd never concede. He swallowed his disappointment. "This is a surprise."

"As it was meant to be. Hello, Lucas." Lana stood, balancing on delicate stilettos and clad in an expensive designer suit Cia would have sniffed at righteously.

Funny. He'd never noticed what Lana wore, other than to figure out the best way to get it off without ruining it, as she was ridiculously fussy about her clothes. Again, hindsight. Couldn't go home to her husband with buttons missing. "Is something wrong?"

With a glance at Helena, she said, "Can I buy you a cup of coffee?"

Yeah. Go out in public with Lana while still married to

Cia. Exactly what he needed. Actually, even a private conversation with Lana sounded less than fun, but as he took in the classy blonde who'd thanked him for his time and effort with lies, he realized he was over it.

And he was curious what she wanted. "Helena's coffee is better than any coffeehouse's. I have a few minutes. Let's sit in the conference room."

Lana followed him to the conference room across from the receptionist's desk, which he'd chosen due to the glass walls in case she thought there was a chance in hell he'd pick up where they'd left off.

He had a strong sense of propriety, not a shallow love for appearances as Cia liked to accuse him of.

Helena entered with two cups of coffee and left them on the table, along with an array of creamers and sugars. Lucas waited for Lana to take a seat and then chose a perpendicular chair.

"What can I do for you?" he asked politely.

Two artificial sweeteners and four creamers. Lana hadn't changed the way she drank coffee and likely nothing else, either. She took her time stirring, then looked up. "I came to apologize."

Lucas raised an eyebrow. "For which part?"

"All of it. I was lonely. Bored. Feeling adventurous. Take your pick. My shrink would agree with all of them. I'm not asking you to understand why I did it. Just to believe I'm sorry I hurt you."

"You didn't hurt me." He laughed and hated that it sounded forced. "You lied to me. You used me. Then you unleashed your husband on me to finish the evisceration job you started. That was the most unforgivable part."

He took a deep breath. Maybe he wasn't as over it as he'd imagined.

She sipped her coffee, as if for fortification, and blinked her baby blues. "I'm here to apologize for that, too," she said.

"And to tell you the truth. I didn't unleash my husband on you. All the rumors and hits to your business, I did that. Not Henry."

"What?" Shock froze his tongue, preventing him from voicing anything else. No. Not over it *at all*.

"Henry will be fifty-eight in December. I had no illusions about being in love when I married him and neither did he. When I told him about you, he patted my hand and said it was cheaper than a divorce, then went back to work. I played him up as the jealous husband because, well, I wanted you to believe I had worth to him."

"Why?" he prompted when she paused.

"Because you're so hard to faze, Lucas. Emotionally. Do you feel anything at all? I wanted you to love me and you didn't. I thought…maybe if you believed he loved me, you'd see something desirable in me, too. Only it didn't work. I was heartbroken. Devastated that it was just all fun and games to you."

"It was fun," he reminded her harshly. She had a lot of nerve, talking about love when they'd been nowhere near serious. "It could have been more, maybe. Eventually. At least I thought it could."

Genuine sadness laced her small smile. "Could have been. Maybe. Eventually. That's how it is with you. No commitment. So I lashed out. Tried to ruin you. Instead, you fell in love with someone else, blew past all my efforts to destroy you and went on to be happy without me."

A catch in her throat cut off the sentence and a catch in his gut kept his resounding "No" from being voiced.

He wasn't happy.

The rest of it was true. He was in love with Cia, and he needed her, like a tree needed water. She brought out all the best parts of him and kept him on his toes. She challenged him and made him feel alive.

He'd given her up, so sure that if she didn't need him, they had no reason to be together.

Ironic how Lana hadn't accused him of marrying Cia on the rebound after all. Instead, she'd put a microscope on his marriage, and the view shook his spine something fierce.

She coughed and touched a finger to the corner of her eye. "I'm sorry, and I'm not going to bother you anymore. I'm in a place now where I can be happy for you."

And he was in a place where he could accept Lana had cut him deeper than he'd been willing to admit, spilling over into his relationship with Cia and causing missteps visible only in hindsight. *Hindsight.* The word of the day.

"Okay." He stood so fast the rolling chair shot away from the backs of his legs. "Thanks for coming by. You didn't have to, and I appreciate it."

Surprised, she glanced up. "Rushing me out? I guess I don't blame you. Good luck, Lucas. You deserve a much better life than what I could have given you."

In his head, the word *life* became *wife.* He agreed. He deserved a better wife than one who betrayed him the way Lana had. But his wife deserved a better husband than one who had betrayed her. Like he'd done to Cia. He'd done all she'd accused him of, and more, and probably not as subconsciously as he'd insisted.

He'd refused to see the truth. He'd been so busy trying to have what Matthew had had that he'd missed the most critical element. It was clear now why his brother hadn't been able to live in the house he'd built with Amber, why he'd taken off despite being a Wheeler.

Love made a person do crazy, irrational things. Things he'd never do under normal circumstances, like offer a short-term wife millions of dollars to make it long-term. Instead of blowing off Cia's broken heart like a complete moron, he should have just opened his mouth and admitted he wanted to alter the deal because he loved her and couldn't live without her.

It might not have changed the outcome. But it might have.

Love. That was the reason he couldn't move on this time. He'd been too afraid of it, too much a coward to examine what he was feeling, and it would serve him right to have lost Cia forever. But he wasn't going down without a fight.

He hurried to his office to start on the Lucas Wheeler Philosophy of Cia Wheeler. He had to get it right this time.

Something was wrong with Fergie. Cia had tried everything, but the bird wouldn't eat. The blob of gray feathers sat in the bottom of the cage and refused to acknowledge the presence of her owner. It had been like this since the day she'd moved back into her condo.

Every morning, she rushed to Fergie's cage, convinced she'd find the bird claws up and stiff with rigor mortis, which would be about right for a companion she'd anticipated having for fifty years.

One more thing ripped from her fingers.

"You have to eat sometime," she told Fergie. Not that she blamed her. Cia had no appetite, either, and after cooking in Amber's gourmet kitchen, the one in her condo, which she'd been using for years, wasn't the same. "We'll try again tomorrow."

At quarter till nine, she went to bed, where she would likely not sleep because she refused to turn on the TV and refused to acknowledge she'd grown used to it.

She didn't need the TV, and she didn't need Lucas Wheeler. For anything, least of all to "help" her find another shelter site. She had an internet connection and lots of patience. Okay, maybe not so much patience. Tomorrow she'd investigate using another real estate professional. A female.

Cia stared at the dark ceiling and shifted for the hundredth time into yet another uncomfortable spot on the hard mattress. It was just so quiet without the TV. Without the rustle of sheets and the deep breathing of a warm, male body scant inches away.

Not a night went by without a stern internal reminder of how much better it was to be alone, instead of constantly looking over her shoulder for the guillotine that would sever her happiness.

A knock at the front door interrupted her misery. Grumbling, she threw on a robe and flipped on a light as she crossed the small condo. A peek through the peephole shot her pulse into the stratosphere.

Lucas.

With a sheaf of papers in his hand. The divorce papers. He was dropping them off—personally—this late?

Hands shaking, she unlatched the door and swung it open. "What are you doing here?"

"Hello to you, too." He captured her gaze, flooding her with a blue tidal wave of things unsaid. Unresolved.

The porch light shone down, highlighting his casual dress. Cargoes and a T-shirt, which meant he hadn't come straight from work. Was he not working all hours of the night anymore? Dark splotches under his eyes and lines of fatigue in his forehead told a different tale.

She set her back teeth together. She had to get out of the habit of caring.

"Come in, before I let in all the mosquitoes in Uptown." She stepped back and allowed him to brush past her, to prove his raw Lucas-ness didn't have any power here. His heat warmed her suddenly chilled skin, and the quick tug in her abdomen made a liar out of her.

A squawk stopped his progress midstride. Fergie flapped her wings and ran back and forth along one of the wooden dowels anchored across the top of her cage. "Lucas, Lucas, Lucas," she singsonged.

Cia glared at her miraculously revived bird. "I didn't know she could say that."

"Took her long enough." He grinned, and his eyes lit up. All the butterflies in her stomach took flight. "We've been working on it."

So. Fergie and Lucas had been buddy-buddy behind her back. She sighed. Maybe Fergie would eat, now that her precious Lucas was here. Traitor.

She waved at the couch. "Sit down."

He sank into the giant white sectional, and it shrank as his frame dominated the space. Then he spilled his masculinity into the rest of the room, overwhelming her.

Why had he come here, invading her refuge?

Luckily, he'd had the wisdom to move them into Matthew's house—his house now—instead of moving in here for the duration. The separation would have been a hundred times more difficult if she'd had to wash his presence from the condo. No way she could have. She would've had to move.

Might still have to, just from this visit.

"Will you sit with me?" He nodded to the couch.

"I prefer to stand, thanks. Besides, you're not staying long. Are you dropping off the papers?"

"In a way," he said. "But first, I'd like to tell you something. You know my great-great-grandfather founded Wheeler Family Partners back in the eighteen hundreds, right?"

When she nodded, he went on, "Back then, there weren't many buildings. Mostly land. That's true real estate, and it's in my blood. I used to think real estate was about deals. A piece of paper, signed and filed. Then I was done, ready to move on to the next deal. But that's not who I am anymore. I'm in the business of partnering with people to build something real. Something permanent. That's why I grew WFP without Matthew. Not because I got lucky or worked hard. I fell in love with someone who challenges me to be more. Who taught me the value of wholehearted commitment."

¡Dios mío!

"Is *that* where you were going?" She laughed, and it came

out more like a sob. So now he was in love with her. Conveniently. "You came to deliver divorce papers and tell me you decided you're in love with me. Anything else?"

He came off the couch in a rush, feet planted and eyes blazing. Involuntarily, she backed up from the heat of his anger. *This* was Lucas mad. Before, by the pool, was nothing in comparison.

"I'm not here to deliver divorce papers." He held them up and flicked his other hand. A lighter appeared between his fingers, flame extended.

Before she could blink, he set the papers on fire.

Smoke curled away from the burning pages, and her divorce deal turned to ash. He blew out the fire before it reached his fingers and threw the charred corners on her pristine coffee table, metal glinting from his third finger with the motion. He was still wearing his wedding ring.

"What did you do that for?" she demanded, pulse pounding. "I have a copy in the other room, and you're not leaving here until you sign it."

His taut frame still bristled as he dismissed the demand with a curt slice of his hand. "I am not divorcing you. Period." He took a deep, steadying breath. "Cia, listen for a minute. I handled it all wrong. I'm sorry. I cut down what mattered most to you and undermined your goals with the shelter, trying to force you to need me. I was too much of a dingbat to realize I'd done everything except the one thing you really wanted."

"Oh, what's that?" she asked. Tears stabbed at her eyes, burned down her throat.

"You stuck your heart out and then yanked it right back so quickly, I almost didn't see it. You don't give a guy a chance to think about what to do with such a gift, and I'm sorry it took me so long to figure out what would be enough." He inched toward her slowly, giving her time to move. Or to stay. "You want someone to love you. You want *me* to love you."

Her lungs contracted as his heart splashed onto his face.

This was definitely not some conveniently discovered feeling calculated to get his way. He'd never looked at her with such fierce longing coupled with aching tenderness.

And yet, he'd always looked at her like that. She'd never dared examine it. Never dared hope it meant more than warm feelings for the woman he was sleeping with.

When he'd taken all the steps he could, she hadn't moved. He swept her up in his arms.

"Darlin'," he whispered into her hair. "Let me love you."

She shut her eyes and breathed in Lucas. Breathed in the acrid, charred scent of burned paper as his body cleaved to hers and he held her. It would be so easy to plunge into this new Lucas, the one who opened up and poured out poetry and promises like sap from a felled tree.

With her stomach and heart twisting, she broke his embrace. "That's not what I want."

"Stop pretending." Ferocity leaped back into his expression. "You're so afraid, you either fake everything or you fight it, as if that will insulate you from hurt. Nothing will. But being alone hurts in a different way."

His blue laser beams punched right through her, past the flesh and bone. She'd struggled so hard to be whole, to heal from losing pieces of her soul. First, when her parents died and after, when she tried to replace the loss with disastrous relationships.

And here she was, with no empty space. No room for anyone, not even this surprising, layered man who stood before her, asking for something she couldn't give.

"I am afraid." Had she said that out loud?

"I know, honey. I know all about fear. Do you think it was easy for me to come here with nothing to give except myself? Jewelry and spectacular sex are much easier to offer than risking you'll accept plain old me. But I'm hoping it's enough, because I can't live my life without you."

He was saying all the right things. Except he was first and

foremost a salesman, and she'd experienced his stellar ability to sell himself firsthand. "You wanted me to be needy. But not anymore?"

"Yeah. I wanted you to need me and told myself fulfilling your needs was my half of the partnership. A total lie. It was so I didn't have to do the work. So I could keep from investing emotionally. The worst part is, I was already in deep and couldn't tell you how much I need *you*. You're right. Need is dangerous." He inclined his head in deference. "I can't survive without you. I'm completely addicted to you. And I love you too much to let you go."

The sentiment darted right through her flimsy barriers and spread with warmth into the emptiness she would have sworn wasn't there.

Lucas had known, though, and burrowed right past the pretense, past all the lies she told herself. It was frightening to consider just being real for once and more frightening still to consider giving up her defenses. "How can I know for sure this isn't all going to evaporate one day?"

"I don't have a crystal ball. All I have is right here." He held his hands wide, palms up. "Can you forgive me?"

She shut her eyes against the raw emotion spilling from the sea of blue trained on her face. No sales pitch there. Just a whole lot of Lucas, showing her the inner reaches of his heart. "This is a lot to take in. Without the divorce, I don't get my money. How can I live with that?"

His expression grew cunning. "How can you live with yourself if you do get your money? You don't want to be a slave to need, yet you're willing to be one to your grandfather."

She flinched. "What are you talking about?"

"You're dependent on your grandfather and his money to grant you a measure of control over a life that can't be controlled." He advanced on her, backing her up until she hit the wall. "I'm not above stacking the deck to get what

I want, and I want you, Cia Wheeler. I dare you to take a risk on us. I dare you to stare your grandfather in the eye and tell him to keep his money, because you're keeping your marriage."

Vocalized in Lucas's whiskey-smooth voice, her name sounded beautiful. Exactly right. It was too much. He saw too much, wanted too much. He made her want too much.

"How can I?" she whispered.

"Simple. You have needs, whether you like it or not. They're part of being human, so you have to make a choice. Do you need your grandfather to take care of you financially? Or do you need to take a chance on a new deal with me? A mutually beneficial deal, because, honey, you need me as much as I need you. The question is, can you admit it?"

There it was. He'd drawn the line, given her a choice. Maybe it was that easy to just say *yes*. But it couldn't be. "What if I don't want kids?"

He flashed a grin. "What if I do? What if I don't want you to keep a single stitch of your wardrobe? What if I want to put on clown makeup and join the circus? What if—"

"Okay. I get it." And he got her. Not so difficult to believe after all, not when it was Lucas. That's why the betrayal had hurt so much, because he'd twisted the knife with expert knowledge. "You're saying we'll figure it out."

"Together. I love you and that will never change. It's the only guarantee I've got. Well, I can also guarantee we'll fight over the radio station. But I'm willing to overlook your terrible taste in music if it means I get a real wife out of the deal. Do I?"

Real. Everything she'd been afraid to want until Lucas. The divorce deal was a flawed shield against a real relationship, but fear of losing something meaningful had squelched all her courage to reach for that dream.

She'd done her best to get rid of Lucas before he could hurt her, but he kept coming back. Maybe it was finally time to stop fighting it. Time to admit she loved him fiercely.

Could she take a chance on a marriage deal? Could she risk the possibilities, bad or good?

"No." Mind made up, she inspected him through narrowed eyes and crossed her arms. "How is that fair? You get a real wife in exchange for exposure to my excellent taste in music. Yet I'll be forced to listen to songs about cheating, honky-tonks and cheap beer? No deal. Find a pen and sign the copy of the papers right now unless you can agree to find a type of music we both like."

His gaze played over her face, and when he smiled, the sun rose. No point in denying it. She'd given a huge piece of her heart to Lucas a long time ago, and he was offering to fill that hole with himself. Love had healed her, and now, she could let him do that.

"Opera?" he suggested and yanked her into his arms, engulfing her in the scent of clean pine. The scent of her real husband.

His mouth captured hers before she could argue opera was more a type of theater than a type of music. Lucas kissed her, and her heart became whole, then swelled, too big for her chest.

She pulled back a tiny bit, unwilling to be too far from him. "I really, really hope you meant it when you said you love me, because if you want a real wife, you're going to have to suffer through a big, formal wedding. And I'm asking your mother to help plan it."

He groaned. "I meant it. You know you'll have to suffer through a real honeymoon in exchange, right?"

"With lots of real sex? *Dios,* the things I do for you." With a tsk, she smiled. "I must love you a lot."

"Well, then. Since we're already married, the big, formal wedding is merely symbolic. So the honeymoon comes first." He peeled back her robe and rolled his eyes at the tank top underneath. "Please. I'm begging you. Let me buy you some nice, tasteful sleepwear not made from cotton."

"Not unless you let me teach you to dance." His hands slid under the tank top and claimed her body, just like he'd claimed her heart. "Lucas," she breathed.

Fergie squawked, "Lucas, Lucas, Lucas."

Lucas laughed against Cia's mouth. "That's a deal."

Even with Fran's help, the wedding plans stretched over the course of two months. The real story was far too incredible, so Lucas smoothed over everyone's questions with the partial truth—Cia'd had a change of heart about including everyone in their marriage celebration, and she wanted a lavish second ceremony.

Finally, after endless rounds of making decisions and sampling cake and addressing invitations, Cia clutched Abuelo's arm and walked down the aisle to her husband. Then, nearly five hundred guests accompanied them to an extravagant reception, where the bride and groom danced to every song, be it fast or slow.

Lucas twirled Cia to one of his favorite country numbers and she sang along, not ashamed to admit she kind of liked it, twangy guitars and all. He gathered her close and smiled. "Was it worth it? The big wedding?"

"It's everything I dreamed it would be. Exhausting but so wonderful."

That morning, she'd begun to suspect the exhaustion wasn't due to frantic wedding plans but another reason entirely. But she'd had no time to slip away and buy a pregnancy test. Tomorrow was soon enough to confirm it.

She couldn't wait to find out for sure. A whole, intact heart allowed for plenty of possibilities, and, finally, she was in a place where the thought of a baby didn't scare her blind. And if the test came back negative, they'd try some more. It was all in the journey and the pleasures to be had along the way.

When the music ended, Lucas escorted her to the table, and Fran flashed yet another proud smile. Cia touched the pearls around her neck and grinned at Fran and Andy in turn. She'd gained a family along with a husband.

Well, most of a family—Matthew hadn't come back for the wedding and it weighed on Lucas. Hopefully she could cheer him up tomorrow with the news he'd started on the next generation of Wheelers a little earlier than expected.

Abuelo approached the table and took Cia's hand. "I'm afraid this old man must retire for the evening, my dear. Lucas, I'll be in your office a week from Monday to sign the papers. I'm a little sad to see the Manzanares complex change hands, but I couldn't be happier with the deal you negotiated."

"Anything for family. I'm glad to be of service." Lucas clasped Abuelo's outstretched hand and wished him a good evening.

Only after a knockdown, drag-out fight, which Cia refused to lose, had Lucas agreed to still represent Abuelo in the sale of Manzanares, even though he hadn't followed through with the divorce. Seriously, her husband took integrity to a whole new level. When Cia pointed out she couldn't trust any other real estate broker with Abuelo's business except Lucas, he conceded.

Abuelo hadn't budged on changing the terms of the trust, despite Cia's zealous pleas, but she was okay with that. In lieu of wedding gifts, Cia and Lucas had asked for donations to the newly formed Wheeler Family Foundation, helmed quite expertly by Fran Wheeler, and the balance grew by leaps and bounds daily.

Every time Cia launched into an impassioned explanation about the work she and Fran were doing, and every time someone handed her another check, she could feel her mother smiling down in approval. Nothing could bring back her parents, but trusting Lucas with her heart had finally allowed Cia to close that chapter and embrace the next one.

She dreamed of forever, and Lucas Wheeler was exactly the man to give it to her.

* * * * *

IMPROPERLY WED

BY
ANNA DEPALO

A Harvard graduate and former intellectual property attorney, **Anna DePalo** lives with her husband, son and daughter in New York City. Her books have consistently hit bestsellers list and Nielsen BookScan's list of top one hundred bestselling romances. Her books have won the *RT Book Reviews* Reviewers' Choice Award, the Golden Leaf and the Book Buyer's Best, and have been published in more than twenty countries. Readers are invited to reach her at www.annadepalo.com, friend her on Facebook or follow her on Twitter, www.twitter.com/ anna_depalo.

This one is for You, the reader,
the reason I write,
and for my editor, Elizabeth Mazer

One

"If any of you can show just cause why they may not lawfully be married, speak now or else forever hold your peace."

Belinda smiled encouragingly at Bishop Newbury.

The reverend returned her smile and opened his mouth to continue…before fixating on something in the pews over Belinda's shoulder.

Belinda heard it then, too. The footfalls sounded ever closer.

No…it couldn't be.

"I object."

Belinda heard the commanding words fall like an anvil on her heart.

A sick feeling gripped her. She closed her eyes.

She recognized that voice—its tone bland but edged with mockery. She'd heard it a million times in her dreams… her most illicit fantasies—the ones that left her blushing and appalled when she woke. And when she hadn't heard it there, she'd had the misfortune of catching it from a distance at a society event or in a television interview or two.

There was a rustling and murmuring in the congregation. Beside her, Tod had gone still. Bishop Newbury looked quizzical.

Slowly, Belinda turned. Tod took his cue from her lead.

Even though she knew what—no, *who*—to expect, her eyes widened as they met those of the man who should have been a sworn enemy to a Wentworth like her. Colin Granville, the Marquess of Easterbridge, heir to the family that had been locked in a feud with hers for centuries… and the person who knew her most humiliating secret.

When her eyes connected with his, she felt longing and dread at the same time. Even under cover of her veil, she could tell there was challenge and possessiveness in his gaze.

He loomed large, even though he wasn't up at the altar with her. His face was hard and uncompromising, his jaw square. Only even features and an aquiline nose saved him from looking harsh.

His hair was the same inky dark brown that she remembered and a shade or two darker than her own chestnut. Brows winged over eyes as dark as they were fathomless.

Belinda raised her chin and met his challenge head-on.

How did one crash a wedding? Apparently, the ticket was a navy business suit and canary-yellow tie. She supposed she should be glad he'd at least settled on formal attire.

Then again, she'd hardly seen Colin the real-estate mogul in anything other than a power suit that did nothing to disguise his athletic build. Well, except for that one night…

"What is the meaning of this, Easterbridge?" her uncle Hugh demanded as he rose from his seat in the first pew.

Belinda supposed someone should be standing to defend the honor of the Wentworths, and Uncle Hugh—as the head of the family—was the logical choice.

She scanned the settled mass of New York and London high society. Her family seemed aghast, but other guests looked fascinated by the unfolding drama.

Her bridesmaids and groomsmen appeared ill at ease, even her friend, Tamara Kincaid, who was always self-assured.

Off to the side of the church, her other close friend and wedding planner, Pia Lumley, had blanched.

"I say, Easterbridge," Tod spoke up, irritated and alarmed. "You were not invited today."

Colin shifted his gaze from the bride to her intended, and his lips curled. "Invited or not, I would hazard to guess that my position in Belinda's life entitles me to a say in these proceedings, wouldn't you?"

Belinda was acutely aware of the hundreds of pairs of interested eyes witnessing the show unfolding at the altar.

Bishop Newbury frowned, clearly perplexed, and then cleared his throat. "Well, it appears I'm compelled to resort to words that I've never had to use before." He paused. "Upon what grounds do you object to this marriage?"

Colin Granville, Marquess of Easterbridge, looked into her eyes.

"Upon the grounds that Belinda is married to me."

As the words reverberated off the soaring walls of the cathedral-size church, gasps sounded all around. Behind Belinda, the reverend began to cough. Beside her, Tod stiffened.

Belinda's eyes narrowed. She could detect mockery in Colin's expression. It lurked in the area around his eyes and in the slight lift to the end of his mouth.

"I'm afraid you must be mistaken," Belinda stated, hoping against hope that she could prevent this scene from getting worse.

As a matter of precise accuracy, she was correct. They had been married oh-so-briefly, but no longer were.

Still, Colin looked too sure of himself. "Mistaken about our visit to a wedding chapel in Las Vegas over two years ago? Regrettably, I must disagree."

There was a collective gasp from the assembled guests.

Belinda's stomach plummeted. Her face felt suddenly hot.

She stopped herself from replying—for what could she say that wouldn't add to the damage? *I'm sure my brief and secret marriage to the Marquess of Easterbridge was annulled?*

No one was supposed to know about her impetuous and hasty elopement.

Belinda knew she had to move this scene to a place where she could face down her demons—or, rather, one *titled* demon in particular—in a less public way. "Shall we resolve this matter somewhere more private?"

Without waiting for a response, and with as much dignity as she could muster, she gathered up the skirt of her wedding dress in one hand and swept down the altar steps, careful not to make eye contact with anyone among the congregated guests as she held her head high.

The sun shone through the church's large stained-glass windows. She walked intermittently through beams of sunlight slanting through the air.

Outside, Belinda knew, it was a perfect June day. Inside, it was another story.

Her perfect wedding was ruined by the man whom family and tradition dictated she should loathe most in the world. If she hadn't been wise enough before to think he was despicable—on that one night in particular—she certainly did now.

When she drew abreast of the marquess, he turned to follow her across the front of the church and through an open doorway that led into a corridor with several doors. Behind Colin, Belinda heard Tod, her erstwhile groom, follow.

When she stopped in the corridor, she heard a louder rustling and murmuring break out in the church. Now that the principal parties had exited the area of worship, she assumed the congregants felt at greater liberty to voice their whispers. She could only hope that Pia would be able to quiet this affair, though she was realistic enough to believe, too, that the effort would be mostly in vain. In the meantime, she could hear Bishop Newbury state to the wedding guests that there had been an unexpected delay.

She ducked into an unoccupied room nearby. Looking around, she concluded from the sparse furnishings and lack of personal belongings that the room probably served as a staging area for church functions.

Turning around, Belinda watched both the groom and her alleged husband follow her into the room. Colin closed the door on the curious faces still looking at them from the main area of the church.

She threw back her veil and rounded on Easterbridge. "How could you!"

Colin was close, and she was practically vibrating with tension, her heart beating loudly. Until now, Colin was the embodiment of her biggest secret and her greatest transgression. She'd tried to avoid or ignore him, but today running was out of the question.

Outrage was, of course, not only the logical but also the easiest emotion to adopt.

"You had better have a good reason for your actions, Easterbridge," Tod said, his face tight. "What possible explanation can you have for ruining our wedding with these outlandish lies?"

Colin looked unperturbed. "A wedding certificate."

"I don't know what alternate reality you've been living in, Easterbridge," Tod replied, "but no one else is amused by it."

Colin merely looked at her and raised an eyebrow.

"Our marriage was annulled," she blurted. "It never existed!"

Tod looked crestfallen. "So it's true? You and Easterbridge are married?"

"We *were*. Past tense," Belinda responded. "And only for a matter of hours, years ago. It was nothing."

"Hours?" Colin mused. "How many hours are in two years? Seventeen thousand four hundred seventy-two, by my calculation."

Belinda rued Colin's facility with math. She'd been stupidly enamored by it—by *him*—at the gaming tables before their impetuous Las Vegas elopement. And now it had come back to haunt her. But how could it be true that they'd been married for the last two years? She'd signed the papers—it was all meant to be wiped away.

"You were supposed to have obtained an annulment," she accused.

"The annulment was never finalized," Colin responded calmly. "Ergo, we are still married."

Her eyes rounded. She was a person who prided herself on remaining unruffled. After all, she'd faced down the occasional recalcitrant client in her position as an art specialist at renowned auction house Lansing's. But if her brief history with Colin was anything to judge by, the marquess had an unparalleled ability to get under her skin.

"What do you mean by *not finalized?*" she demanded. "I know I signed annulment papers. I distinctly remember doing so." Her brow furrowed with sudden suspicion. "Unless you misrepresented what I was signing?"

"Nothing so dramatic," Colin said with enviable composure. "An annulment is more complicated than simply signing a contract. In our case, the annulment papers were not properly filed with the court for judgment—an important last step."

"And whose fault was that?" she demanded.

Colin looked her in the eye. "The matter was over-looked."

"Of course," she snapped. "And you waited until today to tell me?"

Colin shrugged. "It wasn't an issue till now."

She was flabbergasted by his sangfroid. Was this Colin's way of getting back at her for leaving him in the lurch?

"I don't believe this." Tod threw up his hands, his reaction echoing her feelings.

She had decided to proceed without legal counsel in her annulment with Colin, even though she'd had only a cursory understanding of family law. She hadn't wanted anyone—even a family attorney—to know of her incredible lapse in judgment.

Now she regretted the decision not to hire a lawyer. Clearly she'd committed another error in judgment. Not only had she not made sure her annulment had been properly finalized—because she'd wanted to forget about the whole sorry episode in Las Vegas as soon as possible—but as a result she'd put her trust in Colin to see the annulment through.

Colin's gaze swept over her. "Very nice. Certainly a

departure from the red sequin ensemble that you wore during our ceremony."

"Red is an appropriate color when marrying the devil, wouldn't you agree?" she tossed back.

"You didn't act as if I were the devil at the time," he responded silkily, his voice lowering. "In fact, I recall—"

"I wasn't myself," she bit out.

I was out of my mind. That's right, she thought feverishly. Wasn't insanity a basis for annulment almost everywhere?

"Insane?" Colin queried. "Already trying to create a watertight defense to bigamy?"

"I did not commit bigamy."

"Only through my timely intervention."

The man was infuriating. "Timely? We've been married two years according to your calculation."

Colin inclined his head in acknowledgment. "And counting."

She was incredulous at his audacity. But then she supposed that, as her spouse, Colin felt he took precedence over Tod, an *almost* husband. And he'd be right, damn him. Even physically, Colin was more imposing. He was the same height as Tod but more muscular and formidable.

She rued her continuing awareness of Colin as a man. Still, it was a situation she intended to rectify forthwith to the extent she could.

"How long have you known we were still married?" she demanded.

Colin shrugged. "Does it matter if I arrived in time?"

She smelled a rat from his evasive response. *He'd wanted to create a scene.*

Still, he gave nothing away.

"You'll be hearing from my lawyer," she stated.

"I look forward to it."

"We're getting an annulment."

"Not today, however. Not even the state of Nevada works that fast."

He had a point there. Her wedding day was well and truly ruined.

She stared at him in impotent fury. "There are grounds," she insisted, reassuring herself. "I clearly must have been insane when I married you."

"We agreed on lack of consent due to intoxication, you'll recall," he parried.

"Yes, yours!" she retorted, annoyed by his continued sangfroid.

He inclined his head. "By our mutual agreement, due to a better alternative."

"Fraud should have sufficed," she responded tightly. "You completely misrepresented your character to me that night in Las Vegas, and after today, no one would disagree with me. This latest bit of Granville chicanery is for the history books."

He lifted an eyebrow. "Chicanery?"

"Yes," she insisted. "Delivering the news on my wedding day that you were derelict in filing our annulment papers."

"No need to impugn my ancestors by association," he responded calmly.

"Of course, there is," she contradicted. "Your ancestors are why we're in this current mess. They're the reason why—" she gestured in the direction of the church "—the crowd out there was electrified by the news that a Wentworth had married a Granville. What are we going to do?"

"Stay married?" he suggested mockingly.

"Never!"

Belinda turned to exit just as Uncle Hugh and Bishop Newbury barged in.

As she brushed past her uncle, she heard her relative demand, "I hope you have a good explanation, Easterbridge, though I can't imagine what it is!"

Apparently, all hell had broken loose in the hallowed sanctum.

Revenge.

A sordid word.

Still, revenge hinted at personal animosity. Instead, Colin mused, the Wentworths and Granvilles had been after each other for generations.

Perhaps *feud* or *vendetta* would be more appropriate.

His relationship with Belinda was intimately intertwined with the Wentworth-Granville feud. The feud was the reason that his and Belinda's passion for each other in Las Vegas had been infused with the thrill of the forbidden. It was also why Belinda had run out on him the next morning.

Ever since, he'd been set on a path to make Belinda acknowledge the visceral connection between the two of them—despite the fact that he was a Granville. His plan for doing so involved complicated maneuvers to vanquish the Wentworths, once and for all, and thus end the Wentworth-Granville feud.

Colin gazed at the panoramic view afforded by the floor-to-ceiling windows of his thirtieth-floor duplex condominium, waiting for the visitor who would inevitably arrive. The Time Warner Center, at one end of Columbus Circle, afforded a wealth of privacy as well as luxury to well-heeled foreigners seeking a pied-à-terre in New York City.

He slid his hands into his pockets and contemplated the

treetops of Central Park in the distance. Because it was a Sunday, he was in shirtsleeves rather than a business suit. It was a beautiful sunny day, much as yesterday had been.

Yesterday, of course, was what had almost been his wife's wedding day.

Belinda had appeared divine in her wedding dress, though her expression hadn't been celestial or angelic when she'd confronted him. Rather, she'd looked as if she was torn between cheerfully throttling him and dying of mortification.

Colin smiled at the image that crossed his mind. She had a passionate nature beneath her prepossessed exterior, and it drew him to her. He wanted to strip away the smooth veneer to the substance of the woman beneath.

If yesterday was any indication, Belinda hadn't changed much in two years. She had just as much passion—around him, anyway. Her erstwhile fiancé didn't seem to bring out the same fire. She'd been cool and collected by Dillingham's side, beautiful but detached. The smooth porcelain-doll facade had been in place—at least until he had interrupted the wedding service.

Her rich dark hair had been swept up and away from a face that was still arrestingly lush. Dark brows arched delicately over hazel eyes, an aquiline nose and lips too full for decency. Her ivory wedding dress had hugged a curvaceous figure. Its short lace sleeves and the lace over the décolleté were the only things that saved it from being immodest.

The moment she'd turned away from the altar and toward him, he'd felt a wave of heat and a tightening of the gut, even with the whisper of her veil between them.

Colin clenched his jaw. Belinda had looked breathtaking, just like on their wedding day. But when she'd married him, she'd been full of excitement and anticipation, eyes alight and those sinful lips spread in a dazzling smile. None of that stuffy, stilted Wentworth hauteur, just a stunning blend of passion and sensuality. The remoteness hadn't emerged until the following morning. But even now, Colin was pleased to see he could still get a reaction out of her.

After their confrontation in the church staging area, Belinda had swept out of the room. Colin wouldn't be surprised if she'd gotten into a cab and gone directly to her attorney's office. His mocking suggestion that they remain married had apparently been the last straw, as far as his wife was concerned.

The wedding reception had gone on, he'd heard. Belinda's wedding planner and friend, Pia Lumley, had seen to it at the Wentworth family's request. Regrettably, however, none of the three principal characters—the bride, her husband or the groom—had been present.

Colin stared broodingly at the magnificent view from his windows.

The enmity between the Wentworths and Granvilles ran deep. The two families were longstanding neighbors, landowners and, most importantly, rivals in England's Berkshire countryside. From skirmishes over property lines to allegations of political treachery and dastardly seduction of female relations, the flare-ups between the families had entered into folklore.

He, of course, as the current titular head of the Granville family, had written a fitting chapter to the long-running story by eloping in Las Vegas with Belinda Wentworth.

Over the years, he had found Belinda intriguing. Of course, he'd been curious about her. When he'd seen his opportunity to get to know her better, he'd taken it—first at a friend's cocktail party in Vegas and soon afterward, in a casino.

By the end of the night at the Bellagio casino, he'd

known he wanted Belinda like he'd wanted no woman before her. There had been something about her, and it went beyond the both of them being former competitive swimmers and current opera fans.

She was a dark and striking beauty, more than a match for him in wits. Of course, that same wit was what had made her floor him, as no woman had, at the end of the evening with the announcement that she couldn't sleep with him without a marriage certificate.

Of course, he hadn't been able to resist the challenge. Perhaps his winnings at the gaming tables had made him believe he could win no matter what the odds. He'd been willing to take the gamble for a night in bed with Belinda.

And she *hadn't* disappointed.

He felt a tightening in his gut even now at the memory, more than two years on.

And then yesterday, he'd used the element of surprise to his advantage by crashing Belinda's wedding. He'd only recently discovered that she was to be wed. He'd also guessed that nothing short of a public spectacle would have caused Belinda's wedding plans to fall apart. If he'd given her advance warning, she might have attempted to persuade him to finalize an annulment with no one being the wiser.

Tod Dillingham, who was concerned with status and appearances, would not know how to forgive a public transgression like yesterday. At least, Colin was banking on it.

At the chime of the apartment door, he turned away from the view. *Just in time.*

"Colin," his mother announced as she sailed in, "an incredible rumor has reached me. You must deny it immediately."

Colin stepped aside to let her in. "If it is incredible, why are you here seeking a denial?"

His mother's flair for drama never ceased to amaze him. Fortunately, these days he was usually at a safe remove, since she considered her London flat to be home base. On the other hand, it was his bad luck that a trip of hers to New York in order to visit friends and attend a party or two happened to coincide with Belinda's wedding date. He wondered idly if his younger sister, Sophie, was enjoying a London temporarily free of their mother's presence.

His mother tossed a glance back at him, a sour expression on her face. "Now is no time for you to be jesting."

"Was I?" he mused as he shut the door.

"Tosh! The family name is being besmirched." His mother put down her Chanel bag and settled herself in a chair in the living room, after giving her coat to the housekeeper who magically materialized for a moment. "I demand answers."

"Of course," Colin responded, remaining standing but folding his arms. He acknowledged the housekeeper with a grateful nod.

His mother looked incongruous in the contemporary setting. He was much more used to her in a traditional English sitting room, surrounded by chintz prints and stripes, with old and faded family photos adorning the console table and piano. Certainly she was used to a complete staff of servants.

He and his mother both waited, until his mother raised her eyebrows.

Colin cleared his throat. "What is the rumor precisely?"

"As if you didn't know!"

When he continued to remain silent, his mother sighed with resignation.

"I've heard the most horrible gossip that you disrupted the nuptials of the Wentworth chit. What's more, you apparently announced you were married to her." His mother held up her hand. "Naturally, I cut off the horrible harridan who was repeating the vicious rumor. I informed her that you would never have put in an appearance at a Wentworth wedding. Ergo, you could not have stated that—"

"Who was this teller of tall tales?"

His mother stopped, frowned and then waved a hand dismissively. "A reader of Mrs. Jane Hollings, who writes a column for some paper."

The New York Intelligencer.

His mother looked at him in distracted surprise. "Yes, I believe that's it. She works for the Earl of Melton. Whatever could Melton be thinking to own that rag of a paper?"

"I believe that tabloid turns a healthy profit, particularly online."

His mother sniffed. "It was the downfall of the aristocracy when even an earl went into trade."

"No, World War I was the downfall of the aristocracy," Colin contradicted sardonically.

"You can't possibly have turned up uninvited to the Wentworth nuptials," his mother repeated.

"Of course not."

His mother relaxed.

"When Belinda Wentworth's nuptials actually took place two years ago, I was very much invited—as her groom."

His mother stiffened.

"My station as a marquess, attributable to centuries of proper inbreeding," he continued wryly, "forced me to prevent a crime from being committed when it was within my means to do so once word reached me of Belinda's intention to marry again."

His mother sucked in a sharp breath. "Are you saying that I have been succeeded as the Marchioness of Easterbridge by a Wentworth?"

"It is precisely what I'm saying."

His mother looked as if she were experiencing vertigo. The news seemed to hit her with the force of a stock-market crash. Naturally, Colin had been counting on it; otherwise she would have been distinctly not amused by his insouciance.

"I don't suppose she changed her name to Granville in that chapel in Las Vegas?"

Colin shook his head.

His mother shuddered. "Belinda Wentworth, Marchioness of Easterbridge? The mind revolts at the thought."

"Don't worry," he offered, "I don't believe Belinda has used the title or has any intention of doing so."

If Belinda did use the title, his mother would be forced to style herself as the *Dowager* Marchioness of Easterbridge in order to avoid confusion. It would be viewed as adding insult to injury, Colin was sure.

His mother looked exasperated. "What on earth possessed you to marry a Wentworth in the first place?"

Colin shrugged. "I imagine you could find the answer among the multitude of reasons that other people get married." He was unwilling to divulge too much of his private life to his mother. Like hell was he going to talk about *passion*. "Why did you and Father marry?"

His mother pressed her lips together.

He'd known his question would end her query. His parents had married at least partly because they were social equals breathing the same rarefied air. As far as he could tell, it hadn't been a bad marriage until his father's death five years ago from a stroke, but it had been a proper and suitable one.

"Surely you can't mean to stay married."

"Never fear. I wouldn't be surprised if Belinda was consulting her lawyer as we speak."

Colin wondered what his mother would say if she knew that Belinda wanted out of their marriage but he didn't.

At least, not yet—not until his goal was reached.

In fact, he thought, he needed to call his lawyer and find out how the negotiations for his purchase of the property in question were going.

When the deal went through, Belinda would have no choice but to engage him—face matters without running or dodging.

Two

She'd made all the right moves in life…until a night in Las Vegas with Colin Granville.

Belinda tossed a sweater into the suitcase on her bed with more force than necessary.

She'd read history of art at Oxford and then worked at a series of auction houses before landing her current gig as a specialist in impressionist and modern art for posh auction house Lansing's.

She was usually punctual, quietly ambitious and tastefully dressed. She considered herself to be responsible and levelheaded.

In the process, she'd made her family happy. She'd been the dutiful child—if not always doing what they dictated, then at least not rebelling.

She was never the subject of gossip…until this past weekend. One glaring misstep was now the subject of breathless coverage in Mrs. Hollings' Pink Pages column in *The New York Intelligencer*:

It was to be the society wedding of the year.
Except—oh, my!
In case word hasn't reached your tender ears yet, dear reader, this town is abuzz with the news that the Wentworth-Dillingham wedding was crashed by none other than the Marquess of Easterbridge, who proceeded to make the astonishing claim that his short-lived marriage to the lovely Ms. Wentworth two years ago in Las Vegas— of all places!—had never been legally annulled.

Belinda winced as the words from Mrs. Hollings' column reverberated through her mind.

Mrs. Hollings had simply fired the first salvo. *Damn the social-networking sites.* The fiasco at St. Bart's Church had gone viral in the past three days.

She didn't even want to think about her family's continued reaction. She'd avoided calls from her mother and Uncle Hugh in the past few days. She knew she'd have to deal with them eventually, but she wasn't prepared to yet.

Instead, yesterday she'd commiserated over the phone with her closest girlfriends, Tamara and Pia. They'd both been full of sympathy for Belinda's situation, and they'd admitted that the would-be wedding had brought them troubles of their own. Tamara had confessed that she avoided one of the groomsmen at the wedding, Sawyer Langsford, Earl of Melton, because their families had long cherished the idea that the two would wed. Meanwhile, Pia had admitted that she'd discovered one of the wedding guests was her former lover, James "Hawk" Carsdale, Duke of Hawkshire, who had left her without so much as a goodbye after one night three years ago, when he'd presented himself as merely Mr. James Fielding.

In short, the aborted wedding had been a disastrous day for her and her two girlfriends.

Fortunately, Belinda thought, she had a ticket out of town. Tomorrow morning, she would be leaving her tidy little Upper West Side one bedroom for a business trip to England. Even before the wedding that wasn't, she and Tod had decided to postpone a honeymoon for a later date—one that was more convenient for their mutual work schedules. And now she was glad she already had a business trip planned. She couldn't outrun her problems, but some space and distance from the scene of the crime—namely, New York—would help clear her mind so she could come up with a plan.

Ironically, while her wedding date to Tod was supposed to seal her image as the perfect and dutiful society bride, it had done the exact opposite, thanks to Colin's appearance. Her wedding was to have been her apogee, but instead it had been her downfall.

Still, an annulment or divorce should be easy enough to obtain. People got them every day, didn't they? She herself had thought she'd received one.

She paused in the process of packing, sweater in hand, and gazed sightlessly at the clutter on top of her dresser.

She recalled how she'd stared at the annulment papers when they'd arrived for her signature and then pushed aside the quick stab of pain that they had engendered. They were simply a reminder of the blemish on the resume of her life, she'd told herself. But no one needed to know about her appalling mistake.

Belinda dropped the sweater into her suitcase and swallowed against the sudden panicky feeling in the pit of her stomach. She cupped her forehead, as if she could will her proverbial headache away.

But she knew there was no hope of making a six-foot-plus wealthy marquess disappear from her life with a *poof!*

Even before that fateful night in Vegas, she'd run into Colin at social functions occasionally over the years and had found him, well, compelling. But she was too aware of the history between their two families to ever talk directly to him. On top of it all, he was too masculine, too sternly good-looking, too everything. She, who prided herself on her propriety and self-control, couldn't risk spending time with someone who made her feel so…unsettled.

But then she'd been sent on assignment to Las Vegas to appraise the private art collection of a multimillionaire real-estate developer. When she'd run into Colin at the developer's cocktail party, she'd felt compelled for business' sake to socialize with him. She hadn't planned on discovering, much to her chagrin, how charming he was and how much she was attracted to him.

He was like a breath of home in a new place—pleasantly familiar—and yet he stirred a response in her like no one ever had. In the process of idle cocktail party chitchat and banter, she discovered they'd both been standout swimmers in school, they were both partial to operatic performances at New York's Lincoln Center and London's Royal Opera House and they were both active in the same charities to help the unemployed—though Colin sat on the board, while she was more of a foot soldier volunteering her time.

Belinda had thought their similarities were almost disconcerting.

Toward the end of her stay in Vegas, she'd run into Colin again in the lobby of the Bellagio. She'd been momentarily uncertain what to do, but he'd made the decision for her. The ice had already been broken at the recent cocktail party, and what's more, it turned out they were both staying at the Bellagio.

Frankly, she'd been in a partying mood—or at least one for a celebratory drink or two. She'd landed a deal with Colin's real-estate developer friend for a big auction sale of artwork at Lansing's. She knew she had Colin partially to thank. His smooth mediation of her conversations with the developer at the party had certainly been helpful.

Buoyed by a surge in magnanimity, she'd agreed to have a drink with Colin. Their drinks had naturally progressed to dinner and then time at the gaming tables, where she'd been impressed by Colin's winnings.

At the end of the evening, it had seemed like the most natural thing in the world to continue up in the elevator with him to his luxury suite.

She'd teasingly suggested that she couldn't sleep with him unless they were married. She'd gambled on her pronouncement being the end of the matter. After all, she'd recently broken up with a boyfriend of more than a year with nothing to show for it.

Colin, however, had shocked her by upping the ante and daring her to go to the Las Vegas Marriage License Bureau with him. They'd turned around and headed back downstairs.

She'd been by turns amused and horrified by their escapade, especially when they'd started hunting for a chapel. She'd never been in an iconic Las Vegas wedding chapel. One had been too easy to find that night.

Later, of course, she'd blame her uncharacteristic actions on having had a drink or two and on the crazy Vegas environment. She'd point the finger at just having turned thirty and losing another boyfriend. She'd place fault on the increasing pressure from her family to marry well and soon, and on the fact that most of her wellborn classmates from Marlborough College were already engaged or married. She'd even blame her surge of goodwill toward Colin, who'd helped her land business at the cocktail party. Basically, she'd found everyone and everything at fault—most of all herself.

In the morning, her cell phone had rung, and she'd blearily identified the call as being from her mother. It had been as if someone had doused her with icy water while she'd still been half-asleep. She'd come back to reality with a shock, and had been truly horrified by what she'd done the night before. She'd insisted on a quick and quiet annulment without anyone being the wiser.

At first, Colin had been amused by her alarm. But soon, when it had become clear that her distress wasn't temporary, he'd become closed and aloof, thinly masking his anger.

Belinda dropped her hand from her forehead, and in the next moment, she was startled by the ring of her cell phone.

She sighed. She supposed it was a good thing to be jostled out of unhappy memories.

Locating the phone on top of her dresser, she confirmed what the ring tone was telling her—it was Pia calling.

She put a Bluetooth device in her ear for hands-free listening so she could continue packing while she talked.

"Aren't you supposed to be in Atlanta for a wedding?" Belinda asked without preamble once she had her earpiece in place.

"I am," Pia responded, "but I have until the end of the week before the pace picks up for Saturday's main event."

She and Pia and their mutual friend, Tamara, had gotten to know each other through charitable work for the Junior League. All three of them had settled in New York in their twenties, soon after university. Though they'd chosen to live in different Manhattan neighborhoods, and were busy pursuing different careers—Tamara's being in jewelry design while wedding planning had always been Pia's dream—they had become fast friends.

Though Tamara was the daughter of a British viscount, Belinda had not met her as part of the aristocratic set in England because Tamara had grown up mostly in the United States, after her American-born mother had divorced her titled husband. Too bad—her free-thinking bohemian friend would have been a breath of fresh air in Belinda's stilted, structured adolescence. Tamara had never met a trend that she didn't want to buck—a trait that Belinda couldn't help but admire. Pia was more like herself, though her friend came from a middle-class background in rural Pennsylvania.

"Don't worry," Belinda joked, guessing the reason for Pia's call, "I'm still alive and kicking. I intend to be granted my freedom from the marquess if it's the last thing that I do."

"Oh, B-Belinda, I-I-I wish there was something I could do," Pia said, her stutter making a rare appearance.

"Colin and I made this mess, and we'll have to be the ones to clean it up."

Belinda regretted the repercussions for Pia's wedding-planning business from the nuptial disaster on Saturday. She'd thought only of helping her friend's career when she'd asked Pia to be her wedding planner instead of her bridesmaid—despite knowing Pia was a dyed-in-the-wool romantic. Unfortunately, none of her plans for Saturday had worked out well.

Damn, Colin.

Since she'd had a three-way phone conversation with Pia and Tamara only yesterday, and Pia had just arrived in Atlanta for business today, Belinda sensed there might be more reason for her friend's call than an opportunity to chat.

Because she was not one to skirt an issue, unless it involved her *husband*—not to be confused with her *groom*—she went straight to the point. "I know you wouldn't be calling without a reason."

"W-well," Pia said delicately, "I wish this conversation could take place at a later time, but there is the issue of what announcement to send, if any, with regard to Saturday's, er, interrupted nuptials. And then, of course, the wedding gifts—"

"Send them all back," Belinda cut in.

She was an optimist but also a realist. She didn't know for sure how long it would take to bring the marquess to heel at least long enough to grant her an annulment or divorce.

"Okay." Pia sounded relieved and uncertain at the same time. "Are you sure, because—"

"I'm sure," Belinda interrupted. "And as far as a statement, I don't think one is necessary. A wedding announcement would no longer be appropriate obviously, and anything else would be unnecessary. Thanks in part to Mrs. Hollings, I believe everyone is in the know about Saturday's events."

"What about you and Tod?" Pia asked. "Will you be able to, ah, patch things up?"

Belinda thought back to the events of Saturday.

Outside the church, Tod had caught up with her, apparently having exited the confrontation with Colin soon after she had. They'd had a short and uncomfortable conversation. While he had tried to maintain a stiff upper lip, Tod had still seemed flabbergasted, annoyed and embarrassed.

She'd handed his engagement ring back to him. It

had seemed like the only decent thing to do. She'd just discovered she was still married to another man, after all.

Then she had ducked into the white Rolls Royce at the curb, relieved to have attained privacy at last. She had been quivering with emotion ever since Colin's voice had rung out at the church.

Belinda sighed. "Tod is perplexed and angry, and under the circumstances, I can hardly blame him."

She winced when she thought about her glaring omission—not telling him about her elopement. Her only excuse was that she could hardly bear to think about it herself. It was too painful.

She hadn't been able to live down her uncharacteristic behavior, and then it had come barging in in the form of a tall, imposing aristocrat who aroused passionate reactions in her.

Pia cleared her throat. "So matters between you and Tod are…?"

"On hold. Indefinitely," Belinda confirmed. "He's waiting for me to resolve this situation, and then we'll decide where we'll go from there."

Pia said nothing for a moment. "So you don't want to issue any public statement…for clarification?"

"Are you volunteering to be my publicist?" Belinda joked.

"It wouldn't be the first time I issued a public statement or a press release for a bride," Pia responded. "Media relations is part of the job for society wedding planners these days."

Belinda sighed. "What could I say, besides confirming that I am in fact still married to Easterbridge?"

"I see your point," Pia conceded, "and I don't disagree. But I thought I'd give you the opportunity to respond to Mrs. Hollings if you want to."

"No, thanks."

The last thing Belinda wanted was for this scandal to play out in the media. After all, a public statement by her might just invite Easterbridge to issue his own *clarifications.*

She would try to deal with Colin privately and discreetly—even if she had to go beard the lion in his den. She wanted to avoid further scandal, if possible. She knew it was a slippery slope from retaining lawyers to sending threatening letters and ultimately going through an ugly and public divorce.

"What the devil has gotten into you, Belinda?" Uncle Hugh said, coming around his desk as Belinda stepped into the library of his town house in London's Mayfair neighborhood.

The mark of disapproval was stamped all over her uncle's face.

She was being called to account. She, Belinda Wentworth, had done what none of her ancestors had—betrayed her heritage by marrying a Granville.

Belinda knew when she'd gone to London on business that she'd be compelled to pay a visit at the Mayfair town house. She had been able to escape in-depth conversations—and explanations—with her relatives directly after the wedding by departing the church forthwith and having Pia run interference for her at the show-must-go-on reception afterward. Her family had also been preoccupied with trying to save face with the assembled guests—to the extent such a thing was possible.

She glanced above the mantel at the Gainsborough painting of Sir Jonas Wentworth. The poor man was probably turning in his grave.

The London house had been in the Wentworth clan

for generations. Like many other highborn families, the Wentworths had fought tooth and nail to hang on to a fashionable Mayfair address that carried a certain cache, if no longer necessarily signifying generations of quality breeding due to the growing number of new money.

Though the Wentworths were not titled, they descended from a younger branch of the Dukes of Pelham and had intermarried with many other aristocratic families over the years—save, of course, for the despised Granvilles. Thus, they considered themselves as blue-blooded as anybody.

"This is quite a tangle that you've created," her uncle went on as a servant rolled in a cart bearing the preparations for afternoon tea.

Belinda worried her bottom lip. "I know."

"It must be resolved forthwith."

"Of course."

As the servant left the room, Uncle Hugh gestured for Belinda to sit down.

"Well, what are you going to do to fix this mess?" he asked as they both sat, she on the sofa and he in a nearby armchair.

By force of habit, Belinda leaned forward to fix tea. It gave her something to do—and the illusion of being in control while not meeting Uncle Hugh's gaze.

"I intend to obtain an annulment or divorce, of course," she said evenly.

Despite her self-assured attitude, there was nothing *of course* about it.

She surveyed the tea tray. A proper English tea was more than loose tea and hot water. There were the customary finger sandwiches, buttery biscuits and warm scones.

Really, she could drown herself in scones right now. Crumbly blueberry ones…rich raisin ones…decadent chocolate-chip ones—

No, not decadent. Definitely not decadent. It came too close to mimicking the behavior that had gotten her into her current fix with Colin.

She was decidedly not into decadent behavior, she told herself firmly.

Nevertheless, an image flashed into her mind of lounging on a king-size bed with Colin Granville, sharing champagne and strawberries high above the flashing lights of Las Vegas.

Her face heated.

"…a youthful indiscretion?"

She fumbled in the process of pouring hot water into a cup.

She jerked her head up. "What?"

Her uncle raised his eyebrows. "I was merely inquiring whether this unfortunate situation came about due to a youthful indiscretion?"

She knew she must look guilty. "Can I claim so even though I was thirty at the time?"

Uncle Hugh regarded her with a thoughtful but forbearing expression. "I'm not so old that I don't re-member how much partying and club-hopping can go on in one's twenties or beyond."

"Yes," Belinda said, more than ready to accept the proffered excuse. "That must be it."

Her uncle accepted a teacup and saucer from her.

"And, yet, I'm surprised at you, Belinda," he went on as he took a sip of his tea. "You were never one for rebellion. You were sent to a proper boarding school and then to Oxford. No one expected this scenario."

She should have guessed that she would not be let off the hook so easily.

Belinda stifled a grimace. Marlborough College's most famous graduate these days was the former Kate

Middleton, Duchess of Cambridge, who would mostly likely be queen one day. *She,* by startling contrast, had failed miserably on the matrimonial front. She now had the wreckage of not one but two wedding ceremonies behind her.

She hated to disappoint Uncle Hugh. He had been a father figure to her since her own father's death after a yearlong battle with cancer when she'd been thirteen. As her father's older brother, and the head of the Wentworth family, her uncle had fallen naturally into the paternal role. A longtime widower, Uncle Hugh had been unable to have children with his wife and had remained single and childless since then.

On her part, Belinda had tried to be a good surrogate daughter. She'd grown up on Uncle Hugh's estates—learning to swim and ride a bicycle during her summers there. She'd gotten good grades, she hadn't acted out as a teenager and she'd kept her name out of the gossip columns—until now.

Uncle Hugh sighed and shook his grayed head. "Nearly three centuries of feuding and now this. Do you know your ancestor Emma was seduced by a Granville scoundrel? Fortunately, the family was able to hush up matters and arrange a respectable marriage for the poor girl to the younger son of a baronet." His eyebrows knitted. "On the other hand, our nineteenth-century land dispute with the Granvilles dragged on for years. Fortunately, the courts were finally able to vindicate us on the matter of the proper property line between our estate and the Granvilles'."

Belinda had heard both stories many times before. She opened her mouth to say something—*anything*—about how her situation with Colin was different.

"Ah! I see I've finally run you to ground."

Belinda turned in time to watch her mother sail into

the room. She abruptly clamped her mouth shut to prevent herself from groaning out loud. *Out of the frying pan and into the fire.*

Her mother handed her purse and chiffon scarf to a servant who hastened in from the doorway before turning for a discreet retreat. As usual, she looked impeccably turned out—as if she'd just come from lunch at Annabelle's or one of her other customary jaunts. Her hair was coiffed, her dress was timelessly chic and probably St. John and her jewels were heirlooms.

Belinda thought that the contrast between her and her mother could hardly be more pronounced. She was casually dressed in chain-store chinos and a fluttery short-sleeved blouse that were paired with a couple of Tamara's affordable jewelry pieces.

Even aside from the accoutrements, however, Belinda knew she did not physically resemble her mother. Her mother was a fragile blonde, while she herself was a statuesque brunette. She took after the Wentworth side of the family in that regard.

"Mother," Belinda tried, "we spoke right after the wedding."

Her mother glanced at her and widened her eyes. "Yes, darling, but you gave me only the vaguest and most rudimentary of answers."

Belinda flushed. "I told you what I knew."

Her mother waved a hand airily. "Yes, yes, I know. The marquess' appearance was unexpected, his claims outlandish. Still, it all begs the question as to how precisely you've been married two odd years with no one being the wiser."

"I told you the marquess claims that an annulment was never finalized. I am in the process of confirming that claim and rectifying matters."

She had not hired a divorce lawyer yet, but she had phoned an attorney in Las Vegas, Nevada, and requested that Colin's claim be verified—namely, she and Colin were still married.

Her mother glanced at Uncle Hugh and then back at her. "This scandal is the talk of London and New York. How do you plan to rectify that matter?"

Belinda bit her lip. Obviously, her mother, having met with resistance to her first line of inquiry, had moved on to another.

It was ironic, really, that she was being subjected to questioning by her mother. She had turned a deaf ear to her mother's personal affairs over the years, though they had been the subject of gossip and cocktail-party innuendo. She hadn't wanted to know more about *affaires de coeur,* as her mother was fond of referring to them.

Her mother looked fretful. "How will we ever resolve this with the Dillinghams? It's disastrous."

"Now, now, Clarissa," her uncle said, leaning forward to set down his teacup. "Histrionics will not do a bit of good here."

Belinda silently seconded the sentiment and then heaved an inward sigh. She and her mother had never had an easy relationship. They were too different in personality and character. As an adult, she'd been pained when her mother's behavior had been shallow, selfish or self-centered, and often all three.

As if on cue, her mother slid onto a nearby chair, managing somehow to be graceful about it while still giving the impression that her legs would no longer support her during this ordeal. "Belinda, Belinda, how could you be so reckless, so irresponsible?"

Belinda felt rising annoyance even as she acknowledged

she'd been asking herself the same question again and again. She *had* acted uncharacteristically.

"You were expected to marry well," her mother went on. "The family was counting on it. Why, most of your classmates have already secured advantageous matches."

Belinda wanted to respond that she *had* married well. Most people would say that a rich and titled husband qualified as good enough. And yet, Colin was a detested Granville and thus one who was not to be trusted under any circumstances.

"We spent a long time cultivating the Dillinghams," her mother continued. "They were prepared to renovate Downlands so you and Tod might entertain there in style once you were married."

Belinda didn't need to be reminded of the plan, contingent on her marriage to Tod, to update the Wentworths' main ancestral estate in Berkshire. She knew the family finances were, if not precarious, less than robust.

Truth be told, neither she nor Tod had been swept away by passion. Instead, their engagement had been based more on practicalities. She and Tod had known each other forever and had always gotten along well enough. She was in the prime of her friends' matrimonial season, if not toward the end of it, at thirty-two. Likewise, she knew Tod was looking for and expected to marry a suitable woman from his highborn social set.

Tod had said he would wait for her to resolve the situation. He had not said how long he would wait, however.

Her mother tilted her head. "I don't suppose you could lay claim to part of Easterbridge's estate for being accidentally married for the past two years?"

Belinda was appalled. "Mother!"

Her mother widened her eyes. "What? There have been plenty of real marriages that have endured for less time."

"I'd have more leverage if Easterbridge were divorcing me!"

Belinda recalled the marquess' jesting offer to remain married. It was clear she'd have to be the one to initiate proceedings to dissolve their marriage.

"You didn't have time to sign a prenuptial agreement at that wedding chapel in Las Vegas, did you?" her mother persisted and then sniffed—ready to answer her own question. "Why, I wouldn't be surprised if Easterbridge carried a standard contract in his back pocket."

"Mother!"

Uncle Hugh shook his head. "A man as sharp as Easterbridge would have seen to it that his property was not vulnerable. On the other hand, we wouldn't want the marquess to make any claim to Wentworth property."

Her mother turned back to her. "It's a good thing that none of the Wentworth estates are in your name."

"Yes," Uncle Hugh acknowledged, "but Belinda is an heiress. She stands to inherit the Wentworth wealth. If she remains Easterbridge's wife, her property may eventually become his to share, particularly if the assets are not kept separate."

"Intolerable," her mother declared.

For her part, Belinda didn't feel like an heiress. In fact, from all of her family's focus on making a good match, she felt more stifled than liberated by the Wentworth wealth. True, she was the beneficiary of a small trust fund, but those resources only made it bearable for her to live in Manhattan's high-rent market on her skimpy art specialist's salary.

She'd been reminded time and again that her task was to carry the Wentworth standard forward for another generation. She was never unaware of her position as an only child. So far, however, she could not have made a bigger mash of things.

"I'll deal with the marquess," Belinda said grimly, stopping herself from her nervous habit of chewing her lip.

Somehow, she had to untangle herself from her marriage.

Three

"Thank you for meeting me today," she said, somewhat incongruously, as she stepped into a conference room in Colin's business offices at the Time Warner Center.

She was hoping to keep matters on a polite and productive footing. Or at least to start that way.

Colin gave a quick nod of his head. "You're welcome."

Belinda watched as Colin's gaze went unerringly to her now ring-free hand.

Her heart beat loudly in her chest.

She'd wanted a meeting place that was private but not too private. She knew Colin owned a spectacular penthouse high above them in the same complex—it was one of the unavoidable pieces of information that she'd come across about him in the news in the past couple of years—but she'd shied away from facing him there. And her own apartment farther uptown was too small.

It would have been hard enough to confront Colin under

any circumstances. He was wealthy, titled and imposing—
not to mention savvy and calculating. But he was also her
former lover and could lay claim to knowing her intimately.
Their night together would always be between them. She'd
seen what they could do with a hotel room... What they
could do in his apartment didn't bear thinking about. At
all. Ever.

Belinda scanned him warily.

He wore a business suit and held himself with the easy
and self-assured charm of a sleek panther ready to toy with
a kitty. He carried the blood of generations of conquerors
in his veins, and it showed.

Belinda felt awareness skate over her skin, a good deal
of which was exposed. She was dressed in a V-neck belted
dress and strappy sandals, having arranged to have this
meeting during her lunch break at Lansing's.

Colin gestured to the sideboard. "Coffee or tea?"

She set down her handbag on the long conference table.
"No, thank you."

He perused her too thoroughly. "You are rather even-
keeled, in sharp contrast to last week."

"I've chosen to remain the calm in the storm," she
replied. "The rumors have run amok, the groom has
decamped for the other side of the Atlantic and the wedding
gifts are being returned."

"Ah." He sat on a corner of the conference table.

"I hope you're satisfied."

"It's a good start."

She quelled her ire and looked at him straight on. "I am
here to make you see reason."

He was ill-mannered enough to chuckle.

"I know you're busy—" *too busy to have obtained an
annulment, obviously* "—so I'll go straight to the point.
How is it possible that we're still married?"

Colin shrugged. "The annulment was never finalized with the court."

"That's what you said." She smelled a rat—or more precisely, a cunning aristocrat. "I hope you fired your lawyer for the matter."

She took a steadying breath. The lawyer she had recently consulted had confirmed that, as far as state records showed, she and Colin were still married because there was no record of an annulment or even of papers being filed.

One way or the other, she had to deal with matters as they unfortunately stood.

"It's futile to look back," Colin remarked, as if reading her mind. "The issue is what do we do now."

Belinda widened her eyes. "Now? We obtain an annulment or divorce, of course. New York recently did me the enormous favor of introducing no-fault divorce, so I'll no longer have to prove that you committed adultery or abandoned me. I know that much from some simple research."

Colin looked unperturbed. "Ah, for the good old days when marriage meant coverture and only a husband could own property or prove adultery."

She didn't appreciate his humor. "Yes, how unfortunate for you."

He lifted his lips. "There's only one problem."

"Oh? Only one?" She was helpless to stop the sarcasm.

Colin nodded. "Yes. A no-fault divorce can still be contested, starting with the service of divorce papers."

She stared at him dumbly. What was he saying?

She narrowed her eyes. "So you're saying…"

"I'm not granting you an easy divorce, in New York or anywhere else."

"You ruined my wedding, and now you're going to ruin

my divorce?" she asked, unable to keep disbelief from her voice.

"Your wedding was already ruined because we were still married," Colin countered. "Even if I hadn't interrupted the ceremony, your marriage to Dillingham would have been considered void ab initio due to bigamy. It would have been as if the marriage ceremony had never occurred."

Belinda pressed her lips together.

Colin raised an eyebrow. "I know. It's rather inconvenient that your marriage to Dillingham would have been the one to have been declared legally nonexistent."

"You ruined my wedding," she accused. "You chose the precise wrong moment to make your big announcement. Why crash the ceremony?"

"Shouldn't you be thanking me for preventing a crime from being committed?"

She ignored his riposte. "And to top it off, you ruined my marriage by not making sure the annulment was properly finalized."

"Your marriage to whom? The one to Tod that never existed? Or ours? Most people would say that not finalizing an annulment is the way to avoid ruining a marriage."

She wasn't amused by his recalcitrance. She'd come here to get him to agree to a quiet dissolution of their union.

Colin rubbed his chin. "I can't understand how you managed to keep our Las Vegas wedding a secret. Did Dillingham even know?"

Belinda reddened. "Tod is standing by me."

"That means no." Colin let his gaze slide over her hand. "Also, you're not wearing his ring. Just how...*closely* is he standing by? Or does his support amount to waiting in the wings until this whole messy divorce business is taken care of? But just how long is he willing to wait?"

"As long as it takes," she shot back.

They stared at each other, and Belinda forced herself not to blink. The truth was she had no idea how long or how short Tod would wait. The wedding fiasco had been quite a blow.

Colin tilted his head and contemplated her. "You didn't even tell him that you already had one wedding behind you. Were you afraid of what an Old Etonian like Dillingham would think of the quick Vegas elopement in your past?"

"I'm sure he would have been bothered only by the fact that the groom had been you," she retorted.

"Right, competitive," Colin said, nodding even as he twisted her meaning. "But then there's the fact that you lied on your marriage license."

Belinda's flush deepened.

It was true that she had omitted to list the Las Vegas ceremony when applying for a marriage license in New York. Her union with Colin had been a marriage of brief duration that had been contracted in another state and, she believed, had ended in an annulment.

Didn't an annulment usually mean that a marriage had never existed?

Belinda rallied her reserves.

"You know quite a bit about dissolving a marriage even if you haven't accomplished it successfully yourself," she retorted. "Have you talked to a lawyer already?"

"You have. Why shouldn't I?" he returned rather cryptically.

"That's the difference between you and Tod. He hasn't spoken with an attorney." The last thing she needed was for the Dillinghams to resort to legal means to recoup their costs for the wedding fiasco.

Colin twisted his lips. "Pity. Because if he had, his lawyer would have told him just what my lawyer told me.

If I choose to fight your divorce suit, you'll remain my wife for quite a while longer."

"So you plan to fight it?"

"With everything I've got."

"I'll win eventually."

"Maybe, but I'm sure the Wentworths won't appreciate the notoriety."

He was right, Belinda thought with a sick feeling. If this scandal deepened, her family would be horrified. And she felt ill just thinking of the Dillinghams' reaction.

"You're the Marchioness of Easterbridge," Colin said, driving his point home. "You might as well start using the title."

Marchioness of Easterbridge. She was glad her ancestors weren't around to hear this.

"It's a good thing you chose to keep your surname on the Nevada marriage license," Colin continued. "Otherwise, you'd have been erroneously representing yourself as Belinda Wentworth rather than Belinda Granville for more than two years."

"I remember choosing to keep my name," she shot back. "I wasn't so completely off kilter that I don't remember that detail."

Somehow, it had been acceptable to marry Colin but not to take the Granville name.

Belinda Granville. It sounded worse than Marchioness of Easterbridge. Easterbridge was simply Colin's title, whereas Granville had been the surname carried by his devious ancestors.

"Why are you doing this?" she blurted. "I can't understand why we shouldn't have a civilized divorce—or better yet, annulment."

He sauntered toward her. "Can't you? Nothing has been civilized between the Wentworths and the Granvilles for generations. The ending of our…encounter in Las Vegas is further evidence of it."

Her eyes widened. "So it all goes back to that, doesn't it?"

He stopped before her. "I intend to make a conquest of the Wentworths once and for all—" his gaze slid down her body "—beginning and ending with you, my beautiful wife."

Disaster preparedness.

He'd laid the groundwork, Colin thought. He'd spent two-plus years planning for this moment, making sure he'd anticipated every likely contingency.

"Excellent," Colin said into the phone. "Did he ask many questions?"

"No," his deputy responded. "Once he knew you were willing to meet his price, he was pleased."

And now, he was satisfied himself, Colin thought.

"I believe he assumed you were a Russian oligarch looking to make a prime purchase."

"Even better," Colin replied.

If he knew Belinda, in the past few weeks she'd been quietly working to find a way to disengage herself from their union with as little fanfare as possible. But now he held a trump card.

After ending the call, he looked up at his two friends. When his cell phone had buzzed, and he'd seen who was calling, he'd been too impatient for answers to ignore the call despite the presence of company on a Thursday evening.

From their seats in upholstered chairs in the sitting room of Colin's London town house, Sawyer Langsford, Earl of Melton, and James Carsdale, Duke of Hawkshire, exchanged looks. They all happened to be in town at the same time and had met for drinks. Having removed their jackets, they all sat around with loosened ties.

Like his two fellow aristocrats, Colin had had a more peripatetic existence than most, so his accent was cosmopolitan rather than British. Still, despite all being well-traveled—or maybe, because of it—he, Sawyer and Hawk had become friends. Thus it seemed oddly appropriate that the three of them would become romantically entangled at the same time.

Sawyer had unexpectedly gotten engaged to Tamara Kincaid, one of Belinda's bridesmaids. Hawk was intently pursuing Pia Lumley, Belinda's wedding planner, in an effort to smooth out his bumpy history with her.

Both of his friends were enjoying rather more success romantically than Colin at the moment—though unsurprisingly, Belinda's friends had proven challenging to woo, as well. Colin had an advantage in that Belinda was already his wife. Yet the fact that she now refused to communicate with him except through lawyers was a decided obstacle.

But no matter. He and Belinda were still married, and with his business deal today, she'd have to deal with him sooner rather than later.

"What game are you playing, Easterbridge?" Hawk inquired.

"A rather high-stakes one, I'm afraid," Colin said in a faintly bored tone. "I'm sure you want no part of it."

Hawk raised an eyebrow.

Sawyer shrugged. "You've always played your cards close to your chest, Colin."

"Simply doing my best to burnish the Granville surname." And what better way to varnish it than to be responsible for finally vanquishing the family foes, the Wentworths?

Colin hadn't given much thought to his fellow Berkshire landowners over the years. This was the twenty-first century, after all, and civility toward one's neighbors, barring direct provocation, was the norm. Besides, in his rather small aristocratic world, it was considered downmarket to openly not get along.

He'd been willing to let bygones be bygones for most of his thirty-seven years, not interacting with the Wentworths but not engaging in open feuding, either. He'd been disposed to maintain a status quo of wary distance because not much had been at stake.

But then he'd unexpectedly come into contact with Belinda in Las Vegas. He was as susceptible as the next man to a leggy brunette with flashing eyes.

He'd been intrigued by Belinda Wentworth whenever he'd occasionally chanced to cross her path over the years. It hadn't happened often. She was a good half-dozen years younger, so their childhoods in Berkshire had not overlapped much. He'd been sent up to Eton at the age of thirteen to continue his studies, and had only rarely returned home. By the time he'd begun to establish his real-estate empire, Belinda had been off at school herself.

But then, an opportunity had presented itself at a Vegas cocktail party to speak with Belinda and he'd been pleased, not least of all because his curiosity had been stoked.

Nothing had happened that night but banter and conversation, but it had definitely whetted his appetite for more. When he'd encountered Belinda in the hotel lobby of the Bellagio, a couple of days after the cocktail party, he hadn't let the opportunity that he'd been hoping for slip by. He'd invited her to have a drink. Drinks had become dinner, and then they'd wound up in the casino, where he'd been able to exhibit his skill at the gaming tables.

By that time, of course, he'd *really* wanted Belinda.

She'd been a desirable woman who pushed all the right buttons for him. By the end of the night, he'd had a sense of rightness and anticipation.

She'd followed him into the elevator leading to his luxury suite. But then she jokingly suggested that she'd have to marry him first.

The gauntlet had been thrown down.

He'd studied her. She looked relaxed and uninhibited but not as if she'd crossed the line to being intoxicated.

The elevator doors opened, and they stepped out onto the penthouse floor.

He turned to her and took a step closer.

"It doesn't seem right to marry you when I haven't even kissed you," he murmured in a low voice.

Belinda's hazel eyes twinkled. "I'm not putting out anymore without a promise. You know, like the song 'Single Ladies.'"

Her tone was joking, but he detected an underlying note of seriousness.

"Someone hurt you."

She shrugged. "Not badly."

Colin experienced a sudden surge of anger at an unnamed jerk.

Blast, he was far gone.

One kiss.

He cupped Belinda's face and ran his thumb over her mouth. She closed her eyes on a sigh, and he bent his head to sip from her pink lips.

She tasted sweet, so sweet. Their breaths mingled.

He sunk into the kiss, heedless of the fact that they were next to the elevator and the doors could open at any moment.

He'd always been daring. He'd had to take risks to expand his real-estate empire. In his personal life, he'd skydived, bungee jumped and usually done whatever was the thrill in vogue—much to the chagrin of his mother, who hadn't liked seeing the heir or, subsequently, the holder of the marquessate, risking his neck.

"This is Vegas, and you know what that means," he said after the kiss ended.

Belinda had looked at him inquiringly.

"There must be a wedding chapel nearby."

The lark had started that way and just gained momentum.

They'd gone downstairs again, and sure enough, they'd located a wedding chapel without too much trouble.

He'd never met a woman before who was willing to up the ante with him. It was a powerful aphrodisiac.

And then back at the hotel, when they'd finally gone to bed, she'd stunned him with how natural and uninhibited she was.

In the morning, however, he'd been met with a completely different person from the hot woman with whom he'd gone to bed.

His pride had been stung. He'd been thinking about their day and the ones after that, and she hadn't known how to get rid of him fast enough.

In that moment, of course, the Wentworth-Granville feud had become personal. He'd vowed to end the stalemate between the families, once and for all.

He played to win. It was why he'd engaged in a secret purchase of some prime London real estate, unbeknownst to the Wentworths.

"Be careful, Easterbridge," Hawk said, recalling him from his thoughts. "Even seasoned gamblers have their losses."

Sawyer nodded. "I haven't bested you at poker anytime

lately, but on the other hand, one could argue that just means you're overdue for a dry spell."

Colin quirked his mouth. "I'm happy with the cards that I'm holding at the moment."

Four

Seven months later

*S*oon she'd be free.

Or at least single again—she wasn't sure if she'd ever be free of family obligations and expectations. For one thing, her family still had the expectation that she would marry again—and marry well.

As she steered her rental car up the drive of the private estate, Belinda forced herself to relax.

Nevada was known for granting quick and simple annulments. Fortunately for her, because she and Colin had married right here in Las Vegas, she didn't even have to establish the usual six weeks' residency in Nevada in order to take advantage of the court system.

Colin had kept her on the hook long enough, she'd decided. She'd waited until her June wedding fiasco had faded from everyone's memory. She'd spent months stewing, not wanting more of a scandal but not knowing how to avoid one, either. Now she hoped to quietly have her marriage to Colin dissolved.

She was going for broke trying to get an annulment rather than a divorce. Nevada made it a relatively simple matter to obtain an annulment, unlike New York. With an annulment, it would be as if her marriage had never existed.

Unfortunately, her relationship with Tod had been a casualty of the past several months of her wait-and-see approach. They'd had a parting of the ways, and she could hardly blame him. Who wanted to wait around while his fiancée continued to be married to another man?

She'd gone scouring for a work assignment in Nevada so she could obtain her annulment without tipping anyone off as to her real purpose. Fortunately, something had fallen into her lap. An anonymous collector wished to have his private collection of French impressionist art appraised.

She'd do her work, and in the meantime, she already had a meeting scheduled with a lawyer tomorrow to see about the paperwork for her annulment.

She emerged from her car in front of an impressive Spanish-style hacienda and breathed in the warm air. She looked around the drive, which was alive with the color of cactus flowers. The weather in this suburb of Las Vegas was mild and lovely in March—a contrast to what she was used to in New York or back home in England. Just a slight breeze caressed her arms, which were bare in the sleeveless wheat-colored belted dress that she wore.

She'd been told that the mansion was more of an investment property than anything else and that its owner resided elsewhere. Still, it seemed to be very well maintained. Clearly the owner was someone willing to invest plenty of time and effort in his property.

She looked around. There were no other vehicles visible in the drive, but she had been told that a small staff made sure that the estate ran properly.

Within moments, however, the housekeeper with whom she had spoken through the intercom at the front gate opened the arched aged-wood front door. The middle-aged woman greeted her with a smile and ushered her inside.

After declining any refreshment, Belinda let the housekeeper give her a short tour of the lower level of the house. As an art appraiser, she often found it helpful to see how clients lived generally. The rooms here were large and tastefully decorated but devoid of personal memorabilia—like a staged photo shoot for a home-furnishings catalog. She supposed she shouldn't be surprised, because the mansion was just an investment property.

After a quarter of an hour, she followed the older woman upstairs to what she was told functioned more or less as the art gallery.

When the housekeeper pulled open the double doors, Belinda stepped inside the vast room—and immediately sucked in a breath.

She identified a Monet, a Renoir and a Degas. They were lesser known works, of course, since the most famous ones hung in museums around the world. Still, from her point of view as an art expert, there was no such thing as an obscure Renoir.

More importantly, she recognized the paintings as works that had come to auction in the past few years— *her auctions.* The auctions she'd organized had gone so well as to earn her a promotion at Lansing's.

She'd wondered then whom the mysterious buyer or buyers had been. In her line of work, it wasn't unusual for a buyer to wish to remain unknown, sometimes using a business entity through which to make purchases. But whoever the owner was, Belinda had envied him or her even then.

The paintings were beautiful—dappled, romantic works of art. She wished *she* had had the money to purchase them. She admired the sensibility of the owner and the good sense shown in the way of the paintings' display.

The room was a mini-museum. It was large, had white walls and sported temperature control. The few pieces of furniture were arranged so that no matter where one sat, one had an excellent view of the paintings on the walls.

The housekeeper gave her a smile and then a polite nod. "I'll leave you to your work."

Belinda glanced at the older woman, who looked indulgent at how overwhelmed she was. "Thank you."

After the housekeeper departed, Belinda walked to the center of the room. She stood there for a moment, turning first to the Renoir and then to the Monet. She sat down on a nearby chair for further contemplation.

She was delighted that the paintings had found a place together. They were some of those she'd loved best among those that she'd been fortunate enough to have cross her desk. She'd performed her role well and sold them to the highest bidders for excellent prices. She had scattered them far and wide—or so she thought.

But now she could have her cake and eat it, too—sort of. They were all here.

The Monet was of a man and women in close conversation against a green landscape. The Renoir was a couple dancing in a close embrace. And the Degas was a ballerina figure in pirouette.

After minutes had ticked by, she stood up and moved to the Renoir to inspect it more closely.

The brushstrokes were, of course, exactly as she remembered them.

She heard the door of the room open, and before she could turn around, a voice reached her.

"I believe they're worth more than I paid for them."

The tone was dry, amused...and familiar.

She froze, and then a second later as she pivoted, her eyes collided with the Marquess of Easterbridge's.

"You."

Colin's lips tilted upward. "I believe the correct term is husband."

"How did you get in here?" she demanded.

He looked amused. "I own this house."

Belinda stared at him, her mind reeling as she tried to absorb his words.

Colin looked fit and healthy, and he dressed like an aristocrat at play. He wore a white shirt with rolled cuffs and dark trousers with a thin belt. She assumed they were all ordered from a Savile Row tailor that the Granvilles had patronized for generations.

As usual, Colin was cool and self-possessed. There wasn't a trace of the cat who ate the canary, though she supposed he was entitled to the feeling right now.

"Returning to the scene of the crime?" she asked, desperate to mask how he had rattled her.

She wouldn't give him the satisfaction of immediately launching into an angry polemic about how he had tricked and cornered her.

His eyes gleamed. "The wedding, you mean? It's our third anniversary, you know."

She tossed her hair and feigned indifference. "Really? I didn't recall. All I'm waiting for is the chance to celebrate our annulment."

Colin sauntered farther into the room. "So that's why you're back in Las Vegas?"

"Whether you cooperate or not," she stated unequivocally.

Colin continued to look unperturbed. In her dreams, he wouldn't respond to the service of annulment papers on him. There'd be an uncontested dissolution of their marriage. Of course, in her dreams, she also regularly had a disturbing replay of their passionate night in Vegas.

He gestured around them. "I hope you enjoy examining these works of art."

She regarded him suspiciously. "What are you up to?"

He gave her a small smile. "Isn't it obvious?"

"You lured me here."

"On the contrary, you came willingly in order to obtain an annulment." He regarded her. "I will admit to guessing that you'd probably make your way back to Vegas sooner or later. I thought I'd make the trip worth your while."

"And so you're having some impressionist art work appraised?" she mocked. "Are you planning to sell them?"

Despite herself, she felt sad that he might sell and split up these beautiful paintings. If only she had the means to offer to buy them herself.

Colin tilted his head. "No, I have no intention of selling. At the moment, I'm far more interested in cultivating my investments."

She felt palpable relief, even though she told herself again that what he did, or didn't do, was of no matter to her. "You recently bought these paintings. Why would you want them appraised? There hasn't been enough time for any significant appreciation." She pursed her lips. "They are authentic, you know. I can personally vouch for it."

"Ah, authenticity," he murmured. "It's what I look for."

She shifted, aware that he might be talking about something other than the paintings.

Colin tilted his head. "As I said, I wanted confirmation

that I paid a good price. Like most of my investments, I think they're worth more than I bought them for—at least, now."

Again, Belinda experienced the uncomfortable feeling that there was a subtext to his words that she didn't wholly understand.

"You can't put a precise number on art, though many people try to," she responded. "Beauty is in the eye of the beholder after all."

"So I've understood," he responded, his tone soft.

She watched him look her over, down to the tips of her toes. His gaze started with her face—she only wore light makeup—traveled down to her dress, lingered at her bust and ended with her peep-toe floral-print sandals.

She felt the weight of that look on her breasts and at the juncture of her thighs, even before it made her strangely unstable on her legs.

It was an appreciative look—and enough to belatedly bring out her combative instinct.

"Why are you doing this?" It was time to drop all pretense.

"Perhaps I would like to lay claim to being the one who finally buried the Wentworth-Granville feud." To his credit, he didn't pretend to misunderstand her meaning, but his gaze remained enigmatic.

"If you want to end this feuding between *us,* all you have to do is sign the dissolution papers."

"Hardly any valor to lay claim to in that—it's far too passive."

"You could always divorce me on the grounds of adultery," she suggested hopefully.

She tossed out the rude comment as a gambit and then regretted it when Colin looked keen and possessive.

"Yours or mine?" he asked.

"Mine, of course."

"You're a terrible liar."

"I don't know what you mean."

"Of course you do. You never slept with Dillingham."

His audacity took her breath away.

"Really," she answered with scorn. "And how would you know that? Confident that you ruined me for any other man?"

His smile was deceptively slow and mild. "No, but a marriage contracted to save the family farm is rarely full of passion."

Belinda sucked in a breath.

"And then there's the fact that you had sex with me here in Vegas three years ago only after we were married. What did you say you'd come to understand? You were looking for a man who played for keeps? I guessed that you were likewise making Tod wait."

Belinda realized she was chewing on her bottom lip and abruptly stopped—to anyone who knew her well, her habit was a giveaway that she was nervous. Three years ago, she'd still been smarting from being tossed aside by a boyfriend.

"Except I ruined matters for you with Dillingham, didn't I?" Colin continued. "And now, in desperation, Uncle Hugh has taken matters into his own hands. I bet you had no idea the Wentworth financial affairs were quite so desperate."

Her eyes widened. "What do you mean?"

She should have figured that Colin had an ace up his sleeve. After all, she'd seen his successful streak at the poker tables three years ago. And she knew from his real-estate holdings that he had an uncanny ability with numbers and investing.

"Have you spoken with your uncle lately?" he countered.

"No." Belinda searched her brain. "What's wrong with Uncle Hugh?"

"Nothing, but he has given up his Mayfair town house."

Belinda knew her uncle moved around on a regular basis. "There's nothing unusual—"

"Permanently."

Belinda stilled. "Why would he do that?"

"Because the Mayfair town house now belongs to me."

Belinda shook her head. "That's impossible."

Just a few months ago, she'd been at the Mayfair address that had belonged to the Wentworth family for generations. True, her uncle had seemed preoccupied and worried, but she'd never imagined—

"On the contrary, you'll find the deed has been properly recorded...unlike our annulment. Your uncle may still reside there on his estates, but it's at my discretion."

Belinda looked at him with stupefaction. "Why in the world would Uncle Hugh sell the town house to you? You're the last person in the world to whom he'd sell."

"Simple," Colin responded in a dry tone. "He wasn't aware I was the ultimate buyer. The town house was sold to one of my companies. Presumably he didn't know I was the principal shareholder. I imagine he thought he was selling to one of those newly minted Russian oligarchs who prize privacy as well as London real estate."

She stared at Colin in astonishment. It couldn't be...

Colin shrugged. "It was a quick sale for an agreeable price. Your uncle was apparently looking for a quick infusion of cash."

"What does that have to do with me?" she demanded defiantly.

"I also already owned the larger of the two Berkshire estates."

Belinda's shoulders lowered. The Wentworth family

had, somewhat unusually, two estates in Berkshire. The smaller of the two was of more recent origin, having come into the family through the marriage of her great-great-grandmother. The larger—which Colin apparently now owned, if his claims were to be believed—had been in the family since the days of Edward III. Downlands, as it was called, bordered Granville land, and had been the subject of a prolonged property-line dispute with Colin's family in the nineteenth century.

Belinda's head buzzed. She had no responsibility for the Wentworth estates, she told herself. After all, she had her life in New York as an art dealer. She was far from the family fray—or was she?

"I suppose you acquired the Berkshire estate through a similar anonymous purchase? The privately held company that you used for the transaction wouldn't be LG Management, would it?" She named the mysterious company that she had been told owned the Las Vegas hacienda that they were in.

Colin inclined his head. "LG Management, yes." He quirked his lips. "Lord Granville Management."

Belinda's eyes narrowed. "How clever of you."

"I'm glad you think so."

Her mind raced even more. How was it possible that the family holdings had been so diminished and she had been unaware of it? Was the family's financial situation that dire?

"How did you pay for your lavish wedding to Tod?" Colin asked, seemingly reading her mind.

Belinda started guiltily. "It's none of your business."

Colin thrust his hands in his pockets. "I imagine that in the customary way the Dillinghams bore some of the cost, but as far as the Wentworth share, I can't imagine that you shouldered the entire burden."

The truth was that she had paid for a portion of her wedding. But when Uncle Hugh and her mother had insisted on a lavish affair, she'd given in—on the condition that they bear the additional expense.

"I imagine that Hugh saw your nuptials as Napoleon's escape from Elba," Colin said, connecting the dots for her. "It was his last, desperate gamble to save the family legacy through a fresh infusion of cash from the Dillinghams. Unfortunately, it instead became his Waterloo."

She stared at Colin in disbelief. It was inconceivable that a Granville owned Wentworth land now. But then again, she imagined that some people found it hard to comprehend that a Wentworth—namely, her—was married to a Granville.

But all was not lost, she told herself.

"Even if you own both properties," she countered, "as your wife, I have a claim to them. We are married, after all."

She'd learned *something* from consulting a matrimonial lawyer.

Colin's eyes gleamed with reluctant admiration. "Yes, but only to half the property at most, in all likelihood. And at best, you might be able to get a legal accounting, but then you'd only be entitled to a portion of the cash value from the sale of the estates to a third party."

The rat. Colin would rigorously litigate. She should have known better than to try to best Colin at his own game. Business moguls like him kept schools of corporate lawyers well-fed.

"What about the property that you acquired through your business during our nonmarriage?" she challenged. "Wouldn't that be considered marital property subject to division in a divorce? We don't have a prenuptial agreement."

"Since our marriage has been brief and defunct from day one—" he didn't say thanks to you, though Belinda felt the words as an accusation "—it's unlikely that a court would view those as up for grabs. In any case, I assume your first priority would be trying to get back the Wentworth estate."

Belinda tried to keep the defeat out of her shoulders, because he was right.

"It seems we're at an impasse."

"You've obviously given this thought," she accused.

"Quite, but then three years is a long time to ruminate… about having a wife without conjugal rights."

Belinda felt the flush crawl up her face. "What makes you think I give a fig for what happens to some old buildings and parcels of land an ocean away?"

"Oh, you do," he returned silkily. "The Mayfair town house and the Berkshire estate are where you spent your childhood."

Belinda bit her bottom lip.

"I only observed you from afar," Colin added mockingly, "but I was aware enough of your comings and goings to understand that much."

He was right, damn him.

She recalled running through the halls of the Mayfair town house when she was four or five, and later, learning to ride a horse on the Berkshire estate. And then there had been the innumerable dinner parties. She'd watched her mother get ready for them by donning an expensive gown and selecting the jewels from the family safe. When she was still an adolescent, she'd been invited to join those dinner parties. It was where she'd first met artists of national and international importance and learned the love of art that she'd turned into a career.

Still, she knew enough not to give away too much. "What do you want?"

"I want the woman I married. The one who made decisions for herself, instead of following in her family's footsteps. For a wife like that, I might be willing to come to some sort of compromise about the disposal of my properties."

"I'm not into rebellion enough to be your wife."

"Oh, you're more of a rebel than you think," Colin returned smoothly, stepping closer.

Belinda lifted her eyebrows in mock inquiry.

"One can even say your move to New York, distancing yourself from the other Wentworths, was a small act of rebellion."

She felt strangely exposed.

"It's your choice," Colin said. "You can choose to be a Princess Leia or a Han Solo. You can choose to be a stick-in-the-mud and annul our marriage for another safe and family-approved husband, or you can be someone who lives life according to her own terms. Which is it going to be?"

"Frankly, it's like being offered a bargain by Darth Vader," she tossed back, covering her sudden confusion.

Colin's eyes crinkled, and then he laughed.

Belinda swallowed. Despite her flippant response, Colin's words hit close to home. But then, what did he know of her life? She wasn't a stick-in-the-mud, damn it. She was just responsible.

This conversation was enough to make a girl long for some shopping therapy.

"What's in this for you?" she asked.

"I told you. I'm cultivating an investment."

She fought the urge to stamp her foot in frustration. "I don't know what that means."

"Does it matter?" he retorted. "Your side of the game is clear. You can do as your family dictates and end our marriage, but that may leave the Wentworth heritage solely in my hands. Is that what you want?"

What she wanted? She had no idea, not anymore. There was too much at stake, and he was far too attractive, standing so close to her, looking so powerful and in control.

"The other option is better," he tempted. "By staying married to me, you can both rebel and play the role of dutiful daughter or niece at the same time. It's rare that such an opportunity presents itself."

She tried to wrap her mind around what he was saying.

"Stay married to me, and you can move these paintings to Downlands."

"To Downlands?" she challenged, licking suddenly dry lips. "Downlands is no longer mine."

"It could be solely yours," Colin countered, his voice low and smooth, "if we remain married. I'll sign that contract."

She wasn't ready for this. She needed time to process… think…

But Colin wasn't giving her time or space. He stepped closer, within touching distance.

She felt a sizzle skate along her nerve endings.

His hair was short and silky, like mink, and his eyes were dark and gave nothing away. She noticed the tiny crinkles at the corners of his eyes that had grown infinitesimally more pronounced from three years ago.

She shifted her gaze downward, over the hard planes of his cheekbones and nose, to his mouth. For a hard man, he had soft lips.

As she well knew. On their wedding night, he'd kissed every inch of her, doing a leisurely survey, as she had lain on black satin sheets, the petals from the roses that he'd hastily procured for their ceremony haphazardly scattered around them.

He'd used the petals to tickle and arouse her until she'd moaned and writhed, practically panting for him to take her.

He'd been equally affected. His heart had beat hard and fast, and when he'd slid inside her, there hadn't been a moment's doubt about how much he wanted her.

It had been the most decadent thing she'd ever done in her life.

Colin's lips moved. "You look practically slumberous."

She jerked her gaze upward and then felt red-hot heat stain her cheeks.

He looked amused but intent. "What were you thinking about? Remembering the last time we were in Vegas?"

Remember? She could feel him in every pore, like an airy caress.

"It was a mistake," she said automatically.

"How do you know?" he responded. "You refuse to test the proposition."

"I don't need to touch fire again to know I'll get burned."

She realized instantly that her analogy was off, because his eyes kindled.

"Interesting choice of words," he murmured. "Is that what we were? Did we go up in smoke?"

"I didn't say—"

He rested his finger against her lips, stopping her words. They both went still, searching each other's eyes.

He lowered his hand only to trail his finger down her chin and then her throat, in a light caress.

He slid his hand to cup the side of her neck, and his thumb found and came to rest on her pulse.

The rapid beat of her heart was a giveaway as to how affected she was, and they both knew it.

"It was good, wasn't it?" he asked, rubbing soothingly over her rapid pulse. "The best sex ever."

She swallowed, and her lips parted. She had tried not to think about it, but yes, it had been the most sensational night of her life.

"Should I feel flattered?" she challenged.

He laughed. "Maybe lucky is more like it, since similar nights can be yours for free."

"Everything has a price."

"I'm willing to keep paying."

"And what will *I* have to pay?"

"Next to nothing compared to what you'll receive… and what we can create together. What we have created together, remember?"

She sucked in a breath. "It was Vegas. It makes you do crazy things."

"We're back here, breathing the same air. And it's our anniversary."

Dear Lord. "Our families are enemies. It was forbidden sex, nothing more."

"We're married. I'm legally yours and you're legally mine."

"Only because you haven't fought fair."

"You said that you wanted a man who played for keeps, because you'd been burned before. Yet you threw me back the next morning."

"So what is it you want now, revenge sex?"

He smiled enigmatically. "Is that going to be your excuse if it's just as explosive?"

She started to turn her head to the side, but his mouth came down on hers before her denial was complete.

Three years. Three years she'd lived with the memory

of what it was like to kiss and be possessed by Colin Granville, Marquess of Easterbridge.

In one moment, however, the memory was washed away by an even more vivid reality.

If Colin had been demanding, she might have had a better chance of resisting him. But he kissed her languidly, as if he was enjoying a sweet drink and had all the time in the world.

He tasted minty and warm. He slid his tongue into her mouth and coaxed her into deepening the kiss.

Belinda felt every sensation as if she was doing tequila shots without the lime. It was heady, and there was no respite.

Colin slid his hand to her rear end, bringing her flush up against his undeniable arousal, and his other hand slid around her back, molding her to him.

Belinda could feel everything through the thin fabric of her matte jersey dress. She became aware of her nipples jutting and pressing into the unyielding wall of his chest.

She'd been hoping her memories were exaggerated, but Colin lived up to billing and more.

Being in his arms was an intoxicating mix of the dangerous—as if she was walking on a precipice and he was tempting her into unknown and risky territory—and the comforting. He was solid and capable and made her feel oddly free, as if with him, at least, she could finally and truly be herself.

Strange. She shouldn't feel as if he was someone to whom she might shift her burden. He was a Granville, she reminded herself, and she still wasn't sure what game he was playing. And it didn't help that she'd just confirmed she had a visceral sexual reaction to him.

She stilled and then pulled away.

Colin let her go reluctantly.

They stared at each other, both breathing deeply.

Colin's eyes glittered, but then he gained mastery of himself and banked the fires.

Belinda could only imagine what she looked like. Her lips tingled from his kiss, and she fought a sudden unsettling urge to slip back into his arms for more.

She started to raise her hand to her lips, belatedly realized Colin caught the movement and then abruptly stopped herself.

She bent and grabbed her purse, then turned on her heel and hurried to the door.

She didn't care that she was fleeing—and he was letting her.

He spoke behind her. "The paintings—"

"The price is too high."

Five

Belinda glanced around the elegantly appointed Mayfair town house. Her visit was like her last…with one important difference.

The town house no longer belonged to the Wentworths, as it had for generations, but was merely on loan. Despite the illusion of permanence afforded by the decor of family antiques, everything was ephemeral.

Her uncle continued to reside here at the Marquess of Easterbridge's pleasure. Uncle Hugh could have the heirloom Persian rug pulled out from under him at any moment.

"Tell me it isn't true."

She said the words without preamble after appearing unannounced in the library. She knew this conversation was too important to have over the phone. She'd arranged a flight to London as soon as she could, right after flying back to New York from Vegas without making any progress on an annulment.

Uncle Hugh regarded her from behind his desk. "Whatever are you talking about, my dear?" He shook his head. "I didn't even know you were in London. You do lead the peripatetic existence these days, don't you?"

"I just arrived this morning." Belinda glanced around her. "Tell me you did not sell this house."

After a moment, Uncle Hugh visibly crumbled. "How did you find out?"

"Does it matter?" she responded.

After she'd taken off from the hacienda, she'd considered that Colin might call her uncle himself to mention their meeting in Vegas and to reveal himself as the cloaked buyer. She'd dreaded that he'd go public with the news. But judging from her uncle's reaction, he hadn't done anything—so far.

Upon reflection, she realized that she should have known Colin would leave it to her to make the shocking revelation to her uncle that his buyer was the Marquess of Easterbridge. *Of course.*

Still, she wondered what it signified. Did Colin intend to derive every satisfaction from vanquishing her uncle, including having Belinda confront her relative, or did he think it was more merciful for her to deliver the news rather than for him to reveal it himself?

"I was assured of discretion," Uncle Hugh said, his tone defensive. "I am continuing to live here and at the estate in Berkshire, and nobody needs to be the wiser about the change in ownership."

Belinda looked at him with a sinking heart. "Assured of discretion for how long and by whom? The Russian billionaire to whom you thought you sold the property for investment purposes?"

Uncle Hugh nodded. "The agreement was for me to

continue to live here for years." He paused. "How did you find out? If you know, then—"

"You fell into a trap. A layer of corporate entities obscured his identity, but the buyer is none other than the Marquess of Easterbridge."

Uncle Hugh looked flabbergasted and then bowed his head and clasped his forehead with his hand.

"Why didn't you tell me the family finances were so dire?" Belinda demanded.

"There's nothing you could have done."

"How did we reach this pass?"

She had a right to know, especially since she was on the spot for getting them out of this quagmire. At least, the smaller of the Berkshire estates remained in Wentworth hands, so her family would never be completely without a home, but their identity was tied up in the properties that they no longer owned.

Her uncle glanced up and shook his head, his look beseeching. "Our financial investments have not done well in the past few years. There are also family members with significant allowances. Your mother…"

Neither of them needed to say more. Belinda was well aware of her mother's lavish lifestyle. She made no mention, however, of Uncle Hugh's own expensive tastes. Of course, her uncle would not view them as such. After all, what was the cost of a bespoke suit to one who had worn them for all his adult life?

As for herself, Belinda supplemented her modest salary at Lansing's with a small trust fund that her grandparents and father had left her, so she had not needed to draw an allowance. If she had known the specifics, however, she would have gladly turned over her trust fund to save the family ship from sinking. At the same time, she doubted it would have done much good aside from buying them a small amount of time.

Belinda studied her uncle. He'd always loomed large in her life—someone to look up to. She'd grown up under his roof. But now he appeared diminished by more than merely his years. The shoe was on the other foot now, and Belinda felt uncomfortably like she was chastising a child.

Uncle Hugh bent his head. "It's all ruined."

"Not quite."

She knew what ruin felt like—her wedding day had been a disaster—so her heart went out to her uncle. At the same time, she stopped herself from pointing out that while she had been castigated for marrying a Granville, Uncle Hugh had sold the family estates to one, albeit inadvertently. Who had committed the greater transgression?

Her uncle glanced up. "What do you mean?"

"I mean Colin is reluctant to grant me a divorce, though he ultimately may not have a choice." Nothing was ever quite as lost as one believed, she was discovering.

Uncle Hugh brightened. "We may have some leverage."

"I knew you'd think so," she commented drily.

"Yes, yes." Her uncle looked more animated by the second. "You must stay married to him."

Belinda bit her lip. Stay married to Colin? She'd avoided dwelling on the possibility since leaving Vegas.

Uncle Hugh sat up straighter. "Tell him that you'll stay married on condition of his signing over the properties to you."

"What?" she asked, sliding into a seat because she didn't like the direction this conversation was taking. "What possible motivation would he have for doing so? He'd likely think I'd divorce him as soon as I had the deeds to the properties, and he'd be right!"

"Then negotiate," her uncle replied, setting his hands on his desk. "Have him turn over the properties one by one."

Belinda's stomach felt as if it were a roller coaster. "A postnuptial agreement?"

"Exactly." Her uncle nodded. "It's done all the time."

Belinda worried her lip. Why was it up to her to save the family fortunes?

Colin was right—this *was* her chance to be the rebel and the dutiful child all at once. But she never would have dreamed that Uncle Hugh would latch on to the idea with such enthusiasm. This is the most her family had ever asked of her. It was all preposterous and outrageous. Yet she found herself considering it.

"Why would Colin want to stay married to me?" she rejoined.

Her uncle looked at her keenly. "Now there's a question for the marquess. You're an attractive girl. And perhaps he wants to save face with society. After all, you did almost marry another man while you remained his wife. If you and the marquess live as man and wife for a period of time, it'll stamp out the taint."

Belinda felt her shoulders slump. She didn't believe Colin cared a fig about society—after all, *he* was the one who had generated a scandal by interrupting her wedding. But soothing the blow to his pride? Yes, *that* she could believe. She had rejected Colin after their Vegas wedding. She'd fled, fearful of what she'd done, and had beat a hasty retreat down the reckless path she'd traveled in one night.

If she had instigated Colin's drive for revenge, wasn't she responsible for rectifying the fallout?

The thought swept through Belinda's mind. Her world

was no longer a neat painting but one streaked with bold and unexpected new colors.

She was no longer faced with the relatively simple matter of dissolving her marriage to Colin. The Wentworth heritage was in Granville hands. And the responsible streak in her wouldn't let her walk away without making an effort to save it, especially if she'd had a hand in bringing about the current situation.

Still, even if she was responsible, could she play a high-stakes game with a seasoned gambler?

Her cell phone buzzed, interrupting her thoughts, and she fished it out of her handbag to glance down at a text message.

Meet @ Halstead—DH

Belinda's mind churned. The message could be interpreted as a summons, a request or a question. Halstead Hall was the family seat in Berkshire of the Marquess of Easterbridge. Though Belinda didn't recognize the phone number, there was no mistaking whom the text was from. Colin had cleverly signed himself as *DH—darling husband* in text parlance.

There was one way to find out the answer to the question of whether she was up to the task of saving the Wentworth family fortune.

Her campaign would be if not exactly snatching victory from the jaws of disaster then at least surviving to fight another day.

"I'll remain married to you."

Belinda felt like a defeated army general being summoned for the signing of a peace treaty, all of whose terms had been dictated by the other side. Her job was to salvage what she could.

In a nod to the nippy March weather, her armor was a cowl-neck sweaterdress and knee-high boots.

Colin stood beside the fireplace in a drawing room of Halstead Hall. He wore a knit pullover over wool trousers—typical English country-gentleman attire.

He raised an eyebrow.

"I have certain conditions, however," she said from a few feet away, having declined a seat.

She tried not to look around, because she feared she might be daunted. She'd never been inside Halstead Hall before, but of course she was familiar with the house and surrounding estate. Together they formed a Berkshire landmark, and she'd grown up literally next door.

The house was an immense monolith with a beauty all its own. It had been started in the sixteenth century and added onto ever since. There were enough turrets, arched entries and paned windows to impress the most discerning *cognoscenti,* let alone the typical tourist.

Belinda had found it almost comical to be greeted at the door by the housekeeper and addressed as Lady Granville. Obviously, Colin had informed his staff about what to expect after she'd texted him back and accepted his invitation to meet—or perhaps, more accurately, set down arms—at Halstead Hall. To her credit, the housekeeper had acted as if Belinda's arrival at the front door was already an everyday occurrence.

Belinda knew she had taken on quite a bit by meeting Easterbridge in his bastion. But if nothing else, their recent encounters had shown her that negotiations would take place on his terms. The ball was, quite literally, in his court.

If the outside of Halstead Hall was an impressive testament to centuries of wealth and power, then the inside bore witness to the current occupant's money and prestige. Everything had been updated for modern comfort but was still in keeping with the house's history and majesty. The whole vast interior had central heat, twenty-first century plumbing and insulation and barely a creaky floorboard.

There were finely wrought plaster ceilings, and antique furniture and marble busts. She recognized paintings from Rubens and Gainsborough, among others.

It was all in depressing contrast to the Wentworth properties. She'd grown up with her great-grandmother's Victorian china, but not wealth of the caliber that existed at Halstead Hall. She knew that Downlands needed a long-overdue modernization of its plumbing and heating, and the Mayfair town house required a new roof.

"Of course you have conditions," Colin said smoothly. "Would one of those be having a wedding ceremony that does not involve a Vegas chapel?"

"No, definitely not." She didn't appreciate his sardonic humor. It was bad enough that she had come back to him with proverbial hat in hand. "I said I'd stay married to you—not that I'd marry you again."

She'd already survived an elopement and a wedding. She didn't want to push her luck. Because let's face it, she and the altar had a love-hate relationship.

His reaction wasn't what she'd anticipated. It was cool and calculating, despite a certain intensity in his gaze.

"There's a difference?" he asked mockingly.

"Of course," she replied. "Can you imagine what our two families would do if they had to sit across a church aisle from each other?"

"Make peace and attribute it to divine intervention?" he quipped.

"Quite the opposite, I'm sure."

"It might make for a good show."

"I'd rather take my chances with an Elvis impersonator."

"You almost did."

"Don't remind me." She'd declined—just barely—the offer of an Elvis wannabe to witness her elopement.

"So what are your conditions?"

"I want you to sign over the Wentworth properties to my name."

"Ah." Colin's eyes gleamed, as if he'd been expecting her demand.

Belinda raised her chin. "It's a fair bargain. After all, they are what is keeping this marriage alive."

Colin tilted his head. "Considering how weak your bargaining position is, it's an impressive demand. After all, your only bargaining chip is to threaten to dissolve our marriage, but then you wouldn't necessarily wind up with the Wentworth estates anyway."

Belinda felt her face heat but stood her ground.

She'd learned a few things during her years as an art specialist. One of them was to start bargaining by asking for more than one could possibly hope to get. It was up to him to make a counteroffer.

"And more than that," Colin continued, "what assurance do I receive that you won't go running off to Vegas for a dissolution the moment that I do sign the properties over to you?"

"You have my pledge."

Colin laughed. "You're delectable, but you are a Wentworth."

Belinda ignored how her pulse skittered and skated over the word *delectable*. "And you're a Granville."

"It does come down to that, doesn't it?"

She shot him a distinctly unamused look.

"I'll suggest a compromise."

"Oh?" *Here it comes.*

"Yes," he continued. "I'll sign the properties over to you one by one on a schedule. The longer we're married, the more you receive if we divorce."

Belinda felt a sense of relief wash over her. Colin was suggesting exactly what her uncle had in London three days ago.

Still, it rankled that the two men had pigeonholed her—and that they thought alike.

She had to admit, however, that the plan made a crazy sort of sense. After all, given her preference, she'd get an annulment or divorce tomorrow, while Colin wouldn't. This way, they got a marriage for some indefinite duration—not for forever, but on the other hand, not over tomorrow.

"One property every six months," she said, forcing herself to put down the demand without blinking.

To her surprise, Colin didn't blink, either. But then, she thought, he was a seasoned gambler.

Finally, he lifted the side of his mouth. "You're a good negotiator."

"I appraise and auction artwork for a living."

He inclined his head. "We're alike in that way, I suppose. We're both skilled in the art of the deal."

She didn't want to discover she had one more thing in common with him. They already had too much.

"You haven't said whether you agree to my terms," she reminded him.

He tilted his head. "One year for each, and at the end of two, both the Mayfair town house and the Berkshire estate are yours."

She opened her mouth to protest. *Two years?*

And yet, she acknowledged, it was a rather fair offer.

Two years would still leave her plenty of time to get on with her life after her marriage was officially over.

"Agreed." Still, she perversely pushed the envelope. "And what's to prevent me from divorcing you at the end?"

Colin smiled enigmatically. "Perhaps I'm banking on the fact that you won't want to."

He surprised her by departing from the script that she'd been preparing for ever since her conversation with her uncle. He was supposed to say that he was trying to repair the blow to his ego and remove the taint on his name. She, in return, was supposed to be in the position of disdaining his shallow motives.

Instead, his bravado took her breath away.

"The position of marchioness comes with benefits," he said in a low, seductive voice. "Estates, cars, travel…"

"I've seen plenty of money and fame. I come across it regularly as part of my job at Lansing's."

He shrugged, easy and self-assured. "What else can I tempt you with?"

"I'm surprised you didn't put yourself at the top of the list," she challenged.

Colin laughed. "Okay, *me*."

Good Lord. She hadn't done a good job of resisting him for one night three years ago in Vegas. How was she going to erect a wall against him for the long haul?

Colin was suddenly looking at her with a renewed intensity. "It was good, wasn't it? We were good."

"I was out of my mind—"

"With passion, don't deny it."

"I'd had a couple of drinks—"

"One Kamikaze?" he queried.

"The name says it all. And don't forget most of a Sex on the Beach."

He waved away her response. "It was hours earlier."

"They created a nice buzz."

Colin smiled. "It wasn't sex on the beach, but it was close, wasn't it? There was the scent of sun and surf. Then I realized it was you."

She resisted putting her hands over her ears. "Don't remind me!"

She'd never worn that perfume again. It carried too many memories.

She wasn't sure whether to take him seriously. He would say anything to win, except she wasn't quite sure what the endgame was.

"Why are you doing this?" she blurted.

She'd demanded an answer to that question before, but this time it was a metaphorical stamping of the foot.

"Perhaps I enjoy the challenge of going where no Granville has gone before."

"Straight to hell?" she asked sweetly.

Colin laughed.

"One of your villainous ancestors seduced a Wentworth heiress," she reminded him.

"Seduction—is that what she claimed?" he scoffed. "More likely, she had fallen for the handsome lad before her family packed her off to God knows where."

"Of course that story would be the Granville version."

"Sad to say, the poor lad ultimately didn't get a chance to marry her. I've accomplished what no Granville has before."

"It'll be a Pyrrhic victory."

Colin smiled. "I'll be the judge of that."

Belinda felt his words like a caress.

He suddenly straightened and then walked over to a nearby console table.

No doubt the table was an original eighteenth-century piece, Belinda thought with bemusement. The Granville wealth dwarfed the Wentworths' and probably had as well in her ancestors' heyday. She admired now the strength of her forebears in standing up to—some would say, *running afoul of*—the highest-ranking nobility in the vicinity.

Colin slid open a drawer and withdrew a small velvet pouch. Then he crossed to her.

Belinda found herself holding her breath as Colin loosened the pouch by its drawstring and then neatly deposit its contents into the palm of his hand.

She widened her eyes. He held two simple gold bands, one a large plain one with a slight groove at the edges and the other a smaller one etched with a feminine pattern.

They'd picked those rings out together just before their Vegas wedding ceremony.

Colin's gaze met hers, and she felt heat and promise in his look.

Then the side of his mouth teased upward. "To seal our bargain."

Belinda watched with sudden dry mouth as he slipped the bigger band on his finger. Then he slid the empty pouch into one of his pockets.

With slow deliberation, he lifted her hand, his grip sure and firm, and slid the smaller wedding band onto her finger.

Belinda tried to keep her hand steady, fighting a tremor.

She knew what she was doing, she told herself. She was strong and capable.

Still, she sucked in a breath when Colin raised her hand to his lips. He kept his eyes on hers as he very properly blew a kiss right over the back of her hand.

She felt relief—and yes, a twinge of disappointment

that she quickly banished—before Colin surprised her by turning her hand over.

He leisurely kissed first the pad of one finger and then another, and Belinda felt her heart quicken.

When he was done, he closed his eyes and pressed his lips into her palm.

Belinda took short and shallow breaths.

She felt his warm, soft lips like an erotic brand that sent pulsing sensation down to the tips of her toes.

Why, oh why did Colin know so unerringly how to get under her defenses? He certainly lived up to billing as the descendant of conquerors. Whenever she thought she knew what to expect, he caught her off guard.

Yet despite his calm facade, she could tell he was affected, too. He held himself with a leashed stillness and intensity.

He'd take her right here if she agreed.

The thought raced through her mind, and Belinda felt herself melt. She remembered how passionate their night in Vegas had been. The images were emblazoned on her memory in vivid 3-D, though she'd tried hard over the years not to play that particular movie.

Colin opened his eyes and raised his head, and she ran her tongue over her lips.

He watched the action like a bee drawn to pollen. She knew if he kissed her, her lips would certainly feel bee-stung.

He never did anything in half measures, she realized. In that respect, he'd acted true to form in his current take-no-prisoners battle with the Wentworths.

Belinda straightened her spine and extricated her hand from his.

Colin might be an expert at seduction, but he was also

the one who had plotted the ruination of her family for his own nefarious purposes—and she was his pawn. She might allow her uncle to manipulate her for their family's sake, but she would not allow her husband to control her, as well—certainly not now, before their agreement was officially in place.

Colin's lips quirked with dry humor. "We can always select rings that are more to your liking. Garrard has been the Granville family's jewelers for over a century. Naturally, you can also have your pick from the Granville heirlooms."

"These are fine," Belinda responded, curling her fingers into the palm of the hand that he had kissed.

She wanted the reminder of how their relationship had started with a hasty trip to a Vegas chapel. Somehow, she knew she'd need the clue in the weeks and months to come.

"You'll also need a proper engagement ring."

Belinda was glad the sexual tension had eased, but somehow she still felt under siege. "I'm surprised you don't already have one picked out. This meeting has all the markings of a victor arranging to inventory his spoils."

Unconscionably, Colin grinned. "So you see yourself as a spoil of war? Strangely, I find the analogy to Helen of Troy more compelling."

"The face that launched a thousand ships?" she parried. "I doubt you have a thousand warships to launch."

Colin laughed. "I'll have to be more inventive, then."

Belinda became aware of the pounding of her heart.

Colin had been inventive enough already. She really didn't want him to be any more so.

He bent his head to kiss her, and she took a step back.

She felt her heart skitter. "I'll need some time to adjust—"

At that moment, there was a tap on the door to the drawing room, which was followed by a cough as the door opened.

Belinda was grateful for the interruption.

A butler somberly announced, "The Dowager Marchioness of Easterbridge, has arrived, sir."

Six

Colin bit back an oath.

His promising interlude with Belinda had been cut short.

His mother came and went from Halstead Hall at her leisure, but she refused to use twenty-first century technology like email or text messaging to presage her arrival. *Too common,* she'd sniff.

From the look on Belinda's face, Colin could tell she was as surprised and nonplussed as he was by his mother's unexpected arrival—but for different reasons, he was sure.

"Colin, what is the meaning of this?" his mother said as she sailed into the room. "*Dowager?* Kindly instruct your staff that I haven't been relegated…"

The words trailed off as his mother stopped, realized who else was in the room and widened her eyes.

Colin stepped forward.

"May I introduce my wife, Belinda?" he said, neatly sidestepping the issue of titles and surnames.

After all, one was the Marchioness of Easterbridge and the other the Dowager Marchioness of Easterbridge.

One word of difference disguised the vast gulf between the two women.

Colin watched his mother's face turn different shades before she opened and closed her mouth.

He raised his eyebrows. "Belinda is residing here."

Under any other circumstances, it would have been a rather comical statement to make about one's wife, but all three of them knew there was nothing ordinary about this situation. Why pretend otherwise?

"I thought you meant to find a suitable bride," his mother breathed.

Obviously, Colin thought wryly, he wasn't the only one prepared to drop all pretense.

"Belinda is suitable, Mother."

"She's a Wentworth," his mother responded flatly.

"Well, in that regard, you are correct," he quipped. "Belinda chose to keep her maiden name upon our marriage."

Apparently anything could be forgiven these days except a family feud. A divorcée, a single mother and the descendant of coal miners had married the heirs to thrones across Europe, but if there was bad blood and scandal between neighbors, then all bets were off.

"How do you do?" Belinda spoke up.

Colin noticed that she maintained an admirable poise under the circumstances, but he wondered whether her question was tongue in cheek.

It was clear to everyone that the older marchioness was doing exceedingly *unwell* at the moment.

He scanned Belinda's face, but she didn't glance at him. Instead, she kept her gaze fixed on his mother.

"Colin is correct that I did retain my surname," Belinda said. "It should be quite easy to avoid confusion, I think, if you remain Lady Granville, and I am styled as Lady Wentworth."

His mother gave a haughty stare. She was dressed in tweeds, silks and pearls, and her clothes underlined her expression. "Yes, but you would still be the Marchioness of Easterbridge, would you not?"

Colin tried to avoid looking long-suffering. He detested the way some women were able to throw proverbial knives at each other. His mother excelled at it.

"I am sure, Mother," he said, an edge to his voice, "that you will make Belinda feel comfortable. She needs to learn her way around, and our house is vast." He'd put a subtle but noticeable emphasis on the word *our*. This was Belinda's home now, too, and his mother would need to reconcile herself to the reality.

Belinda turned to face him. "My job is in New York. How will I manage to be employed at Lansing's and reside here?"

"Yes, Easterbridge," his mother joined in. "Do tell us, dear."

Colin lifted the side of his mouth. He had somehow managed to shift the conversation so that Belinda and his mother were aligned against him. If he had any idea how he'd done it, he'd pat himself on the back.

He shot Belinda a glance. "You can arrange a transfer to the London office of Lansing's. We can spend our weekdays in London and retire to Halstead Hall for weekends."

Brilliant. He was satisfied that he'd walked the tightrope—that is, until he saw Belinda's expression.

She turned from him to his mother, a tight smile on her face. "However, a transfer may be difficult to obtain, so I may be based in New York indefinitely." She tossed him a pointed look. "Colin and I haven't yet discussed our living arrangements in depth."

"You will continue to have a career?" his mother asked cryptically.

Belinda kept her smile. "Yes, at least until I am entitled to receive back my family's property under the terms of the postnup."

His mother looked horrified.

Colin was almost amused by Belinda's determination. He'd married no retiring English rose.

He folded his arms. "Are you shocked by the fact that we didn't have a prenuptial agreement, Mother, or by the fact that we're negotiating a postnuptial one?"

"I should have known a Wentworth would be in this for money," his mother sniffed.

"I would toss him back if it weren't for the properties I stand to regain," Belinda said cheerily.

His mother looked pinched. "My son is not a fish."

"Of course not," Belinda replied before he could say anything. "I don't catch fish—or kiss frogs for that matter."

Colin gave her a sardonic look. "Thank you for clarifying the issue."

At least she was willing to allow he wasn't a frog—while refusing to be cast as a money or title hunter.

His mother looked from one to the other of them until her eyes came to rest on him. "I will see you at dinner, Colin."

She turned on her heel and headed to the door. The subtext of her words, of course, was that she intended to rest until this evening and, with any luck, awaken to the realization that this was all a terrible nightmare.

When the door shut, Colin addressed Belinda. "Well, that went rather well."

She shot him an ironic look. "I'm looking forward to dinner."

Dinner was a pained affair.

Colin watched his younger sister, Sophie, concentrate on spearing her food and chewing while she cast the occasional glance around the table.

Sophie was eight years younger than he was and thus more of Belinda's contemporary than his own. His mother had suffered a miscarriage between their two births and then had had difficulty conceiving again.

As was his mother's preference, dinner was a formal affair in the main dining room, though it was only four who were present for the meal.

Still, even the arrangement of the seating had been a fraught affair. One of his aides had come to see him about it before the appointed dinner hour.

He'd instructed that he'd take his usual seat at the head of the table, and Belinda would be seated to his right. Because of Belinda's presence, his mother had been moved to his left and Sophie farther down the table.

Colin glanced at his sister again. He doubted that Sophie minded being away from the fray. And fortunately, there was plenty of spacing between the seats at the long Victorian dining table.

Colin heaved an inward sigh. He had hoped that the spacing would stop the ladies from lobbing dinner rolls at each other, and so far dinner had been a tame affair—*too tame*.

Conversation had been desultory.

His mother was trying to ignore Belinda, and Sophie was a reluctant participant.

Sophie resembled him in coloring, but she'd had more trouble escaping their mother's influence—no doubt partly because she was younger, and his mother had her own hopes for her only daughter.

Colin looked from his sister to Belinda. They should be at least vaguely familiar with each other. After all, they were only a few years apart in age and had grown up in the same social circles.

He cleared his throat. "Sophie, I would have thought you and Belinda were acquainted."

His sister jerked her head up and gave him an alarmed look. Her eyes darted to their mother before returning to him. "I believe that Belinda and I have been at some of the same social functions, but we hardly spoke."

Everyone, of course, knew why.

The friction between the Granvilles and the Wentworths was legendary, and judging from the conversation tonight, it was also in their blood to be unable to communicate.

Colin would not be deterred. "My sister is a graphic designer, Belinda. She's always coming up with new prints inspired by famous artists."

Belinda and Sophie exchanged wary looks.

"Actually, my designs are influenced by *manga*," Sophie said. "I've visited Japan several times."

"I've been to Japan for Lansing's," Belinda responded.

Sophie nodded…and the conversation lapsed.

Colin firmed his jaw.

He guessed he wouldn't be able to unearth the witty Belinda tonight even if he had professional digging equipment. The same went for Sophie.

His mother was, of course, a lost cause.

No, the only things that glittered about the women

tonight were their clothes and their jewels. Belinda's
beaded top caught the light, competing with his mother's
five-carat ruby necklace.

He suddenly saw the months stretching ahead of him
like a dusty desert road. If his family and Belinda could
barely talk then he'd have to keep them away from each
other.

He could easily do so, of course. He owned several
houses, and Halstead Hall was quite large. But it rankled
that he'd have to resort to it.

This should have been a moment to savor because
Belinda was his.

She'd set down her weekend bag in a guest suite when
she'd arrived earlier today, but in his mind, now that she'd
agreed to remain his wife, it was only a matter of time
before he seduced her into thinking that heading back to
bed with him was a good idea.

He studied his wife. Her dark hair was loose around her
shoulders and just caressing the tops of her breasts. Her
lips were full and glistening pink, and her profile straight.
The soft lines of her cheek and jaw were outlined by the
light and shadows of the dining room.

He wanted her.

They had explosive chemistry in bed, and he was
looking forward to enjoying it again.

On the other hand, *explosive* could hardly be used to
describe dinner.

It was time, he decided, to ignite the fuse on the
proverbial bomb.

He cleared his throat, and three pairs of eyes fixed on
him.

"Belinda and I have been invited to the Duke of
Hawkshire's wedding to Pia Lumley," he said. "It will be
our first public outing as a couple."

Aside, of course, to their literal outing as man and wife at the Wentworth-Dillingham near-miss of a wedding last year, he added silently.

His words rang out like the peal of cathedral bells—though Hawk and Pia were in actuality getting married in a local parish.

Belinda's eyes widened.

Colin could tell it hadn't occurred to her that Pia and Hawk's wedding was next week, and now that she'd agreed to their bargain, they'd be attending together as husband and wife.

His mother, on the other hand, looked aghast.

He guessed she was thinking that next week didn't give her enough time to change his mind or do damage control.

Colin took a last bite of his food, satisfied that he'd taken control of matters.

"By God, you've done it." Uncle Hugh smiled, slapped his knee and then grasped the arm of his leather chair.

Belinda regarded her uncle from where she was sitting on the sofa and had to agree. On the other hand, she and Uncle Hugh almost certainly had different ideas about what his words connoted.

"I hope you're satisfied." The words were a strange echo of the ones that she'd slapped Colin with.

She was back in Uncle Hugh's Mayfair town house after a night at Halstead Hall.

Except, of course, it wasn't her uncle's town house any longer.

Belinda glanced around the sitting room. Her uncle was looking several shades more robust than he had mere days ago, when he'd declared that all was lost. Her mother was as elegant as ever as she sat sipping tea next to Belinda on the sofa. On the surface, there was nothing to distinguish this gathering from hundreds that they'd had in this house before.

But now Belinda *knew* Colin owned these walls.

The town house was furnished with a few antiques but certainly nothing that would impress a marquess used to even grander quarters. Without the family history here that the Wentworths had, what possible use could Colin have for this house?

I intend to make a conquest of the Wentworths once and for all.

Colin's words had become more of a reality than she could possibly have predicted.

When she'd arrived at Halstead Hall two days ago to meet with Colin, she'd immediately been shown to a guest suite, and it had been easy to avoid Colin with the interference of his mother and his sister in the house.

The morning after the stilted family dinner, she'd made her excuses and departed for London and eventually New York to settle her affairs and attend to business, particularly now that she knew she'd be spending more time in England for the foreseeable future.

Colin hadn't appeared happy about her departure, but if he sensed that her work wasn't as pressing as she made it seem, he'd said nothing. Besides, she knew he had his own business matters to attend to.

He seemed content to bide his time, but she knew he was intent on seducing her. They were engaged in a game of cat and mouse, really.

Recalling Belinda back from her thoughts, her mother set down her cup and saucer on a nearby table. "When I asked how you planned to quell the scandal *du jour,* I had no idea that you would do so by staying married to Easterbridge."

"What did you expect me to do, Mother?" Belinda asked.

She'd always felt as if she had a damned-if-you-do, damned-if-you-don't relationship with her mother.

She'd expected her mother to be overjoyed. Uncle Hugh certainly was. But then, her uncle was a lot closer to the family's bills and financial statements than her mother. He was the gatekeeper, while the idea of being financially responsible was one her mother had never grasped.

Her mother sighed. "What will your life be like?"

What, indeed. Belinda had asked herself the same question numerous times since agreeing to remain married to Colin.

She was having a hard time seeing what their marriage would be like. Perhaps, like most couples, they'd have to make things up as they went along.

Belinda bit her lip. What if she became pregnant with Colin's child?

She could only imagine what their two families would think about the joining of their bloodlines and what kind of life their child would have caught between the feuding families.

Belinda gave a slight shake of her head. No, she and Colin had an agreement, and at the end, they would go their separate ways. Implicit in that understanding was the fact that they would plan not to have children.

She was thirty-three. Even if Colin turned the property over to her in two years, she'd be thirty-five and still have some time ahead of her.

She recalled Colin's words when she'd asked what would prevent her from obtaining a divorce eventually. *Perhaps I'm banking on the fact that you won't want to.*

She experienced a strange quiver. She wasn't sure if she

still completely understood Colin's motives, and that was troubling.

Her mother exchanged looks with Uncle Hugh and then addressed her. "Perhaps you might see Tod...in order to make amends."

Belinda's jaw dropped. "Make amends?"

"Yes, darling, in order to keep your options open. You will, after all, be a single woman again some day."

Belinda was flabbergasted. Here she'd been concerned about the possibility, however unlikely, of conceiving a child with Colin, and her mother was already thinking about her *next* husband.

Her mother had obviously not given up on the Dillinghams.

"You know I won't be around forever," Uncle Hugh joined in, "and Tod would make a good steward of the Wentworth estates."

"There are practically no Wentworth estates at the moment," Belinda retorted. "It's all in Granville hands."

It wasn't technically true. They still had one estate in Berkshire left, as well as a couple of rental buildings, but it hadn't been in the family that long. Still, at least they wouldn't be homeless, thank goodness, if Colin turned them out.

"This arrangement with Colin need be only a bump in the road," Uncle Hugh went on. "Surely once it's over, you'll wish to return to your rightful groom and pick up where you left off."

Belatedly, Belinda recognized just how much animosity her uncle harbored toward Colin, who'd divested him of the Wentworth patrimony. Uncle Hugh was ready to shoo her back in Tod's direction at a moment's notice.

Her mother was worse. She was almost suggesting that

Belinda befriend Tod and keep her options open, as it were, even before her marriage to Colin ended.

"Tod is no longer in the picture," Belinda responded flatly.

She reached forward and set her teacup down with more noise than necessary.

"Now, now, Belinda," her mother said in a soothing voice, "no need to get snappish. Your uncle means well."

"We're thinking of your best interests."

"Are you?" Belinda said as she stood up. "Then why is it up to me to save the family fortunes?"

She turned then and walked out the door.

She would head back to her London hotel, and then fly to New York to settle her affairs there.

Life had just taken a detour—one that led to Halstead Hall.

Seven

Belinda's eyes misted as Pia reached the front of the church.

Pia looked beautiful in her wedding gown, holding a tightly bunched bouquet of red roses. A delicate tiara graced her coiffure. It was a gift from Pia's groom, Hawk, for their wedding day.

In a nod to her groom's country, Pia had made a fashion-forward choice from a British designer. In a bow to tradition, however, the dress had lace elbow-length sleeves and a full skirt. The ensemble was light and ethereal, like Pia.

Belinda adjusted the skirt of Pia's dress and then took the bouquet from her friend's hands, all the while steadfastly refusing to make eye contact with Easterbridge, standing a few feet away, next to the groom.

The service was being held in the parish church near Silderly Park, the Duke of Hawkshire's estate in Oxford.

Belinda was Pia's lone attendant. Because Tamara was

several months' pregnant, she had bowed out of being part of the wedding party and had instead chosen to remain comfortably seated among the wedding guests.

To Belinda's discomfiture, however, Colin was acting as Hawk's best man. Belinda wondered if Pia's romantic nature was at work in the choice. After all, not so long ago, Pia had suggested that Easterbridge was drawn to Belinda like a moth to a flame.

Pia gave her a bright and tremulous smile before facing the minister.

Belinda was truly happy for her friend. But much as she hated to disillusion Pia, Belinda didn't think she and Easterbridge bore even a passing resemblance to Romeo and Juliet—though their families, she admitted to herself, might rival the Montagues and Capulets.

Belinda kept her eyes firmly on the Anglican minister as he began to speak. When the time came for the couple to recite their vows, though, her gaze drifted of its own volition to Easterbridge's.

"Wilt thou have this woman to be thy wedded wife..."

Colin's face remained cool and fixed, but his eyes were hot as they looked into hers.

"Wilt thou love her, comfort her, honour, and keep her in sickness and in health, and, forsaking all other, keep thee only unto her, so long as ye both shall live?"

Belinda felt herself heat, as if she could feel Colin's caress as well as see it. Every bone in her body seemed to melt under Colin's gaze.

The memory of their own wedding rose between them. It had been just the two of them, the officiant and standby witnesses called in by the chapel. Their service had been a lighthearted, can-you-believe-we're-actually-doing-this reverie. They'd both been looking forward to consummating their marriage.

"Wilt thou have this man to be thy wedded husband…?"

Once upon a time, Belinda thought, she'd answered yes to that question to the man standing a few feet from her and eating her up with his eyes.

"Wilt thou love him, comfort him, honour, and keep him in sickness and in health, and, forsaking all other, keep thee only unto him, so long as ye both shall live?"

Pia had chosen to modernize the traditional vows by omitting a reference to *obey* and instead using vows that mirrored the groom's.

Colin smiled ever so slightly.

Belinda raised her chin a fraction. Was he recalling that she similarly had chosen not to obey? It was a good thing, because the very next morning she'd chosen not even to *keep* him.

She recalled Colin's puzzlement and then thin-lipped control when she'd nearly bolted from their hotel room, horrified at her rash actions.

She had never imagined Easterbridge would agree to obtain a marriage license before she slept with him. She'd followed through rather than changed her mind because she'd been irresistibly drawn into his orbit by that point and Vegas was an uninhibited gambler's paradise.

It had been irresistibly seductive to be wanted so much. And now that Easterbridge was staking his claim on her again—moving heaven and earth to do so, in fact—she felt almost…cherished.

Belinda tingled down to the tips of her toes. Her gown was a modest peach chiffon confection, but under Colin's gaze, she felt as if she were wearing a revealing sexy ensemble, and enjoying its effect.

Colin looked as if he could lift her up right now and carry her down the aisle and directly to a bed—*his bed.*

At least, Belinda thought, she'd gotten desire if not love.

Easterbridge had given a vow to *love* her, but he couldn't have meant it—not after knowing each other so briefly.

She held back a sigh. It would be wonderful if a man could vow to love her and mean it. She'd never had the opportunity to test the proposition with Tod because their ceremony had been cut short. And with Easterbridge...

Because she felt unexpectedly teary, she drew herself up straighter.

Rats.

She would not give Easterbridge the satisfaction of seeing her get emotional. Though it was not unusual, of course, to cry at a wedding, she knew Colin would wonder if it was Pia's happiness or her own memories that had caused her tears.

Fortunately, she was able to make it through the rest of the ceremony without a hitch.

Later, at the wedding breakfast at Silderly Park, she found Pia and hugged her again.

Tamara walked up to them just as the quick embrace ended.

"I'd join the hug, too," Tamara quipped, looking down at her stomach, "if I didn't have a basketball in my way."

"I'm so very happy for you, Pia," Belinda said, blinking more rapidly than usual and then casting a glance at Tamara. "And for you, too, though you look ridiculously radiant as a pregnant lady."

"Only because my morning sickness has stopped." Tamara turned to Pia with a smile. "I suppose we'll need to address you as *Duchess* from now on."

"No, *ma'am* will do," Pia teased.

As a duchess, Pia outranked both Belinda and Tamara, who were marchioness and countess, respectively.

Belinda was sincerely glad that Pia and Tamara had found happiness with Colin's friends, the Duke of

Hawkshire and the Earl of Melton. Still, though to the outside world she might be a marchioness, Belinda knew that, unlike Pia and Tamara, her marriage wasn't built to last.

Sure, both Pia and Tamara had encountered roadblocks on the way to a happy marriage. Pia had had a fling with Hawkshire years before—when he'd represented himself as simple Mr. James Fielding—that had ended with her feeling discarded until their reunion years later gave him a second chance to earn, and this time, keep her love. Tamara, in contrast, had entered into a marriage of convenience with Melton that had turned into a love match. But Belinda doubted that a similar happy ending was in store for her and Easterbridge.

As if reading her mind, Pia leaned in conspiratorially. "What is happening with you and Easterbridge?"

"It's your wedding day," Belinda protested. "Let's not talk about other matters."

"I'm already pulling rank as a newly minted duchess," Pia teased.

Belinda knew Pia meant well, and since Tamara looked on with interest, she reluctantly gave in. "I suppose then that this is as good a time as any to tell you I'm no longer pursuing a way to dissolve my marriage to Easterbridge."

Pia clasped her hands together. "Oh, Belinda, that's wonderful news. You and Colin have decided to try to make it work."

Tamara looked doubtful. "I'm not so sure Belinda regards it as happy news, Pia. In fact, I'm guessing there's more to the situation than she's saying."

Pia widened her eyes. "Is that true?"

Belinda sighed. "I did warn you this wasn't a fitting discussion for a wedding day."

Pia touched her arm. "Oh, no."

"Let's just say Colin has plenty in common with Sawyer and Hawk in the complicated courtship department."

Pia looked surprised and Tamara resigned.

"He's blackmailing you?" Tamara hazarded a guess.

Belinda raised her eyebrows. "Why use an ugly word like *blackmail* when *proposition* will do?"

Tamara's eyes narrowed. "Just what is Easterbridge offering you?"

"Colin is now the proud owner of the Wentworth family town house in Mayfair, as well as the old estate in Berkshire."

Pia gasped, and Tamara's expression turned to one of sympathy.

Belinda resisted the urge to rub her temples. "Apparently, my uncle believed that the corporate entity to whom he was selling was a cloak for a wealthy foreigner who preferred anonymity. He didn't know it was Easterbridge until I broke the news to him recently."

"Uh-oh."

Belinda shot Pia a glance that said she agreed with the sentiment. "Of course, this change of ownership is all hush-hush. No one is supposed to know about it, and Uncle Hugh is continuing to reside at the town house in London."

"Well, don't worry," Pia said, "as far as I know, Mrs. Hollings hasn't gotten wind of this angle to the story."

Belinda frowned. "What do you mean by angle?"

Pia and Tamara exchanged looks, as if debating who was going to tell her.

"Out with it."

Pia pasted on a smile. "Mrs. Hollings published news in her gossip column this morning that you had moved into Halstead Hall and that you and Colin have decided to make a go of your marriage."

Belinda closed her eyes. "Oh, Pia, on your wedding day!"

"It's all right," Pia soothed. "My wedding will no doubt feature prominently in tomorrow's column. Mrs. Hollings' column is actually what prompted me to ask about you and Colin."

Belinda sighed. "I didn't want to trouble you with my news in the days before your wedding, and Tamara is pregnant and has other things on her mind."

The truth was also that she was still coming to terms with her new status quo with Colin.

Belinda had no idea how Mrs. Hollings got her information. The woman seemed to have sources everywhere. On the other hand, Belinda acknowledged that she herself had not gone to great trouble to conceal her steps, either. She had appeared on Colin's doorstep last week with weekend bag in hand and had let it slip at work that she'd been at Halstead Hall. For better or worse, she was going to be Colin's wife for the next two years, and word was bound to get out sooner or later.

She knew her marital status had been a source of speculation and interest at Lansing's, and elsewhere in New York and London. Everybody was aware of the debacle at St. Bart's last year—some had even been eyewitnesses.

She supposed that the silver lining to Mrs. Hollings' gossip column today was that her work colleagues would stop conjecturing about her marital status and see her as settled into married life.

Tamara fished a cell phone out of her small handbag. She scrolled down and then handed her phone to Belinda.

Belinda read the text with unease.

This columnist has it on good authority that a certain marquess and marchioness are nesting in Berkshire near H****. Could it be that a little birdie will hatch next spring?

Belinda mentally winced.

She handed the phone back to Tamara. "Isn't there something you can do to stop Mrs. Hollings? Doesn't she work for Sawyer's media outlets?"

Tamara shrugged as she put away the phone. "Mrs. Hollings is a renegade. Sawyer believes in the separation of the news and business sides of his companies. He won't interfere to kill an individual story."

Belinda grimaced at Mrs. Hollings' words. *Hatch a little birdie?* She hadn't even slept with Colin again—yet. She'd arrived back in England from New York just in time for Pia's wedding.

"What are you going to do?" Tamara asked.

Belinda lifted her shoulders. "What can I do? Nothing. No annulment, no divorce."

"So that's it? You plan to stay married...until death do you part?"

"Not quite," Belinda admitted, hedging. "I've talked Easterbridge into a sort of postnuptial agreement. The longer we stay married, the more Wentworth property I can walk away with in a divorce."

In fact, Easterbridge had had a short agreement drawn up by his solicitor while Belinda had gone back to New York. She'd had her lawyer review it, and the agreement had been signed just yesterday.

Pia looked deflated. "Still, perhaps Colin really does care for you, because what other incentive would he have for agreeing to such an arrangement?"

"Hardly," Belinda responded.

Tamara tilted her head. "And so, you're planning to stay the course in this marriage until you gain title to all the Wentworth property?"

"Exactly."

Belinda watched Pia and Tamara exchange another look.

"Just be careful," Tamara finally spoke. "Take it from me, this marriage of mutual convenience situation can be trickier than you think."

Belinda knew Tamara was remembering her own predicament with Sawyer, when her future husband had also made marriage a condition to the both of them getting what they wanted.

Belinda bit her bottom lip. "I've already learned my lesson, remember? I eloped with Easterbridge once. It's not the type of mistake that I intend to make again."

She knew she had to keep her guard up with Colin. She didn't have a crystal ball or good insight into his motivations.

Pia looked doubtful. "Well, this time you're already married, so the only thing that can happen is—"

Warningly, Tamara gave a quick shake of the head.

"—anything," Belinda acknowledged, finishing for her.

At the wedding reception, Colin barely took his eyes off of Belinda. He stood to one side of the ballroom and took a sip of his wine. He knew he had unmasked desire on his face. He was committing the unbelievably gauche sin of lusting after his own wife at a social event, but he didn't give a damn.

After Pia and Hawk's wedding ceremony, followed by a traditional wedding breakfast, everyone had repaired and refreshed in time for an elegant black-tie dinner-dance in Silderly Park's ballroom.

When Colin had first caught sight of Belinda tonight, she had stunned him with a body-hugging gown of crimson satin. She wore a large ruby-and-diamond pendant necklace and matching earrings. A delicate flower-motif tiara nested in her upswept hair.

He'd presented her with the jewels when she'd arrived at their hotel for the wedding. He'd texted her in advance to ask the color of her dress, and if she'd wondered why he bothered asking, she hadn't let on. He meant tonight to be a statement to everyone that Belinda was his marchioness. Not only were many entrants in *Debrett's Peerage* in attendance, but he thought he'd spotted a photographer for *Tatler,* the society glossy.

Across the room, Colin stared at the ruby pendant resting in the deep V of Belinda's cleavage. It twinkled and taunted him. If he thought he'd been tempted this morning during the wedding ceremony, he was certainly in purgatory now as a result of her crimson fire ensemble. It was all he could do not to sweep up Belinda and carry her away from the conversation that she was having with a Spanish countess.

Belinda had arrived from London only this morning and had parked her bags in their hotel suite with just enough time to get ready for the wedding. He'd missed her this past week. If anything, their recent skirmishes had increased his desire for her.

Colin handed his empty glass to a passing waiter and walked deliberately toward his wife.

At the last moment, Belinda turned her head and spotted him. She widened her eyes.

"Hello, darling," he said, leaning in to give her a quick peck on the cheek before she could move away.

The Spanish countess smiled at both of them.

"Colin, may I introduce you to—"

"We already have made each others' acquaintance," he interrupted smoothly. "Pleased to see you again, Countess."

"Likewise, my lord."

He cupped Belinda's elbow. "You would not mind if I lure my beautiful wife away for a dance…"

The countess smiled again and inclined her head. "Of course, not."

"Oh, but—"

Colin turned Belinda in the direction of the dance floor. "The next song is about to begin."

After a moment's resistance, Belinda let him guide her toward some other couples.

When they reached the dance floor, he turned her to face him.

She frowned up at him. "Neatly done."

It wasn't a compliment. Nonetheless, he smiled easily. "Thank you. I assume you know how to waltz?"

"Yes." She wrinkled her nose. "I was forced to take comportment lessons as a teenager."

His smile widened into a grin. "I can see the results. Your manners are exquisite, particularly toward me."

"Sarcasm is not appreciated," she grumbled.

He slipped his hand around her waist, and when she laid her hand in his, he pulled her closer.

She sucked in a startled breath. "Of course a romantic like Pia would want the waltz played at her wedding."

"Lucky me."

He'd been itching to touch her all evening, even if it was through the satiny barrier of her dress.

The music began, and they started gliding in circles around the dance floor, keeping time with the other couples.

Colin's eyes stayed on Belinda's as the world receded around them and they were swept away by the notes of "Waves of the Danube."

Her eyes were more amber than green. They reflected

her emotion in a way that she probably wouldn't be happy about but that was fascinating and useful for a gambler at heart like him.

Right now, her eyes were telling him that she was affected by their nearness although she was trying hard not to let it show.

He could feel her body heat under his hand at the small of her back. Her lips were slightly parted and carried a lustrous red shimmer that called to him.

The look of her lips just saved him from being entranced by the ruby practically tucked in her bodice. If it was gauche to gaze hungrily at one's wife, then staring at her cleavage was beyond the pale.

"If you keep regarding me that way, we may go up in flames," she said sharply.

"You're the one wearing red."

"Yes, it was clever of you to lend me jewels that are magnificent as well as a flashing fire alarm right over my cleavage."

He choked back a laugh. "Someone needs to put a warning sign on you."

"More like a stamp of ownership—"

He inclined his head and didn't deny it—so she had understood his intentions with his gift.

"—As well as a clever excuse for you to stare at my breasts."

He looked down just to annoy her. They still hadn't broken a step of the dance, and she kept a smile fixed firmly on her face.

"It is a stunning ruby," he murmured, "surrounded as it is by diamonds and the pillow of your creamy breasts. I was imagining the same when I chose the necklace and the tiara from among the jewelry in the family safe.

The earrings, however, I picked out myself this week at Garrard."

She shot him a look of liquid fire that nevertheless said she didn't know how to react. Should she be angry with him for his sexual banter, thank him for his gift or give in to the attraction that was undeniable between them?

The dance came to an end at that moment. He reluctantly loosened his hold on her, and stepped back.

"Walk with me in the garden."

She looked at him in surprise. "What? It's cold outside."

"Hawk has a greenhouse. It's where the head gardener works his magic for the estate grounds."

"I hardly think—"

"We're supposed to convince people tonight that we've decided to make a real go of our marriage."

It was a weak excuse. Still, she could not have missed the curious looks they'd received throughout the day.

She sighed.

"You know you want a breather. It's become a terrible crush in here." Particularly for them—a couple who was one of the interesting sideshows of the evening.

She contemplated him for a second, and then a look of resignation crossed her face. "Fine. I'll make a dignified exit with you."

They walked through the ballroom and out the French doors to a terrace warmed by heated lamps. From there, it was a short stroll to the greenhouse.

They discovered that Hawk's heated sanctuary had drawn other curious guests. They had come to admire some of the estate's more exotic plants and small blooms.

He and Belinda wandered along, stopping occasionally for her to appreciate a particular plant species—and for him to pretend to.

The greenhouse door opened and closed a couple of

times until Colin glanced around to discover that he and Belinda were alone except for another couple at the other end of the glass building. He could barely hear their voices.

"I believe Hawk's gardener has been experimenting to create hybrid roses," Belinda remarked.

She was looking down at a wood work table strewn with various gardening tools, plants and neatly marked glass jars.

He studied her profile. "I wouldn't be surprised. Max, my gardener, has done the same at Halstead Hall."

She cast him a look from under her lashes, as if wondering whether his comment was meant to be a reproach—his house, which was now her own as well, had the same cottage industry in place and she didn't seem to know it—or whether it was yet another meaning-laden invitation to make herself at home in his life.

The scent of roses and other blooms hung around them in the warm, humid air. Colin would never have thought that a greenhouse would be a sexually stimulating environment, but it was.

He let his fingertips trail up Belinda's arm in a light caress, and watched goose bumps appear. *Fascinating.*

She didn't look up at him, but there was a new stillness to her.

Testing, he stepped closer and cupped her upper arms from behind her. He bent and breathed in the soft air by her temple.

"What are you doing?" There was a catch in her voice.

"What does it seem as if I'm doing?" he responded, his voice laced with laughter and seduction. "I'm trying to determine your scent."

"There are other people here."

"Surely they won't mind if I try to distinguish my wife's scent from among those intermingled in the air."

"They'll misconstrue your actions."

"Is that my fault?" he murmured, teasing.

The greenhouse door opened and closed again, and this time, they were well and truly alone.

He stroked her arms. Belinda had the softest skin. He'd thought so before, but now, touching her, the tactile sensation brought the realization rushing back to him. Blood rushed to his head and other parts of his anatomy.

He let his lips skim the column of her neck.

"I don't think you'll be able to pick up my scent in a place as aromatic as this."

"Tiger lily," he announced, and then breathed in deep. "It's soap or body wash or some type of lotion."

She glanced back at him, her look astonished. "How did you guess?"

He crinkled his eyes as he held back a grin. "It's not a shy scent—"

"Oh."

"—and I noticed some tiger-lily products among your cosmetic products back at the hotel."

"Oh!" Her eyebrows drew together.

"I'm not nearly so omniscient about taste, however."

"Clearly."

"For that, there's only one way for me to find out."

Before she could react, he turned her toward him.

He settled his lips on hers and tasted her as if he had all the time in the world. He explored with his tongue, coaxing a reaction from her and inviting her to be a full participant with him.

After a moment, she relaxed in his arms, though she still didn't give him the uninhibited reaction he was looking for.

She tasted faintly of sweet wine and delicacy.

He worked hard to lower her defenses. His hands smoothed over her back, molding her to him.

She was a fantastic kisser. He'd learned that back in Vegas, and he got further glimmerings of her potential now.

He skimmed his hands above the back of her dress. He pressed and rubbed her muscles, soothing her.

Belinda made a low sound of pleasure.

Of course, he'd suggested the greenhouse in order to have a private moment, but he knew, even in his current aroused state, that he couldn't simply lower her to the floor here and make love to her.

Then again, he *could* lock the greenhouse door...

He undid the hook at the back of her dress and then lowered the zipper, relaxing her bodice.

Belinda sighed, and the cups of her gown fell away from her breasts.

Colin feasted on the sight.

Belinda's lips were parted and glistening, her eyes half-closed. The tips of her breasts were drawn tight, beckoning to him.

He bent and lowered his mouth to one rosy bud.

Belinda's knees buckled, nearly taking them both down to the floor.

Colin drew his brows together, concentrating on the task at hand—giving and receiving pleasure.

He breathed deeply, and Belinda moaned.

Suddenly, the greenhouse door opened and shut. A moment later, the air around them changed and cooled. Distantly, there was the sound of voices.

Belinda pulled away from him with a jerk and gathered her bodice to her chest.

He knew he should have locked that door when he'd had the chance.

She looked disheveled and reached to pull up her zipper. "We can't do this!"

"Reluctantly, I have to agree. We're no longer alone."

"Our postnup hasn't been signed," she countered.

"Is that what you're waiting for?"

"That's what *we're* waiting for," she corrected.

Clearly, she meant to hold him off on sex until the agreement was signed.

Colin breathed in deep and took a moment to bring himself back from acute arousal. Damn, it hurt.

No doubt about it. He'd have to raise hell to get their agreement finalized as soon as possible.

Belinda glanced from side to side and then shot him a repressive look. "I have to get out of here."

Colin smiled sardonically. He needed to get out of here, too. They had to leave before he got them to take up where they had unsatisfyingly left off—agreement or no agreement.

He raised her chin and touched the pad of his thumb to the corner of her mouth.

Her eyes widened.

"Your lipstick is smeared, and your color is high—"

She lowered her shoulders.

"—and sooner or later you're going to wind up in my bed."

She froze and then abruptly pulled away from him. "Yes, but for now, I need to freshen up and get presentable again."

She headed to the greenhouse door, and he followed her at a more leisurely pace.

He knew Belinda desired him—Granville or not.

His job was to make her *acknowledge* it. He felt as if he was on the verge of attaining a goal that he'd been pursuing ever since their night in Vegas.

Soon—very soon—Belinda would be his not only in name.

<u>Eight</u>

Belinda looked around her lavish bedroom at Halstead Hall. She had known luxury in the past, but this was at a whole other level.

The bedroom curtains were of silk damask, the walls were painted a celestial blue and the furniture was all carved wood antique. Her bed was large and canopied, the fireplace mantel was marble and a Victorian vanity table graced the far wall. The view out the windows was, of course, the best in the house. The vista was of the back lawn and wooded area.

This bedroom and its adjacent sitting room comprised the traditional quarters of the Marchioness of Easterbridge. The marquess' rooms were next door. Belinda had no doubt that Colin hoped to persuade her to go there at the first opportunity.

The fact that their postnuptial agreement had yet to be signed had bought her a reprieve. But Belinda had heard from her lawyer, and knew Colin was working diligently on getting the agreement finalized ever since Pia's wedding last week.

Belinda got goose bumps just thinking about it. She'd slept with Colin once, and it had been an earth-moving event for her.

She sucked in a deep breath. Her interlude with Colin in the greenhouse was still fresh in her mind. She remembered the feel of his mouth on her breast and of his hands on her skin. They'd been imprinted on her memory and came to her at night, unbidden.

She *couldn't* let him get under her skin so easily. She reminded herself of all his misdeeds—most of all, secretly buying up Wentworth properties.

She was just a tool to him. He was either toying with her or she was part of a grand plan that she wasn't totally privy to—or both.

Fortunately, she'd kept herself occupied enough to avoid dwelling on matters and to stay out of Colin's way.

In the past week, she'd flown to New York, tidied up her affairs there and asked for some time away from work until she was settled at Halstead Hall.

Her superiors at Lansing's had already broached the subject of transferring her to the London office on a permanent basis. Apparently, they were easily impressed by Colin's wealth and title and by the social and business connections implied by them. Everyone was intent on making nice and assumed moving her to London was what *she* wanted, too.

For now, she'd let her work colleagues think what they would, but she knew that she'd eventually have to clarify matters before she really was transferred to London.

She wanted to disrupt her life as little as possible, as vain a hope as that might be, even though she'd chosen to remain married to Colin. She knew Colin spent a good deal of time in New York seeing to his business interests. Let him accommodate *her* in his life, as well.

After glancing at her watch, Belinda left her bedroom and headed downstairs for a late lunch. Colin was still in London, roughly an hour's commute away, attending to pressing work matters.

She turned a corner in the hallway and steeled herself when she realized Colin's mother was coming her way.

The dowager marchioness had moved out of the house when her husband had died, ceding Halstead Hall to Colin as a principal residence and staying primarily at an address in London's tony Knightsbridge neighborhood. Belinda had gleaned that much from Colin and the staff.

Regardless, however, the marchioness was visiting here today, and by the looks of it, she was just as surprised and nonplussed about encountering the newest member of the family as Belinda was about meeting her.

Colin's mother must have just arrived, Belinda thought. According to the staff, the dowager was used to availing herself of Halstead Hall during travels and in lieu of a hotel when visiting the neighborhood.

The dowager marchioness inclined her head at the same time as Belinda nodded in greeting.

The older woman didn't crack a real smile. "Settling in?"

"Yes, thank you." Belinda was sure the news wasn't welcome.

"You'll want to speak to the chef about the menu for next week's dinner party," the other woman said, coming to a stop. "And the housekeeper, Mrs. Brown, is looking for direction as to how you wish your work space organized. I believe a number of social invitations are awaiting your response."

Having stopped, too, Belinda pasted a smile on her

face. "I am looking forward to meeting with Mrs. Brown tomorrow."

"Excellent."

"I'll speak with the chef."

"You are unused to how we run things at Halstead Hall."

It was hard to argue with the facts. "Yes, I would say so."

"An important realization."

"One of many, I hope."

With that, the dowager marchioness sailed on, and the two of them passed each other like two ships with canons manned but holding most of their fire—at least for now.

Belinda sighed. She wondered how many such skirmishes she was destined to have.

As if fate laughed, she descended the stairs and ran into Sophie.

The other woman looked uneasy. "Good afternoon."

"Good afternoon."

"I just arrived. I came to Halstead for the weekend to pick up some of my things, and I plan to leave tomorrow."

Colin's sister stopped as if out of breath—and as if belatedly realizing that her words could be construed to mean that she was gathering up her belongings and clearing out now that Belinda was living in the house.

What could she say in response, Belinda thought, that could not also be misconstrued? *Take your time? Let me know if I may be of help?*

She sensed that Sophie didn't bear her as much hostility as her mother but, rather, was finding the whole situation awkward and strange.

Belinda could hardly blame her. She and Colin's sister were contemporaries, but they'd never had any real interaction. Public events such as Royal Ascot and Wimbledon were big enough to lend themselves to selective socializing by Granvilles and Wentworths alike.

Belinda opened her mouth and voiced the first passably sensible thought that occurred to her. "I've yet to discover an art room in the house."

"There isn't one," Sophie said.

"Didn't you ever have one?" Belinda asked curiously. "With your profession…"

"I did most of my work outside the house and then took many of my things with me when I moved into a London flat. Mother didn't approve of graphic des—"

Sophie cut herself off.

Belinda was glad *she* wasn't the only person or thing that Colin's mother frowned upon. "Perhaps I'll create a room, then. I'm sure the youngest Granville cousins would appreciate it, and the staff must have children and grandchildren who would."

Seemingly despite herself, Sophie showed a spark of interest.

Belinda felt surprisingly heartened at the positive sign. She and Colin's sister were both in artistic professions, and she wouldn't be surprised if Colin's sister had an appreciation for nineteenth- and twentieth-century artwork. Maybe the next two years wouldn't be as bad as she'd feared.

"Sophie?"

The dowager marchioness's voice sounded from above them, and Sophie shot Belinda a rueful look before heading up the stairs.

Belinda continued on to the dining room.

Perhaps, she thought, all was not lost. Or at least, she'd survived another day…

There was something incongruous about a marquess doing his own grocery shopping. Belinda watched Colin eye a display of imported tapenade and other spreads.

She'd been at Halstead Hall a couple of days when Colin had returned. When he'd realized she was making a trip to the supermarket, he'd decided to come along—to her chagrin.

She pulled a crunchy French loaf from a bin and deposited the bread in her shopping cart. She rolled her cart a few feet, and stopped next to Colin.

Her brow furrowed. "How often do you run out to buy your own milk?"

Colin looked amused. "Now and then."

She searched his face.

"More so now," he teased, "that there's a marchioness who insists on selecting her own brand of jam."

"Except I didn't know I was a marchioness for all of the past three years."

"If William and Catherine can be caught buying their own produce at the market," he joked with a reference to the British royals, "then I suppose a marquess can, too."

"We are in Waitrose, however," she countered. "I refuse to be too impressed."

She knew just as well as he did that the upscale supermarket chain, run by a workers' cooperative, was popular in well-heeled social circles.

Colin smiled. "I'll just have to keep trying, then."

Her eyes skated away from his as she was conscious of the air between them changing.

She continued on with her cart, and Colin turned to follow.

She scanned the shelves, glad for the distraction. While it was safe to think of Colin as all aristocratic hauteur, she had to admit that he'd pleasantly surprised her with today's outing.

They continued on through Waitrose, stopping to chat with the occasional local who recognized Colin as the local marquess. At each conversation, Colin introduced her as his wife. There were no looks of surprise, presumably because everyone in this corner of Berkshire was well aware of the recent notoriety of the Marquess and Marchioness of Easterbridge.

Belinda was relieved not to have to offer any delicate explanations about how she'd become Colin's wife—particularly since there'd been no recent wedding celebration. Or at least, she corrected with an inward wince, there had been no wedding in which she'd been the bride and Colin had been the *groom*.

Still, even though their grocery shopping went smoothly, she was glad when they reached the checkout.

They stood in line like everyone else. Colin paid by credit card and then declined assistance to their car by one of the baggers.

"No need," Colin said to the teenager. "I'll have no problem handling these bags myself."

When they exited the supermarket, she followed Colin to their vehicle, where he loaded their purchases. Then she waited while he began to wheel their empty cart back toward Waitrose.

He'd only gone a few feet, however, when a petite older woman, well-dressed and carrying a Chanel purse, stopped him.

"Young man, would you mind assisting me inside with a return purchase? If you could simply bring your cart over here." She gestured to the back of her car.

Belinda realized that the woman had mistaken Colin for a Waitrose employee or manager. Perhaps the Chanel lady thought that Colin was reporting for his shift and had decided to tidy up the parking lot by taking an empty shopping cart inside with him.

Belinda opened her mouth. "Oh, but—"

She cut herself off as she caught Colin's eye and his slight shake of the head.

She gave an almost imperceptible lift of her shoulders.

Within minutes, Colin had loaded the woman's medium-size espresso maker into the cart.

Belinda watched as the older woman followed Colin toward the store entrance.

They'd only gone a few yards when a real Waitrose employee spotted them, froze and then hurried over.

On a mischievous impulse, Belinda started forward herself.

"Oh, dear," she announced in a voice meant to carry.

Colin and the Chanel lady turned back toward her.

"So sorry," she said, looking at Colin apologetically, "but I forgot to tip you."

Colin cast her a droll look, and she returned it with an impish smile before lifting her handbag from her shoulder.

A male Waitrose employee stopped before them. "May I be of assistance, my lord?"

Belinda caught the sudden arrested expression on the other woman's face. The *my lord* was, of course, a giveaway. Only certain members of the aristocracy were addressed in that fashion.

"Oh, my." The Chanel lady looked abashed as she glanced from Colin to Belinda and back. "I had no idea. I'm new to the area—"

"May I introduce you to the Marquess of Easterbridge?" Belinda deadpanned.

The older woman's eyes widened as she continued to regard Colin.

"I'm happy to be of assistance, madam."

"I—oh, goodness."

"It's all right," he said smoothly. "I usually go by the code name Colin."

The Waitrose employee looked baffled.

Belinda nearly giggled.

Colin bent toward her and murmured, "If you can go by the alias Belinda Wentworth, why can't I be Chuck the grocer?"

"First of all, your name is not Chuck," she whispered back. "And secondly, you're to the manor born."

"So are you."

She cast him a sidelong look. "It's different. I didn't grow up as the heir, nor am I the current holder of a marquessate."

Colin looked ready to say more, but she turned back to the other woman.

Belinda leaned forward conspiratorially. "He's a good-looking clerk but not nearly as impressive as a lord, don't you think?"

If possible, the other woman looked even more flustered. She glanced up at Colin. "My husband and I would be delighted to have you over for tea, my lord. To thank you for your assistance, of course."

Colin scanned the cart beside him. "I suppose espresso is out of the question?"

The woman tittered. "The coffeemaker can be replaced."

Belinda smiled. "We're most appreciative of the invitation."

Colin sighed. "May I introduce my wife…?"

He proceeded to do so.

The store employee looked undecided as to what to do.

Colin gave him a small nod. "If you would be so kind as to assist this lovely lady inside with her purchase?"

"Yes, of course, my lord."

"Excellent."

Belinda waited beside Colin as the older woman and

the store employee moved off and then turned back with him to their car.

Colin spoke first. "Thank you for accepting an invitation to tea."

"You're welcome," Belinda responded tongue-in-cheek. "Except she didn't get your address."

"I'm sure a few inquiries will yield my coordinates at Halstead Hall."

"How often have you done that?"

"What?"

She waved a hand back toward where they had come. "You know, *that*."

"It happens from time to time."

"It was a rather nice thing to do," she allowed. "Rather classy to not immediately correct her misimpression but just offer your assistance."

She tried hard not to feel charmed, but still felt herself slipping.

"She called me *young man*," Colin remarked as he walked beside her. "I suppose it's all a matter of perspective, but still it's worth a few points in my book."

"It's no more than you deserve," she scolded with mock humor, "for taking a trip to the supermarket dressed so unassumingly that you might be mistaken for anyone."

"Would you prefer I wear a pin declaring me a lord? Or better yet, a Granville?"

"Please."

Colin gave an uneven grin. "I suppose it would be easier than facing the awful possibility that not all Granvilles are died-in-the-wool villains."

They reached their car, and Colin pulled open the passenger door for her.

Belinda glanced up at him but found her gaze skittering

away again. They were getting into uncomfortably deep waters.

"Now, about that tip that you owe a certain good-looking store employee..."

There was laughter in Colin's voice, and it brushed tantalizingly across her skin as he let her pull the car door closed.

From the doorway, Colin watched Belinda exchange smiles with his cousin's nine-year-old daughter.

Daphne was standing before an easel, and Belinda was encouraging the girl, as well as pointing out a few ways to deepen the painting.

The empty playroom next door to what traditionally functioned as the nursery, on the third floor of the house, had been turned into a painting studio and an arts-and-crafts room. Canvas covered the wood floor, and the curtain-free windows offered an unobstructed path for the morning sunlight.

A half-dozen children moved about. Everyone wore paint-smeared smocks over casual clothes and sneakers or clogs. Some retrieved art supplies and others stood intently before easels. One child was the ten-year-old daughter of his stable manager, and another was the housekeeper's grandson. There was also Daphne's seven-year-old younger sister, Emily.

Belinda had suggested setting up an art playroom once she'd heard there were definitely children in his extended family and among the family of the staff. The art classes had been a big hit. At least those Granvilles below the age of twelve had taken to Belinda naturally. And Sophie had admitted to spending some time in the art room working with the kids alongside Belinda.

Colin thrust his hands into his pockets. Belinda's guard

was down, probably because she hadn't yet noticed his appearance in the open doorway.

He took the opportunity to study her.

Similar to the kids, she was dressed down in jeans and a pullover lavender top. The jeans showed off a pert rear end, though her smock obscured the rest of what Colin knew to be a delicious figure. Her hair was caught back loosely, but tendrils escaped to caress and frame her face.

Colin felt a tightening in his gut.

Daphne gave an impish grin, and Belinda laughed down at her. It was clear Belinda was in her element—spattered with paint and laughing. And she was relaxed, naturally, all because she thought he wasn't there.

In the next moment, however, she glanced up and caught his eye. She froze, and he gave her a mocking salute with a lift of his lips.

For him, every look and glance was overlaid with the memory from Vegas of kissing her luscious pink lips, smoothing his hand down a satin thigh and tracing a path along the tender skin of her abdomen.

Belinda quickly looked down to answer another of Daphne's questions.

When Daphne finally moved off, Colin sauntered in.

Belinda glanced at him warily.

"Who knew that what was missing was an art room?"

She gave him a tart look. "Well, it does already possess a double-height library, two wine cellars and a private theater."

He let his eyes crinkle. "Welcome to the ancestral pile."

"Is there any element I've overlooked?"

"No worries. You've added the missing element. An art room."

"You're the one who has a Renoir hanging in the master suite."

"Perhaps I was hoping to tempt you."

Belinda reddened. "Thank you, but I'm perfectly content with reproductions in books."

He laughed softly. "Any time you change your mind…"

"I won't."

"The agreement is awaiting your review and signature."

They both knew which contract he was referring to. It was the postnuptial accord that she had set up as the final barrier between them.

Belinda turned away. "Yes, I know. I'll get to it as soon as I have the chance."

"Don't wait too long."

He laced the words with promise. He watched Belinda's profile stain with heat again before she walked over to help another child.

Colin watched her go.

He'd stayed away in London and New York on business for a week, he'd taken cold showers and pressed his attorney to act fast. Let Belinda feel some of his urgency.

He knew he had to keep up the heat. He *would* seduce his wife back into his bed.

And then his plan to make Belinda acknowledge she wanted a Granville—that their night in Vegas was no fluke—would be achieved.

Frankly, his sanity was starting to depend on it.

Nine

When Colin had suggested they attend a performance at Covent Garden, Belinda had been unable to resist agreeing. She knew *Aïda* was playing. She'd always thought the opera was unbearably beautiful.

One of the things she'd always loved about the southern corner of Berkshire where Downlands and Halstead Hall were located was that it was just a short trip to London, making a night in town more than possible.

She was happy and excited when Colin bought tickets for good seats, which she knew were expensive and often hard to come by. She wanted to think he'd thought of her when doing so, but she was also enough of a realist to remember Uncle Hugh's words: since Colin had suffered a blow to his ego when she'd nearly walked down the aisle with another man, of course he'd be eager to line up public engagements for the two of them.

She dressed with care in a one-shouldered midnight-blue cocktail dress and croc-embossed peep-toe pumps. She had caught back her hair in a loose knot. She knew Colin would be in a suit and tie.

In fact, her heart palpitated excitedly as she came down the main staircase at Halstead Hall, all the while aware of Colin, handsome and distinguished, looking up at her from the landing.

Their postnup had just been finalized—she'd reviewed and signed it—so there was nothing barring Colin from her bed anymore. She also knew this was the twenty-first century and a marquess couldn't just order her around. Still, she knew that she was morally obligated to stand by her agreement.

She tried to focus on the fact that she had signed a contract. She wouldn't let herself think about standing face-to-face with Colin in his bedroom, his hot eyes on her while his hands skimmed over her sensitized skin, making her desperate with the desire for him to undress her.

She wouldn't think about the pleasure to be found in his arms.

No, she wouldn't.

Because they dined at home, they went directly to London's Royal Opera House in Covent Garden for the performance. Colin drove them in his Aston Martin, eschewing the services of Halstead Hall's resident driver.

Inside the opera house, the crowd was already milling. Colin introduced her to a couple of acquaintances who greeted him, and Belinda thought she did a credible job of smiling and being an appropriate consort.

When she and Colin eventually ended their conversations and made their way up to their seats in a front box, she had trouble relaxing. She almost wished Pia and Tamara were there for support. At least their husbands were friends of Colin's with whom she was familiar and comfortable.

When she and Colin took their seats with a close view of the stage, Belinda caught her breath. No need for opera glasses, she thought whimsically. The view was spectacular.

She perused her program until, minutes later, the lights blinked and dimmed, signaling the beginning of the performance.

She was just sliding into the start of the opera when Colin clasped her hand, folding it gently into his. She couldn't help focusing on the contact.

His hand was bigger, tougher and rougher than hers. It was an apt metaphor for their relationship, she thought. Yet, his clasp was surprisingly gentle, and his lightest touch had an electric effect on her.

She felt tossed by a storm of emotion mimicking the drama onstage. There were two shows here tonight—the one in which the singers participated, and Colin's private one for her benefit.

He traced over her hand with his thumb—an airy and rhythmic movement that might be mistaken for a soothing motion but that caused a quickening tempo of tension inside her.

She stole a glance at him from the corner of her eye. He faced forward and his face gave nothing away—except he continued his light touch on her hand.

She admitted that Colin had quite charmed her lately. Logically, she wished it were otherwise, but she was finding him hard to resist.

Belinda parted her lips on a sigh as she focused on the stage again.

The military commander, Radames, was caught between his love for Aïda, a captured princess, and loyalty to his Pharaoh—whose daughter, Amneris, had unrequited love for her father's commanding officer.

Belinda felt her heart clench as the opera built to its tragic climax. She almost couldn't bear to watch the final scene, where Radames and Aïda were destined to die together.

She swallowed hard against the lump in her throat and blinked rapidly. Belatedly, she became aware of Colin squeezing her hand, his thumb smoothing over the pulse at her inner wrist.

The audience burst into applause as the final scene faded to its close. Belinda bit her lip and distractedly accepted Colin's offer of a tissue. She felt silly—she'd known how Verdi's opera ended. But still, she cried.

She told herself that the image of star-crossed lovers was iconic. Radames and Aïda were the Romeo and Juliet of another era. Neither couple bore any resemblance to her and Colin—*not in the least*.

"Did you enjoy the performance?" Colin asked, his voice deep and low.

"I loved it," she croaked.

He chuckled then, and she gave a weak laugh—because her tears clashed with her statement.

"Let's get home."

Belinda felt a rush of emotion at Colin's words. It was the first time he'd used the word *home* with her to refer to Halstead Hall, but of course she knew what he meant without thought. Had she already started to think of Halstead Hall as home?

They rode back in companionable silence, making desultory conversation.

"I thought I'd make you happy with tickets to *Aïda*," Colin joked at one point, "but it would seem you prefer to cry when you go to the opera."

"You weren't unaffected by the performance, either," she parried. "You wouldn't be an opera fan otherwise."

He cast her a sidelong look, taking his eyes off the road for a moment. A smile played at his lips. "I was enjoying watching you as much as the opera singers on stage."

She heated. "You were not watching me!"

"How do you know?"

She bit her lip, because of course she had been found out. The only way she could know for sure that he hadn't been watching *her* was by being aware of *him*.

"I know," she insisted. "You were too busy playing with my hand."

Colin laughed, low and deep, and then faced the road again.

Belinda glanced out the window. They were speeding toward Halstead Hall and already the air between them had become more intimate.

When they arrived at the house, everything was still and dark. Colin had told the butler not to await their return from London. Some of the staff, of course, had the day off.

Belinda hesitated in the hall, unsure of what to do.

"Nightcap?" Colin asked, offering a solution to her problem.

"All right." She nodded, willing to put off the climb up the stairs to their adjoining suites.

She followed him into the library, where she disposed of her evening bag and coat while Colin busied himself at the side bar.

When Colin returned, she gratefully accepted the glass of clear liquid on ice from him.

"Cheers," he toasted, raising his glass. "To new beginnings."

She took a sip at the same time as he did, and her eyes widened. "Water?"

"Of course."

He took her glass from her and set both glasses down on his nearby desk.

This was not what she'd envisioned when he'd suggested a nightcap. She'd pictured imbibing something strong—to fortify her.

Colin trailed one finger up her arm to her shoulder. "It's a good thing neither of us has had a real drink."

"Why?" she asked, stumbling over the word. "So we don't do anything rash and regret it again?"

He gave a small smile. "No, so we won't have any excuses when we do."

Belinda's heart beat a staccato rhythm in her chest. "We have to stop this."

"Do we?" he joked, and then looked around. "Last time I checked, we were married. We even live here."

"The marquess ravishing his wife in the library? It sounds like a bad round of Clue."

"If I weren't so aroused right now, I might suggest we play."

"Isn't that what we're doing? Playing?" she parried. "This is a game."

"Then why am I so deathly serious?"

"Because you play to win."

"Exactly. Kiss me."

"Rather direct," she tried. "I would have thought you'd have more subtle lures in your repertoire."

"I do, but I've waited three years."

"Perhaps the first time was a fluke."

"Does this feel like a fluke?" He took her hand and placed it on his chest. "Touch me, Belinda."

Belinda's head buzzed. She felt the strong and steady beat of his heart beneath her palm. The contact with him was intoxicating, just like at the opera.

"We may have been born and bred to be enemies," he said, "but in this, we're one."

"It's just passion…"

"Enough to build on."

Colin bent his head slowly, tilting it first in one direction and then in another, as if deciding how he wanted to kiss her.

Belinda felt as if the moment drew out forever.

When he finally settled his lips on hers, it was with soft but insistent pressure, and Belinda unconsciously parted her lips.

He tasted faintly minty and all male, a flavor that only fueled and deepened her desire. His hands settled on her shoulders, where they molded and relaxed her.

She'd closed the door on their past. She'd tried not to dwell on how hotly passionate their night in Vegas had been. Now, however, she recalled vividly how he'd kissed every inch of her.

Her nipples became pronounced, her hips heavy with desire.

Colin moved his hands down her back.

"I don't know where the zipper is," he murmured between kisses.

"That's the point," she said against his mouth.

"I don't want to ruin your lovely dress. It fits you like a glove, and with any luck, there'll be other evenings when you can wear it to bring me to my knees."

She fought against the feelings that his words evoked. "You are not literally on your knees."

He pulled back to gaze into her eyes. "Would you like me to be?"

She trembled because she remembered the previous time that Colin had called her bluff. They had walked into a wedding chapel.

He trailed a finger lazily down from her collarbone to her cleavage, just skirting the tip of one breast.

"If I were on my knees," he said in a deep voice, "I think my lips would reach right here."

He touched the sensitive skin of her midriff.

She found herself holding her breath.

"On the other hand, if you bent forward," he continued, "my mouth would close over here."

His thumb skimmed over her nipple, and Belinda gasped and her eyes went wide.

"Would you bend over for me?"

"I—it's a theoretical question," she responded thickly.

"But it doesn't have to be."

He settled his lips on hers again, and Belinda's response was muted.

This time, rather than holding still, he folded her into his arms, and she slid her hands around his shoulders.

Colin found the zipper hidden in the side seam of her dress. He lowered it slowly, and cool air hit her skin.

Colin trailed his lips across her jaw to the delicate shell of her ear and then down toward her throat.

Images, words and scents from their night in Vegas came back to her. They'd been joking and teasing…until suddenly they weren't. Instead, they'd lain back on the bed, entangled in passion.

It had been the best sex of her life. Colin had been tender, prepared and patient—that is, he had been until a powerful climax had shaken him and sent her over the top with its aftershocks.

And now he was doing it again.

The dress slipped away from her.

Colin took a step back so that he perched on the corner of his desk. "Come here. Please."

If he'd been arrogant or impatient, she'd have had a

chance at resisting him. Instead, she took two steps forward and fit in the space created by his legs.

He leaned forward, and his lips nuzzled her cleavage.

Belinda's eyes drifted closed.

He licked first the tip of one breast and then of the other, stoking a fever of emotion inside her.

She moaned, and her fingers spread through his hair.

Colin settled his mouth on one breast, and Belinda arched up to him.

She felt deliciously alive, her body humming with desire. She rubbed against Colin's erection, the evidence of his burgeoning passion.

Colin groaned and turned his attention to her other breast.

It was all too much and yet not enough, Belinda thought hazily. It was consuming and liberating.

Their clothes fell away from them, one by one, until only Colin's trousers remained as a barrier between them.

With her gown and panties pooled at her feet, he lifted her, not breaking their kiss.

Her high-heeled pumps hit the library floor with a thud, one after the other.

Colin strode with her across the room and stopped next to the sofa. She slid down his body, feeling every hard plane and muscle on the way, her breasts grazing the sparse hair on his chest, until her feet touched the ground.

A low fire burned in the hearth nearby, casting shadows on the Oriental rug before it.

She looked up at Colin. "I thought we'd be safe in a room without a bed."

He grazed her temple with his lips. "There are ways around it. And we've already tried a bed."

"The Renoir hangs in your bedroom. Isn't that the key to your seduction?"

He gave a choked laugh. "Call it arrogance, call it flying without a net, but maybe I thought I would be enough."

Colin skimmed his hands over her thighs and then up her back.

Together, they lowered to the sofa, and he leaned over her.

His eyes glittering down at her, he cupped her intimately. He parted her folds and dipped inside her. She clenched around him instinctively.

She felt the caress of his thumb at her most intimately guarded place. Her eyelids lowered, and she bit down hard on her lip. Waves of sensation lapped her.

"You drive me crazy when you do that."

"Oh." Then she realized she wasn't sure what he meant. "Oh?"

"I keep thinking of sucking on that pouty lower lip of yours."

Unthinkingly, she bit her lip again.

"I want you." Already shirtless, he stood up and disposed of his trousers, and then sheathed himself with protection that he retrieved from a pocket.

The flames from the fire cast their flickering shadows on him, showing him in all his bronze glory.

He was magnificent—primed and male and wanting her. *Right now.*

Liquid fire coursed through Belinda.

Colin lowered himself to her, settling himself between her legs.

"I'm sure this sofa is an antique," she protested.

"Then it's been witness to plenty."

Without another word, he glided inside her, causing them both to sigh.

It had been so long—three years—that Belinda found

herself trembling. A tremor went through Colin, too. She could feel it.

He began a rhythm that she soon took up in counterpoint, her fingers finding traction on the dips and plateaus of the muscles of his back.

They both moaned.

"That's right," Colin urged.

"Yes." The blistering word was all she could manage.

The sofa groaned and creaked with their increasingly urgent movements.

They were so hot for each other that it was a wonder their coupling wasn't over in minutes.

She was impressed by Colin's control in order to give and receive pleasure. He was making it good for her, just as he had in Vegas.

Waves lapped her with increasing strength until she felt herself undulating with climax.

She cried out and Colin held her, soothing her.

Minutes later, he built his rhythm again, until he suddenly stilled and gave a hoarse groan.

Belinda followed him over the edge again on a throaty cry.

Afterward, they lay together, spent and breathless.

If there was any doubt, Belinda thought, about their first time being a fluke, it had been put to rest.

Ten

"Congratulations, Melton."

Colin glanced around him after offering the words. He and Sawyer, along with Hawk, were sitting in the library of Sawyer's London abode, a luxury flat in Mayfair. Tamara, Sawyer's wife, had come home from the hospital yesterday, after giving birth to Viscount Averil. She, Pia and Belinda had gone to the nursery with the baby.

"Thank you," Sawyer said in acknowledgment of his words. "In lieu of cigars, I'll suggest a round of scotch."

"It is a rather stupendous occasion," Hawk remarked.

"Rather," Colin commented. "The newly arrived viscount is in fine form, though he came a little early."

Belinda had received a call that Tamara had given birth, a few days after the trip to Covent Garden. Colin had driven them to London at one of the earliest opportunities.

Still, his brief time at Halstead Hall with Belinda had been spectacular, Colin thought with an inner grin. Three years had not dimmed his memory of their wedding night in Las Vegas, and the night of the opera had been a fitting sequel.

He felt a bone-deep sense of rightness—like turning up an ace at the end of a card game. Certainly, it wasn't a feeling that he'd gotten with any other woman.

Now all that remained was to get Belinda to acknowledge aloud that he, a dreaded Granville, had the same effect on her. It was all that remained, but it was a tall order.

"The baby's arrival caught both me and Tamara by surprise," Sawyer said, breaking into Colin's thoughts. "Though since he weighed seven pounds, perhaps it was a good thing that Tamara didn't go on for even another week."

"Thanks to Tamara's dual citizenship," Colin remarked, "the little viscount will also be an *American* heir to the earldom."

Sawyer rose and headed to the bar. "I'm sure one of my ancestors is rolling in his grave right now. Probably one of those who was among George III's cronies."

"No doubt."

"Tamara rather liked the idea of—"

"—snubbing one of your starchy ancestors?" Hawk finished.

Sawyer turned back and smiled. "I'm just relieved we were within walking distance of a hospital when Tamara went into labor. And now with the baby, we're heading in a new direction."

Hawk addressed Colin. "Speaking of new directions, you and Belinda appear to be on more amicable footing these days, Easterbridge."

Colin cast him a droll but forbearing look. "You mean she doesn't seem to be on the verge of doing me in?"

Sawyer looked up, pausing in the act of pouring scotch into a double old-fashioned. "One can't help but note the subdued fireworks."

"Meaning there still are some?"

Hawk tilted his head. "I'm surprised I haven't enjoyed more barbed comments between you and Belinda up to now."

"Yes, rather unsporting of me not to provide more entertainment," Colin commented drily.

"We do have empathy for you, Easterbridge," Sawyer put in, walking back with three glasses in his hands, "because we were in your shoes ourselves not too long ago."

Colin knew that neither Hawk nor Sawyer had had a smooth path to the altar with their wives. And yet, both were happily married now.

"Still, it is interesting to watch how the mighty have fallen," Hawk added with a grin, accepting a glass.

Colin quirked a brow. "What makes you think I've fallen—or even kneeled?"

Hawk and Sawyer exchanged looks before Hawk looked back at Colin with a sly smile. "Then I'll look forward to witnessing it happen when it does."

Colin felt his cell phone vibrate, fished it out of his pocket, and glanced down for a moment at the screen.

"Congratulate me, gentlemen," he announced, accepting his own glass from Sawyer. "You're looking at the new owner of the Wentworth's Elmer Street property."

Hawk's eyebrows shot up. "You've bought another Wentworth property in London?"

"Only a minor one."

"And let me guess," Sawyer said, "you did not reveal yourself in this real-estate deal, either."

"Only to those who know the exact constituency of the firm Halbridge Properties," Colin returned blandly.

Hawk shook his head in resignation. "You got Halbridge from combining Halstead and Easterbridge, I suppose. Clever."

Colin said nothing.

"You're in deep waters," Hawk commented finally.

Sawyer nodded his head in agreement. "Be careful, Easterbridge. Much as I admire your prowess in business, you're in uncharted territory here."

"I'm used to high stakes," Colin replied blandly, raising his glass in anticipation of a toast to the new arrival. "Bring it on."

Belinda looked down at the newborn Viscount Averil sleeping in his crib and her heart constricted. Tamara and Sawyer had named the baby Elliott, but by virtue of his father's name and position, he carried a courtesy title and thus was styled Elliott Langsford, Viscount Averil.

Belinda cast a glance around the nursery, done in shades of soft gray and white, before looking down at the baby again. She, Pia and a proud but tired Tamara hovered over the crib.

Two days ago, Belinda reflected, she'd again had the best sex of her life. It had been glorious, liberating and disconcerting at the same time. If she was in the same room as Colin, she wanted to throw herself at him. And from the looks of him, Colin stood ready to catch her at a moment's notice.

Yet, she knew it was temporary. Their agreement was for two years. There would never be a sleeping baby with downy skin making soft breathing noises, his torso rising and falling with every rapid beat of his heart. She and Colin had used protection to ensure it.

Belinda swallowed. She told herself that her emotion stemmed from the fact that she wouldn't be a mother at least until after she and Colin parted ways. Of course, she didn't want to become pregnant. *Of course*—it wasn't part of her understanding with Colin.

"Should we sit down?" Pia whispered, looking from Tamara to Belinda and back.

Belinda shot Tamara a look of concern.

Tamara's smile was weary but transcendent. "Only if I have a donut pillow to sit on."

Pia giggled and then all three of them moved toward the doorway and into the adjacent playroom.

Tamara sat in a rocking chair while Pia removed a stuffed giraffe from its position and sat on a toy chest.

Belinda made herself comfortable in a perch on a child-size chair.

She looked around the brightly colored playroom, a contrast to the nursery next door. "You know," she quipped, "I think I need to get back to playing with a primary palette and get away from all this impressionist stuff."

Tamara and Pia laughed.

Tamara gestured to the bookshelves set against a far wall. "Your watercolors await you. We're stocked for kids of all ages."

Pia tilted her head to the side. "Speaking of playing, you and Colin are acting positively cozy. Did I imagine it, or did he give you a warm kiss soon after you walked in the door together?"

Belinda flushed.

Pia was a true romantic, but Belinda didn't want to give her friend false hope. The truth was that she and Colin had become lovers. *But* they didn't have a permanent relationship, despite being married.

Tamara sat up straighter. "Something tells me that Belinda is looking at Colin more kindly these days."

Pia clapped her hands. "Oh, good. I always thought you and Colin should—"

"It's not what you think," Belinda said.

Tamara arched a brow. "Worse?"

How had her friend guessed? She was susceptible to Colin, more so than she had wanted to admit.

Belinda hesitated and then confessed, "Diary, I slept with him."

Pia gasped.

Tamara laughed. "We've all been there and now I have a baby to prove it."

Exactly, Belinda thought. In contrast, there'd be no baby for her—at least with Colin. She shifted in her seat.

"Just be careful," Tamara said. "I'm afraid that Colin is cut from the same cloth as his two counterparts sitting downstairs—Pia's husband and, much as I love him, mine. In other words, he should come with a warning label."

She hardly needed the warning, Belinda thought, when the sensible part of her wholly agreed.

"The path of true love never runs smooth," Pia offered.

Belinda knew Pia wouldn't be quelled in her romantic notions, but neither would the continuing complicated history of the Granvilles and the Wentworths.

Two days after visiting Sawyer and Tamara, Belinda prepared to attend a dinner-dance with Colin on an estate near Halstead Hall in honor of a new exhibition of eighteenth-century Chinese art. The guests were to be treated to an advance private viewing.

Belinda wondered if Colin had wanted to accept the invitation to please her, because he knew art was her passion as well as her career.

She scanned the contents of her closet. She moved aside one hanger after another. Though Colin had announced she had her own funds as the Marchioness of Easterbridge, she had decided to wear a gown that she already owned.

She didn't really have time to shop. What's more, she already owned a small but formal wardrobe because her career required her to attend the occasional black-tie affair. She'd paid for her designer wardrobe by carefully budgeting her funds and shopping the sales.

After debating a few minutes, she chose a floor-length beige tulle and beaded dress that cleverly skimmed her curves. Its color matched and blended with her skin tone.

Later that night, Colin's reaction didn't disappoint.

When she walked into the parlor where he was awaiting her, his face took on an appreciative expression.

Belinda felt her pulse pick up—and not only because of the look on Colin's face. If she thought she'd ever get used to him in a tuxedo, she was being proved mightily wrong.

He had an old-world elegance. His hair gleamed glossy dark in the light, and he looked impossibly broad and masculine in his suit.

The chauffeur appeared in the doorway. "I will await you outside at the car, my lord."

Colin's eyes flickered away from her for an instant. "Very well, Thomas."

Belinda composed herself. The flower-motif tiara that Colin had previously given her was nestled in her upswept hair.

"You look…" Colin's voice trailed away, as if he'd been robbed of words. "Ethereal."

She felt the words like a caress. "Thank you."

"I have something for you."

She watched as he reached for a velvet case on a nearby table and then approached her.

He opened the case for her inspection, and her breath caught.

"Yet again, it appears we're on the same wavelength," he commented, his tone deep.

The velvet case contained a dazzling diamond choker. The styling marked it as vintage, probably from the Victorian or Edwardian era.

"It came into the family by way of my great-great-grandmother." There was a smile in Colin's voice. "She wasn't a Granville by birth."

Belinda glanced up at him. "It's lovely." She swallowed. "I'll need a moment to put it on."

"No need," he said, the words falling easily from his lips. "I'll help you."

She searched his gaze, and what she saw there sent her heart into deep beats.

Colin set the box down and removed the diamond sparkler. It gleamed with white fire in the light.

She held herself still as he leaned close.

The cool diamonds slid against her skin, and a moment later, Colin's warm fingers touched her as he worked to fasten the jewelry at her neck.

Belinda felt her nipples tighten in reaction, and warmth pooled within her.

When his job was done, Colin paused, his lips hovering inches away from hers.

Her breath hitched in response.

They remained that way for only a fraction of a minute, but it seemed like forever.

"I'm looking forward to this evening," Colin said huskily.

Yes. No, no. What was wrong with her?

He had her so confused and sexually aware that she couldn't think straight.

Colin straightened and gave her a lopsided smile. "I believe I'll let you deal with the matching earrings yourself."

The spell was broken. Belinda took a step back.

In the next moment, Colin reached for another velvet box, she turned toward a nearby oval mirror and the housekeeper simultaneously walked in to announce that rain was threatening and umbrellas were advisable.

Soon after, Belinda and Colin departed for the party. The short drive was uneventful, and since this wasn't her first social engagement with him, she soon found herself relaxing and enjoying the party when they arrived.

Two of Colin's married cousins were present—parents of children that she'd entertained in the art room. After some awkward chitchat with her, they and their spouses appeared to lower their defenses—if only because she'd so effectively entertained the junior members of the family.

A little while later, she was turning away from a conversation with a British viscount and his wife when she spotted a familiar figure and froze.

Tod.

She was aghast.

She had no idea that he would be here tonight. She glanced over at Colin and realized that he had noted Tod's presence, too.

Belinda stifled the impulse to bolt. She supposed it was inevitable that she and Colin would run into Tod at some point. London was not that big of a town. Still, did it have to be right now?

Tod approached her. "Lady Wentworth—or is it more proper to address you as Lady Granville?"

Within a moment, Colin had walked over to them and

gave Tod a sharp nod of acknowledgment. "In either case, she is the Marchioness of Easterbridge."

Belinda looked at Colin. Must he refer to the elephant in the room so bluntly? All three of them knew she remained Colin's wife. Tod had asked a fair question given that she'd retained her maiden name and a number of people knew it.

Still, annoyed as she was with Colin, she couldn't help comparing the two men as they stood side by side. Tod seemed somehow diminished in Colin's presence. He was not quite as broad, but there was also a subtle distinction in bearing. Colin exuded power.

Of course, the physical differences were only part of the story. Tod had given in to familial pressure by heading to the altar with her. In contrast, Colin had eloped with her in Las Vegas, driven by passion and acting in careless defiance of what his family might have thought.

Tod turned toward her. "Would you like to dance?"

"Her next dance is taken." Colin spoke before she could.

Belinda felt her annoyance kick up a notch. Before she could say something, however, Colin and Tod faced off.

Tod raised his eyebrows. "The dance after that, then."

"It is taken, as well."

"Belinda can speak for herself."

"There's no need when I've already answered you."

Belinda looked from Colin's set expression—he looked practically menacing—to Tod's clenched jaw. They seemed as if they were moments away from coming to blows. What's more, they were attracting curious looks from nearby guests.

"First you lock her into marriage," Tod muttered, "and now you're shuttering her away from the world?"

"In fact, Dillingham, you will notice if you look around you that Belinda is attending a social event." Colin's tone was icy.

"So it's me that you object to?"

"And as for marriage," Colin went on flatly, ignoring the question, "Belinda and I eloped because we couldn't keep our hands off each other."

Belinda gasped.

Colin's words were a thinly disguised insult. The implication, of course, was that she and Tod *had* been able to keep their hands off each other.

It didn't help that there was truth behind Colin's words.

Belinda could see a muscle flex in Tod's jaw, and Colin's hand had clenched at his side.

She quickly stepped between the two men.

"This is outrageous," she announced. "Stop this minute, both of you."

Because she'd had enough, she turned on her heel and stalked off.

As Belinda made her way through the crowd, trying not to draw attention to her hot face, she fumed about the imbecility of men.

To think that she'd befriended some of the extended Granville clan this evening. She'd even started believing that Colin might be more than an overbearing, conniving Granville.

Of course, Belinda thought, the only thing that people would remember now was Tod and Colin's tense standoff. The exchange had stopped short of being a full-blown scene, but she'd seen the looks on the faces of some nearby guests.

She'd agreed to remain married to Colin, but he didn't have a license to embarrass her—them—on his path to vanquish the Wentworths.

Belinda managed to avoid Colin—and Tod—for the rest of the party by making conversation with one fellow guest after another. As was customary at these formal functions, she and Colin, as husband and wife, were not seated next to each other at dinner. And neither, thank the fates, was she seated near Tod.

When it was time to depart, she and Colin had reunited for only the most desultory conversation. They rode home in silence in their chauffeured car.

And when they arrived back at Halstead Hall, she sprinted lightly up the stairs to her suite while Colin stopped to speak with the butler.

Finally closeted in her rooms, Belinda felt her nerves ease for the first time in hours. She sat down at her vanity and removed her jewelry.

She stared at her face in the mirror. The woman who looked back at her was composed, belying the roil of emotions inside her. Her makeup was still in place, her hazel eyes luminous but wide—as if she was still trying to process tonight's drama.

At any moment, she expected to hear Colin's tread in the hallway as he made his way to his own suite, but she heard nothing.

Belinda pressed her lips together. The longer that Colin remained downstairs, the more her anger grew.

How dare he?

After debating for several minutes what to do, she rose and turned and made her way out of her suite and downstairs.

When she reached the lower level, she could hear movement from the library, but otherwise the house was quiet.

She walked into the library, and Colin looked up.

He had a decanter in one hand and a glass in the other. His tuxedo tie hung loose around his neck. Despite looking uncharacteristically careworn, however, he was still devastatingly attractive.

"Drink?" he offered.

She shook her head.

"As you wish," he said, returning to the task of pouring himself one.

His abruptness was startling. It was unlike Colin to be anything but effortlessly well-mannered, even when he was vanquishing an opponent.

"You were an absolute boar to Tod."

"Was I?" Colin returned. "I suppose you mean the animal and not that I bored him to death, however appealing the thought might be."

Belinda pressed her lips together.

Colin turned back toward her and took a sip of his drink. "Were you also afraid I'd gore him?"

"Only with your rancid wit."

"Ouch." Colin shook his head. "And what about the way you wound me, my dear wife?"

Belinda blinked.

"I'm a servant who awaits your next word and hangs on your every glance."

"That's the most ridiculous thing I've ever heard."

Colin quirked a brow. "Is it?"

He set down his glass and come toward her.

Belinda forced herself to stand her ground. "Our agreement does not give you license to be rude to Tod."

"Doesn't it?" Colin asked. "And what about the fact that you almost wed him while you were still married to me?"

"I didn't know that we were still married."

"But now you do."

He was talking circles around her, and she tried to formulate a response that would expose his illogic. Just because she knew now what she didn't know then, she wasn't at fault, was she?

Colin appeared to anticipate her argument as he came to a stop before her. "It happened without your knowing, but now we must all be cognizant of the fact that it did happen, and also that you remain married to me."

Colin was jealous. And it rendered him surprisingly vulnerable.

The realization flashed through Belinda's mind unbidden and unwanted. To stay mad at Colin, she didn't need a surprising insight into his perspective.

He touched her upper arm and a shot of sensation went through her. She knew Colin had noticed the reaction in her, too.

"It's always there between us, isn't it?" he murmured.

It was hard to argue with the truth.

He gave a self-derisive chuckle. "Definitely inconvenient at times."

"Like right now."

He shook his head. "I need to kiss you."

Colin claimed her lips before she could react.

Her moan remained stuck in her throat. Instead, she found herself wrapping herself around him even as his arms bound her to him.

They kissed frantically, kindred souls finding each other and trying to meld. Sexual union was only part of it.

Colin divested her of her gown and she kicked off her shoes.

"I wanted to wring Dillingham's pretty little neck when he wanted to dance with my nearly naked wife."

"I know." And she did—now. Oh, she still had the lingering remnants of anger, but she was more under-standing.

They frantically worked at removing Colin's tie and then he shrugged out of his jacket and shirt.

She moved her fingertips over the smooth planes of his chest and then down to the hair above his groin.

He undid his belt and shed his trousers and shoes.

They were both nearly without clothes now.

He was fully aroused, his erection pushing against his briefs.

She caressed him through the fabric, letting her hand wander and explore.

"Yes, touch me," he said harshly.

She slid the briefs off of him and then kneeled and slowly caressed him with her lips.

"Belinda, sweet—"

She savored her effect on him until Colin pulled her up and tugged off her panties. They lowered to the sofa.

Belinda felt Colin's delicious weight press her back against the pillows. She wrapped her legs around him.

She thought dimly that Colin's library was fast becoming their favorite place. They really couldn't be bothered with a trek to bed most of the time.

Colin kissed along her jaw and down the side of her neck. His hand stroked up and down her thigh and then cupped her breast.

Their breathing deepened and mingled as Belinda's world shrank to the two of them and their need for each other.

Colin stopped only to reach for protection and then gathered her to him.

"You know," he teased, his voice rough with passion, "before you, I never considered the library to be a sexy place."

She batted her lashes. "Do you want me to play the role of the sexy librarian?"

He gave a bark of laughter. "Why not? You've already been my Las Vegas seductress."

"Your lucky charm and arm candy at the gaming tables?"

"Come here."

Colin claimed her in a blaze of passion that matched her own. And Belinda's last thought was that if she couldn't resist him now, she could never resist him.

She shut off her mind before she could follow that thought to its logical conclusion…

Eleven

As Colin rode his polo horse across the field, holding his mallet at the ready, Belinda fanned herself with her event program.

April was the beginning of polo season, and the weather was mild.

But the sight of Colin exerting himself, his legs encased in form-fitting riding breeches as he rode to and fro to help his team best their opponents, was having an odd effect on Belinda's body temperature.

They were on polo grounds near Halstead Hall for an event to raise money for a local children's hospital. Even though the sporting event was for a good cause, the players on the field played ferociously.

Competitiveness was part of Colin's nature, Belinda realized. Moreover, he was born and bred to win.

A week had passed since Belinda's path had unexpectedly crossed with Tod's and had set her and Colin into an emotionally and sexually charged confrontation.

The power balance between them had been altered. Colin's reaction that night a week ago had been so stark—almost pained—that it had pierced her heart. He was under her spell as much as she was under his. They were two bodies circling around each other in an intimate dance.

Since then, she was cognizant of the fact that he was a Granville, that they had a postnup and that he held Wentworth property in the palm of his hand. But she was also aware of her power—and of the fact that the relationship really came down to the two of them.

They had, in the past week, been unable to keep their hands off each other. She had lost track of where and when they had been intimate. Certainly they had been at night in his bedroom, which she had essentially moved into, but also in the library, in the sitting room and—she flushed at the recollection—even in the stables after they had gone horseback riding.

Colin was filling her mind as well as possessing her body. She was losing sight of the reason she was staying married to him—to get the Wentworth property back.

Her cell phone buzzed, and Belinda retrieved it from her handbag to realize that she had missed a call from Uncle Hugh because she had had her ringer turned off. She quickly listened to the phone message and its summons to Downlands.

She frowned. Uncle Hugh didn't sound in ill health, but he hadn't given a precise reason for his call, either. She wondered what was going on.

She sighed, pushing aside an uneasy feeling. There was no way around it. She would have to go see him and find out what the issue was. Fortunately, it was a short trip from Halstead Hall to Downlands.

She looked up and saw Colin walking off the polo field toward her. The skin at the open collar of his shirt glistened with perspiration, and there were damp patches on his clothes. She knew he would smell all male, and her body began to hum in response.

He stopped, leaned down and brushed his lips across hers.

When he straightened, he smiled. "We won."

"Did you? I didn't notice."

His smile widened. "We'll have to work on your appreciation for the sport of kings."

"Why?" she asked innocently, looking at him through her lashes. "Would you rather I didn't focus on you instead?"

"Well, in that case, I can hardly argue."

He bent down and kissed her again.

Belinda's mind swam as she was quickly surrounded by his scent, his touch and his taste. He was quickly becoming addictive.

"We're in public," she managed when he drew back.

"To the victor go the spoils, as they say." He looked wicked. "Can I interest you in a trip to the stables?"

She tried and failed to look prim. "We've already been there."

"Go with what works."

She felt herself flush. "I really can't at the moment. I received a rather cryptic message from Uncle Hugh, and I need to check on him at Downlands and make sure nothing is seriously amiss."

"I'll wait for you at Halstead Hall, then."

There was promise in his words.

When Belinda arrived at Downlands, she found Uncle Hugh pacing in the library.

She'd had so many happy moments in this house while growing up. Downlands was smaller and less impressive than Halstead Hall, but it boasted light and airy rooms, courtesy of an Elizabethan frame that had been added, and lovely gardens. It was hard to believe the place had been sold.

"What is the matter?" Belinda asked.

Uncle Hugh turned toward her, looking agitated.

When her uncle didn't immediately answer, she truly began to worry. "Unless it's life or death, I'm sure—"

"Your husband bought and sold the Elmer Street property."

"What?" Belinda tried and failed to wrap her mind around what her uncle had just said. "Bought and sold? When and how?"

She hadn't even known the Elmer Street property had been on the market. It was a four-story residential building in Covent Garden that was rented out. The rentals had probably made it a more difficult property to sell.

Uncle Hugh rubbed his hands together. "I sold it to a company called Halbridge Properties. I just discovered the firm is another front for your husband, and he, the bounder, has promptly turned around and tried to sell the Elmer Street address to someone else."

Belinda felt her heart plummet. "You sold another Wentworth property?"

She felt betrayed—by all sides. Hadn't she put herself on the line trying to get back ownership to property that her uncle had already unwittingly sold to Colin? How could her uncle do this to her?

She spoke the last thought aloud. "How could you sell another property?"

"Belinda, please. You have no idea how dire our finances are."

"Apparently not."

Uncle Hugh continued to look distressed.

"And to be taken by Colin, again."

At this, her uncle flushed.

In Uncle Hugh's defense, Belinda had to admit that her uncle was probably not the only one to have been roundly bested by Colin. She'd seen firsthand what a good gambler Colin was. And his skill extended to real estate. He was London's most famous landowning marquess.

He was also the man who'd made tender and passionate love to her.

All along, however, he'd been intent on buying and selling yet another Wentworth parcel.

She felt betrayed and, worse, sullied.

"How is your relationship with Easterbridge?" her uncle asked suddenly. "You had no idea about Halbridge Properties and its recent purchase?"

This time, it was her turn to feel uncomfortable. She thought about Colin making sweet love to her. She'd thought they were growing closer, she'd thought that…

Never mind. It was clear that all the while, Colin was keeping her in the dark about his machinations with respect to the Wentworths.

Uncle Hugh tilted his head, his expression betraying a mixture of desperation and cunning. "There's always room for negotiation between a husband and wife. You worked your magic on Easterbridge before, perhaps…"

Uncle Hugh let the sentence trail off, but Belinda nevertheless understood his meaning. He had hopes that she could seduce back the Elmer Street property from Colin, too.

If she needed any further evidence, her uncle's implication highlighted how much her marriage to Colin was viewed simply as a means to an end by her family. *She* was merely a tool.

Belinda wanted to say that the way she was feeling right

now, the Berkshires would turn into the Sahara before she'd sleep with Colin again.

She swung toward the door. Yet again, she thought grimly, she was destined for a confrontation with Colin.

Colin turned toward the door of his home office at Halstead Hall.

When he saw Belinda, a swell of pleasure coursed through him. She was still dressed in the attire she'd had on at the polo field earlier—knee-high black boots and a tweed dress cinched by a thin belt. He couldn't wait to undress her.

He'd just had time to shower and put on some clean clothes, but he'd be happy to strip down again for her if it meant getting her into bed—or for that matter, even without a bed.

In fact, he was tempted to lock his office door right now...

He cut the distance between them.

"How could you?" Belinda demanded.

In the process of bending to kiss her, Colin pulled back and arched a brow. "How could I what?"

"You bought, and then promptly turned around and sold, the Elmer Street property without anyone being the wiser."

He stilled. She'd caught him off guard. He'd meant to tell her and explain why his actions made sense, but now he had to improvise.

"How did you find out?" he asked without inflection.

"Uncle Hugh informed me."

"Fine chap, Uncle Hugh."

Belinda continued to frown at him. "A business associate of his discovered the truth. He investigated

Halbridge Properties and told Uncle Hugh who the true owner was."

"Of course," Colin said drily. "Why am I not surprised Uncle Hugh has been keeping his ear to the ground? Or should I say, more accurately, has friends doing it for him?"

"Yes, well, at least he has the Wentworth family interests at heart!"

"Does he?" Colin countered. "He sold the property in the first place. And in this case, I agree with him. The Elmer Street property is not in good shape. It needed to be sold, and the proceeds need to be used to upgrade the other Wentworth properties."

If possible, Belinda looked more irate. "So you admit that you intended to sell as soon as you bought the property?"

He said nothing, and she read her own meaning into his silence.

"Does everything with you come down to a decision based on numbers?" she asked. "What about emotion and sentiment? I can't believe you are the same person who eloped with me in Vegas."

Colin tightened his jaw. "What makes you think marrying you wasn't my biggest gamble?"

"So that's what it was to you?" she countered. "Another calculation of risk and potential payoff?"

He thought he was doing her—and the Wentworths—a good turn by bringing some sanity to their financial chaos. Of course, he'd anticipated that Belinda's initial reaction might be negative, so he'd been looking for the right moment to explain. But now she'd discovered matters for herself in the worst way possible, and she showed no signs of being able to see his side.

"I said it was a gamble, not that emotion didn't enter

into it," he responded. "The Elmer Street property is of sentimental value to you? You never even lived there."

She tilted up her chin. "It's been in the Wentworth family for two generations."

"And that line of thinking demonstrates precisely why the Wentworths found themselves in a financial fix."

"I'm a Wentworth." She placed her hands on her hips. "We had an agreement. You promised not to sell Wentworth property."

"I promised to sign over to you the Wentworth property that I owned. The Elmer Street property is one that I subsequently bought."

Belinda fumed. "No wonder Uncle Hugh didn't suspect you were the buyer. He thought you were bound by our postnuptial agreement."

"I am bound by it, and I haven't broken it."

"You still violated the spirit, if not the letter, of our agreement. We agreed to stay married partly to keep Wentworth property together."

"And it will. The proceeds from the sale of the Elmer Street address will be well-spent on upgrades to the other Wentworth properties."

"What guarantee do I have that you'll actually use the money to renovate the other properties? After all, you sold the Elmer Street house without informing me."

Colin felt his annoyance spike. All he was trying to do was help her loony relatives out of their financial quicksand. "I didn't promise a day-to-day update on the management of the properties."

"There is nothing to say, then, is there?" she countered.

Belinda turned on her heel and walked toward the door.

Belinda watched Uncle Hugh frown.

"There are rumors and gossip in the press that you left

Colin," Uncle Hugh said, grasping the arms of his chair, "and they depict you in an unflattering light, I'm afraid."

Her mother, sitting gingerly to Uncle Hugh's right, nodded in agreement.

Frankly, Belinda didn't give a fig about rumors. She was more miserable than she could ever remember being, including when she'd bolted from a certain Vegas hotel room.

They were in the parlor of Uncle Hugh's Mayfair town house—or rather, her husband's Mayfair house. It was all such a tangle.

After leaving Halstead Hall yesterday, she had spent the night at Tamara and Sawyer's empty London flat. Tamara hadn't hesitated to lend her the apartment as a place to stay, particularly since she, Sawyer and the baby were back at the family seat in Gloucestershire.

Her friend had been a bit curious about the reasons behind Belinda's unexpected phone call, but the emotions had been too raw for Belinda to talk about them.

She was fortunate, Belinda thought, that no one had been witness to her sleepless, teary night. She'd tossed and turned to no avail, and the tears had continued to seep from under her lids.

By dawn, she had been unable to escape the truth.

She loved Colin's intelligence, his humor, and, yes, his sexual skill. They had common interests, but more importantly, they complemented each other in personality. He made her feel more alive.

She had fallen in love with Colin.

It was why his betrayal was like a dagger to the heart.

But obviously, she was nothing more than a conquest to him. If he cared for her, he wouldn't have been so cavalier about his disposal of the Elmer Street property.

Uncle Hugh drummed his fingers on the arms of his chair.

He had come down to London from Downlands earlier in the day. Upon learning that Belinda was in town, too, he had suggested that she take tea with him and her mother.

Uncle Hugh glowered. "I'm sure the stories in the press were planted by the Granvilles. Well, they might have gained the initial upper hand in the media, but we'll win the war."

Belinda felt her heart squeeze. Had Colin retaliated in the press, making sure he fired the first salvo in a divorce battle?

Uncle Hugh rubbed his hands together. "We'll hire the best lawyers to contest Colin's sale. We'll claim he violated your postnuptial agreement. We'll request that you be granted all of the original Wentworth property in a divorce. When the property is back under my stewardship, I'll see to it that the Granvilles aren't allowed to touch it again."

"No."

The word caught her by surprise almost as much as it did her uncle and her mother.

Everyone stopped.

"No?" Uncle Hugh asked, his brow furrowing. "What do you mean, no?"

Belinda took a deep breath. "I mean I'll never give up control of the Wentworth estates."

Uncle Hugh relaxed. "Well, of course not, dear girl. Isn't that what we're trying to arrange, with any luck, and the help of a few good solicitors?"

Belinda suddenly saw things with a clarity that had hitherto eluded her.

Belinda knew in her heart that her uncle would simply start selling or mortgaging the properties to the hilt if he had control. Uncle Hugh was not competent to manage the Wentworth estates.

In a way, Belinda realized, Colin had done her and the Wentworths an immense favor. If Uncle Hugh hadn't unwittingly found an eager buyer in Colin, he may have stripped the properties to the point of default and foreclosure. And then the Wentworths would certainly have fallen out of favor with the upper crust. They would have stopped receiving party invitations and gotten the cold shoulder in certain quarters.

Her family had been keen for her to marry Tod, and she'd assumed they'd simply wanted her to make a good match. She hadn't been aware of how desperate they had been for her to save the family fortunes.

There was a big difference, she thought, between making it known that you were expected to marry up, and being sacrificed to save the family from financial ruin—again and again.

She loved her family, but they were human and flawed— very flawed.

What was it that Colin had said? She had a choice between being a stick-in-the-mud or a free agent.

Her uncle continued to look uncomprehending. "Of course, you'll have a property manager in me, or Tod when you marry him."

"No, Uncle Hugh," she said firmly. "Tod is out of the picture—for good. What's more, if and when I divorce Colin and have control of the Wentworth property again, we'll do things my way."

What a novel thought—her way.

Her mother looked quizzical. "Belinda, this is absurd."

"No, it's not," she responded and then stood to leave. "I think it's the best idea I've had in a long time. In fact, I'm rather looking forward to becoming a real-estate mogul."

Her husband had taught her a lot. And one of those things was that she had more power than she thought she had.

She had just asserted her power with her family. Now she had to decide what to do with respect to Colin.

She'd been unfair to him, she realized. He should have told her about the Elmer Street property, but with new insight, she understood why he had acted as he had with respect to the disposal of the building.

The only question was, how would she mend fences with him, and would he want her back after she had seemed to side with Uncle Hugh?

Twelve

"Mother, what have you done?"

"Never fear, dear. It's all about the media these days."

"Believe it or not," he said patiently, "I'm one of those relics who still believes in a reality apart from public perception."

"Nonsense. What an antiquated idea."

The irony, of course, Colin thought, was that *he* had brought the Granvilles into a new millennium, shoring up the family wealth through shrewd real-estate holdings.

They were sitting at lunch in a room with French doors that offered a panoramic view of the gardens of Halstead Hall. At one time, the room had functioned as the music room, but these days it served as the family's informal dining room.

He'd been informed by a member of the staff shortly before lunch that his mother had arrived and would be joining him for the meal. As usual, his mother had presented herself impeccably groomed, pearls in place.

He, meanwhile, felt uncharacteristically scraggly and under the weather. He hadn't shaved that morning, and though he wore his usual work-at-home attire of trousers and open-collar shirt, he felt unkempt.

He knew the cause of his mood, however. She had left two days ago.

His mother took a sip of her tea. "You know, you really could take a cue from your friend Melton. He's a media person, isn't he?"

Colin wondered sardonically if his mother included following Sawyer as an example in the marriage department. After all, Tamara, the earl's wife, was a maverick American by upbringing, though her father was a British viscount. On top of it all, she remained one of Belinda's closest friends.

"Melton will be hurt to discover that you didn't use one of his media outlets as your mouthpiece for a public statement," Colin drawled. "I will assure him, however, not to take the matter personally."

The dowager marchioness waved a hand dismissively. "I still begrudge that horrid columnist of his, Mrs. Hollings. How dare she perpetuate the story of your appearance at the Wentworth-Dillingham nuptials?"

"How nice of you to retaliate by *not* feeding her salacious gossip about Belinda."

"It's the least I could do," his mother sniffed. "And I don't understand what you're upset about. What did I say that wasn't true? Belinda left you after you bought some burdensome property and thus gave much-needed financial assistance to the Wentworths."

"I'm not sure Belinda would characterize matters in quite that way."

The marchioness raised her eyebrows. "Precisely my point."

In the two days since Belinda had left Halstead Hall, he'd had time to reflect and, frankly, brood. It had been hell and he'd been unable to work.

He'd started to think that Belinda had a point. He'd been so fixated on the bottom line that he'd somehow failed to appreciate how much Belinda cared about other things. Of course, family, history and sentiment were important to her. She was, after all, a lover of impressionist art, the epitome of nineteenth-century romance.

His mother sat up straighter. "We need to move quickly and gain the upper hand so that the press and public opinion are on our side. I'm only thinking of your reputation."

"My reputation doesn't need saving."

He needed saving. He needed Belinda to save his cerebral and mercenary gambler's soul.

Because he loved her.

The realization hit like a sledgehammer. He was flummoxed, right before exploding joy and worry hit.

It was a hell of a moment to have an epiphany, considering his mother was in the room. But there was no other explanation for the way he'd been feeling since Belinda had departed.

His mother looked at him consideringly. "Colin, you could have your pick of brides."

"Yes, and how could I forget that the story you planted in the press also listed the names of one or two women."

His mother's eyes gleamed. "Suitable ones. As I said, you could have your pick."

"But I want just one," he replied. "I can't believe you'd turn your back on Belinda so easily. The rest of the family has warmed to her."

"She's still a Wentworth."

"It's past time to bury the hatchet. The hostilities have lasted longer than the War of the Roses."

"Of course, the hostilities are over," his mother replied, frowning. "You have won. The Wentworths are in your debt."

"Have I won?" he asked softly.

His mother closed her eyes.

"Accustom yourself to the idea, Mother. Belinda is the Marchioness of Easterbridge, and if she'll have me, she'll remain so."

He knew with a sudden clear insight that, without Belinda, his seeming victory over the Wentworths would be hollow.

As Belinda opened the apartment door, her mouth dropped. "How did you find me?"

Colin's mouth lifted sardonically. "A little birdie told me."

"Sawyer," she guessed.

Colin inclined his head. "It is his flat, after all."

"I detest the way you blue bloods band together."

"And right now," he guessed, "you especially detest me."

She let her silence speak for itself. Of course, she was furious and hurt. Why shouldn't she be? She'd been falling for him while he'd been toying with her.

How could she castigate Uncle Hugh for his bad judgments, she thought, when she'd made worse decisions?

And yet, she found herself drinking in the sight of Colin. His hair was mussed, when it ordinarily looked smooth, and his jaw was shadowed, when he was normally groomed.

"May I come in?" he asked, his manner steady.

"Do I have a choice?"

"Sawyer has graciously lent me his apartment, too, while I'm in London."

"How kind of him." She lifted her chin. "One wonders at the need for it, considering just how many properties you have acquired lately."

"The Mayfair town house is rented out."

"Oh, yes, how can I forget? Your act of noblesse oblige. Uncle Hugh sends his regards."

Colin bit off a helpless laugh. "I suppose I deserve that."

"Surely your mother and sister would offer you a sofa to sleep on in London."

"Perhaps Sawyer thought my home was here with you."

Belinda felt suddenly flush with emotion.

"With so many properties at your disposal?" she forced herself to scoff.

Colin looked at her steadily. "As a matter of fact, those properties are the reason I'm here."

She tensed. "I thought you would have let your attorney do the talking."

He grimaced. "Do we have to have this discussion on the doorstep?"

Reluctantly, she moved out of the way.

He stepped inside and removed his overcoat. It was an overcast day, typical of London but not rainy—yet. Under his coat, he wore a white open-collar shirt over dark trousers.

Belinda was glad she was presentable herself, though she'd had to use cucumber patches for her puffy eyes this morning. She had, however, showered and dressed. She'd donned a blue belted shirtdress, tights and flats shortly before Colin's arrival.

After Colin folded his coat and placed it on a nearby chair, she turned and walked farther into the flat, leaving him to follow her.

She stopped in the parlor and turned back to face him.

Despite appearing a bit careworn, he was still imposing—tall, broad and ruthless. And yet she remembered his achingly soft caresses and his whispered words of promise.

Like a bad angel, she thought with a twist of the heart.

"The Elmer Street property is not being sold," he announced.

She blinked.

It had not been the announcement that she'd expected from him. She had thought he was here to negotiate with her about their future.

"I thought it was a done deal," she finally said.

"The sale was in contract, but the parties had yet to sign."

"Oh." She paused. "What made you change your mind?"

He searched her eyes. "I decided it would be better to sell the property to you—"

She frowned.

"—for one pound sterling. Have you got it in your purse?"

Her heart skittered. "Is this some attempt to modify our postnuptial agreement?"

"Yes, for forever."

Her eyes went wide.

Colin stepped toward her, and she caught her breath.

He acted like his usual commanding self, but his face told a different story. It spoke of stark need and naked emotion.

"What are the terms?" she asked with a catch in her voice.

"Name them." He searched her face. "In fact, my plan is to sign over all the Wentworth property to you today for a nominal amount…and for accepting me back, if you'll have me."

Belinda felt emotion clog her throat. Still, she managed to say, "Of course, you would never be caught without a plan."

Colin lifted his mouth in an uneven grin. "A gambler always has a strategy, and I believe this is one of my better ones."

"Oh?" she asked, matching his tone. "Then far be it for me to stand in the way of its execution."

"Excellent." He went down on bended knee and took hold of her hand. "Belinda, would you do me the great honor of remaining my wife?"

She blinked back tears. "Even better."

"I love you passionately."

"Best. Definitely the best plan you've ever had." She smoothed away an errant tear. "I love you, too, so I suppose there's nothing for it but to remain married to you."

It was hard to say who moved first, but in the next moment, they were in each others' arms and kissing passionately.

It was a long moment before they came up for air.

"You know we'll scandalize both our families by staying married to each other," she remarked.

"Who cares? We withstood their attempts to pull us apart."

She nodded. "It's the awful interfamily feud."

Colin smiled, his eyes twinkling. "We're putting it to rest. In fact, I suggest we make love not war right now."

"We're in Sawyer's flat."

Colin looked around them. "Looks good to me. Can you think of something better to do on a wet and overcast day?"

"Colin…"

Belinda laughed as he tugged her down with him to the deep rug before the fireplace, pulling a blanket off the sofa as he did so.

It wasn't long before the weather was forgotten for more interesting pursuits....

Later, Belinda snuggled with Colin on the sofa, watching the rain beat against the windows of Sawyer's London flat.

Colin cleared his throat. "I let revenge take over for three years. It was convenient not to look beyond that overruling motivation."

"Because I walked away." She said the words without rancor, as merely a statement of fact.

Colin lifted the corner of his mouth. "You didn't just walk. You ran."

"What?" she joked. "In three-inch platform heels and a red sequin minidress?"

"The minute I saw you, I wanted to strip you out of them."

She gazed at him through her lashes. "And you did."

"You couldn't have chosen a better seduction ensemble if you had tried," Colin teased. "What were you thinking?"

Belinda heated. "I was thinking that I was in Vegas and I was going to have a good time."

"Ah," he said, nodding with understanding. "You were already starting to do things your way without knowing it."

"And maybe, just maybe, when I saw you, I made sure to stay put until you spotted me in the hotel."

"Ah." Colin nodded with satisfaction. "Finally, a confession. Here's mine—I knew you were staying at the Bellagio."

Belinda's eyes widened. "No doubt your ego was in full bloom."

He placed her hand on his chest. "But my heart shriveled on the vine for the next three years."

She turned her head to look up at him. "Did you ever discover how our annulment was never finalized in Nevada?"

"The biggest confession of all," Colin admitted. "I did not authorize my attorney to file the annulment papers."

Belinda gasped and then laughed in disbelief. "I always suspected as much!"

"I tried to find every which way to get you back. I even pursued the end of the Wentworth-Granville feud in order to get you back. Why do you think I became a collector of impressionist art?"

Belinda's eyes shone. "Me?"

Colin nodded.

Belinda swallowed against the well of emotion. "Oh, Colin, how sweet and romantic."

He brushed her lips with his.

"I'm sorry for running out on you in Vegas." When he made to speak, she pressed a finger to his lips. "In the morning, I was afraid of the floodgates that you opened in me, and I didn't know how to deal with the situation. You were willing to take risks that I wasn't. You were more than I expected, and more than I could handle at the time."

When she lowered her hand, he stole another quick kiss.

"You handled me fine." His eyes glinted. "And I'd say you took a big risk by eloping with me. You just needed me to get used to jumping into the deep end once in a while in your life."

She laughed. "I'm sure you'll give me plenty more chances to do it."

"I was a lord who was missing his heart, and didn't know it."

"The majority of Wentworths would agree that you were heartless," she allowed.

"Only because you'd stolen my heart." He looked deeply into her eyes. "And you absconded to New York with it."

Belinda's lips twitched. "Uncle Hugh would claim you're the thief who stole the Wentworth family patrimony—the London town house, the Berkshire country estate..."

"But what you didn't understand is that you always had the more valuable property in your possession, and I was just trying to get my heart back."

"You took the family jewel, the Berkshire estate."

"The only jewel I stole was you."

"I guess I'll have to change my name to Granville, then."

Colin gave a small smile. "I guess you'll have to, if you want to."

"What? And risk giving people, including your mother, conniptions at being styled Belinda Wentworth, Marchioness of Easterbridge?"

"I wouldn't mind as long as you remained the lady of my heart."

"Oh."

"Would you like to renew our vows?"

Belinda swallowed against the lump in her throat. "I've been a disaster at weddings, in case you haven't noticed."

He gave her a swift kiss. "What matters is that you're a winner at marriage."

"It's nice of you to think so."

He gave her an intimate smile. "I'm betting on it."

Belinda smiled. "Then, yes, I'll marry you again."

"The local parish church would do nicely. The locals will love the show."

"Even if I'm not dressed in red sequins?" she joked.

"Especially if I avoid a white Elvis suit."

She laughed.

"I started out trying to put the Wentworth-Granville feud to rest by vanquishing the Wentworths. Instead, by falling in love, we'll be the means together to end the feud in a far more satisfactory way."

Belinda couldn't agree more. "I can't wait to get started together on your next strategy."

Epilogue

It was the Christmas season in snowy Berkshire, and Belinda was surrounded by those who loved her and whom she loved in return.

What else could a woman ask for?

She surveyed the scene in the sitting room at Halstead Hall. A huge tree hugged one corner of the room, a bright star at the very top and foil ribbon gracing the boughs.

Colin was speaking with Hawk near the tree, but in the next moment, his eyes connected with hers.

A look ripe with emotion and understanding passed between them. Colin's face said that he adored her—and he couldn't wait to get her alone.

Then he winked, and Belinda's smile widened.

She was six months pregnant with twins—a boy and a girl—and this time next year, they would be parents like their friends. It was nice to get a reminder that even in her current state, her husband still, well, *lusted,* for her.

On the floor in front of one of the sofas, Pia played with her son, William, the seven-month-old Earl of Eastchester—the courtesy title used by the eldest son of the Duke of Hawkshire. She laughed along with Tamara when William snagged a ball that had been rolled his way by Tamara's fifteen-month-old son, Elliott Langsford, Viscount Averil.

Off to one side, Tamara's husband, Sawyer, stood with a toddler's juice box in hand, surveying the action.

This time next year, two children would become four, Belinda thought. She'd be playing on the floor along with Pia and Tamara, though it was hard to believe these days since her view of her feet had already disappeared.

She and Colin hoped to make this Christmastime gathering an annual event with the two couples whom they considered the best of friends.

And fortunately, they both continued to mend fences with their families. She and Colin had had a lovely, formal wedding at the local parish church in Berkshire and a reception at Halstead Hall. She'd worn a designer sleeveless gown with white gloves that had drawn a gratifyingly stunned response from Colin. For his part, Colin had exuded a quiet male authority in a morning jacket and red cummerbund.

They had even invited Mrs. Hollings to the wedding. She had turned out to be a sixty-something woman who was a British subject by birth but had lived in New York for years. She also had impeccable sources.

For Belinda, the third time had been the charm, because though both Wentworths and Granvilles had attended, there had been no hiccup in the proceedings. Of course, it had helped that the two families had followed tradition and occupied opposite sides of the church aisle.

Now, however, that Belinda was pregnant with Wentworth-

Granville offspring, even the fact that she'd legally changed her name to Belinda Granville had apparently faded into the background. Even Colin's mother had become reconciled, though, of course, to her, the expected grandchildren were simply Granvilles.

Hawk bent down to help his son, and Colin came over to her and slipped his arm around her back.

"Happy?" Colin asked her.

"Of course," Belinda said. "And it's wonderful to have our friends here with us."

Colin smiled. "Even though both our families are set to arrive the day after Christmas for Boxing Day?"

"They'll behave, or else," she threatened with mock humor.

"If Uncle Hugh bests my mother at chess again, there may be blood on the Persian rug."

Belinda laughed. "Who knew they'd have something in common?"

Uncle Hugh continued to reside at the Mayfair town house and the estates nearby in Berkshire. Eventually the property would pass to Belinda's children, as was always intended.

The Elmer Street property had been sold—Belinda herself had pushed for it—and the proceeds used to upgrade the Berkshire estates and the Mayfair town house.

Belinda knew she was lucky.

She had asked for and gotten a transfer to the London office of Lansing's. She had worked there for several months and given notice only two weeks ago. She hoped, though, to keep her hand in the art world somehow. There were many priceless works of art at Halstead Hall to give her inspiration.

For the moment, however, she had her hands full with the babies' impending arrival, her work with the staff at

Colin's various properties and her charitable and other endeavors as the Marchioness of Easterbridge.

"Life is good," she announced.

"But not like a dappled impressionist painting," Colin teased. "It's more like a work of modern art. It's what you make of it. It's all in the eye of the beholder."

"Kiss me," she said, "and I'll tell you what I make of it."

Colin's eyes twinkled. "I'd love to."

And they sealed their future with a kiss.

* * * * *

A BREATHLESS BRIDE

BY
FIONA BRAND

Fiona Brand lives in the sunny Bay of Islands, New Zealand. Now that both of her sons are grown, she continues to love writing books and gardening. After a life-changing time in which she met Christ, she has undertaken study for a bachelor of theology and has become a member of The Order of St Luke, Christ's healing ministry.

For the lord. Thank you.

on finding one pearl of great value,
he went and sold all that he had and bought it.
—Matthew 13:46

One

With a wolf-cold gaze, Constantine Atraeus scanned the mourners attending Roberto Ambrosi's funeral, restlessly seeking…and finding.

With her long blond hair and dark eyes, elegantly curved body and rich-list style, Roberto's daughter Sienna stood out like an exotic bird among ravens.

His jaw compressing at the unmistakable evidence of her tears, Constantine shook off an unwilling surge of compassion. And memories. No matter how innocent Sienna looked, he couldn't allow himself to forget that his ex-fiancée was the new CEO of her family's failing pearl empire. She was first and foremost an Ambrosi. Descended from a once wealthy family, the Ambrosis were noted for two things: their luminous good looks and their focus on the bottom line.

In this case, his bottom line.

"Tell me you're not going after her now."

Constantine's brother Lucas, still jet-lagged from a long-haul flight from Rome to Sydney, levered himself out of the Audi Constantine had used to pick up both of his brothers from the airport.

In the Sydney office for two days of meetings, Lucas was dressed for business, although he'd long since abandoned the jacket and tie. Zane, who was already out of the car and examining the funeral crowd, was dressed in black jeans and a black shirt, a pair of dark glasses making him look even more remote.

Lucas was edgily good-looking, so much so that the media dogged him unmercifully. Zane, who was technically their half brother, and who had spent time on the streets of L.A. as a teenager before their father had found him, simply looked dangerous. The outer packaging aside, Constantine was confident that when it came to protecting his family's assets both of his brothers were sharks.

Constantine shrugged into the jacket he'd draped over the back of the driver's seat as he watched Sienna accept condolences, his frustration edged by a surge of emotion that had nothing to do with temper.

Grimly, he considered that the physical attraction that had drawn him away from The Atraeus Group's head office on Medinos, when his legal counsel could have handled the formalities, was clouding his judgment.

No, that wasn't it. Two years ago Constantine had finally learned to separate sexual desire from business. He was no longer desperate.

This time if and when Sienna Ambrosi came to his bed, it would be on his terms, not hers.

"I'm not here to put flowers on Roberto's grave."

"Or allow her to grieve. Ever heard of tomorrow?" Lucas shrugged into his jacket and slammed the door of the Audi.

Constantine winced at Lucas's treatment of the expensive car. Lucas hadn't been old enough to remember the bad old days when the Atraeus family had been so poor they hadn't been able to afford a car, but Constantine could. His father's discovery of a rich gold mine on the Mediterranean island of Medinos hadn't altered any of his childhood memories. He would never forget what it had felt like to have nothing. "When it comes to the Ambrosi family, tomorrow will be too late." Resignation laced his tone as he eyed the press gathering like vultures at a feast. "Besides, it looks like the story has already been leaked. Bad timing or not, I want answers."

And to take back the money Roberto Ambrosi had conned out of their dying father while Constantine had been out of the country.

Funeral or not, he would unravel the scam he had discovered just over a week ago. After days of unreturned calls and hours of staking out the apparently empty residences of the Ambrosi family, his patience was gone, as was the desire to finish this business discreetly.

Lucas fell into step beside Constantine as he started toward the dispersing mourners. Grimly, Constantine noted that Lucas's attention was fixed on the younger Ambrosi daughter, Carla.

"Are you certain Sienna's involved?"

Constantine didn't bother to hide his incredulity.

Just what were the odds that the woman who had agreed to marry him two years ago, knowing that her father was leveraging an under-the-table deal with his, hadn't known about Roberto's latest scam? "She knows."

"You know what Roberto was like—"

"More than willing to exploit a dying man."

Constantine made brief eye contact with the two bodyguards who had accompanied them in a separate vehicle. The protection wasn't his choice, but as the CEO of a multibillion-dollar corporation, he'd had to deal with more than his share of threats.

As they neared the graveside, Constantine noted the absence of male family members or escorts. The wealthy and powerful Ambrosi family, who had employed his grandfather as a gardener, now only consisted of Margaret—Roberto's widow—the two daughters, Sienna and Carla, and a collection of elderly aunts and distant cousins.

As he halted at the edge of the mounded grave, the heavy cloud, which had been steadily building overhead, slid across the face of the midday sun and Sienna's dark gaze finally locked with his. In that fractured moment, something close to joy flared, as if she had forgotten that two years ago, when it had come down to a choice between him or the money, she had gone for the cash.

For a long, drawn out moment, Constantine was held immobile by a shifting sense of déjà vu, a powerful moment of connection he had been certain he would never again feel.

Something kicked in his chest, an errant pulse of emotion, and instead of dragging his gaze away he allowed himself to be caught, entangled...

A split second later a humid gust of wind sent leaves flying. In the few moments it took Sienna to anchor the honeyed fall of her hair behind one ear, the dreamy incandescence that had ensnared him—fooled him—so completely two years ago was gone, replaced by stunned disbelief.

A kick of annoyance that, evidently, despite all of his unreturned calls, Sienna had failed to register his presence in Sydney, was edged by relief. For a moment there, he had almost lost it, but now they were both back on the same, familiar page.

Constantine terminated the eye contact and transferred his attention to the freshly mounded soil, now covered by lavish floral tributes. Reasserting his purpose, reminding himself.

Roberto Ambrosi had been a liar, a thief and a con man, but Constantine would give him his due: he had known when to make his exit.

Sienna, however, had no such avenue of escape.

Sienna's heart slammed hard as Constantine closed the distance between them. Just for a few moments, exhausted by sadness and worn-out from fighting the overwhelming relief that she no longer had to cope with her father's gambling addiction, she had let the grimness of the cemetery fade.

She'd trained herself to be a relentlessly positive thinker, but even for her, the wispy daydream had been unusually creative: a reinvention of the past, where love came first, instead of somewhere down a complex list of assets and agendas. Then she had turned and for a disorienting moment, the future she had once thought was hers—and which she had needed with a fierceness that still haunted her—had taken on dazzling life. Constantine.

The reality of his clean, powerful features—coal-black hair brushing broad shoulders and the faintly resinous male scent that never failed to make her heart pound—had shocked her back to reality.

"What are you doing here?" she demanded curtly. Since the embarrassing debacle two years ago, the Ambrosis and the Atraeuses had preserved an icy distance. Constantine was the last person she expected to see at her father's funeral, and the least welcome.

Constantine's fingers closed around hers. The warm, slightly rough, skin-on-skin contact sent a hot, tingling shock through her. She inhaled sharply and a hint of the cologne that had sent her spiraling into the past just seconds ago made her stomach clench.

Constantine was undeniably formidable and gorgeous. Once he had fascinated her to the point that she had broken her cardinal rule. She had stopped thinking in favor of feeling. Big mistake.

Constantine had been out of her league, period. He was too rich, too powerful and, as she had found out to her detriment, utterly focused on protecting his family's business empire.

Bitterly, she reflected that the tabloids had it right. Ruthless in business, ditto in bed. The CEO of The Atraeus Group was a catch. Just don't "bank" on a wedding.

He leaned forward, close enough that his cleanly shaven jaw almost brushed her cheek. For an electrifying moment she thought he was actually going to kiss her, then the remoteness of his expression wiped that thought from her mind.

"We need to talk." His voice was deep and curt—a cosmopolitan mix of accents that revealed that, his Mediterranean heritage aside, he had been educated in the States. "Five minutes. In the parking lot." Jerking her fingers free, Sienna stepped back, her high heels sinking into the soft ground.

Meet with the man who had proposed one week, then discarded her the next because he believed she was a calculating gold digger?

That would be when hell froze over.

"We don't have anything to discuss."

"Five minutes. Be there."

Stomach tight, she stared at the long line of his back as he strolled away through the ranks of marble headstones. Peripherally she noticed Lucas and Zane, Constantine's two brothers, flanking him. Two security guards kept onlookers and the reporters who inevitably hounded the Atraeus family at bay.

Tension hummed through her at the presence of both brothers and the security. The bodyguards were a reality check, underlining the huge gulf between her life and his.

She registered a brief touch on her arm. Her sister, Carla. With an effort of will, Sienna shook off the shock of Constantine's presence and her own unsettling reactions. Her father's sudden death and the messy financial fallout that followed had consumed every waking moment for the past few days. Despite that, all it had taken had been one fractured moment looking into Constantine's gaze and she had forgotten where she was and why.

Carla frowned. "You look as white as a sheet. Are you all right?"

"I'm fine." Desperate to regain her equilibrium, Sienna dug in her purse, found her compact and checked her makeup. After the tears in church and the humid heat, any trace of the light makeup she had applied that morning was gone. Her hair was tousled and her eyes were red-rimmed—the exact opposite of her usual cool, sophisticated façade.

Carla—who was far more typically Medinian than Sienna in appearance with glossy dark hair and stunning light blue eyes that stopped people in their tracks—watched the Atraeus brothers, an odd expression in her eyes. "What are they doing here? Please don't tell me you're seeing Constantine again."

Sienna snapped the compact closed and dropped it into her purse. "Don't worry, I'm not crazy."

Just confused.

"Then what did they want?"

Carla's clipped demand echoed Sienna's question, although she couldn't afford the luxury of either anger or passion. For the sake of her family and their company, she had to be controlled and unruffled, no matter how worried she felt. "Nothing."

Constantine's series of commands replayed itself in her mind. Another gust, this one laced with fat droplets of rain, snapped her numbed brain back into high gear. Suddenly she formed a connection that made her pulse pound and her stomach hollow out.

Oh, damn. She needed to think, and quickly.

Over the past three days, she had spent long hours sifting through her father's private papers and financial records. She had found several mystifyingly large deposits she couldn't match to any of the business figures. Money had come in over a two-month period. A very large amount. The money had been used to prop up Ambrosi Pearls' flagging finances and cover her father's ongoing gambling debts, but she had no idea of its source. At first she thought the money had to be winnings, but the similar amounts had confused her. Roberto Ambrosi had won large sums of money in the past, but the amounts had differed wildly.

Now Constantine wanted a conversation.

Desperate to deny the conclusion that was forming, and to distract Carla, who was still locked on the Atraeus brothers like a heat-seeking missile, she craned around, searching for their mother. "Mom needs help."

Carla had also spotted the reporter chatting to Margaret Ambrosi, who was exhausted and still a little shaky from the sedatives the doctor had prescribed so she could sleep. "Oh, heck. I'll get her. It's time we left anyway. We were supposed to be at Aunt Via's for lunch ten minutes ago."

A private family lunch at the apartment of their father's

sister, Octavia, not a wake, which Sienna had decreed was an unnecessary luxury.

The last four days since her father had collapsed and died from a heart attack had been a roller-coaster ride, but that didn't change the reality. The glory days of Ambrosi Pearls, when her grandfather had transferred the company from the disaster zone Medinos had become during World War II to Sydney, were long gone. She had to balance the need to bolster business confidence by giving the impression of wealth and stability against the fact that they were operating on a shoestring budget. Luckily, her father had had a small insurance policy, enough to cover basic funeral expenses, and she'd had the excuse of Margaret Ambrosi's poor health to veto any socializing.

Her gaze narrowed. "Tell Via I'm not going to be able to make it for lunch. I'll see you at home later on."

After she had gotten rid of Constantine.

Constantine sent a brooding glance at the sky as he unlocked the Audi and settled in to wait for Sienna.

From the backseat Zane crossed his arms over his chest and coolly surveyed the media who were currently trying to bluff their way past Constantine's security. "I can see she still really likes you."

Constantine stifled his irritation. At twenty-four, Zane was several years his junior. Sometimes the chasm seemed much wider than six years. "This is business." Not pleasure.

Lucas slid into the passenger-side seat. "Did you get a chance to discuss the loan with Roberto?"

The words *before he died* hung in the air.

Constantine dragged at his tie. "Why do you think he had the heart attack?"

Apparently Roberto had suffered from a heart condition. Instead of showing up at Constantine's house, as arranged for the meeting that he himself had requested, he had been seated at a blackjack table. When he hadn't shown up, Constantine had made some calls and found out that Roberto had gone directly to the casino, apparently feverishly trying to win the money he needed.

Constantine had sent his personal assistant Tomas to collect Ambrosi, because going himself would have attracted unwanted media attention. Tomas had arrived to find that seconds after a substantial win the older man had become unwell. Tomas had called an ambulance. Minutes later Roberto had clutched at his chest and dropped like a stone.

Constantine almost had a heart attack himself when he had heard. Contrary to reports that he was ruthless and unfeeling, he had been happy to discuss options with Roberto, but it was not just about him. He had his family and the business to consider and Roberto Ambrosi had conned his father.

Lucas's expression was thoughtful. "Does Sienna know that you arranged to meet with her father?"

"Not yet."

"But she will."

"Yep." Constantine stripped off his tie, which suddenly felt like a noose, and yanked at the top two buttons of his shirt.

He wanted to engage Sienna's attention, which was the whole point of him dealing with the problem directly.

It was a safe bet that, after practically killing her old man, he had it by now.

Thunder rumbled overhead. Sienna walked quickly toward her car, intending to grab the umbrella she had stashed on the backseat.

As she crossed the parking lot a van door slid open. A reporter stepped onto the steaming asphalt just ahead of her and lifted his camera. Automatically, her arm shot up, fending off the flash.

A second reporter joined the first. Spinning on her heel, Sienna changed direction, giving up on the notion of staying dry. Simultaneously, she became aware that another news van had just cruised into the parking lot.

This wasn't part of the polite, restrained media representation that had been present at the beginning of the funeral. These people were predatory, focused, and no doubt drawn by the lure of Constantine and the chance to reinvent an old scandal.

The disbelief she'd felt as she'd met Constantine's gaze across her father's grave increased. How dare he come to the funeral? Did he plan to expose them all, most especially her mother, to another media circus?

With an ominous crash of thunder, the rain fell hard, soaking her. Fingers tightening on her purse, she lengthened her stride, breaking into a jog as she rounded the edge of a strip of shade trees that bisected the parking lot. She threw a glance over her shoulder, relieved that the rain had beaten the press back, at least temporarily. A split second later she collided with the solid barrier of a male chest. Constantine.

The hard, muscled imprint of his body burned through the wet silk of her dress as she clutched at a broad set of shoulders.

He jerked his head at a nearby towering oak. "This way. There are more reporters on the other side of the parking lot."

His hand landed in the small of her back. Sienna controlled a small shiver as she felt the heat of his palm, and her heart lurched because she knew Constantine must have followed her with the intent of protecting her. "Thank you."

She appreciated the protection, but that didn't mean she was comfortable with the scenario.

He urged her beneath the shelter of the huge, gnarled oak. The thick, dark canopy of leaves kept the worst of the rain off, but droplets still splashed down, further soaking her hair and the shoulders of her dress.

She found a tissue in her purse and blotted moisture from her face. She didn't bother trying to fix her makeup since there was likely to be very little of it left.

Within moments the rain slackened off and a thin shaft of sunlight penetrated the watery gloom, lighting up the parking lot and the grassy cemetery visible through the trees. Without warning the back of her nose burned and tears trickled down her face. Blindly, she groped for the tissue again.

"Here, use this."

A large square of white linen was thrust into her hand. She sniffed and swallowed a watery, hiccuping sob.

A moment later she found herself wrapped close, her face pressed against Constantine's shoulder, his palm hot against the damp skin at the base of her neck. After a moment of stiffness she gave in and accepted his comfort.

She had cried when she was alone, usually at night and in the privacy of her room so she wouldn't upset her mother, who was still in a state of distressed shock. Most of the time, because she had been so frantically busy she'd managed to contain the grief, but every now and then something set her off.

At some point Constantine loosened his hold enough that she could blow her nose, but it seemed now that she'd started crying, she couldn't stop and the tears kept flowing, although more quietly now. She remained locked in his arms, his palm massaging the hollow between her shoulder blades in a slow, soothing rhythm, the heat from his body driving out the damp chill. Drained by grief, she was happy to just be, and to soak in his hard warmth, the reassurance of his solid male power.

She became aware that the rain had finally stopped, leaving the parking lot wreathed in trailing wisps of steam. In a short while she would pull free and step back, but for the moment her head was thick and throbbing from the crying and she was too exhausted to move.

Constantine's voice rumbled in her ear. "We need to leave. We can't talk here."

She shifted slightly and registered that at some point Constantine had become semi aroused.

For a moment memories crowded her, some blatantly sensual, others laced with hurt and scalding humiliation.

Oh, no, no way. She would not feel this.

Face burning, Sienna jerked free, her purse flying. Shoving wet hair out of her face, she bent to retrieve her purse and the few items that had scattered—lip gloss, compact, car keys.

Her keys. Great idea, because she was leaving now.

If Constantine wanted a conversation he would have to reschedule. There was no way she was staying around for more of the same media humiliation she'd suffered two years ago.

"Damn. Sienna…"

Was that a hint of softness in his eyes? His voice?

No. Couldn't be.

When Constantine crouched down to help gather her things, she hurriedly shoveled the items into her bag. The rain had started up again, an annoying steamy drizzle, although that fact was now inconsequential because every part of her was soaked. Wet hair trailed down her cheeks, her dress felt like it had been glued on and there were puddles in her shoes.

Constantine hadn't fared any better. His gray suit jacket was plastered to his shoulders, his white shirt transparent enough that the bronze color of his skin showed through.

She dragged her gaze from the mesmerizing sight. "Uh-uh. Sorry." She shot to her feet. She was so not talking now. His transparent shirt had reminded her about her dress. It was black, so it wouldn't reveal as much as white fabric when wet, but silk was silk and it was thin. "Your conversation will have to wait. As you can see, I'm wet."

She spun on her heel, looking for an avenue of escape that didn't contain reporters with microphones and cameras.

His arm snaked around her waist, pulling her back against the furnace heat of his body. "After four days of unreturned calls," he growled into her ear, sending a hot shiver down her spine, "if you think I'm going to cool my heels for one more second, you can think again."

Two

Infuriated by the intimacy of his hold and the torrent of unwanted sensation, Sienna pried at Constantine's fingers. "Let. Me. Go."

"No." His gaze slid past hers.

Movement flickered at the periphery of Sienna's vision, she heard a car door slam.

Constantine muttered something curt beneath his breath. Now that the torrential downpour was over, the media were emerging from their vehicles.

He spun her around in his arms. "I wasn't going to do this. You deserve what's coming."

Her head jerked up, catching his jaw and sending a hot flash of pain through her skull, which infuriated her even more. "Like I did last time? Oh, very cool, Constantine. As if I'm some kind of hardened criminal just because I care about my family—"

Something infinitely more dangerous than the threat of

unwanted media exposure stirred in his eyes. "Is that what you call it? Interesting concept."

His level tone burned, more than the edgy heat that had invaded her body, or the castigating guilt that had eaten at her for the past two years. That maybe their split had been all her fault, and not just a convenient quick exit for a wealthy bachelor who had developed cold feet. That maybe she had committed a crime in not revealing how dysfunctional and debt-ridden her family was.

Her jaw tightened. "What did I ever do to truly hurt you, Constantine?"

Grim amusement curved his mouth. "If you're looking for a declaration, you're wasting your breath."

"Don't I know it." She planted her palms on his chest and pushed.

He muttered a low, rough Medinian phrase. "Stay still."

The Medinian language—an Italian dialect with Greek and Arabic influences—growled out in that deep velvet tone, sent a shock of awareness through her along with another hot tingling shiver.

Darn, darn, darn. Why did she have to like that?

Incensed that some crazy part of her was actually turned on by this, she kept up the pressure, her palms flattened against the solid muscle of his chest, maintaining the bare inch of space that existed between them.

An inch that wasn't nearly enough given that explosive contact.

Maybe, just maybe, the press would construe this little tussle as Constantine comforting her instead of an undignified scuffle. "Who called the press?" She stabbed an icy glare at him. "You?"

He gave a short bark of laughter. "*Cara,* I pay people to keep them off."

She warded off another one of those hot little jabs of response. "Don't call me—"

"What?" he said. "Darling? Babe? Sweetheart?"

His long, lean fingers gripped her jaw, trapping her. He bent close enough that anyone watching would assume their embrace was intimate, that he was about to kiss her.

A bittersweet pang went through her. She could see the crystalline depths of his eyes, the tiny beads of water clinging to his long, black lashes, the red mark on his jaw where her head had caught him, and a potent recollection spun her back to the first time they had met, two years ago.

It had been dark but, just like now, it had been raining. Her forward vision impeded by an umbrella, she had jogged from a taxi to the front door of a restaurant when they had collided. That time she had ended up on the wet pavement. Her all-purpose little black dress had been shorter, tighter. Consequently the sexy little side split had torn and her umbrella and one shoe had gone missing in action.

Constantine had apologized and asked if anything was broken. Riveted by the low, sexy timbre of his voice as he had crouched down and fitted the shoe back on her foot, she'd had the dizzying conviction that when she had fallen she had landed in the middle of her favorite fairy tale and Prince Charming had never looked so good. She had replied, "No, of course not."

Although, she had whimsically decided, when he left her heart could be broken.

The pressure of Constantine's grip on her arms zapped her back to the present. A muscle pulsed along the side of his jaw and she was made abruptly aware that, his mystifying anger aside, Constantine was just as disturbed as she.

"*Basta*," he growled. Enough.

Constantine jerked back from the soft curve of Sienna's mouth and the heady desire that, despite all of his efforts, he had never been able to eradicate. "You're wearing the same dress."

"No," she snapped back, informing him that in the confusion of the collision she had been as caught up by the past as he. "That was a cocktail dress."

"It feels the same." Wet and sleek and almost as sensual as her skin.

"Take your hands off me and you won't have to feel a thing."

Her voice was clipped and as cool as chipped ice, but the husky catch in her throat, her inability to entirely meet his gaze, told a different story.

He should let her go. She was clearly shaken. Lucas had been right—on the day of her father's funeral he should show compassion. But despite the demands of common decency, Constantine was unwilling to allow her any leeway at all.

Two years ago Sienna Ambrosi had achieved what no other woman had done. She had fooled him utterly. Touching her now should be repugnant to him. Instead, he was riveted by the fierce challenge in her dark eyes and the soft, utterly feminine shape of her body pressed against his. And drawn to find out exactly how vulnerable she was toward him. "Not until I have what I came for."

Her pupils dilated with shock, and any lingering uncertainty he might have entertained about her involvement in her father's scam evaporated. She was in this up to her elegant neck. The confirmation was unexpectedly depressing.

She blushed. "If it's a discussion you want, it will have to wait. In case you hadn't noticed, we're both wet and this is my father's funeral." She shoved at his chest again.

His hold on her arms tightened reflexively. The sudden full-body contact sent another electrifying shock wave of heat through Constantine, and in that moment the list of what he wanted, and needed, expanded.

Two years ago passion had blindsided him to the point that he had looked past his parents' stormy marital history and the tarnished reputation of the Ambrosi family in an attempt to grasp the mirage. He didn't trust what he had felt then, and he trusted it even less now. But he knew one thing for sure: one night wouldn't be enough.

Sienna threw a glance over her shoulder. "This media craziness is all your fault. If you hadn't turned up, they wouldn't have bothered with us."

"Calm down." Constantine studied the approaching reporters. "And unless you want to be on the six o'clock news, stay with me and keep quiet. I'll do the talking."

The two dark-suited men who had been flanking Constantine earlier materialized and strolled toward the reporters.

In that moment Sienna realized they had been joined by a television crew.

The barrage of questions started. "Ms. Ambrosi, is it true Ambrosi Pearls is facing bankruptcy?"

"Do you have any comment to make about your father allegedly conning money out of Lorenzo Atraeus?"

Several flashes went off, momentarily blinding her. An ultraslim, glamorous redhead darted beneath one of the bodyguard's arms and shoved a mike in her face. Sienna recognized the reporter from one of the major news channels. "Ms. Ambrosi, can you tell us if charges have been brought?"

Shock made Sienna go first hot then cold. "Charges—?"

"Unless you want a defamations suit," Constantine interjected smoothly, "I suggest you withdraw those questions. For the record Ambrosi Pearls and The Atraeus Group are engaged in negotiations over a business deal. Roberto Ambrosi's death has complicated those negotiations. That's all I'm prepared to say."

"Constantine, is this just about business?" The red-headed reporter, who had been maneuvered out of reach by one of the bodyguards, arched a brow, her face vivid and charming. "If a merger of some kind is in the wind, what about a wedding?"

Constantine hurried Sienna toward a sleek black Audi that had slid to a halt just yards away. "No comment."

Lucas climbed out of the driver's seat and tossed the keys over the hood.

Constantine plucked the keys out of midair and opened the passenger-side door. When Sienna realized Constantine meant her to get into the car, with him, she stiffened. "I have my own—"

Constantine leaned close enough that his breath scorched the skin below her ear. "You can come with me or stay. It's your choice. But if you stay you're on your own with the media."

A shudder of horror swept through her. "I'll come."

"In that case I'm going to need your car keys. One of my security team will collect your car and follow us. When we're clear of the press, you can have your little sports car back."

Suspicion flared. "How do you know I have a sports car?"

"Believe me, after the last few days there isn't much I don't know about you and your family."

"Evidently, from the answers you gave the press, you know a lot more than I do." She dug her keys out of her purse and handed them over. As badly as she resented it, Constantine's suggestion made sense. If she had to return to the cemetery to pick up the car later on, it was an easy bet she'd run into more reporters and more questions she wasn't equipped to answer.

Seconds later she was enclosed in the luxurious interior of the Audi, the tinted windows blocking out the media.

She reached for her seat belt. By the time she had it fastened, Constantine was accelerating away from the curb. Cool air from the air-conditioning unit flowed over her, raising gooseflesh on her damp skin.

Nerves strung taut at the intimacy of being enclosed in the cab of the Audi with Constantine, she reached into her purse and found her small traveling box of tissues. Pulling off a handful, she handed them to Constantine.

His gaze briefly connected with hers. "*Grazie.*"

She glanced away, her heart suddenly pounding. Hostilities were, temporarily at least, on hold. "You're welcome."

She pulled off more tissues and began blotting moisture from her face and arms. There was nothing she could do about her hair or her dress, or the fact that the backs of her legs were sticking to the very expensive leather seats.

She glanced in the rearview mirror. Her small sports car was right behind them, followed by the gleaming dark sedan, which contained the second of Constantine's bodyguards and his brothers. "I see you still travel with a SWAT team."

Constantine smoothly negotiated traffic. "They have their uses."

She flashed him a cool look. There was no way she would thank him yet, not when it was clear that Constantine's presence had attracted the press. Until he had showed up, neither she nor any member of her family had been harassed. She studied the clean line of his profile, the inky crescents of his lashes and the small scar high on one cheekbone. Unbidden, memories flickered—the dark bronze of his skin glowing in the morning light, the habit he'd had of sprawling across her bed, sheets twined around his hips, all long limbs and sleek muscle.

Hot color flooded her cheeks. Hastily she transferred her gaze to the traffic flowing around them. "Now that we're alone you can tell me what that media assault was all about." The very fact that Constantine had interceded on her behalf meant something was very wrong. "Conned? Charges? And what was that about negotiating a deal?"

With her background in commercial law, Sienna was Ambrosi Pearls' legal counsel. At no point in the past two years had her father so much as mentioned The Atraeus Group, or any financial dealings. After the loan Roberto had tried to negotiate had fallen through, along with her engagement, the subject had literally been taboo.

Constantine braked for a set of lights. "There is a problem, but I'm not prepared to discuss it while I'm driving."

While they waited in traffic her frustration mounted. "If you won't discuss it…" her fingers sketched quotation marks in the air, "then at least tell me why, if Ambrosi Pearls is supposed to have done something so wrong, you're helping me instead of throwing me to the media wolves?"

"In an instant replay of the way I treated you two years ago?"

The silky edge to his voice made her tense. "Yes."

The lights turned green. Constantine accelerated through the intersection. "Because you're in shock, and you've just lost your father."

Something about the calmness of his manner sent a prickle of unease down her spine, sharpened all of her senses.

His ruthless business reputation aside, Constantine was known to be a philanthropist with a compassionate streak. He frequently gave massive sums to charities, but that compassion had never been directed toward either her or her family.

"I don't believe you. There's something else going on." During the short conversation during which he had broken their engagement, Sienna had tried to make him understand the complications of her father's skyrocketing gambling debts and the struggle she had simply to support her mother and keep Ambrosi Pearls afloat. That in the few stressful days she'd had before Constantine had discovered the deal, the logic of her father asking Lorenzo Atraeus for a loan had seemed viable.

She had wasted her breath.

Constantine had been too busy walking out the door to listen to the painful details of her family's financial struggle.

"As you heard from the reporters, there is very definitely 'something else going on.' If you'll recall, that was the reason our engagement ended."

"My father proposed a business deal that your father wanted."

"Reestablishing a pearl facility on Medinos was a proposal based on opportunism and nostalgia, not profit."

Her anger flared at the opportunism crack. "And the bottom line is so much more important to you than honoring the past or creating something beautiful."

"Farming pretty baubles in a prime coastal location slated for development as a resort didn't make business sense then and it makes no sense now. The Atraeus Group has more lucrative business options than restoring Medinos's pearl industry."

"Options that don't require any kind of history or sentiment. Like mining gold and building luxury hotels."

His gaze briefly captured hers. "I don't recall that you

ever had any problem with the concept of making money. As I remember it, two years ago money came before 'sentiment.'"

Sienna controlled the rush of guilty heat to her cheeks. "I refuse to apologize for a business deal I didn't instigate." Or for being weak enough to have felt an overwhelming relief that, finally, there could be an answer to her family's crippling financial problems. "My only sin was not having the courage to tell you about the deal."

She stared out of the passenger-side window as Constantine turned into the parking lot of a shopping mall. It was too late now to admit that she had been afraid the impending disgrace of her father's gambling and financial problems would harm their engagement.

As it turned out, the very thing she had feared had happened. Constantine believed she had broken his trust, that her primary interest in him had always been monetary. "I apologized for not discussing the deal with you," she said, hating the husky note in her voice, "but, quite frankly, that was something I would have assumed your father would have done."

Constantine slotted the Audi into a space. She heard the snick as he released his seat belt. He turned in his seat and rested an arm along the back of hers, making her even more suffocatingly aware of his presence.

"Even knowing that my father's lack of transparency indicated he was keeping the deal under wraps?"

A dark sedan slid into a space beside the Audi. One of Constantine's bodyguards, with Lucas in the passenger seat and Zane in the rear. A flash of cream informed her that her sports car, driven by the second bodyguard, had just been parked in an adjacent space.

Feeling hemmed in by overlarge Medinian males, Sienna released her seat belt and reached for her purse. "I didn't understand that you were so against the idea of re-establishing a pearl industry on Medinos."

Stupidly, when she hadn't been frightened that she would lose Constantine and burying her head in the sand, she had been too busy coping with the hectic media pressure their engagement had instigated.

Life in a fish tank hadn't been fun.

"Just as I couldn't understand why you failed to discuss the agreement, which just happened to have been drawn up the day following our engagement announcement."

Her gaze snapped to his. "How many times do I have to say it? I had nothing to do with the loan. Think about it, Constantine. If I was that grasping and devious I would have waited until after we were married."

A tense silence stretched, thickened. Now she really couldn't breathe. Fumbling at the car door, she pushed it wide.

Constantine leaned across and hauled the door shut, pinning Sienna in place before she could scramble out. The uncharacteristic surge of temper that flowed through him at the deliberate taunt was fueled by the physical frustration that had been eating at him ever since he had decided he had to see her again.

The question of just why he had taken one look at Sienna two years ago and fallen in instant lust, he decided, no longer existed. It had ceased to be the instant he had glimpsed her silky blond head at the funeral. Even wet and bedraggled, her eyes red-rimmed from crying, Sienna was gorgeous in a fragile, exotic way that hooked into every male instinct he possessed.

The combination of delicacy paired with sensuality, in Anglo-Saxon terms, was crazy-making. He was at once caught between the desire to protect and cushion her from the slightest upset and the desire to take her to bed and make love to her until she surrendered utterly.

It was an unsettling fact that he would rather argue with Sienna than spend time with any other woman, no matter how gorgeous or focused on pleasing him she might be.

"Now that's interesting. I assumed that the reason you stayed quiet about the loan was that your father needed the money too badly to wait."

Her face went bone-white and he knew in that instant that he had gone too far.

Then, hot color burned along her cheekbones and the aura of haunted fragility evaporated. "Or maybe I was simply following orders?"

His gaze shifted to her pale mouth, the line of her throat as she swallowed. "No," he said flatly.

Sienna had been Roberto's precocious second-in-command for the past four years. She had run the family's pearl house with consummate skill and focused ambition while her father had steadily gambled the profits away at various casinos. The last time she had taken an order from Roberto, she had been in the cradle. If she had a weakness, it was that she needed money.

His money.

And she still did.

She pulled in a jerky breath. He felt the rise and fall of her breasts against his arm, the feathery warmth along his jaw as she exhaled. The light, evocative scent she wore teased his nostrils as flash after flash of memory turned the air molten.

A tap on the passenger-side window broke the tension. One of his security guards.

Constantine released his hold on the door handle, his temper tightly controlled as he watched Sienna climb out and collect her car keys.

Levering himself out of the Audi into the now blistering heat of early afternoon, Constantine gave the guard his instructions. For the past four days he had seldom been without an escort but for the next hour he required absolute privacy.

Peeling out of his damp jacket, he tossed it behind the driver's seat. He frowned as he noticed Lucas speaking with Sienna. From the brevity of the exchange he was aware that his brother had simply offered his condolences, but Sienna's smile evoked an unsettling response.

The fact that Lucas was every inch a dangerous Atraeus male shouldn't register, but after the charged few moments in the Audi, the knowledge of just how successful his brother was with women was distinctly unpalatable.

Constantine strolled toward Sienna as she slid her cell phone out of her purse and answered a call.

Lucas waylaid him with a brief jerk of his chin. "Are you sure you know what you're doing?"

"Positive."

"It didn't look like a business discussion back at the cemetery, and it sure as hell didn't look like a business discussion just then."

Constantine knew his gaze was cold enough to freeze. "Just as long as you remember that Sienna Ambrosi is my business."

Lucas lifted a brow. "Message received."

Jaw tight, Constantine watched as Lucas climbed into the passenger-side seat of the dark sedan. He lifted a hand as the car cruised out of the parking lot. Maybe he hadn't needed to warn Lucas off, but the instinct to do so had been knee-jerk and primitive. In that moment he had acknowledged one clear fact: for the foreseeable future, until he had gotten her out of his system, Sienna Ambrosi was his.

While he waited for Sienna to terminate her call, he grimly considered that fact, sifting through every nuance of the past hour. The tension that had gripped him from the moment he had laid eyes on Sienna at the funeral tightened another notch.

Constantine knew his own nature. He was focused, single-minded. When he fixed on a goal he achieved it. His absolute commitment to running the family business was both a necessity and a passion and he had never flinched from making hard choices. Two years ago, severing all connection with Sienna and the once pampered and aristocratic Ambrosi family had been one of those choices.

Sliding dark glasses onto the bridge of his nose, Constantine crossed his arms over his chest and studied the pure line of Sienna's profile, the luscious combination of creamy skin and dark eyes, her soft pale mouth.

Until he had been handed an investigative report he had commissioned on Ambrosi Pearls and had discovered that Sienna had been linked on at least three occasions with Alex Panopoulos, a wealthy retailer.

He still remembered the moment of disorientation, the grim fury when he'd considered that Panopoulos could be Sienna's lover.

He had soon eliminated that scenario.

According to the very efficient private eye employed by the security firm, Panopoulos was actively hunting but the Greek hadn't yet managed to snare either of the Ambrosi girls.

Sienna registered Constantine's impatience as she ended her conversation with Carla, who had been concerned that she had been caught up in the media frenzy in the parking lot.

Constantine lifted a brow. "Where do we talk? Your place or mine?"

Sienna dropped her phone back into her purse. After the tense moments in the car and the sensual shock of Constantine invading her space, she couldn't hide her dismay at the thought of Constantine's apartment. Two years ago they had spent a lot of time there. It had also been the scene of their breakup.

The thought of Constantine in the sanctuary of her own small place was equally unacceptable. "Not the apartments."

"I don't have the apartment anymore. I own a house along the coast."

"I thought you liked living in town."

"I changed my mind."

Just like he had about her. Instantly and unequivocally.

He opened the door of her small soft-top convertible. Feeling as edgy as a cat, her stomach tight with nerves, she slipped into the driver's seat, carefully avoiding any physical contact. "Carla's taken Mom to a family lunch at Aunt Via's apartment, so they'll be occupied for the next couple of hours. I can meet you at my parent's beach house at Pier Point. That's where I've been staying since Dad died."

Constantine closed her door. Bracing his hands on the window frame, he leaned down, maintaining eye contact. "That explains why you haven't been at your apartment, although not why you haven't been returning my calls at work."

"If you wanted to get hold of me that badly you should have rung my mother."

"I got through twice," he said grimly. "Both times I got Carla."

Sienna could feel her cheeks heating. After Sienna's breakup with Constantine, Carla had become fiercely protective. Constantine hadn't gotten through, because Carla would have made it her mission to stop him.

"Sorry about that," she said, without any trace of sympathy in her voice. "Carla said there had been a couple of crank calls, then the press started bothering Mom in the evenings, so we went to stay at the beach house."

Constantine had also left a number of messages at work, which, when she had been in the office at all, Sienna had ignored. She had been feverishly trying to unravel her father's twisted affairs. Calling Constantine had ranked right up there with chatting to disgruntled creditors or having a cozy discussion with IRD about the payments Ambrosi Pearls had failed to make.

"If Pier Point is hostile territory, maybe we should meet on neutral ground?"

Was that a hint of amusement in his voice?

No, whatever it was Constantine was feeling, it wasn't amusement. There had been a definite predatory edge to him. She had seen a liquid silver flash of it at the gravesite, then been burned by it again in the parking lot.

The foreboding that had gripped her at the cemetery returned, playing havoc with her pulse again.

Suddenly shaky with a combination of exhaustion and nerves, she started the car and busied herself with fastening her seat belt. "The beach house is far enough out of town that the press isn't likely to be staking it out. If this conversation is taking the direction I think it is, we'd better meet there."

"Tell me," he said curtly. "What direction, exactly, do you think this conversation will take?"

"A conversation with Constantine Atraeus?" Her smile was as tightly strung as her nerves. "Now let me see… Two options—sex or money. Since it can't possibly be sex, my vote's on the money."

Three

Money was the burning agenda, but as Sienna drove into Pier Point, with Constantine following close enough behind to make her feel herded, she wasn't entirely sure about the sex.

Earlier, in the Audi, Constantine's muscular heat engulfing her, she had been sharply aware of his sexual intent. He had wanted her and he hadn't been shy about letting her know. The moment had been underscored by an unnerving flash of déjà vu.

The first time Constantine had kissed her had been in his car. He had cupped her chin and lowered his mouth to hers, and despite her determination to keep her distance, she had wound her arms around his neck, angled her jaw and leaned into the kiss. Even though she had only known him for a few hours she had been swept off her feet. She hadn't been able to resist him, and he had known it.

Shaking off the too-vivid recollection, she signaled and

turned her small sports car into her mother's driveway.
Barely an hour after the unpleasant clash across her father's grave, those kinds of memories shouldn't register.
The fact that Constantine wanted her meant little more
than that he was a man with a normal, healthy libido. In
the past two years he had been linked with a number of
wealthy, beautiful women, each one a serious contender
for the position of Mrs. Constantine Atraeus.

He turned into the driveway directly behind her. As
Sienna accelerated up the small, steep curve, the sense of
being pursued increased. She used her remote to close the
electronic gates at the bottom of the drive, just in case the
press had followed. After parking, she grabbed her handbag and walked across the paved courtyard that fronted
the old cliff-top house.

Constantine was already out of his car. She noticed that
in the interim he'd rolled his sleeves up, baring tanned,
muscled forearms. She unlocked the front door and as he
loomed over her in the bare, sun-washed hall, her stomach, already tense, did another annoying little flip.

He indicated she precede him. She couldn't fault his
manners, but that didn't change the fact that with Constantine padding behind her like a large, hunting cat, she
felt like prey.

"What happened to the furniture?"

The foreign intonation in his deep voice set her on edge
all over again. Suddenly, business agenda or not, it seemed
unbearably intimate to be alone with him in the quiet stillness of the almost empty house.

Sienna skimmed blank walls that had once held a collection of paintings, including an exquisitely rendered
Degas. "Sold, along with all the valuable artwork my
grandfather collected."

She threw him a tight smile. "Auctioned, along with

every piece of real jewelry Mom, Carla and I owned—including the pearls. Now isn't that a joke? We own a pearl house, but we can't afford our own products."

She pushed open the ornate double doors to her father's study and stood aside as Constantine walked into the room, which held only a desk and a couple of chairs.

His gaze skimmed bare floorboards and the ranks of empty built-in mahogany bookshelves, which had once housed a rare book collection. She logged the moment he finally comprehended what a sham their lives had become. They sold pearls to the wealthy and projected sleek, rich-list prosperity for the sake of the company, but the struggle had emptied them out, leaving her mother, Carla and herself with nothing.

He surveyed the marks on the wall that indicated paintings had once hung there and the dangling ceiling fitting that had once held a chandelier. "What didn't he sell to pay gambling debts?"

For a split second Sienna thought Constantine was taking a cheap shot, implying that both she and Carla had been up for auction, but she dismissed the notion. When he had broken their engagement his reasons had been clear-cut. After her father's failed deal he had made it plain he could no longer trust her or the connection with her family. His stand had been tough and uncompromising, because he hadn't allowed her a defense, but he had never at any time been malicious.

"We still have the house, and we've managed to keep the business running. It's not much, but it's a start. Ambrosi employs over one hundred people, some of whom have worked for us for decades. When it came down to keeping those people in work, selling possessions and family heirlooms wasn't a difficult choice."

Although she didn't expect Constantine with his reputation for being coldly ruthless in business to agree. "Wait here," she said stiffly, "I'll get towels."

Glad for a respite, she walked upstairs to her room. With swift movements she peeled off her ruined shoes, changed them for dry ones then checked her appearance in the dresser mirror. A small shock went through her when she noted the glitter of her eyes and the warm flush on her cheeks. With her creased dress and tousled hair, the look was disturbingly sensual.

Walking through to the bathroom, she towel-dried her hair, combed it and decided not to bother changing the dress, which was almost dry. She shouldn't care whether Constantine thought she was attractive or not, and if she did, she needed to squash the notion. The sooner this conversation was over and he was gone, the better.

She collected a fresh towel from the linen closet and walked back downstairs.

Constantine turned from the breathtaking view of the Pacific Ocean as she entered the study, his light gaze locking briefly with hers.

Breath hitching at the sudden pounding of her heart, Sienna handed him the towel, taking care not to let their fingers brush. She indicated the view. "One of the few assets we haven't yet had to sell, but only because Mom sold the town house this week. Although this place is mortgaged to the hilt."

It would go, too. It was only a matter of time.

He ran the towel briefly over his hair before tossing it over the arm of a chair. "I didn't know things had gotten this bad."

But, she realized, he had known her father's gambling had gotten out of hand. "Why should you? Ambrosi Pearls has nothing to do with either Medinos or The Atraeus Group."

His expression didn't alter, but suddenly any trace of compassion was gone. Good. Relief unfolded inside her. If anything could kill the skittish knowledge that not only was she on edge, she was sexually on edge, a straightforward business discussion would do it.

She indicated that Constantine take a seat and walked around to stand behind her father's desk, underlining her role as Ambrosi Pearls' CEO. "Not many people know the company's financial position, and I would appreciate if you wouldn't spread it around. With the papers speculating about losses, I'm having a tough time convincing some of our customers that Ambrosi is solid."

Constantine ignored the chair in favor of standing directly opposite her, arms crossed over his chest, neutralizing her attempt at dominance.

Sienna averted her gaze from the way the damp fabric of his shirt clung to his shoulders, the sleek aura of male power that swirled around Constantine Atraeus like a cloak.

"It must have been difficult, trying to run a business with a gambler at the helm."

As abruptly as if an internal switch had been thrown, Sienna's temper boiled over. Finally, the issue he hadn't wanted to talk about two years ago. "I don't think you can understand at all. Did your father gamble?"

Constantine's gaze narrowed. "Only in a good way."

"Of course." Lorenzo Atraeus had been an excellent businessman. "With good information and solid investment backing so he could make money, then more money. Unlike my father who consistently found ways to lose it, both in business and at the blackjack table." Her heart was pounding; her blood pressure was probably off the register. "You don't know what it's like to lose and keep on losing because you can't control someone in your family."

"My family has some experience with loss."

His expression was grim, his tone remote, reminding her that the Atraeus family had lived in poverty on Medinos for years, farming goats. Constantine's grandfather had even worked for hers, until the Ambrosis had lost their original pearl business when it had been bombed during the war. But that had all been years ago. This was now.

She leaned forward, every muscle taut. "Running a business with a gambler at the helm hasn't been easy."

He spread his palms on the desk and suddenly they were nose to nose. "If it got that bad why didn't you get out?"

And suddenly, the past was alive between them and she was taking a weird, giddy delight in fighting with Constantine. Maybe it was a reaction, a backlash to the grief and strain of the funeral, or the simple fact that she was sick of clamping down on her emotions and tired of hiding the truth. "And abandon my family and all the people who depend on our company for their livelihood?" She smiled tightly. "It was never an option, and I hope I never arrive at that point. Which brings us to the conversation you want so badly. How much do we owe?"

"Did you know that two months ago your father paid a visit to Medinos?"

Shock held her immobile. "No."

"Are you aware that he had plans to start up a pearl industry there?"

"Not possible." But blunt denial didn't ease the cold dread forming in her stomach. "We barely have enough capital to operate in Sydney." Her father had driven what had been a thriving business into the ground. "We're in no position to expand."

Something shifted in Constantine's gaze, and for a

fleeting second she had a sense that, like it or not, he had reached some kind of decision.

Constantine indicated a document he must have dropped on the desk while she'd been out of the room. Sienna studied the thick parchment. Her knees wobbled. A split second later she was sitting in her father's old leather chair, fighting disbelief as she skimmed the text.

Not one loan but several. She had expected the first loan to date back to the first large deposit she had found in her father's personal account several weeks ago, and she wasn't disappointed.

She lifted her head to find Constantine still watching her. "Why did Lorenzo lend anything to my father? He knew he had a gambling problem."

"My father was terminally ill and clearly not in his right mind. When he died a month ago, we knew there was a deficit. Unfortunately, the documents confirming the loans to your father weren't located until five days ago."

Her jaw clenched. "Why didn't you stop him?"

"Believe me, if I had been there I would have, but I was out of the country at the time. To compound the issue, he bypassed the usual channels and retained an old friend, his retired legal counsel, to draw up the contracts."

Constantine ran his fingers around his nape, his expression abruptly impatient. "I see you're now beginning to understand the situation. Your father has been running Ambrosi Pearls and his gambling addiction on The Atraeus Group's money. An amount he 'borrowed' from a dying man on the basis of a business he had no intention of setting up."

Fraud.

Now the questions fired at her by the reporters made sense. "Is that what you told the press?"

"I think you know me better than that."

She felt oddly relieved. It shouldn't matter that Constantine hadn't been the one who had leaked the story, but it did.

Someone, most likely an employee, would have sold the information to the press.

Sienna stared at the figure involved and felt her normal steely optimism and careful plans for Ambrosi Pearls dissolve.

Firming her chin, she stared out at the bright blue summer sky and the endless, hazy vista of the Pacific Ocean, and tried to regroup. There had to be a way out of this; she had wrangled the company out of plenty of tight spots before. All she had to do was think.

Small, disparate pieces of information clicked into place. Constantine not wanting to talk to her at the funeral or in the car, the way he had remained standing while she had read through the documents.

He had wanted to watch her reaction when she read the paperwork.

Her gaze snapped to his. "You thought I was part of this."

Constantine's expression didn't alter.

Something in her plummeted. Sienna pushed to her feet. The loan documents cascaded to the floor; she barely noticed them. When Lorenzo Atraeus had died, he had left an enormous fortune based on a fabulously rich gold mine and a glittering retail and hotel empire to his three sons, Constantine, Lucas and Zane.

It shouldn't be uppermost in her mind, but it suddenly struck her that if Ambrosi Pearls was in debt to The

Atraeus Group, by definition—as majority shareholder—that meant Constantine.

Constantine's gaze was oddly bleak. "Now you're getting it. Unless you can come up with the money, I now own Ambrosi Pearls lock, stock and barrel."

Four

The vibration of a cell phone broke the electrifying silence.

Constantine answered the call, relieved at the sudden release of tension, the excuse to step back from a situation that had spiraled out of control.

He had practically threatened Sienna, a tactic he had never before resorted to, even when dealing with slick, professional fraudsters. In light of the heart-pounding discovery that Sienna hadn't known about her father's latest scam, his behavior was inexcusable. He should have stepped back, reassessed, postponed the meeting.

Gotten a grip before he wrecked any chance that she might want him again.

Unfortunately, Sienna doing battle with him across the polished width of her father's desk had put a kink in his strategy. Her cheeks had been flushed, her eyes fiery, shunting him back in time to hot, sultry nights and tangled sheets. It was hard to think tactically when all he wanted to do was kiss her.

She had never been this animated or passionate with him before, he realized. Even in bed he had always been grimly aware that she was holding back, that there was a part of her he couldn't reach.

That she was more committed to Ambrosi Pearls than she had ever been to him.

To compound the problem, he had mentioned the bad old days when the Atraeus family had been dirt-poor. Given that he wanted Sienna back in his bed, the last thing he needed was for her to view him as the grandson of the gardener.

Jaw tight, he turned to stare out at the sea view as he spoke to his personal assistant. Tomas had been trying to reach him for the past hour. Constantine had been aware he had missed calls, something he seldom did, but for once, business hadn't been first priority.

Another uncharacteristic lapse.

Constantine hung up and broodingly surveyed Sienna as she gathered the pages she had knocked onto the floor and stacked them in a precise pile on the desktop. Even with her dress crumpled and her makeup gone, she looked elegant and classy, the quintessential lady.

A car door slammed somewhere in the distance. The staccato of high heels on the walkway was followed by the sound of the front door opening.

Constantine caught the flare of desperation in Sienna's gaze. Witnessing that moment of sheer panic was like a kick in the chest. He was here to right a wrong that had been done to his father, but Sienna was also trying to protect her family, most specifically her mother, from him. It was a sobering moment. "Don't worry," he said quietly. "I won't tell her."

Sienna stifled a surge of relief and just had time to send Constantine a grateful glance before Margaret Ambrosi stepped into the room, closely followed by Carla.

"What's going on?" her mother demanded in the cool, clear tone that had gotten her through thirty years with a husband who had given her more heartache than joy. "And don't try to fob me off, because I know something's wrong."

"Mrs. Ambrosi." Constantine used a tone that was far gentler than any Sienna could ever remember him using with her. "My condolences. Sienna and I were just discussing the details of a business deal your husband initiated a few months ago."

Carla's jaw was set. "I don't believe Dad would have transacted anything without—"

Margaret Ambrosi's hand stayed her. "So that's why Roberto made the trip to Europe. I should have known."

Carla frowned. "He went to Paris and Frankfurt. He didn't go near the Mediterranean."

An emotion close to anger momentarily replaced the exhaustion etched on her mother's face.

"Roberto left a day earlier because he wanted to stop off at Medinos first. He said he wanted to visit the site of the old pearl facility and find his grandparents' graves. If anything should have warned me he was up to something that should have been it. Roberto didn't have a sentimental bone in his body. He went to Medinos on business."

"That's correct," Constantine said in the same gentle tone, and despite the antagonism and the towering issue of the debt, Sienna could have hugged him.

One of the qualities that had made her fall so hard for Constantine two years ago had been the way he was with his family. Put simply, he loved and protected them with the kind of fierce loyalty that still had the power to send a shiver down her spine. After years of coping with a father who had always put himself first, the prospect of being included in Constantine's family circle, of being the focus of that fierce protective instinct, had been utterly seductive.

That had been the prime reason she had frozen inside when she had found out that her father had done an under-the-table deal with Roberto Atraeus. She hadn't been able to discuss it; she had been afraid to even think about it. She had known how Constantine would react and when the details of the loan had surfaced, the very thing she had feared most had happened. He had shut her out.

She blinked, snapping herself out of a memory that still had the power to hurt.

Constantine checked his watch. "If you'll excuse me, I have another appointment. Once again, my apologies for intruding on your grief."

His cool gray eyes connected with hers, the message clear. They hadn't finished their discussion.

"I'll see you out." Shoving the loan documents out of sight in a drawer, she followed Constantine out into the bare hallway. As much as she didn't want to spend any more time with him, she did want to get him out of the house and away from her mother before she realized there was a problem.

The bright sunlight shafting through the open front door was glaring after the dim coolness of the study.

"Watch your step."

Constantine's hand cupped her elbow, the gesture nothing more than courtesy, but enough to reignite the humming awareness and the antagonism that had been so useful in getting her through the last hour and a half.

Pulse pounding, she lengthened her stride, moving away from the tingling heat of his touch and her growing conviction that Constantine wasn't entirely unhappy with the power he now wielded over Ambrosi Pearls, and her. That behind the business-speak simmered a very personal agenda.

Her stomach tightened at the thought, her mouth going dry as the taut moments in his car replayed themselves. Barely two hours ago Constantine Atraeus, the man, hadn't registered on her awareness. She had blanked him out, along with everything else that was not directly involved with either Ambrosi Pearls or her father's funeral arrangements. Now she couldn't seem to stop the hot flashes of memory and an acute awareness of him. "Thank you for not saying anything about the debt to Mom."

"If I'd thought your mother was involved, I would have mentioned it."

"Which means you do think I'm involved."

Suddenly the whole idea that she could be crazily attracted to Constantine again was so not an issue.

Constantine followed her out into the courtyard and depressed the Audi's key. The sleek car unlocked with an expensive thunk. "You've been running Ambrosi single-handedly for the past eighteen months. And paying Roberto's debts."

She grabbed a remote control from her car and opened the gate at the bottom of the driveway. As far as she was concerned, the sooner he left the better. "By selling family assets, not trying to take more loans when we're already overcommitted."

Constantine's phone buzzed. He picked up the call and spoke briefly in Medinian. She heard Lucas's name and mention of the company lawyer, Ben Vitalis. Business. That explained all three Atraeus brothers being in Sydney at the same time, no matter for how short a period. It also emphasized the fact that Constantine might be here to deal with the mess her father had entangled them both in, but on The Atraeus Group's global radar, Ambrosi Pearls was only a blip.

The tension that gripped her stomach and chest tightened another notch. Which, once again, pointed to the personal agenda.

Constantine terminated the call. "We have a lot to discuss, but the discussion will have to wait until tonight. I'll send a car for you at eight. We can talk over dinner."

She stiffened. Dinner definitely sounded more personal than business, which didn't make sense.

He had been gone for two years. In that time he hadn't ever contacted her. For the first couple of months, she had waited for him to call or to turn up on her doorstep and say he was sorry and that he wanted to try again. The fact that he never had had been an unexpected gift.

She had gotten over him. If he thought she was going to jump feetfirst into some kind of affair with him now, he could think again. "In case you didn't notice, I buried my father today. We have to talk, but I need a couple of days."

Which would give her time to consult their accountant and investigate options. The chance that she could either raise the loan money or make a big sale that quickly was slim, but she had to try. It would also give her time to step back from the mystifying knee-jerk reactions she kept having toward Constantine. She no longer loved him and she certainly did not like him. She could not want him.

Constantine opened the car door. "A few days ago that could have been arranged, but you chose to avoid me. I'm flying out at midnight tomorrow. If you can't find time before then, tomorrow there's a cocktail party at my house, a business meet and greet for The Atraeus Group's retail partners."

"No." As imperative as it was to come to grips with the looming financial disaster, the last thing she wanted was to attend a reception with Constantine, informal or not, at his house. "We'll have to reschedule. In any case I would prefer to talk during business hours."

In a neutral, business setting where the male/female dynamic could be neatly contained.

The businesslike gleam in Sienna's gaze sent irritation flashing through Constantine.

None of this was going as he had envisioned. Not only did he feel like a villain, but she was now trying to call the shots and he was on the verge of losing his temper again, something else that never happened. "We need to talk. When is the reading of the will scheduled?"

"This afternoon, at four."

He saw the moment the reality of her position sank in. If she didn't agree to a meeting he could conceivably send a representative to the reading of the will with the loan documents. It was something he had no intention of doing, specifically because it would frighten her mother.

"You're out of options, Sienna." Constantine slid behind the wheel of the Audi before he caved and started hemorrhaging options that would leave him out of her life altogether.

The engine started with a throaty purr. "Be ready tomorrow at eight."

The following morning, Constantine walked into The Atraeus Group's Sydney office. He was ten minutes late, not quite a first, but close. He had been late once before; two years ago to be exact.

Lucas and Zane, who were both gym freaks, were already there, looking sharp and energized against the clinical backdrop of chrome and leather furniture and executive gray walls. Constantine preferred to jog on the beach or swim rather than subject himself to a rigid workout program. Watching the sunrise and getting sand in his cross trainers was the one break he cut himself in a day that was already too regimented. After a near sleepless night spent pacing, however, this morning he had figured he could forgo his normal dawn run.

He zeroed in on the take-out coffee sitting on his desk and frowned in the direction of his brothers who were both regarding him with the kind of interested gaze that made him wonder if he'd grown an extra head or put his shirt on backward. "What?"

Zane ducked his head and stared hard at the glossy business magazine he was reading, which was odd in itself. His usual reading material involved fast boats, even faster cars and art installations that Constantine didn't pretend to understand. Lucas, meanwhile, hummed snatches of something vaguely familiar under his breath.

His temper now definitely on a short fuse, Constantine drank a mouthful of the coffee, which was lukewarm.

Lucas dropped a section of the morning paper on his desk. "Now that you've had some caffeine you'd better take a look at this."

Even though he had expected it, the photo taken at Roberto Ambrosi's funeral took his breath away. He remembered holding Sienna so she wouldn't walk into the barrage of cameras, but the clinch the reporter had snapped didn't look anything like protective restraint. His gaze was fused with hers, and he looked like he was about to kiss her. From memory, that was exactly how he had felt.

He skimmed the short article, going still inside when he read the statement that he had arrived in Sydney the day before Roberto Ambrosi had dropped dead from a heart attack for the specific purpose of arranging a meeting with the head of Ambrosi Pearls.

The article, thankfully, didn't go so far as to say he had

caused Ambrosi's fatal heart attack, but it did claim a wedding announcement was expected. The tune Lucas had been humming was suddenly recognizable; it had been the *Wedding March*.

He cursed softly. "When I find out who leaked the story to the press—"

"You'll what?" Lucas crumpled his own empty take-out cup and tossed it in the trash bin. "Give them a pay raise?"

Constantine dropped the newspaper on his desk. "Is it that obvious?"

"You're here."

Zane pushed to his feet, the movement fluid. "If you want to step back from the negotiations, Lucas and I can delay the New Zealand trip. Better still, let Vitalis handle the loan."

"No." Constantine's reply was knee-jerk, his gaze suddenly cold enough to freeze, despite the fact that he knew both Lucas and Zane were only trying to protect him.

Zane shrugged, his shoulders broad in his designer jacket. "Your choice, but if you stay in Sydney the press is going to have a field day."

Constantine studied the grainy newspaper photo again. "I can handle it. In any case I'm flying out tomorrow night."

A cell phone vibrated. Lucas's expression was grim as he took his phone out of his pocket. "The sooner the better. You don't need this."

Jaw tense, Constantine stalked over to the glass panels that took up one entire wall of his office, drinking his coffee while Lucas answered his cell.

From here he could see one corner of the Ambrosi building. The office block, dwarfed as it was by the skyscrapers that sprouted near the heart of the Central Business District, clearly undercapitalized one of the more valuable pieces of real estate in town.

Although the monetary value of anything Ambrosi was fast ceasing to hold any meaning for him.

He couldn't stop thinking about the way Sienna had tried to protect her mother yesterday. If she had read the newspaper story, she would hold an even worse opinion of him now, despite the fact that in his own way he had been trying to help her family by keeping the location of her father's heart attack quiet. The furor of Roberto dropping dead in a casino would not help the grieving family or do Ambrosi Pearls any favors.

Not that Sienna was likely to attribute any honorable motivations to his actions.

Lucas terminated his call. "That was one of our security guys. Apparently a news crew has found the location of the Pier Point house. Sienna's down on the beach sunbathing."

Constantine went cold inside. "They must have followed me yesterday." He dropped his now empty take-out cup in the trash.

This morning's story had been buried in the social pages of the paper. If he wasn't fast enough, Sienna could be a lead story by tomorrow morning.

In Sienna's eyes, he was certain that somehow, that, also, would be his fault.

Lucas looked concerned. "Do you want company?"

Constantine barely spared Lucas and Zane a glance. "Catch your flight out. Like I said, I can handle this."

Five

Sienna saw the reporter while he was negotiating the narrow track down to the tiny bay below the Pier Point house. Annoyance flashed through her at the intrusion, and the realization that the reporters had found her family hideaway. No surprises how that had happened, she thought grimly.

To leave the beach she would either have to swim out or climb past the reporter, which meant he would be snapping pictures of her in a bikini all the way. Not good.

She jogged into the water. A leisurely swim later, she pulled herself up onto a small diving pontoon anchored out in the bay.

Slicking wet hair back from her face, she checked out the reporter who was now standing with a forlorn air at the edge of the water. Satisfied that he didn't have a telescopic lens, because if he did he would have had it trained on her by now, Sienna sat down on the bobbing platform and waited for him to leave. If necessary, she could swim to the other end of the bay, climb the rocky slope and walk back to the house.

Long minutes ticked by. She checked her waterproof watch. If he decided to wait her out on the beach, she would have to consider the swim because she was expecting a call in just under an hour back at the house.

She lay down on her back, making herself an even smaller target for the reporter's lens, and forced herself to relax. All last night her stomach churned from the discovery she'd made the previous afternoon that Constantine had been in town when her father had died.

She had spent the night tossing and turning, alternately furious with Constantine because he seemed to be at the center of her entire financial mess, then paralyzed with fear because there didn't seem to be a thing she could do to stop him from taking everything.

As satisfying as it would be to blame Constantine, though, she knew that wasn't fair. Her father, who had been a charming, larger-than-life rogue, had had a number of minor heart attacks over the years. Just recently he had been scheduled for a bypass operation, because his health had gone rapidly downhill. His doctor had specifically told him to stay away from casinos because the stress and excitement were detrimental to his health.

She shielded her eyes from the sun with the back of her hand and smothered a yawn. She allowed her lids to close, just for a few seconds. When she opened them, she was abruptly aware that more than a few seconds had passed.

Cautiously, she scanned the beach, which was empty. The sound that had jerked her out of sleep suddenly fell into its correct context. It wasn't the rhythmic splash of waves against the pontoon. A swimmer, large, male and muscular, was cutting through the water, heading straight for her.

It wasn't the reporter, who appeared to have left the beach. She recognized that smooth, effortless crawl. It was Constantine.

Slipping into the water, she struck out away from the pontoon. If she swam in a semicircle she would be able to avoid Constantine and hopefully get back to the beach before he did. With any luck he would stay aimed at the pontoon and wouldn't realize that she had gone.

Maybe the fight-or-flight reaction was overkill, but dressed in a skimpy pink bikini she preferred to go with the unreasoning panic. If she was going to talk to a mostly naked and wet Constantine, she wanted to be wearing clothes.

Turning her head as she swam, she checked out the pontoon and saw Constantine swimming directly behind her. Her heart pounded out of control. She was good in the water, but Constantine was a whole lot better. When they had been dating he had encouraged her to take a scuba diving course because he had wanted her to share his passion for the sport. After she had qualified he had taken her out a couple of times before they had broken up, making sure she was water fit and proficient with the complex array of scuba gear. She knew firsthand how powerful he was in the water.

The sandy bottom appeared below. She swam a few more strokes then began to wade. The world spun as Constantine swung her into his arms, which was no easy feat. Apart from the fact that he had just swum a good distance, she was not small. She was five foot seven, and lean and toned because she regularly put in time at the pool, swimming laps. She also lifted weights and had progressed to the point where she could almost bench her own body weight, which, according to her gym instructor, was very cool. That all meant that she was a lot heavier than she looked.

She stiffened and tried to shimmy out of his grasp. And tried not to like that he was carrying her. In response, his arms tightened, holding her firmly against his chest.

Avoiding his interested gaze and the fact that he was barely out of breath, she shoved at his slick shoulders. "Okay, tough guy, you can let me go now."

Somewhere it registered that she had said at least some of those words before, the previous day. They hadn't done the trick then, either. She spied batteries and what looked like a camera memory stick scattered on her beach towel. There were some interesting scuffle marks in the sand. "What did you do with the reporter?"

"If you're looking for a shallow grave you won't find one. Although I admit I was tempted."

Constantine let her down on the sand. "Honey, I wasn't there when your father had the heart attack," he said quietly. "I didn't know he had a heart condition. He was at a casino instead of attending the meeting he had requested with me when he had the attack. One of my men, Tomas, got him out of there before the newspapers could get hold of the story. Unfortunately, someone leaked details. Probably the same person who went to the newspapers about the loan."

He had tried to protect them. For a moment Sienna's mind went utterly blank. She was so shocked by what he had done that his calling her "honey" barely registered.

She sucked in a deep breath, but the oxygen didn't seem to be getting through. It registered that the fast swim after an almost sleepless night had not been a smart move, her head felt heavy and pressurized, her knees wobbly. When her vision started to narrow and fade she knew she was going to faint for the first time in her life.

"This is not happening." Her hand shot out, automatically groping for support.

Constantine's arm was suddenly around her waist, holding her steady. The top of her head bumped his chin. The scrape of his stubbled jaw on the sensitive skin of her forehead sent a reflexive shiver through her, and suddenly she had her sight back. She inhaled. His warm male scent, laced with the clean, salty smell of the sea, filled her nostrils.

As if a switch had been thrown, she was swamped by memories, some hot and sensuous, some hurtful enough that her temper roared to life. She stiffened, lurching off balance despite the support.

Constantine said something curt beneath his breath. His arm tightened, an iron bar in the small of her back. When she next focused on him, she was sitting on the sand with Constantine holding her head down between her knees.

"I'm okay now," she told him.

The pressure on her neck disappeared. She lifted her head and blinked at the brilliance of sun and sand. Constantine was sitting beside her, his arms resting on his drawn-up knees. The moment seemed abruptly surreal. It suddenly occurred to her how different Constantine was at the beach, almost as if when he walked onto the sand he shed his responsibilities along with his clothes.

A vibrating sound caught her attention, a cell phone ringing. She looked around and spotted his clothes, an expensive suit, shirt and tie and designer shoes lying in an untidy pile on the sand. She made a covert study of Constantine. He wasn't wearing swimming trunks, just dark gray boxers, the wet fabric hugging the powerful muscles of his thighs.

Constantine made no move toward his phone.

"Aren't you going to answer that?"

His expression was surprisingly relaxed, almost content. "No."

"Why not?"

His mouth kicked up at the corner. "I don't answer phones at the beach."

She found herself smiling back at him. In this, at least, they were the same. She regularly "ran away" to the beach, needing the uncomplicated casualness of sun and sand, the feeling of utter freedom the water gave her.

She hadn't ever applied those needs to Constantine, but she did now and a sharp tug of grief for everything they had lost pulled at her. Since the breakup she had been so focused on the things that had gone wrong, she hadn't wanted to remember the wonderful moments.

She sifted sand between her fingers. "Then you should probably go to the beach more often."

His gaze rested on hers with an odd, neutral look. For the first time she acknowledged that when Constantine had walked away from her, his emotional cut-off hadn't been as clinical as she had imagined. He had lost, too.

With a final twitch the phone stopped vibrating.

"Why would you even consider helping my father?" Instead of avoiding his gaze, Sienna let herself be pinned by it. Not because she wanted the contact, but because she needed to establish that Constantine was telling the truth about what had happened.

"I'm not a monster. I was willing to talk."

"You were there to collect." She didn't come right out and say he had killed her father, but the thought loomed large in her mind.

"Now that's where you're wrong." Constantine's gaze was unnervingly direct. "Your father contacted me and made the arrangement to meet. I wasn't there to collect. He wanted another loan."

A few minutes before eight, Sienna stepped into an ankle-length, midnight blue silk shift and ruthlessly squashed the heady sense of anticipation that had been building ever since those few minutes on the beach. She had to keep reminding herself that Constantine was forcing her to meet him at a social event; this wasn't a date.

She checked her makeup, which she'd spent several minutes applying. Her hair was coiled in a classic knot. The Ambrosi pearls she was wearing were the only lavish note. Part of a sample collection they were using to woo a European retail giant, de Vries, the flowerlike cluster of pearls at each lobe and the choker, made from a string of pearl flowers, looked both modern and opulent.

She was attending Constantine's cocktail party at his command, but that didn't mean she couldn't use the opportunity to promote her company. An Atraeus Group meet and greet translated to a room filled with clients and sales contacts Ambrosi Pearls desperately needed.

The car arrived just before eight.

Carla, who had hovered in her bedroom while Sienna had dressed discussing the loan situation, followed her downstairs. Carla was Ambrosi's PR guru, she was also the current Face of Ambrosi, a cost-cutting move that had made sense because Carla was outrageously gorgeous and photogenic.

Carla watched as Sienna checked that she had her phone, credit card and house key. "I'll wait up for you. If you need help, call me or text, and I'll come and get you."

Sienna pinned a determined smile on her face. "Thanks, but that won't be necessary. Believe me, this is strictly business."

She braced for the next confrontation with Constantine as she stepped out into the courtyard. Instead, a lean, dark man who introduced himself as Tomas, Constantine's personal assistant, opened the passenger door of a sleek sedan.

Disappointment flattened her mood as Sienna climbed into the expensive, leather-scented interior. Despite the tension, after the interlude on the beach, she had been certain Constantine had been more than a little interested in picking up where they had previously left off. Evidently, she had been wrong. If Constantine had wanted to underline the power he held, he couldn't have done it more effectively than this.

Twenty minutes later, Tomas turned into a gated drive flanked by security and parked outside an impressive colonial mansion. Sienna took in the sleek, expensive cars that lined the gravel driveway and the lush, tropical garden lit by glowing lights as she mounted the steps to the front door. A brief security check later and she was shown into a chandelier-lit room.

She glimpsed Constantine, dark and brooding in a black suit and fitted black T-shirt, at one end of the crowded room. Jaw firming, she started toward him, her eyes narrowed assessingly as she studied the wealthy, influential crowd. Her heart sped up at the thought that there could even be a de Vries representative here and she would have the opportunity to apply a little direct pressure.

Her way was abruptly blocked by Alex Panopoulos, one of Ambrosi's most prestigious clients.

Panopoulos, the CEO of an Australasian retail empire, had tried to date both her and Carla on several occasions. Since Panopoulos had a reputation as a likeable rogue and a playboy, deflecting him socially hadn't been difficult. He took the rebuffs with good humor; the only problem was he kept bouncing back.

"Sienna." Panopoulos took both of her hands in his. "I was sorry to hear about your father. I was out of the country until this afternoon, otherwise I would have attended the funeral. Did you get my flowers?"

The "flowers" were an enormous arrangement of hothouse orchids that had cost a small fortune and which Carla had given to an elderly neighbor. "Yes, thank you." She flexed her fingers, wondering when he was going to release them. Simultaneously, she sent small darting glances around the room trying to spot the de Vries rep, Harold Northcliffe, a short, plump man who had a reputation for being elusive.

Panopoulos ignored the small movements. "And…how is the business?"

Sienna held on to her professional veneer with difficulty. "We closed today, but otherwise, it's business as usual."

He released one hand and brushed the delicate skin beneath one eye. "With your usual efficiency, no doubt. It's good to take care of business, but I think you also need to take care of yourself."

For a brief moment in time, Sienna almost wished she could have felt something for Panopoulos, even though she knew this was part of his routine, as practiced and slick as his formidable management skills.

Panopoulos smiled, signaling that he was closing in for the kill. "As a matter of fact, I'm very glad we've met tonight. I was hoping you might have dinner with me next week."

Sienna stiffened. Panopoulos was canny. She suspected that he deliberately kept in touch with both her and Carla on a personal level in order to gain an inside track on acquiring Ambrosi, should the business falter. "If you're worried about what the papers are printing, don't be. Ambrosi Pearls will continue to supply your orders."

The calculating glint in his eye grew stronger, more direct. "I'm sure that is so. But it was the future I wanted to discuss."

His grip on her remaining hand tightened. With a start, Sienna realized he meant to lift her fingers to his mouth.

"Panopoulos."

He dropped her fingers as if they had suddenly become red-hot. "Atraeus."

Constantine's gaze briefly locked with hers before he turned his attention back to Panopoulos. "I hear you're joining us on Medinos for the opening of our newest resort complex."

Panopoulos's expression was carefully blank. "I appreciate the opportunity to establish a retail outlet on Medinos. Seven-star hotels are thin on the ground."

"I understand you've made a substantial bid for floor space for the second stage of the resort complex?"

"I spoke with Lucas a few minutes ago. He's set up a preliminary meeting."

"In that case, I'll look forward to seeing you on Medinos next week. Now, if you'll excuse us, Ms. Ambrosi and I have a business matter to discuss."

Panopoulos's gaze narrowed at the smooth dismissal. "Of course."

Constantine's palm landed in the small of her back, burning through the silk and sending a shock of awareness through her as he urged her past Panopoulos.

Seconds later they stepped out of the crowded reception room and onto a deserted patio. Enclosed by walls and cascading foliage, the outdoor space was lushly tropical. A tinkling fountain added an exotic note, and gardenias released their perfume into air that was still sultry from the afternoon storms.

Annoyed by the high-handed way he had dispensed with Panopoulos then marched her away, Sienna stepped back from Constantine, deliberately using a patio chair to create even more space between them. "You shouldn't have done that. I was in discussion with a client. Alex is one of Ambrosi's best custom—"

"What did he want?"

The grim register of Constantine's voice intensified the distracting, humming awareness. The potent attraction made no sense; she should have been over it long ago. "That's none of your business."

"If Panopoulos wanted to discuss Ambrosi, then that is my business."

The soft reminder of just how much power Constantine wielded over her family's company, and her, strengthened the notion that he wasn't in the least unhappy with the situation. "Our discussion was personal. As it happened, he was asking me out to dinner."

"You turned him down."

His flat assertion that she had no interest in Alex contrarily made her bristle. "As a matter of fact, I didn't." Which wasn't a lie, because Constantine had intervened before she could turn him down.

He said something curt beneath his breath. "You're aware that it's Ambrosi Pearls that Panopoulos wants?"

Annoyance exploded inside her, the burst of temper a welcome change from the uncharacteristic jittery angst that had overtaken her since the conversation at her father's gravesite. "Yes. Now, if you'll excuse me—"

"Not yet."

The soft demand froze her in place. Light washed over the sharp cut of his cheekbones, highlighting the irritable glitter of his eyes. In that moment she registered that Constantine wasn't just angry, he was furious.

She had only ever seen him furious once before—the day they had broken up—but on that occasion he had been icily cool and detached. The fact that his formidable control had finally slipped and he was clearly in danger of losing his temper ratcheted the tension up several notches.

A heady sense of anticipation gripped her. She had the feeling that they were standing on some kind of emotional precipice, that for the first time she was going to see the real Constantine and not the controlled tycoon who had a calculator in place of a heart.

Overhead, thunder rumbled; the air was close and tropically hot. In the distance an electrical storm flickered.

Great. Just what she needed, to be reminded of the previous afternoon's encounter and her complete and utter loss of composure.

"Has he proposed?"

Sienna drew in a sharp breath. If she didn't know better, she could almost swear that Constantine was jealous. "Not yet."

"And if he does?"

"If he does…" She searched for something, anything, to say that would reduce her vulnerability. "I'll have to consider saying yes. It's a fact that this time, with a family and business to care for, when it comes to marriage, business does count. Right now, as far as I'm concerned a husband with money would be win-win."

"When Panopoulos finds out how much Ambrosi owes, he won't place your relationship on a formal footing."

Sienna's heart pounded out of control when he shifted the patio chair and glided closer, looming over her in the small courtyard, his breath stirring her hair.

His gaze dropped to her mouth and she was suddenly unbearably aware that he intended to kiss her.

Six

Sienna retreated a step. Big mistake. She had allowed herself to be cornered, literally. One more step and she would come up against the courtyard wall. "I find that remark offensive."

"It would only offend if you'd slept with Panopoulos, and I don't think you have."

Her jaw firmed. She had made a mistake, dangling Panopoulos in front of Constantine, but it was too late to backtrack now. "You can't be sure of that."

"I've been in town for four days. When I wasn't trying to contact you, I made some inquiries. It wasn't difficult to obtain information."

Her stomach sank. With his resources, Constantine would have found it ridiculously easy to discover whatever he wanted to know about her, including the fact that her personal life was as arid as a desert. She seldom dated. She didn't have time to date; she was too busy trying to sell pearls. "You've got no right to pry into my private affairs."

"It's not exactly what I had planned for my leisure time, either, but whether we like it or not, for the foreseeable future, everything to do with Ambrosi Pearls and you is my business. Have you discussed the loan with Brian Chin yet?"

The sudden change from personal to business threw her even more off balance. Brian Chin was Ambrosi's accountant. "I faxed the pages to him this afternoon. He wasn't happy."

An understatement. Like her, Brian had been in a state of shock.

"I take it Chin is still the extent of your financial advice?"

"Brian's been with us for ten years; he's loyal."

"But not a player. He could never control your father."

"Who could?" Even though she felt disloyal to her bluff, charismatic father, it was a relief to finally say the words.

Impatience registered in his gaze. "Then why did you try?"

"Someone had to. Mom doesn't have a head for business. Neither does Carla. If I hadn't stepped in we would have lost everything a long time ago."

"I would have helped."

Her jaw squared. "You had your chance."

His gaze narrowed at her reference to the financial deal that had ended their engagement. "Not under those conditions."

"If you'd bothered to find out anything about me at all, you would have known how important Ambrosi is to me."

"I knew. Why do you think I walked?"

Shock reverberated through her. In a moment of clarity,

she saw herself as she had been two years ago, just seconds ago—driven, obsessed.

The fact that Constantine had ended their engagement so quickly was no longer incomprehensible. She had always known he was ruthless and uncompromising in business; she just hadn't translated that reality to his personal life. He hadn't liked being left out of the picture and he hadn't been prepared to take second place to either her father's gambling addiction or Ambrosi Pearls.

"Finally, you get it."

And suddenly he was close, too close. An automatic step back and the chill of the masonry wall, a stark contrast to the potent heat of his body, brought her up short. Lightning flickered, the display increasingly spectacular, followed by a growl of thunder.

She should shimmy out, slip past him. A quick call to a taxi firm and five minutes on the roadside and she would be on her way home. If Constantine wanted a discussion it would have to be over the phone, or with lawyers present.

His hand landed on the wall beside her head, cutting off that avenue of escape. "Why didn't you tell me what was going on two years ago?"

"And watch you walk away, like you did when you found out about the proposed loan?"

"I told you, I would have helped."

For a moment her mind went utterly blank. Until then she hadn't realized how angry she had been at Constantine for walking away, for choosing not to even try to understand her predicament when she had desperately needed his support. "And then walked? Thanks, but no thanks."

"You could have used professional help for your father and the business."

"He wouldn't accept the first, and we couldn't afford the second."

The pad of his thumb slid along the line of her jaw. Her pulse pounded out of control, her body's response to the sudden stifling intimacy of his touch intense and unsettling.

She felt caught and held by emotions she didn't want to feel: anger, frustration and, unacceptably, a heady, dizzying anticipation. Ever since those loaded moments in his car, she realized she had been waiting for Constantine to make a move on her.

He muttered a short, rough Medinian phrase. "Why are you so stubborn?"

"I guess it's an Australian trait."

Reminding Constantine that after the Second World War, the Ambrosi family had chosen to uproot themselves from Medinos and make Australia their home was a tenuous counterpunch. But in that moment she was willing to grasp at anything that separated her from Constantine.

His hold was gentle enough that she could slide away, walk away if she wanted…

She saw the moment he logged her decision, the intent in his gaze as he angled her jaw so that her mouth was mere inches from his. She also learned something else. If she was still blindly, fatally attracted to Constantine, it was an unsettling fact that he also wanted her, and suddenly there was no air.

Constantine's mouth brushed hers. Sienna jerked back in an effort to control the heat that shimmered through her. She shouldn't want to know what touching him again— kissing him—would feel like when she had spent two years working doggedly to forget. "This isn't fair."

He grinned quick and hard. "It wasn't meant to be."

His hands settled at her waist. Now was the time to pull

back, to insist that they keep their relationship on a business footing.

Instead, seduced by the mesmerizing fact that he did still want her, that if she wasn't careful she could fall for him again, she lifted up on her toes, cupped his jaw and kissed him back.

A bolt of heat seared straight to her loins. She could feel his fingers in her hair, the sharp tug as he pulled out pins, the soft slide of her hair over her shoulders.

He cupped her breast through the double layer of silk and her bra. Her stomach clenched and for a timeless moment she hung suspended. Until a masculine voice registered and she was free, cool air circulating against her overheated skin.

Constantine controlled the savage desire to dismiss Tomas, who was hovering at the entrance to the courtyard.

His PA was under strict instructions not to interrupt this interlude, or let anyone else do so, which meant that whatever Tomas had to say was urgent.

Positioning himself so that he blocked Sienna from Tomas's view, and the curious stares they were now attracting from the handful of guests who had drifted near the French doors, Constantine took the phone Tomas handed him and answered the call.

The conversation with his chief financial advisor was brief and to the point. The legal tangle his father and Roberto Ambrosi had concocted between them had resulted in an unexpected hitch. Lorenzo had signed away water rights Constantine needed for Roberto's bogus pearl enterprise. No water rights meant no marina development, which effectively froze a project in which he had already invested millions.

Constantine terminated the call and handed the phone back to Tomas. Dismissing him with curt thanks, he turned back to Sienna. He had expected that in the brief interval it had taken to deal with the phone call she would close off from him, and he wasn't wrong. Grimly, he noted that in the space of less than two minutes she had smoothed her hair back into an elegant knot, found her evening bag, which she had dropped, and recovered the cool composure that irked him so much.

A jagged flash of lightning signaled that the violent electrical storm had rolled overhead. Sienna, he noticed, didn't so much as flinch. Her gaze was already focused on his room of retailers and, no doubt, the prospect of closing a number of lucrative sales deals.

Not for the first time it occurred to him that he might have more success with Sienna if he had one of her order sheets in his hand.

When she would have strolled past him, using the avenue of an interested group of spectators who had strolled out onto the courtyard to view the pyrotechnics as an escape route, Constantine blocked her way.

"We haven't finished our discussion." He indicated the softly lit decking that encircled the ground level of the house. "We can conclude our business in the privacy of my study."

Sienna teetered on the brink of refusing, the danger inherent in a private meeting suddenly vastly more potent than the financial threat.

In the end, though, she nodded and mounted the veranda steps, eager to at least get under cover. "I take it the phone call was bad news?"

Constantine's calmness was utterly at odds with the white-hot intensity of the kiss. "Nothing that can't be handled."

The call had been bad news, but that suited Sienna. A return to animosity would be a relief, neutralizing the panicked notion that Constantine was intent on maneuvering her back into his bed.

A hot pulse of adrenaline went through her as the thought gathered momentum. She should never have kissed him back. It had been a reckless experiment. She had practically thrown herself at him. Temporarily at least, it had altered the equation between them, giving him a power over her she had vowed he would never again have.

As if to underscore her imminent danger, a deafening clap of thunder sent her wobbling off balance. One stiletto jammed in a knot in the decking timber and in that moment the lights went out, plunging them into darkness.

Constantine's arm curved around her waist. She found herself pressed against the hard outline of his body, her breasts flattened against his chest. She registered the firm shape of his arousal pressed against her stomach. Heated awareness flashed. Reflexively, she shoved at his chest and bent down to release her foot from the stuck shoe. As she straightened, her head connected solidly with Constantine's jaw in a replay of what had happened the previous day.

Constantine lurched off balance. A second white-hot flash illuminated the fact that on this particular stretch of veranda there was no railing to halt his fall, just a sculpted patch of shrubbery. In the next instant they were plunged back into pitch-blackness.

Panic burned through Sienna as she pulled off her remaining shoe, tossed it on the deck along with her evening bag, and gingerly felt her way to the edge of the decking. Hitching her dress up, she climbed into the garden, picking her way through a collection of rocks and succulents, to find Constantine. Lightning flickered again, illuminating him as he pushed into a sitting position.

"Where am I?"

She grabbed his arm. "In the garden."

He rubbed at his jaw, making her feel instantly guilty. That was the second time she had hit him in the same spot.

"Figures."

Bracing her arm around his waist she helped him up, staggering under his weight.

Her dress was catching on the spiky leaves of some tropical flower. Something both crunchy and soft squished under her bare foot. Not a plant.

They stepped onto cool, damp grass. Constantine's arm tightened around her waist, tucking her firmly against his side, until they made their way to a line of solar garden lights that illuminated a path. Seconds later they climbed a shallow series of steps back onto the veranda.

From the controlled tautness of his muscles, the smooth way he moved, Sienna had a sudden suspicion that Constantine no longer needed her support, if he had ever needed it at all.

The click of a door latch punctuated the now distant rumble of thunder. Groping for reference points in the darkness, Sienna's fingers brushed over the smooth painted surface of a doorframe.

Another step and she was inside, her bare feet sinking into thick carpet. The door slammed, cutting off sound. The darkness was warmer and hushed here, scented with the springlike freshness of flowers and a rich undernote of leather. It did not smell like a working environment. "Where are we?"

"My private suite. The study is just down the hall."

Constantine leaned back against the door. Sienna's hand shot out, landing on the taut muscles of his abdomen. His arm tightened around her waist, sealing her against the seductive heat of his chest, and she was made shiveringly aware that Constantine was showing no inclination to move.

Resisting the counterproductive urge to stay put, Sienna disentangled herself and stepped free. She was now certain that, apart from his initial dazed state, there was nothing wrong with Constantine. She peered into the stygian darkness and injected a note of briskness into her voice. "Tell me where you keep a flashlight or candles."

"There's a flashlight in the bedroom."

She was not falling for that one. "In that case you can stay here. I'm going to get help."

And right after she found one of Constantine's minions, she would call for a taxi. He would have all the help he needed. There would be no need for her to come back and check on him.

His fingers locked with hers in the darkness, anchoring her in place. "I don't need help."

Lightning flashed through the leaded sidelights on either side of the door, illuminating the darkening bruise on Constantine's jaw.

She inhaled sharply. "I did hurt you."

"Tell me about it," he murmured and drew her toward him.

His mouth came down on hers, his lips warm and unexpectedly soft. Suddenly, leaving was not an option. Lifting up on her toes, she wound her arms around his neck and returned the kiss with interest. Any idea that Constantine was truly hurt or vulnerable dissolved. If he had been stunned by the fall, clearly the effects had worn off because he was fully aroused.

Long minutes later, he lifted her into his arms, negotiated the hall and carried her into a darkened room, his night vision unerring as he located a couch and set her down on it.

As she went to work on the buttons of his shirt, she felt the zipper of her dress release, then the fastening of her bra. Another long, searing kiss and Constantine peeled both garments away.

Lightning, paler and more distant now, flickered as he jerked his tie free and shrugged out of the jacket and the shirt. His weight came down on her, the bare skin of his chest hot against her breasts. For long breathtaking moments they continued to kiss with a drugging, seducing sweetness that spun her back to long afternoons in her apartment, even longer nights in his bed.

His fingers hooked in the waistband of her panties. She lifted her hips and with one gliding movement she was naked aside from the pearls in her lobes and at her throat.

She had a brief moment to consider that she was on the verge of making a monumental mistake before deciding that after the past two years of worry and work, she could do what she wanted just this once. She could give in to the exhilarating passion she had thought had died when Constantine had walked out on her.

The feel of his trousers against her inner thighs as he came down between her legs was a faint irritation, signaling that Constantine wasn't naked. She had thought, in the brief interval that he had separated himself from her that he would have dispensed with his pants altogether. That small detail faded into insignificance as finally, achingly, they came together.

Until that moment she hadn't realized how much she had missed him, missed this. She had loved the touch, the taste, the feel of him, loved the intimacy of making love, the way he'd made her feel when they'd been together.

Constantine murmured something rough in Medinian. "I knew it. You haven't been with anyone else."

Sienna was momentarily distracted by the satisfaction

in his voice, then his mouth closed over one breast and hot pleasure zapped conscious thought, and she could only clasp his shoulders and move with him.

She heard his indrawn breath. The pressure was close to unbearable, holding her on a knife's edge of expectation, and in a moment of shock she realized he was wearing a condom. She hadn't been aware that he had put one on. Aside from the occasional distant flicker of lightning outside it was pitch-black, and for long, dizzying minutes she'd been blindly absorbed by the overwhelming sensations.

The brief span of time when she had thought he had been undressing was now explained. He had been performing a much more important task.

She should be grateful that he hadn't lost his head the way she had, that he had protected them both, but the knowledge that he had condoms with him was abruptly depressing. A man didn't carry condoms unless he expected, or planned, to make love.

He began to move and her breath hitched in her throat. With every gliding stroke the pleasure wound tighter and tighter. She coiled her arms around his neck, burying her face against his shoulder as the burning tension gathered. Her climax finally hit her in shimmering, incandescent waves. Dimly she was aware of Constantine's release just seconds after her own, the moment primal and extreme.

Soft golden light flooded the room with shocking suddenness. Constantine's gaze locked with hers and any doubt that the lovemaking had been a spur of the moment decision on his part evaporated when she saw the possessive satisfaction in his eyes. However random the events that had precipitated this interlude appeared, he *had* planned to make love to her.

She stirred beneath Constantine's weight, with an effort

of will controlling the intense emotions that had temporarily hijacked her brain, and the hurt. She had wanted to believe that Constantine had been as swept away as she had been.

She pushed at his shoulders. Obligingly, he shifted to one side, allowing her to scramble off the couch.

Feeling exposed and more than a little flustered, she found her dress. Stepping into it, she quickly fastened the zipper. Her bra was hooked over one end of the couch, and she spied her panties beneath an elegant coffee table.

Constantine was in the process of fastening his pants. Cheeks burning, she averted her gaze from his sleek, bronzed shoulders and lean hips. Instead, she snatched up the panties and made a beeline for the bathroom.

Feeling increasingly horrified at her lack of control, she stared at her reflection in the large mirror positioned over a marble vanity. Her hair was disheveled, her skin flushed, her mouth swollen. Constantine might have planned to make love to her, but that didn't change the fact that she had practically thrown herself at him—not once, but twice. And he had been quite happy to take advantage of her vulnerability.

A few minutes later, freshened up, her hair finger combed, she ventured back out into the sitting room. The dress had smoothed out against the warmth of her skin, but she was still minus her shoes and her clutch, which were both outside on the veranda.

Constantine was pacing the room talking into a cell phone, his expression taut. He had pulled on a fresh shirt, which he had left unbuttoned. Her gaze skittered away from the mouthwatering slice of tanned chest and washboard abs. The sexy casualness of his attire emphasized the intimacy of what they had just shared.

Constantine terminated the call and slipped the phone into his pocket.

"Problems?" Suddenly in a hurry to leave, she circled the room, giving the large leather sofa a wide berth as she inched toward the door.

Constantine's silvery gaze tracked her. "A hitch with the new resort."

"Which is why you're flying out tonight."

There was an oddly weighted pause. "You could come with me."

For a brief second, despite the hurt and disillusionment, dizzying temptation pulled at her. "To Medinos?"

He glanced at his watch. "I fly out in three hours. You're welcome to share the flight with me. It makes sense," he concluded smoothly. "We haven't had time to…complete our business. We can pick up where we left off."

In his bed.

Sienna squashed the wild impulse to say yes, to immerse herself even more deeply in a relationship that logic and history dictated was destined to crash and burn.

The sensible response was to refuse, to put their relationship back on a business footing.

Her fingers automatically went to the pearl choker at her throat. She forced herself to breathe, to think. This was no longer just about her.

An Atraeus Resort opening was an A-list event, by invitation only. It would be jam-packed with high-end press and industry professionals. All of the luxury retail giants would be represented, including de Vries.

Despite what had happened on the couch, going to Medinos was an opportunity she couldn't afford to pass up.

She would never have a better chance to push Ambrosi Pearls' new range and secure the sales contract they had been chasing. If de Vries signed even a one-year deal, they could pay off Constantine. They would be free and clear. "All right."

Surprise flared in Constantine's gaze and was just as quickly controlled. "Tomas will take you home so you can pack your bag."

She thought quickly. Apart from the fact that she didn't want to be closeted alone with Constantine on a luxury corporate jet, this was a business trip; she needed time to prepare. Namely to pick up the samples from the vault at the office and make an appointment to meet with the de Vries representative attending the opening. The process of arranging the meeting was a delicate business, which could take days. "I can't go to Medinos tonight. I'll need two days before I leave."

Constantine's gaze narrowed at the sudden crispness of Sienna's voice, at odds with her softly flushed cheeks and tousled hair. His mood deteriorated further as she fingered the silky pearls at her throat for the third time and counting.

When they had been making love, the pearls had seemed to glow in the dark, reminding him that he wasn't just making love to the woman he wanted, he was making love to the CEO of Ambrosi Pearls.

Now she was backing off fast—from the lovemaking and from the unspoken admission he had forced from her that, deny it as she might, she still wanted him.

But at least she had agreed to come to his country, which was progress.

The idea had crystallized when she had stated that she would consider marriage with Panopoulos, then it had set in stone when he had discovered that she hadn't slept with anyone in the two years since their break up.

The primitive surge that had gripped him when he had

realized that Sienna, who had been a virgin when they had first made love, had never belonged to anyone but him, had been profound.

The thought that she could take another lover, possibly Panopoulos, made him break out in a cold sweat. That scenario was unacceptable. "In that case, let me know a departure time and I'll make the company jet available to you."

"No." Her chin jerked up, dark eyes shooting fire at the concept of him paying for her travel, underlining the fact that she was backing off, fast. "I'll book a commercial flight."

In a room filled with soft gold light and pooling shadows, suddenly the Medinian part of her ancestry, the long line of alchemists and merchants stretching back into antiquity, was starkly evident. His jaw tightened as the fascination that had gripped him the first time he had seen her struck him anew. "You can't afford the commercial flight."

By his calculations, he had been paying for everything, including her salary for the past two months.

Her cheeks flushed a deeper shade of pink. "I have money of my own."

"Then at least let me organize your ride home." He took out his phone and dialed Tomas before she could argue.

Seconds later he hung up and followed her out onto the veranda. Sienna had found her clutch and shoes.

Constantine crouched down and gently levered the stiletto heel out of a knot in the decking timber.

She took it from him, her movements brisk. As she slipped her foot into the shoe, she gripped the frame of a nearby window for balance. He caught her studying his reflection in the glass and satisfaction curled through him.

If Sienna had been indifferent to him, he would have

expedited the paperwork, which was cut-and-dried, and walked away. But she did want him. Their chemistry was hot enough to burn.

The fact that he was jealous of Panopoulos didn't please him. The uncomfortable reality that he still wanted Sienna after she had broken his trust two years ago was even more difficult to accept.

There was nothing logical about the emotions. He didn't want the attraction, but it existed, the pull absolute and powerful.

Tomas appeared, a set of keys in one hand. Sienna shot Constantine a bright, professional smile, her gaze missing his by inches as she hurried after Tomas.

As if she couldn't wait to be gone.

Gingerly, Constantine probed at the lump that had formed on the back of his head, clearly from one of his expensive and strategically placed landscape rocks.

He studied the now floodlit grounds and the patch of crushed bromelia balansae.

Damn. He couldn't believe he had fallen into the garden.

Seven

Two days later Sienna disembarked from her commercial flight into the searing heat of Medinos. The ice-blue cotton shift she was wearing was already sticking to her skin as she strolled into the arrivals terminal and found Tomas waiting for her.

Her stomach tensed against a twinge of what was, unacceptably, disappointment. During the flight she had been too wound to sleep, anticipating seeing Constantine when she landed.

Minutes later, with her luggage loaded into the trunk, Sienna slid dark glasses onto the bridge of her nose and settled into the passenger seat of a sleek, modern sedan. While Tomas drove, she stared curiously at limestone villas, fields of olives and grapes and an endless vista of sea and sky.

She had expected Medinos, with its wild, hard country, to be fascinating and she wasn't disappointed. Constantine and his family now owned vast tracts, some in plantations and farms. The original goat farm and market garden on the island of Ambrus was now, of course, a fabulously wealthy gold mine. In fact, the entire island of Ambrus was now owned by the Atraeus family.

From her research on the internet she'd discovered that the main island was large and well populated, although, because the interior was so rugged settlement was primarily on the coast. Other islands of the group were visible as they wound along a high precipitous road, appearing to float hazily in the distance. The lyrical names were as imbued with mystery and magic as the shimmering images: Nycea, Thais, Pythea and, closer in, Ambrus.

Tomas's cell phone rang, the buzz discreet. The low timbre of his voice as he spoke in rapid Medinian briefly spun her back to the explosive interlude with Constantine at his home.

When Sienna had exited the taxi that night after refusing to be driven by Tomas, Carla had been waiting.

Predictably, she had been horrified when she'd learned Sienna had decided to go to Medinos. "Please tell me you're not going with him."

"Don't worry." Sienna kept her voice crisp and light as she struggled to control her blush. "I'm traveling separately. This is business."

Although, very little of what they had done that night had even the remotest connection to business.

Dropping her evening bag on the kitchen table, she filled the electric jug with water and set it to boil. What she wanted was a steadying dose of caffeine but, since she needed to sleep, it was going to have to be herbal tea. As she turned to lean on the table, her reflection in the kitchen window flashed back at her. Tousled hair and bare mouth, the rich luster of pearls making her look more like a courtesan than the CEO of a company.

She had let him make love to her.

Guilty heat burned through her again at the instant, vivid recall of Constantine's mouth on hers, his muscular body pressing her into the soft leather couch.

Carla's expression was taut as she leaned against the frame of the kitchen door, her feet bare, her arms wrapping her thin silk robe closely around her waist. "I knew it. He wants you again."

"No." A little desperately, Sienna searched out painkillers, drank two down with a glass of water, then found mugs and tea bags, glad for the excuse to avoid Carla's too-sharp gaze. "At least, no more or less than he wants any woman."

"So, why does he want you to go to Medinos?"

She set the mugs on the table and dropped in the tea bags. "Not because he wants a relationship."

She poured hot water over the fragrant chamomile. What had happened on the couch had nothing to do with a relationship. It had been sex, pure and simple. Planned sex. Constantine had made no bones about wanting her and she hadn't been able to resist him.

Sienna removed the tea bags and handed Carla her mug. "I'm going to Medinos because a de Vries rep will be at the opening of the new Atraeus Resort. With any luck I can stall Constantine long enough to give us a chance to secure that contract."

A glimmer of hope entered Carla's eyes. She knew as well as Sienna that if they signed with de Vries they would be able to pay off the Atraeus loan outright. They would not lose Ambrosi Pearls.

"Hallelujah," Carla murmured. "Finally some light at the end of the tunnel. I just wish you didn't have to go to

Medinos. I don't trust the Atraeus men, and especially not Constantine. He doesn't have a reputation for revisiting anything—not mistakes, and definitely not affairs. Promise me that whatever you do, you won't let him make you his mistress. Nothing's worth that. Nothing."

Stung by the knowledge that even Carla now labeled her brief engagement to Constantine as an affair, Sienna sipped her tea. "The only liaison Constantine and I will be discussing is a business one."

Carla's cheeks were flushed, her jaw set. "Good. That's what I needed to hear. Be careful."

Sienna intended to be.

She turned her attention back to the glittering Medinian sea and a fishing boat maneuvering alongside a long narrow jetty. They were driving through the outskirts of a city now and the streets were increasingly busy. Olive-skinned, dark-eyed Medinians and brightly garbed tourists mingled, enjoying the brilliant sunshine and the vibrant market-style shopping and street cafés.

Tomas pointed out *Castello* Atraeus, a fortress built on the highest point of the headland, which overlooked the city of Medinos and the bay. Constructed of the same stone that many of the villas and cottages were made of, Sienna knew the original ancient *castello* which had once belonged to a noble family that had since died out, had been almost completely destroyed during the war. Lorenzo Atraeus had bought the ruin with his newfound wealth and had painstakingly rebuilt it, following the ancient designs.

Tomas briefly pointed out other buildings of significance including a magnificent modern library, which Lorenzo had gifted to the city, before driving along a curving stretch of beach. Minutes later, he turned into the lushly planted parking bay of The Atraeus Group's newest hotel—a sleek, luxury, seven-star resort that had only recently been completed.

As Sienna exited the car, her gaze was caught by the island that floated closest to Medinos. "Is that Ambrus?"

Tomas waited for the bellhop to load her bags. "Yes. That is Ambrus."

Looping the strap of her handbag over her shoulder, she walked into the air-conditioned paradise of the hotel's signature cream-and-gold foyer, with its intricately carved frescoes and exquisite mosaics.

Her heart thumped once, hard, when she glimpsed a head of coal-black hair brushing a familiar set of broad shoulders. Constantine was dressed casually in dark pants, a black T-shirt and a loose jacket. In the lush surroundings, he seemed even more darkly masculine and exotic than she remembered. His gaze locked with hers and any idea that this was a chance meeting evaporated.

Feeling overheated and a little flustered because she hadn't expected to encounter Constantine at the front desk, Sienna busied herself signing the register and collecting her key. Constantine spoke briefly with Tomas, directed the bellhop to her suite then insisted on accompanying her.

The lavish ground-floor suite he directed her to had both internal and external access, with huge glass sliding doors that framed an achingly beautiful view of Ambrus. Constantine unlocked the doors to a private patio.

Shielding her eyes against the sun, Sienna stepped outside and stared across the limpid blue water at towering black cliffs. High, rugged hills were bleached the color of ripe wheat by the sun, and the lower slopes were dotted by flashes of white, which she assumed were goats.

She had expected to feel a connection to Medinos. For years, just the name itself had entranced her, although the villa and pearl facility her family used to own were definitely past history.

Sienna logged the moment Constantine moved to stand beside her, her stomach clenching at the faint scents of aftershave and clean male. "Ambrus looks deserted."

Her gaze connected with his. For a split second she was spun back to the interlude at his house, the moment of clarity when the lights had come on and she had seen the possession in his eyes.

He indicated the island. "The mining company operates on the eastern side. There's a construction project for a new resort complex and marina on the northern headland. Other than that, we run goats to keep the weeds down. Your family's old pearl facility is based on the northwestern side."

She stared at the high, stark cliffs, the utter absence of anything as soft and tamed as a sandy beach. She knew there were calm bays and inlets—there had to be for the pearl beds—but there was nothing remotely civilized about the southern end.

A discreet tap on her door relieved her of her tingling awareness of Constantine and the hot flashes of memory that kept surfacing. Glad for an excuse to end the unnerving tension, Sienna walked through the elegant sitting room and opened the door so the bellhop could carry her bags inside.

Relieved to see her padlocked sample case stacked on top of her luggage, she tipped the lean young man. The future of Ambrosi Pearls was literally tied up in the contents of that case.

She started guiltily as Constantine prowled up behind her.

His gaze rested broodingly on the sample case, although he couldn't possibly know its contents.

He handed her two cream-colored embossed cards. The first was an invitation to the official opening of the resort that evening, the second an invitation to a luncheon to celebrate the product launch of a new collection of Atraeus gold jewelry the following day. "We won't have time to talk about the loan details today. That discussion will have to wait until this evening."

On the back of both cards, precisely handwritten—no doubt by Tomas or another of Constantine's people—were instructions on dress, reminding her that while Medinos might be a tourist destination, it was closer to the east in its moral codes than the west.

Cheeks flushed, she slipped the cards in her handbag, which was still looped over her shoulder. "Thank you."

Constantine stepped past her and paused at the open door. "I was certain you would appreciate the opportunity to circulate."

Sienna closed the door behind him and leaned against the cool wood waiting for the pounding in her chest to subside.

Constantine had seemed manageable in Sydney—barely. A mere hour ago she had been happily operating under the assumption that on a business footing, at least, she could handle him.

But this was not the Constantine she had known two years ago. The way he had seduced her so easily the other night was a case in point. He had ruthlessly used his fall and the power outage to maneuver her into having sex with him. The fact that she had wanted the sex wasn't at issue as much as the fact that Constantine was harder, sharper, more manipulative and dominant than she had bargained on.

And she was almost certain he knew exactly what she was up to on Medinos.

Eight

<u>**Eight**</u>

Constantine tracked Sienna's leisurely progress across the crowded reception room. Even if he hadn't been informed that she had entered the ballroom of Medinos's newest and most spectacular hotel, it would have been easy to spot her by the turning of heads as she strolled past.

Terminating a conversation, he placed his drink on a sideboard, his temper flashing to a slow burn when he saw what she was wearing.

Her hair was caught up in a knot, emphasizing the dress, which was designed to induce a stroke. A pale champagne halter, the gown was deceptively plain, the silky fabric an almost perfect match for the color of Sienna's skin so that at first glance he had thought she was naked. Added to that, the halter neck meant she wasn't wearing a bra.

His jaw tightened against a throb of mingled desire and irritation. Ankle length and discreetly cut, the gown paid lip service to the dress code he had demanded she follow, while subtly undermining it at every turn.

Beside him Lucas let out a low whistle.

"Look too long," Constantine said calmly, "and I'll put your eyes out."

When he had been dating Sienna, to avoid the press they hadn't gone out together at night. Normally, when he had been in Sydney, he had picked her up from work and taken her back to his apartment, or he'd followed her home to her place. The clothes she'd worn had been elegant, sleek, businesslike and sexy; he had barely noticed them.

The only other clothes he had seen had been her casual at-home gear, a bikini that had driven him crazy and her underwear, which for the most part had been tantalizing, but practical. What Sienna did or didn't have in her wardrobe hadn't interested him. Until now.

Zane, who had flown in from the States that morning for the resort opening, watched Sienna with his usual cool assessment. If Lucas was a shade on the wild side, Zane was worse, but he had the good sense to stay quiet about it. A couple of years on the streets of L.A. after he had run away from his mother's fourth marriage, and before they had managed to track him down, had left their mark. On the surface Zane was cool and calm with a killer charm. He never lacked for feminine company, but it was a fact that he didn't trust any of the women he had dated.

Zane sipped the beer he'd been nursing for the past twenty minutes. "It could be worth it. I notice she didn't bring her accountant with her."

Or anyone else, Constantine thought with grim satisfaction.

Lucas lifted a brow. "No briefcase, either."

No briefcase. No bra.

Zane took another swallow of his beer. "She doesn't look happy to be here."

Rub salt into the wound, Constantine thought bleakly. But at least she wasn't carrying that damned sample case.

"You don't need this," Lucas said bluntly.

Constantine's expression remained impassive. He hadn't discussed what had happened in Sydney, nor would he, but he was aware that Lucas knew exactly how focused he was on the CEO of Ambrosi Pearls.

He could have left the talking to their legal team. The options were clear-cut and his people were very, very good. Unless Sienna produced a large check, The Atraeus Group owned Ambrosi. But since those intense moments across the gravesite, this had ceased to be about the money.

At least for him.

He watched as Sienna paused to talk to an exquisitely dressed Japanese couple, her cool poise at odds with the off-the-register passion and fire that had seared him in Sydney.

The reason Sienna was in Medinos was simple. Aside from the fact that he wanted to make love to her again, he needed to know just how far she would go to clear the debt. The thought that she would agree to sleep with him in order to influence the negotiations wasn't something he wanted to dwell on, but after the debacle two years ago, and the fact that she had let him make love to her so easily the other night, he couldn't afford to ignore the possibility.

"The situation with the water rights has…complicated things," he explained to his brother.

Lucas shook his head. "The only real complication I can see is ten meters away and closing."

Zane finished his beer and set the glass down, his expression wry. "Ciao. Watch your back."

Constantine's gaze narrowed as a male guest moved

in on Sienna. His jaw tightened when he recognized Alex Panopoulos.

His phone vibrated. He registered the Sydney number of the security firm he had used to investigate the Ambrosi family. As he lifted the phone to his ear, Sienna turned to speak to Panopoulos. If he'd thought the front view of the dress was daring, the back of the gown was nonexistent. "It's not my back that's the problem."

Sienna managed to extricate herself from Alex Panopoulos on the pretext that she had to check her wrap. Pausing in a quiet alcove decorated with marble statuary and lush, potted palms, she folded the transparent length of champagne gauze into almost nothing and stuffed it into her evening bag. What she really wanted was a few moments to study the room and see if she could spot Northcliffe, the de Vries rep she was scheduled to meet with in the morning.

She caught a glimpse of Constantine, darkly handsome in evening dress as he talked into a cell phone, and her heart pounded hard.

Nerves still humming, she merged with the flow of guests while she examined that moment of raw panic.

Every time she remembered that she had encouraged Constantine to make love to her, her stomach clenched. Like it or not, where Constantine was concerned she was vulnerable, and the emotional risk of getting too close was high.

A waiter cruised past. She refused an array of canapés, too on edge to either eat or drink until she had identified Northcliffe. Pausing beside a glass display, she studied a series of gorgeously detailed pieces of jewelry, advance samples of tomorrow's product launch. For a timeless moment the room and the nervy anticipation dissolved and she was drawn into the fascinating juxtaposition of lucent tourmaline and smoothly worked gold.

She wasn't a designer. When it came to creating art or beautiful jewelry, she was utterly clueless. Her passion had always been the business side of things. Her father used to jokingly proclaim that she had the heart of a shopkeeper. It was a fact that she was never happier than when she was making a sale.

A faint tingling at her nape made her stiffen.

A glimpse of broad shoulders increased her tension.

If that was Constantine, then he had crossed the room, which meant he had seen her.

"Sienna. Glad you could make it."

She saw taut cheekbones and a tough jaw, but it wasn't Constantine. It was his younger brother, Lucas.

With his slightly battered features, courtesy of two seasons of professional rugby in Australia, and his smoldering bad-boy looks, he was undoubtedly hot.

Lucas had once tried to date Carla. Fatally, he had made his move after Constantine had walked out on Sienna and before Lucas had realized the wedding was off. Carla, who was loyal to a fault, had taken no prisoners and the public spat at a fabulous new nightclub had become the stuff of legend.

Magazines had lined up for the short time both Ambrosi girls had hit the publicity limelight, although Carla had handled the attention a lot better than Sienna. With her PR mind-set she had decided to view the fight with Lucas as a gold-plated opportunity to boost Ambrosi Pearls' profile, and thanks to her, orders had flooded in.

"You know me, Lucas." She checked out the last place she had seen Constantine. "Gold, jewels, objets d'art. I couldn't resist."

"You look like one of Constantine's objets d'art yourself."

Sienna countered his comment with a direct look. The dress she wore was sexier and more revealing than anything she would normally have worn to a business occasion, but in this case it was warranted. The gown had been used in their latest advertising campaign. Harold Northcliffe, who should have received the glossy press kit she had expressed to his Sydney office, would instantly recognize it. The jewelry itself was a set of prototypes they had designed with de Vries and the sophisticated European market in mind. "If you want to score points off me, Lucas, you're going to have to try harder than that. The dress belongs to Carla."

The amusement flashed out of his dark gaze. "It was the jewelry that really caught my eye."

"I didn't know you were interested in jewelry design." Lucas was known as The Atraeus Group's "hatchet man." His reputation was based more on corporate raiding than the creative arts.

"Not normally," he murmured, an odd note in his voice, "but I'm certain Constantine will be. When I first saw you I thought you were wearing a traditional set of Medinian bridal jewels. Quite a publicity stunt considering that you used to be engaged to Constantine."

Dismayed, Sienna touched the pearls at her throat. The pieces she was wearing were based on her grandfather Sebastien's original drawings. The delicate choker consisted of seed pearls woven into classical Medinian motifs, with a deep blue teardrop sapphire suspended from the center. Matching earrings with tiny drop sapphires dangled from her ears, and an intricate pearl bracelet studded with sapphires encircled her wrist.

"Speaking of the devil," Lucas murmured, looking directly over her shoulder.

A hot tingle ran down Sienna's spine. The knowledge that Constantine was directly behind her and closing in was so intense that for a moment she couldn't breathe.

Even though she was prepared, the confrontation was a shock. Dressed in a formal black evening suit, Constantine seemed taller, physically broader and, in that first moment, coldly remote. Although the impression of remoteness disappeared the instant she met his glittering gaze.

"We need to talk."

The curt demand sent another hot tingle through her. She resisted the urge to cross her arms over her chest. Suddenly the dress seemed too thin, too revealing, definitely not her best idea. "That is why I'm here."

A muscle pulsed along the side of his jaw. If she hadn't known he was angry before, she knew it then.

"Outside. Now."

Her jaw tightened at the low register of his voice, the unmistakable whiplash of command. "I don't think so." The last time she had taken orders she had been five and she had *wanted* that Barbie doll.

His hand closed around her arm; his palm burned into her naked skin. A pang of pure feminine fear shot through her, making all the fine hairs at her nape stand on end, but she dug her heels in. To anyone watching they would no doubt appear to be engaged in an intimately close conversation, but Constantine's grip was firm.

When her resistance registered, he bent close. His lips almost brushed her ear and his warm breath fanned her neck, sending another fiery pang through her, this time straight to her loins. She froze, pinned in place by the potent lash of sensation. For a split second she couldn't move. Worse, she didn't want to.

"We're leaving now. If you make a fuss, I'll carry you out and no one will stop me."

"You can't do this."

"Try me."

Wildly she checked for Lucas, but he had conveniently disappeared. "This is assault."

He laughed, and the weird primitive female thing that had frozen her in place and which was probably designed as a survival mechanism for the race so that women would have sex with men even if they were hideous and had no manners at all, dissolved. Suddenly, she was back. "I'll call the police."

"Before or after our business meeting tomorrow?"

Her teeth snapped together at his blatant use of the power he had over both her and Ambrosi. "That's blackmail."

He applied pressure, unceremoniously shunting her out of the room. "Babe, that's business."

Nine

Sienna dug in her high-heels as they entered a deserted gallery with tall, arched windows along one wall, softly lit works of art on the other. "This is as far as I go. We're out of the ballroom, which strangely enough you wanted to leave despite the fact that it's your party. But if we go any farther, I'm afraid no one will hear my screams."

"Calm down, I'm not interested in hurting you."

Ignoring her protest, Constantine swung her up into his arms.

Sienna pushed at his shoulders and attempted to wriggle free. "You could have fooled me."

Constantine strode a short distance then set her down directly in front of a large oil painting, grunting softly when her elbow accidentally caught him in the stomach.

Just when she was congratulating herself on finally ruffling his steely control, one long tanned finger flicked the sapphire teardrop just above the swell of her cleavage. "Part of the new promotion?"

Her cheeks burned with a combination of irked fury and a dizzying heat. "How would you know about that?"

"I'm still on your client mailing list. I get all of your pamphlets."

"I'll have to speak to my assistant."

Better still, she would edit the list herself. Those glossy pamphlets were too expensive to mail out to people who were never going to buy their products.

Constantine's expression was grim. "When you walked into the ballroom wearing Medinian bridal jewels you caused quite a stir. Was that planned, or a coincidence?"

She followed the direction of his gaze. The jewel-bright colors of the large oil painting that loomed overhead came into sharp focus. She studied what was, without doubt, a wedding portrait. "I had no idea these were wedding jewels."

"Or that the press could put two and two together and make ten." Constantine's expression was frustratingly remote. "This isn't a game, Sienna."

She flushed. The only thing she was guilty of was trying to save her family business and she would not apologize for that. "I'm not playing a game or pulling a publicity stunt."

Constantine folded his arms over his chest. "Prove it."

She was tempted to explain nothing, pack her bag and leave on the earliest flight out, but until the loan situation was resolved, she was stuck. "Very well. Come to my room and I'll show you."

Unlocking the door to her suite, she stepped inside and flicked a switch. Lights glowed softly over the marble floors and luxurious white-on-white furnishings.

She set her evening bag on a coffee table flanked by cream leather couches and walked to the wall safe. Punching in her PIN, she dragged out the sample case, which was sitting on top, removed her laptop then quickly shoved the sample case back in the safe, out of sight.

She placed the laptop, a girly pink model with all the latest bells and whistles, on the coffee table. Booting it up, she accessed the jewelry design files, which contained a photographed portfolio of designs that had belonged to her grandfather. She found the scanned page she wanted then removed the jewelry she was wearing and arranged it alongside the laptop. "These jewels are prototypes. They're not in production—"

"Until you locate a buyer."

Sienna drew a calming breath. "—until we have received expressions of interest."

"Otherwise known as a sales order."

Her jaw tightened. "The Ambrosi versions aren't an exact match of the jewels my grandfather sketched. The designs have merely been based on his drawings. We had no idea they were bridal jewelry."

Constantine was oddly still, the pooling lamplight softening the taut line of his jaw, the chiseled cheekbones and the faint hollows beneath. In the lamplight, with his coal-dark hair flowing to his shoulders, he looked fierce and utterly male, much as she had imagined ancient Medinian warriors must have looked. "It seems I owe you an apology."

"Not at all." Grimly, she powered the laptop down and then had to go through the whole risky rigmarole of taking the sample case back out of the safe in order to slot in the laptop.

"Allow me," Constantine said, smoothly taking the sample case from her grasp.

Heart pounding, Sienna reclaimed the case and jammed it back in the safe. If Constantine discovered she was here trying to make a deal with de Vries, that would not be good. With any luck, he hadn't seen the discreet branding on the case because the printed side had been facing away from him when he had taken it from her.

A tiny clinking sound drew her attention. Constantine had picked the necklace up off the coffee table. The delicate combination of pearls and sapphires looked even more fragile against his hands. He gently touched a pearl. Sienna shivered, as if his finger had stroked across her skin.

His gaze connected with hers. "So, who did you wear those pearls for, if it wasn't me?"

"I don't know what you mean." Desperate for a distraction, Sienna walked through to the small adjacent kitchenette and bar, opened a cupboard and found glasses.

After filling the glasses with chilled water from the fridge, she handed one to Constantine, taking care to avoid brushing his fingers.

Constantine finished his drink in two long swallows.

Intensely aware of his gaze on her, she placed her drink on the coffee table and gathered up the sample jewels. The sooner they were out of sight the happier she would feel. If she had understood the potential for disaster inherent in the Medinian designs, she would have stuck to the more modern flower-patterned pearls.

Walking through to her bedroom, she wrapped the jewels in a silk scarf and placed them in the top dresser drawer. She would put them back in the sample case and lock them in the safe once Constantine had left.

When she returned to the sitting room Constantine was pacing. He picked up a small bronze statuette then set it down almost immediately. If she didn't know better, she would think he was nervous.

He glanced at his watch. "Have you eaten?"

The complete change in tack startled her enough that she answered without thinking. "Not since the flight."

"Then I'll order dinner in." He picked up the sleekly modern phone, which was situated on an escritoire.

His suggestion was subtly shocking. Her heart sped up at the thought of spending any more time secluded and alone with Constantine. "No. I'm not hungry."

"You need to eat, and I've made you miss dinner. If you don't want to eat here, we can go somewhere more public."

Sienna considered her options. Constantine had made no bones about the fact that he wanted her. The realization that she was actually contemplating sleeping with him again stopped her in her tracks.

Just days ago she hadn't been ready for a sexual relationship with anyone. Yet, despite being burned twice by Constantine, a stubborn part of her was still dizzily, irresistibly attracted.

Sex had to be out of the question.

She was here on business. For her family and Ambrosi Pearls' sake she had to stay focused.

To shield her blush, she busied herself with the unnecessary job of checking the lock on the safe. "I do need to eat, but not here."

If they ate out it would be easier to avoid talking business and it was a fact that she needed to stall Constantine until late morning at least. By then she would know whether or not de Vries was going to place an order.

"Suits me."

Constantine's unexpectedly mild tone was surprising. For a moment, she thought she saw relief in his gaze, which didn't make sense.

Confused, she walked to her bedroom and grabbed a silk shrug that would cover her bare shoulders and décolletage better than the wrap she'd worn earlier. When she returned to the sitting room, Constantine was replacing the telephone receiver.

"I've booked a table at a small café on the waterfront."

"Sounds great." She sent him her brightest, most professional smile. At this time of year, the height of the tourist season, a waterfront café would be crowded. They would be lucky to hear themselves think, let alone talk. A business discussion would be out of the question.

She picked up her evening bag and her key, and preceded Constantine through the door. She glimpsed their reflection in the ornate hall mirror as they strolled out of the suite. Constantine was tall, broad-shouldered and remote in his formal evening dress. She looked unexpectedly provocative, the soft silk clinging to her curves as she walked.

A powerful sense of déjà vu gripped her as she closed the door behind her, laced with a cocktail of emotions she thought she had dealt with, and dismissed, two years ago.

The image could have been a film clip from the past. They had looked like a couple. They had looked like lovers.

Renewed panic gripped her when she considered that technically they were lovers. That all she had to do was give in to the pressure Constantine was exerting and she would be back in his bed. Again.

The restaurant was tiny and packed with customers but Sienna's relief faded when the two dark-suited bodyguards who had shadowed them since they'd exited the hotel suddenly disappeared and the proprietor led them to a private courtyard. A lone table, which had obviously just been vacated by early diners, was in the process of being set.

Within seconds they were alone.

Girding herself for an unpleasant discussion that would spell the end of Ambrosi, Sienna took the seat Constantine held for her, but instead of launching into business, Constantine seemed content to relax and enjoy the meal. Listening to his casual banter with the proprietor who served them personally and observing his teasing charm when a small child ventured out of the kitchens to chatter shyly at them, she found herself gradually relaxing as well.

An hour later, after dining on creamy goat cheese and figs, followed by an array of fresh seafood including spicy fried squid, the local specialty, Sienna declined dessert.

Her tension snapped back as soon as they reached the enclosed gardens of the resort. The security team melted away once again and she found herself alone with Constantine. Warily, she studied a walled garden with its limpid ornamental pool. Nothing about this part of the resort was familiar. "Where are we?"

"My private quarters. I was about to offer you a nightcap."

Something kicked hard in her chest. Disappointment. "If this is a proposition, believe me, right now sex is the last thing—"

"What if I cleared the debt?"

His words were like a slap in the face, spinning her back two years to the scene in her apartment when Constantine had point-blank accused her of agreeing to marry him in order to guarantee the financial health of Ambrosi Pearls.

It had taken months but she had finally decided that if he didn't know who she was, or what was important to her, that was his problem not hers.

It was difficult to believe that she had ever been naive enough to imagine that he had fallen in love with her, that they had spent six weeks together making love.

Not making love, she corrected. Get it right. Having

sex. Doing exactly what they had done on his couch three nights ago in Sydney.

Constantine hadn't moved. He was simply watching her, his arms folded over his chest, utterly cool and in control. She was suddenly sharply aware that she was being manipulated.

He wanted a refusal.

He had deliberately goaded her in order to get one. Interesting.

Why ask if she would sleep with him for money now, and in such an insulting manner, unless he had finally realized that he had been wrong about her two years ago?

"Last I heard," she said quietly, "you weren't finding it that hard to get a date."

"I take it that's a 'no.'"

"Take that as a definite 'no.'"

"Would the answer have been different if, instead of a temporary arrangement, I'd proposed marriage?"

Bleakly, Sienna decided, that question hurt even more than the last. She scanned the garden in order to get her bearings and find the quickest route back to her room. "There's no point to this conversation since you didn't propose. But since you're so interested…" Hating the huskiness in her voice, she started toward an indentation in the wall that looked like a door. "If I ever do marry, the relationship and my husband will have to fit around my needs."

"I take it that means Ambrosi Pearls?"

A sharp thrill coursed down her spine when she became aware that Constantine had padded up close behind her. As she stepped deeper into the inky shadows that swamped the courtyard, the notion that she was not only being maneuvered but actively hunted, intensified. "Not anymore, since you're intent on relieving me of that particular burden."

Halting at the wall, she studied the door, searching for a way to open it. Like the problems in her life, there did not appear to be a simple answer.

"Interesting," he muttered, "that you should use the word burden. I would never have guessed that you craved freedom."

"Freedom. Now there's a concept." The thought of being free of the debt burden was suddenly, unexpectedly heady, even if it did mean the demise of the company.

Guilt for the disloyal thought fueled her irritation as she pushed at the door. It gave only slightly. Frustration gripped her. She was over being a victim, especially of garden designers. "Please tell me this opens."

Constantine reached down and released a small latch she hadn't noticed in the dark. His arm brushed hers, sending a small shock of awareness through her. Her frustration mounted, both at her knee-jerk response and the fact that the door swung open with well-oiled ease. She was certain that at some level, Constantine was enjoying this and, abruptly, she lost her temper.

Two more steps and the conversation would be over, for tonight. "Back to the hypothetical marriage." As she stepped past Constantine, she deliberately trailed one finger down the lapel of his jacket.

The gesture was intimate, provocative, a dangerous form of payback that registered in the silvery heat of his gaze. "If you are considering a proposal, like I said in Sydney, if the prospective husband just happens to have a healthy bank balance and a flair for financial matters, as far as I'm concerned the situation would be win-win."

Constantine controlled the fierce heat flowing through him as Sienna strode down the path that led back to the resort's main reception area. She mounted a set of stone steps, the champagne silk gown swirling around outrageously sexy high heels. For a split second, the garden lights glowed through the dress, outlining her long, shapely legs, giving the momentary illusion that she was naked.

As distracting as the thought of Sienna naked was, it was the image of her naked and wearing Medinian bridal jewels that was consuming him at that moment.

Constantine briefly acknowledged the security guard he had tasked with protecting Sienna as the man stepped past him and followed her at a discreet distance. There were no serious threats on Medinos but, after the stir she had caused by attending his hotel opening wearing bridal jewels, the paparazzi were bound to hear about it.

Added to that, Alex Panopoulos was here and on the hunt. Constantine didn't regard the Greek as a serious threat, but if he tried to approach Sienna, Constantine wanted to know about it.

When both Sienna and the bodyguard had disappeared from sight, he closed the courtyard door with quiet deliberation and locked it.

It had gone against all of his instincts to let her go, when what he'd really wanted was to cement his claim. But there would be time enough for that, and he knew if he touched her now he wouldn't be content with playing the part of a restrained lover.

He hadn't liked hurting her, but she had pushed him with the jewels and the dress. He had needed to see her reaction to his proposition and he had gotten the result he had wanted. Despite ruthlessly using his company's promotional event to target new sales avenues for Ambrosi Pearls, she had refused to sleep with him to save her company.

What he hadn't bargained on, ever since he had seen her at the funeral, was his own response.

Just days ago he had been certain of Sienna's involvement in her father's scam. But the second she had lifted her head and looked at him at her father's funeral, as if they were still lovers, he had been the one who had been unmasked. He had wanted her whether she was innocent or guilty.

He had studied all of the paperwork and Ambrosi Pearls' financials. There was no tangible link between Sienna and the money Roberto had siphoned out of his father.

Two years ago he had miscalculated. He was determined not to do so a second time.

He wanted Sienna, but as far as he was concerned there were now only two options. It was either strictly business, or bed.

Ten

Dawn streaked the horizon with shades of gold, purple and rose as Sienna walked to the largest of a network of tropically landscaped pools. Shivering slightly at the cool dampness of the morning—supplemented by the resort's sprinkler system, which jetted vaporized water into the air—she eased out of her sandals.

A faint movement caught her eye as she dropped her towel, key and sarong onto one of the resort's deck chairs. The bodyguard who had followed her to her suite the previous night was standing beneath one of the palms. Annoyed, but determined to ignore him so long as he kept his distance, she walked into the water.

She swam energetically for a few minutes then turned on her back to catch her breath. The snick-snick of the sprinklers had stopped, replaced by slow dripping as lush palms shed excess water onto smooth limestone paving.

The deep quiet of the early morning gradually sank in, mending the ravages of a mostly sleepless night.

Constantine had offered to clear Ambrosi Pearls' debt if she slept with him.

Taking a deep breath, she ducked and breaststroked the length of the pool underwater, using the discipline of the physical challenge to cool her escalating temper. When she surfaced at the opposite end her lungs were burning.

On a scale of insults, she guessed it wasn't any worse than the ones he'd leveled at her two years ago, but the fact that he still viewed her that way after all this time was infuriating. If she had wanted to marry money, she could easily have found herself a rich husband by now. She hadn't. Two years after their split, she had barely dated.

Unlike Constantine.

Which brought her back to the manipulation angle.

For reasons of his own, Constantine wanted her off balance. Given his stake in Ambrosi Pearls, the reason couldn't be a business one. He already held all of the cards in terms of money and power. Barring a miracle from de Vries, Ambrosi Pearls was at his mercy; whatever Constantine wanted to happen, would happen. All she could do was plea bargain for her family and the staff.

If it was anyone but Constantine she might assume he wanted revenge, except he could have had that two years ago. All he'd had to do was expose the scandal of her father's dealings and the press would have ripped her reputation to shreds. He had chosen not to do that, saving her that final humiliation.

She frowned, her thoughts going back to Constantine's proposition.

The fact that he had made an offer, couched in business terms, meant he would be prepared to pay, and that, she decided, made him insect material.

Feeling happier with her assessment of him, she swam another length, kicked toward the steps and walked out of the water, slicking wet hair out of her eyes.

Movement sent tension zinging through her. Not the security guy or Constantine. Alex Panopoulos was ensconced on the deck chair next to hers.

He pushed to his feet, her towel in his hands as she approached. "Do you usually swim alone?"

Sienna smiled coolly, her gaze missing his by a calculated few millimeters. "I swim for exercise, not company."

Predictably, he didn't let go of the towel when he handed it over, so that she had to engage in a miniature tug-of-war to pull it free.

Annoyed by the game, and feeling exposed in her bikini when he was fully dressed, she forced another cool smile. "Mr. Panopoulos, if you don't give me the towel, I'll walk back to my suite without it."

"Alex, please." With a shrug he let the towel go. "I was hoping you would agree to be my date at lunch."

"Sorry, I already have a date." She quickly dried off as Panopoulos persevered with a predictable stream of conversation then wrapped the sarong around her breasts.

A flash of movement caught her eye. Constantine, dressed in low-riding gray sweatpants and a soft, faded muscle shirt, as if he'd been jogging, was strolling toward her from the direction of her room. Realization dawned. Constantine's bodyguard had informed him that she had company at the pool.

Constantine nodded at Panopoulos, his greeting curt.

His gaze locked on hers. "Are you ready to go?"

Suddenly any male threat that Panopoulos posed seemed ridiculously tame. Panopoulos's face actually paled as Constantine collected her things.

Sienna scooped up the damp towel. "What took you so long?"

His hand cupped her elbow, and they were moving. She managed to pull free without making it look like a fight. Reflexively, she rubbed her elbow, which tingled with warmth. "Thanks for the rescue, but you don't have to take it this far. I can cope."

Sunlight glanced off the grim line of his jaw. "What did Panopoulos want?"

"That's none of your business."

"If he's bothering you I'll take care of it."

"The same way you deal with newspaper reporters?"

A glint of amusement entered his eyes. "No." Sienna was transfixed by an emotion she absolutely did not want to feel: a primitive surge of satisfaction because her man had stepped in and claimed her.

Her man. Her heart pounded once, hard. She must be out of her mind. She should resent Constantine's actions; she should be fighting with him. Instead her body was in the process of a slow, steady meltdown.

She stopped walking, forcing him to halt. "Why are you having me watched?"

"Not watched, looked after. A couple of the major tabloids have published speculative stories linking us romantically. And Panopoulos hasn't exactly kept his mouth closed about what he wants."

"I can deal with Panopoulos."

His gaze narrowed. "Like you did just then?"

A door slammed. Voices and laughter pierced the air, unnaturally loud in the morning stillness. Sienna was suddenly acutely aware that the sarong had soaked up the dripping moisture from her hair and her bikini and had become transparent where it clung.

Two young children barreled along the path, followed

by their parents. Sienna stepped aside to allow them passage. It was time to take some control back.

She held out her hand, palm up. "Sandals and room key, please."

Annoyingly, Constantine handed them over as if there wasn't an issue. She slipped her feet into the sandals, and wished she had thought to bring dark glasses. They did a great job of shouting "distance," which right now she desperately needed.

The rising sun shone directly in her eyes as she rounded a curve in the path, determined to put some distance between herself and Constantine. Because her feet were wet, her sandals kept slipping, making walking awkward.

Constantine easily kept pace beside her. "Be careful, those pavers are slippery."

"I'm fine."

In an effort to put more space between them, she edged sideways, and then she did slip.

Constantine's hand briefly closed on her arm, steadying her. "Why don't you ever listen?"

She jerked free and stalked the rest of the way to her door. "When you say something I'm interested in hearing, I'll listen."

"That'll be when hell freezes over, then."

The words were bitten out, but laced with an amused exasperation that, frustratingly, charmed her and made her want to bite back and bait him a little more.

Grimly, she fitted the key card in its slot. "You know what, Constantine? Maybe you should stop worrying about what I'm doing and get yourself a life."

"What makes you think I don't get exactly what I want?"

The low, sexy register of his voice froze her in place. Now was the time to back off, to step inside and politely close the door, but his gaze held her locked in some kind of stasis. She knew what it was; she had spent enough time analyzing why she had fallen so hard for Constantine in the first place. It was the alpha male thing; he took control and for reasons unknown, she responded. In this case he had dealt with Panopoulos as easily if he had been shooing a fruit fly away and she couldn't help but be impressed.

"I came over this morning to apologize. I'm sorry about the position I put you in last night, but I had to know. I also owe you an apology for what happened two years ago."

She blinked, struggling with the abrupt mental shift. Of all the scenarios she had gone over in her mind, she had never imagined that Constantine would apologize for their breakup. "What made you change your mind?"

"I did some research—"

"You mean you had me investigated."

"Call it what you like," he said flatly. "All of your financial dealings and business practices are straight down the middle. Roberto was the taker; you were the giver. Nothing in your pattern indicated that you would resort to fraud. And after what happened two years ago, and the fact that you had never tried to contact me again for money or anything else, I decided it didn't make sense that you were involved in this deal."

Sienna briefly saw red over the way he had arrived at his verdict. "Let me get this clear. Because I didn't ask you for money after we split up, I'm okay?"

A pulse jumped along the side of his jaw. "It's standard practice to run security checks on business associates."

"Tell me, did you have me profiled two years ago before you decided to date me?"

"Calm down," he said curtly, as if she was actually going to follow that order.

Fingers shaking with outrage, she started to tap in the

PIN that unlocked her door but before she could complete the sequence, he snagged the key card out of the slot and slipped it into his pocket.

"Oh, this is good. A repeat of the he-man tactics."

His brows jerked together. "What he-man tactics?"

She began to tick them off on her fingers. "The threat over my father's grave, holding me against my will in your car, forcing me to meet you the night after the funeral—"

"I didn't hold you against your will. We were in a supermarket parking lot. If you hadn't avoided me for four days, the meetings would have been conducted in a conventional business setting."

"I had no reason to want to see you. If you'll remember, the last conversation we had wasn't exactly pleasant."

"Which is why I'm apologizing now."

"Two years too late, and it's the worst apology I've ever heard."

His gaze glittered in the dim coolness of the portico that shaded her door. "Nevertheless, you're going to hear the rest of it. I tracked the loan payments. They were all deposited into one of your father's personal accounts, not Ambrosi Pearls' working account."

"That's right, one of Dad's gambling accounts, which was why I couldn't be sure the money wasn't winnings. If you knew that, why ask if I'd sleep with you for money, when you already knew I wouldn't?"

"You weren't involved in your father's loan scam, but that didn't mean you didn't know about it."

"So you tested me." Okay, she had expected that. She understood that a lot of women would be attracted to Constantine simply because he was so rich and powerful. But that didn't excuse him for thinking she could be one of them, or the fact that he still didn't get her.

She met his gaze squarely, which was a mistake, because Constantine's eyes were one of the most potent things about him. They pierced and held with a steady power that had always made her go weak at the knees. "Apology accepted, as far as it went, but I'd prefer that we just stuck to business. Like, for example, what time can we meet today?"

She knew about the official luncheon, because she had an invitation. There was also some kind of photo shoot for Medinos's most famous export, gold, scheduled for later in the day. "I've got meetings most of this morning, so I've slotted you in after lunch."

"Good, because I'm booked to fly out this evening." An early afternoon meeting would also give her the time she needed to meet with Northcliffe and hopefully wrap up the de Vries deal.

"I don't believe you personally wanted the money two years ago," he said abruptly. "What I could never accept was the fact that you gave your loyalty to your father and your company instead of to me."

"I was afraid you'd break the engagement if you found out, which you did, so I guess the lack of trust goes both ways."

His fingers tangled in her wet hair. "Two years ago," he muttered huskily, "I wasn't thinking straight."

Her stomach tensed against the tingling warmth of his touch. "Are you saying you were wrong?"

"I'm saying I shouldn't have let you go."

His answer neatly slid away from the admission she had wanted, but when his palm cupped her nape, a pang of old longing mingled with a raw jolt of desire shafted through her.

Eleven

Constantine's head dipped. Sienna had plenty of time to avoid the kiss, a long drawn out moment to understand that this was exactly the result she had wanted, and then his mouth settled on hers.

Her palms landed on his chest, curled into soft interlock. The hot scents of male and sweat filled her nostrils, triggering memories. Flash after hot flash of his long, muscled body against hers, the damp drag of skin, his hands on her hips, the intense pleasure she'd derived from every touch. The shattering intimacy of making love…

She went up on her toes, leaned into the kiss. A small sound shivered up from deep in her belly. He stepped closer, moving her back a half step until her spine settled against the cool barrier of the door. His hold was loose enough that she could easily pull free. One hand still cupped her nape, the other was spread across the small of her back, but, contrarily, having the choice granted her the freedom to stay.

Somewhere in the back of her mind she was aware that she shouldn't be responding to a man she had spent two years avoiding for a whole list of excellent reasons. Surrendering to him physically went against common sense and plain old-fashioned pride. But a reckless, starved part of her wasn't interested in reason and logic.

Her arms curled around his neck. The unmistakable firmness of his arousal pressed against her belly, sending a shaft of heat through her, and a fierce, crazy elation. Two years, and nothing had changed.

She still wanted him and she had no earthly clue why. For example, why didn't she feel this way about the occasional nice man she had dated since Constantine? Why hadn't she fallen into adoring lust with any one of the hundreds of bronzed, attractive stockbrokers and nine-to-five guys who littered Sydney's Central Business District?

She could have a pleasant, comfortable life with someone who actually loved her. A home, babies…

His mouth slid to her throat. The rough scrape of his jaw sent another raw shudder through her. Gulping air, she dragged his mouth back to hers.

The problem was she responded to Constantine in a way she didn't respond to any other man. It was depressing to think that she might actually be drawn to him because he was so difficult to handle, that after years of suppressing her own desires in order to save Ambrosi Pearls, she needed the battle to feel alive.

Lust was lust, it didn't impress her overly and it had never gotten the best of her before now. She was healthy, with a normal sex drive, but she was also ultrapicky. She didn't just like things so-so; they had to be perfect. Flowers had to be perfectly arranged, her accessories had to complement what she was wearing, otherwise she couldn't concentrate on anything but the fact that something was wrong, even if it was only one minor detail.

A natural extension of that pickiness was that the men in her life had to be right. They had to look right, smell right, feel right, otherwise she just wasn't interested.

Though he was too big, too experienced, too dangerous—nearly more than she could handle—Constantine did smell and taste and feel right, when no one else had ever come close.

His hand slid up over her waist and rib cage. The heat of his palm burned through the sarong as he cupped her breast and gently squeezed. The pad of his thumb rasped over her nipple. A sharp, edgy tension gripped her and for an endless moment her mind went utterly blank. His thumb moved in a lazy circle. The tension coiled tighter, and her mind snapped back into gear.

Oh, no. No way.

She pulled free, banging the back of her head against the door in the process. "I can't do this, not again. I need my key."

When he calmly handed it to her, she lodged it in the lock, tapped in the PIN and shoved the door wide.

She swiped up her towel, which she must have dropped at some point. "That kiss was a mistake. I'm here on business. I can't allow anything to mess that up."

"Don't worry, Ambrosi Pearls will be taken care of."

The breeze plastered the soft tank against the muscled contours of his chest. A resurgence of the hot, edgy tension that had gripped her when he had cupped her breast made her stomach tighten and her nerves hum. "What does that mean, exactly?"

He dipped his head and kissed her again, and like a quivering, weak-kneed fool she let him.

"Simple. I want you back."

Heart pounding, Sienna locked the door. After showering, she blow-dried her hair, applied makeup with fingers that were annoyingly unsteady, then checked her reflection: cream pants, cream camisole, Ambrosi pearl accessories. Cool, calm and classy, the exact opposite of the way she felt.

Constantine wanted her back.

He had said Ambrosi Pearls would be taken care of, although that didn't make sense because the one fact Constantine had always made clear was that he had no interest in committing the cardinal sin of mixing business and pleasure.

After collecting her sample case, she walked to Northcliffe's suite. Just minutes into the meeting, when Northcliffe discreetly checked the time on his watch, Sienna realized her sales pitch wasn't going well.

A short time later, Sienna replaced the sample case in the safe in her room and booted up her laptop. Stunningly, despite keeping her dangling for weeks and showing a good deal of interest, Northcliffe had declined to place an order.

Without a major deal in the pipeline, Ambrosi Pearls was officially in financial jeopardy. With no further sources of revenue, there was nothing to stop Constantine taking the company.

Still in shock at her utter lack of success, Sienna opened up her sheets of financials then put a call through to the company accountant. Sydney was eight hours ahead of Medinos, which meant that her early morning call came in midafternoon for Brian Chin.

After a terse conversation regarding their options—basically none—she asked to be put through to Carla.

Carla was predictably to the point. "Have you talked to Constantine?"

"Not yet, but he has indicated that he will look after the company."

"I'll bet."

They both knew that Constantine was entitled to take the company and break it up if he wanted; after all he had paid for it. If he allowed Ambrosi Pearls to keep trading, that was the best-case scenario.

What worried Sienna most now was that the heavily mortgaged Pier Point house and her mother's small apartment in town, which were both tied in with the company, would go. They had already sold the town house to meet debts. After everything her mother had been through, and in her present fragile state, the thought that she would literally lose everything made Sienna sick to her stomach.

"Did he give you any details about just how he's going to look after Ambrosi Pearls?"

Sienna's cheeks heated. "He didn't go into fine detail." Unless she could count the slow stroke of his fingers at her nape, the glide of his mouth over her throat...

"I'm getting subtext."

"We were...arguing."

There was a taut silence. "He is after you again. I saw the way he was watching you at the funeral. And he went with you to the house afterward. I mean, why was he there at all? Why didn't he just send his legal counsel?"

Sienna finished the call, but Carla's words had sent a small unwelcome shock wave through her. Since she had closed the door on Constantine she had kept herself busy, specifically so she couldn't think, because every time she considered his statement that he wanted her back, her brain froze and her hormones kicked in.

The thought that he had wanted her back before he had landed in Sydney added a layer of calculation to his motives.

He had apologized. Not in a way that made her feel good, but in a factual, male way that told her he was telling the truth. He believed she hadn't been involved in the current scam, but not that she couldn't be an opportunist when it came to money.

He wanted her back, but she couldn't go back into a relationship when she knew Constantine still didn't trust her. Something was going to have to change. He was going to have to change, and she didn't know if that was possible.

The bedside phone rang while Sienna was changing for lunch. Her stomach performing somersaults, because it was most likely Constantine, she picked up the receiver.

It was Tomas.

"Good morning," he murmured in his precise English. "Constantine is busy with meetings until twelve and has asked me to brief you."

"Let me get some paper." Sienna tossed the floaty floral dress she planned to wear over the bed and found a pad and pen in the top drawer of the bedside table. She picked up the phone, expecting to jot down numbers and legal details.

There was a brief pause. "I'm afraid you misunderstand. The briefing concerns lunch."

"Lunch?"

"That's correct."

Tomas followed up with a clipped list of do's and don'ts that sounded like something out of a Victorian diary. Modest dress was essential, with a discreet décolletage and a length preferably below the knee. Low-key makeup and jewelry were advised.

There was a small pause. "There will be a large press contingent at the product launch. Mr. Atraeus has requested that you adhere to his requirements."

The receiver clicked gently in her ear. Sienna listened to the dial tone for several seconds before putting the phone back on its rest.

She stepped out onto her private patio and took a deep breath. Unfortunately, her patio garden, aside from a gorgeous view of Ambrus, also framed the Atraeus fortress where it commanded the headland and a good deal of the island.

Not good.

Her temper still on slow burn, she stepped back inside, repacked the floral dress and shook out a sleek white Audrey Hepburn–inspired sheath that came to midthigh and extracted the flower pearl set from the sample case.

After the disappointment of the meeting with Northcliffe, she had no desire to drink champagne and smile and pretend that everything in Ambrosi Pearls' world was fabulous. Now that the company's fate was sealed, she would have preferred to stay out of the public eye and away from the press.

She had even less desire to follow Constantine's orders.

Minutes later, she checked her hair, which she'd pinned into a smoothly elegant chignon. The style was sophisticated and timeless, a good match for the opulent pearls at her lobes and throat.

The hair and the jewelry were perfect; the dress, however, failed to meet the criteria Tomas had outlined. The scoop neckline displayed a tantalizing hint of golden cleavage, the dress was short enough to reveal the fact that she had great legs, and in no way was the dress inconspicuous.

She sprayed herself with perfume then, on impulse, tucked a delicate white orchid from the tabletop arrangement behind one ear.

The flower transformed the look from sexy sophistication to something approximating bridal.

Satisfied with the result, she slipped into strappy white heels that made her legs look even longer, picked up a matching white clutch and left the room.

Constantine wouldn't miss the message, and that was fine with her. The sooner he realized she would not allow him to control her, the better.

Twelve

Lunch was an elegant affair, with a marquee on the lawn, a classical quartet playing and a well-known opera diva singing.

As Sienna strolled through the garden she spotted Constantine, who was wearing a gauzy white shirt over dark close-fitting pants. He glanced at her. She smiled coolly at a spot somewhere over his left shoulder and pretended she hadn't seen him.

A number of willowy models, dressed as brightly as birds of paradise, swayed through the crowd, weighted down with Atraeus gold. Sienna stiffened as she recognized two prominent gossip columnists sipping champagne, one of whom had relentlessly defamed her following the breakup.

She paused by a heavily guarded display cabinet showcasing exquisite gold and diamond jewelry. The reason for the two armed security guards was clear. Aside from the small fortune in jewelry displayed, the centerpiece was a pale pink baguette diamond ring that glittered with a soft fire. Very rare and hugely expensive.

"Sienna?" The editor of a prominent women's magazine paused beside her, smiling brightly.

Sienna braced herself to make polite, guarded conversation, ignoring a hot pulse of adrenaline when she realized Constantine was walking directly toward her.

The editor briefly studied Sienna's pearl necklace. "I love the pieces you're wearing." She made brief notes about the pearls and Ambrosi Pearls' upcoming collection.

When she moved on, Sienna's attention was drawn back to Constantine who had been waylaid by a pretty woman dressed in an elegant pants suit. She recognized Maria Stefano, the daughter of a prominent European racing magnate, because she had recently been photographed with Constantine at a high-profile charity function.

Maria wound her arms around Constantine's neck and leaned into him for a cooing hug. Constantine's expression as he gazed into her upturned face was amused, bordering on indulgent, and the sudden tension in Sienna's stomach intensified.

Realization hit her like a kick in the chest. She needed to walk someplace quiet and bang her head against a brick wall, because she was jealous of Maria Stefano.

The reason she was jealous was just as straightforward: she was still in love with Constantine.

Her chest squeezed tight. For a long moment she couldn't breathe, then oxygen whooshed back into her lungs, making her head spin. Constantine was single, fatally attractive and hugely wealthy. It was a fact that if he wanted a woman, he usually got her. Over the past two years he had dated a number of women, but until now they had mostly been blank faces and bodies. It had been easy to ignore the gossip because he had never had a steady girlfriend.

A photographer aimed a camera their way. Maria slid her arm around Constantine's waist and posed. By then several other cameras were clicking. Seconds later, Constantine excused himself, cutting the photo session short.

When he reached her side any trace of indulgence was gone. "You don't have to be jealous."

Sienna concentrated on the jewelry in the case and tried to ignore her body's automatic reaction to Constantine's piercing gaze, the clean masculine scent of his skin. "I am not jealous."

"Then stop worrying about other women."

Heat and a totally male focus burned in his eyes. If she'd had any doubt about his intentions or the lovemaking in Sydney, they were gone. He really did want her back.

Although, she was certain that a long-term relationship or marriage were not on Constantine's agenda. All he wanted was a wild, short-term fling.

That he expected her to jump back into bed with him after the sneaky way he had used her financial situation to maneuver her made Sienna so furious she had to unclench her jaw before she could speak. "Why don't we just go to your office now and talk about the loan agreement your father and mine cooked up and see where that takes us?"

Wariness flickered in his gaze. "Not yet," he said mildly. "Unless you came all this way to hand me a check."

"If there was a check, I would have mailed it."

"That's what I thought, in which case we'll stick to the schedule and discuss finances after lunch."

A camera flashed almost directly in her eyes. The photographers who had been so interested in Constantine and Maria were now concentrating on her.

A waiter offered her a glass of champagne. She refused

the drink, although for a split second tipping the chilled contents down Constantine's shirtfront was an irresistibly satisfying image. She had a better idea.

She half turned, brushing close to Constantine as she continued her perusal of the jewelry in the display case.

His gaze dropped to her mouth, and a small hot thrill shot through her. She had been so busy concentrating on Constantine's power and dominance, she had forgotten that she wielded her own power, that two years ago, for a short time at least, he hadn't been able to resist her.

His gaze rested briefly on the white orchid in her hair. "Damn, what are you up to?"

She kept her expression bland. "If you don't want to talk about business now, that's fine by me, but I'm in the jewelry trade and I am here on business. I'd like to take a closer look at the contents of this cabinet."

One hand was casually propped on the display cabinet behind her. To a casual observer they must have looked cozily intimate. For long moments, she thought Constantine was going to refuse, that she had overplayed her hand with the bridal theme—that he could see the sudden crazy plan she had formulated.

Just when she thought he would refuse, he nodded at one of the security guards, who stepped forward and unlocked the case.

Feeling wary but exhilarated, because what she was about to do was risky, she examined the array of beautifully crafted jewelry. Before she could change her mind she selected the largest ring, the pink diamond baguette. As engagement rings went, it would one day make some woman blissfully happy. "Four carats?"

Constantine's gaze was coolly impatient. "Maybe five."

"But then diamond rings aren't your thing, are they?"

He had never given her one, because their engagement had ended before the ring he had commissioned was ready.

After two years the lack of a ring shouldn't matter but in Sienna's opinion, and her mother's, not presenting a ring when he had proposed had been a telling factor.

According to Margaret Ambrosi and Aunt Via if a man didn't humbly offer a ring when he proposed—the best possible ring he could afford—that was a *sign*. The ring wasn't about money; it was about sacrifice. If a man truly loved a woman then he would be more than happy to demonstrate his love to the world by putting his ring on her finger.

To make matters worse, the lack of a ring had somehow made their weeklong engagement seem even more insubstantial. To Constantine the exquisite jewel was just a pretty, expensive trinket, without meaning beyond the calculated profit margin. No sentiment and definitely no emotion involved.

They were almost completely encircled by media now and the security guards weren't happy. Jaw taut, she held the ring out to Constantine. When his hand automatically opened, she dropped it into his palm. She registered the stir of shocked interest, his flash of surprise the moment he logged her not-so-subtle message that this time she wouldn't accept anything less than marriage.

The cool metal of the ring burned Constantine's palm. As his fingers closed around the band, his annoyance—at Sienna for wearing a dress that had every red-blooded man drooling, for wearing the same set of pearls she'd had on when they had made love on his sofa—dissolved.

The reporters and the buzz of conversation faded. He felt as if an electrical charge had just been run through his system, lifting all the fine hairs at his nape.

The bridal white, the pearls and the ring were a statement.

He had gotten the message—loud and clear.

Grimly, he decided he should have expected that she would hit back. In a moment of clarity, he realized that if he had wanted a woman who would allow herself to be dictated to, he would never have chosen Sienna. The CEO of a company that would have been highly successful if Roberto Ambrosi hadn't drained its profits. Sienna was formidable and a handful, and in that moment he was clear on one fact: she was his.

Instead of replacing the ring in the case he clasped her left wrist and slipped the ring neatly on to her third finger. "I would have chosen the white diamond," he murmured.

Shock registered in Sienna's gaze as he slid his arm around her waist, curving her into his side. "Looks like the wedding's on."

His expression controlled, Constantine made brief eye contact with the head of his security team as cameras flashed and the questions started.

Keeping Sienna clamped firmly to his side, he forged a path through the reporters. Moments later, with the help of security, they were clear.

Sienna sent him a stunned look. "Why did you do that?"

"The gesture was self-evident."

She made a strangled sound.

Constantine's jaw tightened. "After what you pulled, both last night and today, no one will believe you didn't angle for marriage."

"You didn't have to compound the issue by putting the ring on my finger."

"It was a spur-of-the-moment thing."

Unlike the past two years which had been ordered and precise, and without any discernible excitement. Seven days ago, he had been okay with that. As the Americans would say, all his ducks had been in a row. Now he wasn't sure if he could live without the chaos. "What I'd like to know is why you decided on the bridal theme?"

For a moment, he was caught between amusement and frustration and a definitely un-PC impulse that would ensure they were front-page news.

The glass doors of the hotel slid open.

Sienna threw him a suspicious glance. "Where are you taking me?"

Constantine felt like saying "To bed," but managed to pull back from that precipice. "The manager's office."

"Oh, goody," she muttered. "I've been wanting to check out all day."

Ignoring startled looks from hotel staff and guests, Constantine hustled Sienna down a corridor and into the large executive suite he had been using as his office, and kicked the door closed behind him.

Sienna spun to face him. "That was a press announcement out there."

He leaned against the door and folded his arms across his chest. "You wanted to play, those are my rules. Last night you turned up at my hotel opening wearing what looked like Medinian bridal jewels. On Medinos that amounts to an engagement announcement."

Her cheeks heated. "I've already told you, I had no idea the jewels we designed on the basis of Sebastien's drawing were wedding jewels! How do you think my family will feel when they open up tomorrow's newspapers and discover we're now supposed to be engaged?"

Her dark gaze held his and another one of those sharp, heady thrills burned through him. The past two years had definitely been flat. "You want me to issue a denial about the engagement?"

"It wouldn't be the first time." She yanked the ring off

her finger and dumped it in his palm. "And in the process it's entirely possible that this time you could look bad."

Given the string of stories dating back to the first broken engagement and the fact that she was presently grieving for her father, make that very bad. Worse, he decided, he would look like a man who couldn't make up his mind or control his woman.

Turning on her heel, Sienna paced to the French doors, which opened out onto a patio. A shadowy movement, visible through the sheer curtains that filtered the overbright sun, stopped her in her tracks.

Constantine dropped the ring in his pocket and strolled behind the large mahogany desk that dominated the room. "If you're thinking of making a break for it, I wouldn't advise it. That could have been a security guard, but more likely it's a reporter trying to get an exclusive through the windows."

Her gaze snapped back to his. "Any publicity generated will be brief. Without a wedding, the story will die a natural death. Just like it did last time."

For a long, drawn out moment silence vibrated between them. Time for a change of tactic.

"All right," he said calmly. "Let's talk. As it happens, now is the perfect time."

He gestured toward one of the chairs grouped to one side of the desk.

A tension he hadn't been aware of eased when Sienna finally moved away from the French doors and took one of the seats he'd indicated. Picking up the briefcase he had deposited in the office earlier in the day, he extracted a set of documents and slid them across the glossy desktop.

Sienna frowned as she skimmed the first sheet. "I don't understand. I thought this would be a straightforward transfer of shares to cover the debt."

She returned her attention to the contract. Overhead a fan slowly circled, with a soft, rhythmic swishing.

Too tense to sit, Constantine took up a position in front of the French doors, standing in almost the same spot that Sienna had, unconsciously blocking at least one exit. He frowned when he realized what he was doing. He guessed, in its crudest form, the paperwork was another form of exit-blocking.

Sienna skimmed the final page of the document. He logged the moment she found the marriage clause.

Shooting to her feet, she dropped the contract on the desk, her eyes dark with shock. "This is a marriage deal?"

"That's correct." Grimly, Constantine outlined the terms, even though he knew that Sienna, with her background in law, would have no problem deciphering the legalese.

Part of the deal was that she signed the transfer of the lease on the old pearl facility on Ambrus and the water rights to The Atraeus Group. In return, her family would retain a minority holding in Ambrosi Pearls. All debts and mortgages would be cleared, including those on the family house in Pier Point and Margaret Ambrosi's city apartment. Constantine had undertaken to reinvest in the company and retain all jobs. With the income from their shares, all three Ambrosi women would be able to live comfortable, debt-free lives.

Sienna shook her head. "I don't understand. If you need a wife, you could have any number of women. You could marry someone who has money—"

Relief loosened the tension that gripped him as he had braced for a refusal. He had known she wanted him, but until that moment he hadn't known whether or not she would agree to marriage. "I want *you*."

"Two years ago you threw everything away because of a loan."

"Two years ago I made a mistake."

He had a sudden flash of the night they'd first made love, the roses and the champagne, the sweetness and laughter when he'd let her seduce him. The chemistry between them had been riveting. He had spent two years without Sienna. Despite his crammed schedule and the fact that he had been absorbed with the challenge of running The Atraeus Group, it suddenly felt like he'd spent two years in a waiting room. "There is nothing complicated about what I want."

Shaking her head, she picked up her clutch, which she'd placed on the desktop. "You and I and marriage… It doesn't make sense."

He covered the distance between them and drew her into a loose hold. She had plenty of time to pull back, and he was careful not to push the physical intimacy, but it was a plain fact that, right now, touching her was paramount. He needed to cement his claim.

Taking the clutch from her, he placed it back on the desk and linked his fingers with hers. This close he could smell the flowery sweetness of her perfume, the faint scent of the orchid in her hair. "We share a common heritage. Marriage made sense two years ago."

"Two years ago we had an ordinary, normal courtship."

"Which is precisely why this should work now."

He lowered his mouth to hers, keeping a tight rein on his desire. One second passed, two. Her lips softened beneath his. She lifted up on her toes, and in agonizingly slow increments wound her arms around his neck and fitted her body to his. His arms tightened around her, exultation coursing through him at her surrender.

His cell phone buzzed, breaking the moment. Curbing

his frustration, Constantine released Sienna to answer the call.

Tomas. He strolled to the window and listened, his attention split as Sienna picked up the contract and studied the pages, her profile as marble-smooth and remote as a sculpture.

She wanted him. He was almost certain that she loved him, but he was aware that neither fact would guarantee her acceptance, and he wasn't prepared to compromise. When serious money had entered his parents' relationship equation, his mother had used the wealth to finance her exit from their lives. His father had remarried, but his wealth had also opened the door to a number of stormy extramarital relationships. With the debacle of his previous engagement to Sienna, Constantine had decided that the one thing he required in his marriage was control.

The contract was cold-blooded, directly counter to the way he felt, but if they were going to do this, he needed clear-cut terms. He would not live the way his father had done, at the mercy of his desires, or allow Sienna to run roughshod over him. This time there would be no gray areas and no hidden agendas.

Sienna's head jerked up as he disconnected the call. The orchid, he noticed, had dropped from her hair and lay crushed on the floor.

Her gaze met his, outwardly calm and cool but dark with emotion. "How much time do I have to think this over?"

Constantine slid the phone into his pocket. "I need a decision now."

Thirteen

Sienna lowered herself into the chair she had previously vacated, the leather cool enough against the backs of her thighs to send a faint shiver down her spine. "What happens if I say no?"

Constantine's gaze was unreadable. "I can have another, more straightforward document drawn up if you don't sign this deal."

The alternative document would be the one she had expected, taking everything—the business, her mother's house and apartment. It would, no doubt, make a large number of Ambrosi employees redundant, and could spell the end of Ambrosi Pearls altogether.

Constantine had made his position clear. There was chemistry enough to smooth the way, but this wasn't a courtship, or even a proposal. It was a contract, a marriage of convenience.

For a moment, after the softness of that kiss, she had

hoped he would say something crazy and wonderful like, "I love you."

Although the time for those words and that moment had been two years ago and they hadn't ensured happiness.

The flowery romantic love that had originally swept her off her feet was long gone, and she wasn't sure she wanted it back. The illusion of love had hurt.

Despite the pragmatism, hope flared. Maybe Constantine didn't love her, but this time, despite the enormity of what her father had done to the Atraeus family, he had fought for her.

Instead of abandoning her to his legal team, he had stepped in and protected her and her family from bankruptcy proceedings and the press. He had also gone to great lengths to protect and care for her mother and make sure she retained an income and her dignity. That counted for a lot.

Sienna aligned the pages until they were neatly stacked. Two years ago she had frozen like a deer in the headlights. She had let her father's actions dissolve her chance at happiness.

Her chin firmed. She didn't like the businesslike approach to something as personal and intimate as a marriage, but she acknowledged that business was Constantine's medium. The explanation for a contract like this, which practically corralled her with obligations to her family, to Ambrosi Pearls and to him, was so that Constantine could feel secure that she was tied in to the marriage. If he needed the extra assurance, that meant she really did matter to him. She didn't know if this would work, but she would never find out if she didn't try.

She took a deep breath. "All right."

Constantine didn't try to kiss her, for which she was grateful, he simply handed her a pen.

When they had both signed the documents, he called in a witness, one of the hotel receptionists. It was all over within minutes.

Constantine's phone buzzed as he locked the documents back in his briefcase. He answered his cell then checked his watch. "I need to be on-site with the contractors on Ambrus in an hour."

She picked up her clutch purse feeling faintly giddy at the leap she had taken. She needed food, and she needed time alone to come to terms with a future that just minutes ago had seemed wildly improbable. "I'll wait here."

"Oh, no, you won't." His jaw was grim. "You're coming with me. Now that we are officially engaged, I'm going to make sure you don't get another opportunity with the press."

Heat blasted off the enormous skeletal structure that was the construction site on Ambrus, shimmering like vapor in the air as the helicopter touched down on a huge slab of concrete.

Hot gusts from the rotors, peppered with stinging dust, whipped at her face and hair, as Constantine helped her out of the chopper. Sienna, who'd had just enough time to change into casual clothes and sneakers, grabbed her briefcase, which she had refused to leave behind.

Constantine would be busy with the contractor who was managing the construction of the hotel complex for a couple of hours, which suited her. There was an office, a modern concrete bunker she had spotted from the air, where she planned to crunch some numbers and catch up on some paperwork. If she found herself with time on her hands, she could always take a walk along the exquisite jewel-like bay.

Clearly, this wasn't a part of Ambrus that had ever been

used for anything more than grazing goats, nevertheless, it was beautiful and from a family history point of view any part of Ambrus interested her.

Anchoring dark glasses on the bridge of her nose, Sienna ducked to avoid the rotors. Constantine's arm clamped around her waist, tucking her into his side as he hustled her beneath the rotating blades. Disorientation hit her along with a wave of heat as she adjusted to his hold.

Ever since she had agreed to the marriage she had been off balance and a little shaky, although Constantine hadn't given her time to think. Ever since they had left the hotel's office, he'd kept her moving. She'd only had bare minutes alone, and that time had been pressurized, because she'd had to change clothes and pack her briefcase in time to make the flight.

She stepped off the concrete pad. Her pristine white sneakers sank into coarse sandy grit and were instantly coated. Automatically, she lengthened her stride, stepping out of Constantine's loose hold, but he kept pace with her easily, underlining the fact that they were now a couple.

Her cheeks burned at the knowledge, although no one in their right mind would attribute her flush to anything but the intense heat. Already her clothes were clinging to her skin and she could feel trickles of perspiration running down her spine and between her breasts.

Behind them the engine note of the chopper changed, the pitch higher, as if the pilot was preparing for takeoff. Sienna brushed whipping tendrils of hair out of her face as the helicopter did lift off then veered back toward the coast. "If that was our ride, how do we get out of here?"

By her reckoning, at this end of Ambrus, they were forty miles at least from Medinos. Not a great distance as the crow flies, but complicated by the barrier of the sea.

Constantine, who had walked on a few steps, calmly

waited for her to catch up. In faded jeans and leather boots, his eyes remote behind dark glasses, he no longer looked like a high-powered business executive but as much a part of the wild landscape as his warrior ancestors must have been. "Don't worry about the transport. I've taken care of it."

Sienna watched the helicopter turn into a small black dot on the horizon and the disorientation hit her again. "I could be crazy to trust you."

Out here there were no taxis and, according to Constantine, no cell phone service until they installed a repeater on one of the tall peaks in the interior. Telephone and internet communication was limited to the satellite connection in the office.

He held out his hand. "You've trusted me this far."

Sienna laced her fingers with his, the sense of risk subtly heightened by the casual intimacy. No matter how right it felt to try again with Constantine, she couldn't forget that just hours ago she had been uneasy about his agenda and certain that no matter how intense the attraction, there was no way a relationship could work.

The office was modern, well-appointed and wonderfully cool.

While Constantine was immersed in a discussion with the site manager, Jim Kady, Sienna appropriated an empty desk. She hadn't yet called either her mother or Carla, because Constantine had asked her to wait until they could inform both of their families. Although with the media stir following Constantine's announcement, she needed to call either that evening or first thing in the morning.

Setting her briefcase down on the desk, she eased out of her sneakers and shook the excess grit into a wastepaper basket. Padding through to the bathroom in her socks, she grabbed paper towels, dampened them then grabbed an extra handful of dry towels. When she returned to the office, Kady had left and Constantine was propped on the edge of the site manager's desk, taking a call.

She sat down, cleaned her shoes and brushed off her socks, which had a brownish tinge. She became aware of Constantine watching her, obviously amused by her perfectionist streak.

"You'll pay for this," she said lightly, trying to defuse the mounting awareness that she was alone with Constantine for the first time since they had signed the agreement.

His expression was oddly intent and ironic. "That I do know."

Her breath caught in her throat and her heart began to pound. It was a weird moment to understand that he liked her quirkiness, that he didn't just want sex and a controllable wife; he wanted her.

The sound of rotor blades filled the air as a helicopter skimmed low overhead.

Constantine checked his watch. "That'll be the engineer."

Relief flooded her. Rescue and reprieve. And the transport was back.

Just over two hours later, when Constantine's meeting was wrapped up, he walked back into the office.

Sienna kept her head down, ostensibly working on Ambrosi Pearls' figures, although it was little more than doodling with numbers. She would no longer be in charge of the major investment decisions, but after years of financial stress and buoyed by the heady opportunities ahead it had been a pleasurable way to pass the time.

The heat hit her like a blow as she stepped outside with Constantine. In the distance the helicopter, which had been sitting on the pad, lifted into the air taking the group of suits attached to the contracting firm back to Medinos. Sienna checked to see if there was a second helicopter, just in case she had missed hearing it come in.

The pad was bare.

Constantine halted beside a four-wheel drive pickup truck that looked like a carbon copy of the truck Kady had parked outside the office, except this one had a bright blue tarp fastened over the bed.

When Constantine opened the passenger-side door, indicating they were driving somewhere, she dug her heels in. "I thought we were going back to Medinos."

"We are, but not just yet. While we're here, I wanted to show you the old pearl facility."

Which meant he had planned this. "If I don't get back soon, I'll miss my flight out."

"The company jet is on the runway at Medinos. You can catch a flight out on that when we get back."

His hands settled at her waist, and suddenly there was no air. He muttered something in Medinian. "I wasn't going to do this yet." Bending, he captured her mouth with his, the kiss hot and hungry and slow.

She froze, for long seconds caught off balance by the ruthless way he was conducting their so-called engagement and her knee-jerk response.

His mouth drifted along her jaw, she felt the edge of his teeth on her lobe. A small smothered sound escaped from her throat. His lips brushed hers again and her arms closed around his neck as she lifted up against him, returning the kiss.

He lifted his head. His forehead rested against hers. "Are you coming with me?"

Sienna let out a breath. This time he was asking, not demanding, but she was also suddenly aware that in spending time alone with Constantine she was agreeing to much more than a sightseeing tour.

The panic she'd felt in the office hit her again. She felt as jittery as a new bride, but she had agreed to marry him and it wasn't as if they hadn't made love before. "Okay."

Feeling distinctly wobbly, she climbed into the truck. Setting her briefcase down on the floor, she fastened her seat belt.

Constantine swung behind the wheel and put the truck in gear. Despite the fact that she had agreed to go with Constantine, the feeling of being herded was strong enough that she was about to demand he drive her back to the mine office when the VHF radio hissed static. Constantine answered the call and the moment passed.

Several minutes later the construction site was no longer visible. There was a rooster tail of dust behind them and the heat shimmer of the rugged island wilderness in front.

Time passed. At some point, lulled by the heat and the monotonous sound of the truck motor, she must have fallen asleep. Straightening, she brushed hair out of her eyes and checked her watch. A good thirty minutes had passed.

She frowned as she studied the road, which was now little more than a stock road running beside a wide, deep green river.

At periodic intervals along the narrow ribbon of road, marker poles had been placed indicating floodwater levels, in places a good meter above the road. There was further evidence of a previous flood and occasional washouts, where portions of the road had been eaten away by the destructive power of the river.

"How far are we from the pearl facility?" The road they were following appeared to be getting narrower.

"Five miles."

Five miles there, then a good thirty miles back to the construction site.

Minutes later, after driving through a deep gorge, Constantine picked up the radio handset again, tried the frequency then set the handpiece down. "That's it. We're out of radio range for the next few minutes. Now we can talk."

His voice was curt as he outlined the business plan for Ambrosi Pearls. He had taken a look at the structure and none of the staff would go, although that would be open for review. Given that the business had been tightly run and had only stumbled because of the debt load imposed by her father, redundancies weren't an option at this point. "Ambrosi Pearls stays in business." There was a brief, electric pause. "But you have to go. Lucas is taking a block of shares. He'll be stepping in as CEO."

Blankly, Sienna wrenched her gaze from Constantine's profile, her mind fixed on his statement that she would have to go.

"Let me get this straight, you want me out of the company completely?"

"That's right, and I'm not asking."

She stared at the stark line of the horizon, rugged hills and more rugged hills threaded by the road they were presently following. She had been braced for demotion. She had not expected to be fired.

She peeled her dark glasses off and rubbed at the sudden sharp ache in her temples. She could feel Constantine studying her, the ratcheting tension.

Although she should have expected this.

Constantine lived on Medinos, therefore it would be difficult for her to remain based in Sydney.

Constantine slowed to a crawl as he drove across a stretch of road that looked like it served a double purpose as a streambed during the wet season. "We signed a contract. You agreed to be my wife."

Her jaw set. "At no point did I agree to give up my job."

Ambrosi Pearls was her baby. She had nursed it through bad times and worse, working crazy hours, losing sleep and reveling in even the smallest victory. She knew every aspect of the business, every employee personally, and their families; they were a tight-knit team. Despite the stress and the worry the company was hers. She was the captain of the team. Ambrosi Pearls couldn't run without her. She felt the cool touch of his gaze.

"I want your loyalties to lie with me, not Ambrosi Pearls. We'll be based in Medinos. Running an Australian business won't be an option."

She stared at the road unfurling ahead, the blinding blue intensity of the sky, the vastness of the sea in the distance. "You run any number of hotels and companies from Medinos."

"Each one has a resident manager. In this case it will be Lucas."

He was right—she knew it—but that didn't make relinquishing Ambrosi Pearls any easier. From childhood she had grown up with the knowledge that, love it or hate it, she would run the family business. "I'm good at what I do. I've studied, trained—"

He braked, allowing a small herd of goats to drift desultorily off the road. "I know how focused you've been on Ambrosi Pearls. No one better."

"Plenty of women juggle a career and marriage."

"Ambrosi Pearls will not be part of this equation."

"Why not?"

His gaze sliced back to hers. "Because I refuse to take second place to a briefcase filled with sales orders."

Sienna jammed her dark glasses back on the bridge of

her nose, abruptly furious at Constantine's hardheaded ruthlessness. "You still don't trust me."

Less than an hour ago she had let him kiss her. He had manipulated her into agreeing to a lot more, despite knowing he was going to sack her while they were driving. "Looking after Ambrosi Pearls has never been just about business. It's part of my family. It's in my blood."

Gaze narrowed, she stared directly ahead, searching for a place where Constantine could comfortably turn the truck around. "I've changed my mind. I want to go back."

"No. You agreed to this."

"That was before you fired me."

"We're spending the night at a beach house up ahead. I'm taking you back in the morning."

Her head snapped around. "I did not agree to that. I do not, repeat, do not, want to spend the night with you. Take me back to the construction site. There must be some kind of regular transport service for the workers. If I'm too late to catch whatever boat or helicopter they use, I'll use the satellite phone in the office to call in my own ride."

"No." His voice was calmly neutral. "The beach house is clean, comfortable and stocked with food."

She could feel the blood pounding through her veins, her temper increasing with every fiery pulse. "Let me guess, no landline, no cell phone network, no internet connection…just you and me."

"And no press, for approximately twelve hours."

With movements that were unnaturally calm, given that she was literally shaking with fury, she unlatched her briefcase and retrieved her cell. She stared at the "no service" message on the screen. Any hope died.

The pearl facility was sited on the western side of the island, tucked into a sheltered bay directly behind the range of hills that was presently looming over them, blocking transmission. "Turn the truck around. Now."

She repeated her request that he turn around immediately.

When he ignored her for the second time, she studied the tough line of his jaw, the dark glasses that hid his eyes, and gauged her chances of yanking the key out of the ignition.

"I don't want to spend the night in some beach house," she said, spacing the words. "I don't want to drive one more mile with you. I'd rather crawl across the island and die of thirst, or swim to Medinos. And if you think I'm going to have sex with you, you can think again. Think dying or rabid thirst, because either of those two things will happen first."

The stare he gave her was vaguely disconcerted, as if he was weighing up which parts of her statements she would actually carry out. It was then she realized that he really did think he was still going to be having sex with her.

He turned back to the road, his jaw set. "We're almost there."

The landscape had changed, flattening out as they neared the coast. Blunt outcroppings smudged with grayish-green scrub and the occasional gnarled olive tree dotted the roadside.

He negotiated another bend and suddenly they were driving alongside the deep, green river again.

Her frustration escalated. Apart from throwing a tantrum, she was almost out of options—and she didn't do tantrums. She liked coolness and precision—pages of neat figures, relationships that progressed logically. She liked forward planning because she liked to win.

Briefly, she outlined plan B. Drive to a place where she could get cell phone service—there had to be a viable high point on this island somewhere—and call in a helicopter. Out here, with the primitive lack of any telephone or power lines, it could land virtually anywhere. If Constantine did what she asked, she wouldn't take this to the police or the newspapers. But if he kept driving all bets were off, and she would sue his ass.

Constantine had the gall to laugh.

A red mist actually swam before her eyes. Her hand shot out and grasped the wheel. He was momentarily distracted while she lunged at the key.

Any idea that she could get out of the truck and make it to a high point on her own was just that, a wild idea. All she wanted was to jolt Constantine out of his stubborn mind-set, stop the vehicle and make him listen.

Constantine jerked her hand off the wheel. Not that that was any big deal, because the maneuver was only a distraction while she grabbed at the elusive prize of the key. Unfortunately, when she had lunged forward, the seat belt had locked her in place, so she'd had to regroup and try again, which had cost her valuable time. Even then her fingertips could only brush the key.

Constantine said something hard and flat. Her head jerked up, not so much at the word, but at the way he'd uttered it.

She saw the washout ahead, which had gouged a crescent-shaped bite out of the road, a split second before the front wheel dropped into the hole. If Constantine had had his full attention on driving, he would have negotiated the hole. A floodplain fanned out on the driver's side. He could have detoured for fifty meters without a problem.

Constantine swung the wheel and gunned the motor, but with the ground crumbling under the rear left wheel there was no way he could pull them back on an even keel.

With a lurch, the truck tilted further.

There was a beat of silence, because Constantine had achieved what she had been trying to do and had turned the engine off. For an endless moment they teetered on two wheels then, with a slow, lumbering grace, the truck toppled sideways.

Fourteen

The distance from the road to the river below wasn't horrendous. From the vehicle it had looked tame, just another eroded riverbank, softened by time and not even particularly steep. But, like the moment when a roller coaster paused on the edge of a drop, no matter how small, the distance suddenly seemed enormous.

Sienna's seat belt held her plastered against the seat as the truck made a clumsy half revolution. Her glasses slid off her nose and a dark shape tumbled past her jaw—her briefcase. The vehicle rocked to a halt. They had stopped rolling, but they had ended upside down, hanging suspended by the seat belts. And they were in the river.

For a heartening moment they bobbed, the murky waterline changing as the truck settled lower. The light began to go as they were almost completely submerged by tea-colored water, tinted, she realized, by the mud that had been stirred up when the truck had disturbed the riverbed.

"Are you all right?"

She turned her head and stared at Constantine. He had a welt on his cheekbone, but otherwise he was in one piece. Apart from the fact that the truck had turned into a submarine and there was something trickling across her scalp—at a guess, blood, which meant she must have banged her head—she was good to go. "Just show me the exit sign."

"Good girl."

The truck was stationary, which meant the roof was sitting on the bottom of the river. That indicated that the depth was shallow, probably not even deep enough to cover the truck fully, but since water was hosing in at various points, getting out was a priority.

A sharp metallic click drew her attention away from the swirling mud and she realized that Constantine had been talking in a low voice. She forced herself to pay attention.

Constantine had already unclipped his seat belt. Using the steering wheel as a handhold, he lowered himself to the roof, which was now their floor, and reversed his position so that he was upright, his back and shoulders wedged against the dash. To do so he had to slide right next to her, because the steering wheel and the gear shift made maneuvering his big frame in the limited space of the cab even more difficult. There was no way he could stand upright.

Constantine leaned across her. She realized he was checking out her door. "The roof crumpled slightly when we went over. Not much, but enough that the doors won't open, so we're going to have to go out through the windows."

He unsnapped her seat belt and caught her as she fell, torpedoing into the deepening puddle of water. With her nose squashed against one rock-hard thigh, she hooked her fingers into the waistband of his jeans and awkwardly jackknifed in the confined space while he kept a firm grip on her waist, holding her steady. She ended up plastered against him from nose to thighs, his arms clamped around her like a vice and with the back of her neck jammed against the edge of the seat. But at least she was finally up the right way, which was a relief, although with her head in the darker floor cavity, the feeling of claustrophobia had increased.

"We're going to have to swim for it, but that shouldn't be a problem since we both know how good you are in the water."

Was that sarcasm? But with water creeping up her ankles she couldn't drum up an ounce of righteous indignation.

Constantine reached across her. She realized he was groping for the window which, luckily, was a manual wind-up type and not electric.

She tried to shuffle sideways, allowing him more room. In the process the top of her foot nudged against a hard object—her briefcase.

She had an instant replay of the sleek, black leather case flying around the cab—the probable cause of the stinging on her scalp. But the injury wasn't what obsessed her in that moment. The accident, stressful as it was, had had a strange effect. Her fury had zapped out of existence and the tension that normally hummed between them was gone. For the first time in two years, stuck upside down in a cab with Constantine as he took control in that calm, alpha way of his, she felt content and almost frighteningly happy.

It was a strange time to realize that despite the constant battles, at a bedrock level she trusted Constantine, and that two years ago when everything had gone wrong this was what she had needed from him.

"You're going out first," he said quietly. "I'll follow."

"No problem." Now that the mud had settled she could see that they were only a couple of feet from the surface. The biggest issue would be the few seconds wait while the cab filled with water. The moment most people would panic would be when the water gushed in. The important thing was to stay calm and hold her breath while the cab filled, because the last she wanted was to swallow a mouthful of river water.

"I'm going to unwind the window. Once the cab is full, you'll have to squeeze out the window. Are you good to go?"

Her head was throbbing a little, but she still felt pumped. Constantine's gaze was inches from hers. With water creeping up her legs and the muscular heat from his body blazing into her, if she hadn't been so at odds with him, she might have given into a *Poseidon Adventure* moment. "Just a second."

She bent her knees and slid down the front of his body. "Don't get any ideas."

She felt around in the water. Her fingers closed around the briefcase handle.

"Leave that."

Leave her laptop underwater? "No. I can use it as a flotation device."

"You can swim like a fish. You don't need a flotation device."

Sienna's head jerked up at his tone, connecting sharply with the back of the seat. A stab of pain shot through her. She had somehow managed to reinjure the same spot, which was now aching. She met his glare with her own version of a steely look. "I don't see why I should lose something I love just because you think it's a good idea." And with any luck the briefcase would be waterproof enough that the laptop would survive.

"I wonder whose idea it was to 'lose' the truck?"

The dryness of his tone flicked her on the raw.

Maybe the briefcase shouldn't be a sticking point, but suddenly it very palpably was. She had lost her company and her career, there was nothing she could do about that, but the briefcase was *hers*. "I'm happy to take the blame for the truck. Just don't blame me for the fact that you haven't gotten around to repairing your road."

"Why did I ever think this was viable?" Constantine jerked her close and pressed a brief, hard kiss on her mouth.

Adrenaline and desire shot through her. Constantine's gaze locked with hers and she had another moment, one that made her heart simultaneously soar and plummet. Her head was stinging and she was angry at the way he had all but kidnapped her, but those considerations were overridden by one salient fact.

No matter what he did, how badly he behaved, she still wanted Constantine. And not just in a sexual way. Her problem was that she wanted all of him—the overbearing dominance and the manipulative way he had pressured her into going into the wilderness with him so he could fire her then keep her prisoner until she forgave him. She wanted the aggravating challenge of his cold, ruthless streak and take-no-prisoners attitude, the flashes of humor. And last, and by no means least, she really, really wanted the heart-pounding sex.

"What now?" he growled, although that didn't fool her. He wanted her, too, and no amount of bad temper could hide that fact.

"Nothing," she snapped back. "As you can see I'm ready to go. I've been ready for ages."

A bare second later water flooded into the cab. The swamping flow would have shoved her sideways but Constantine held her firmly anchored against him. Closing her eyes and holding her breath, she counted and waited until the cold pressurized flow stopped. She opened her eyes on eight. The cab, now filled with water, was dimmer than before, although sunlight shafted through the windows.

Keeping a firm grip on the case, she levered herself out of the window, and kicked to the surface, into blue sky and hot sunlight.

She gulped air and treaded water while she got her bearings. The truck was completely submerged, the only sign of its presence in the river a muddy streak where silt and dirt stained the water. A raw gash on the bank marked the spot where they had gone off the road, but that, she realized was receding.

The current was carrying her downstream at a steady pace. Crumbling banks, eroded by time and scoured by flash floods, rose on either side of her. Despite the sunlight, the water was icy, but that wasn't her biggest problem. Constantine still hadn't surfaced.

Sucking in a breath and, yes, using the case as a flotation device, she kicked toward shore. She could swim against the current, but she would get back to the truck faster by getting onto dry land and jogging back.

Seconds later, her feet found the bottom of the river. Slipping and sliding on rocks, she slogged toward the shore, scanning the smooth green surface as she went. It was entirely possible that Constantine had surfaced for air then gone back down to the truck to retrieve something—maybe the radio set—and she had missed that moment. When she had surfaced she had been too busy hanging on to the briefcase to notice.

Setting the case down she jogged toward the gash in the bank that was now the only marker for the place the truck had gone in, since the muddy streak in the water had cleared. Simultaneously, Constantine surfaced from the now dimly visible shape of the truck, a pack in one hand.

Sienna used the strap of the pack to help pull him to shore. When they stumbled onto the riverbank she dragged the pack out of his hands, dropped it to the ground and checked him out for injuries, relieved when she couldn't see any blood. "Why didn't you surface straightaway?"

He slicked dripping hair back from his face and jerked his chin at the pack. "First aid. Food and clean water. And a portable radio, if it stayed dry."

Explosive anger burned at the back of her throat. Despite his practical reason for staying under and the fact that he had obviously felt confident he could hold his breath for all that time, it didn't change the fact that he could have been in trouble. "That pack wasn't in the cab."

Which meant it had been secured on the truck bed, underneath the flatbed canopy. Instead of following her to the surface he had stayed underwater, holding his breath while he unlaced the tarp, swam beneath it and retrieved the pack. With the swift-flowing current anything could have happened. "I thought you were trapped."

His hands closed around her upper arms, rubbed against her chilled flesh. "It's okay, babe, I had a knife. I cut the canopy open. There was no way I could have gotten trapped."

Babe? Something snapped inside her. "Don't you dare do anything like that again."

Maybe she was overreacting, but the thought that something could have happened to Constantine made her go cold inside. For several seconds she had been forced to consider what life would be like if she did lose him. She hadn't known how much that would matter to her.

She was in love with Constantine. She had to face the fact that if she still loved him after the past two years then it was an easy bet that she would continue to love him, regardless.

She didn't know how long she would feel this way. Maybe sometime in the dim, distant future, whatever it was that sparked her to respond to him would fade and she would love someone else. She was certain love was possible, but she didn't know if she would ever be desperately, hopelessly in love again.

An emotion that made her heart stumble flashed in his gaze. He muttered something in Medinian and hauled her against him. Her arms clamped around his neck as his mouth came down on hers.

Heat radiated from him, swamping her, and the kiss pulled her under. For long seconds she drifted, still locked into the expression she had glimpsed in his eyes. The truth he had hidden from her for two years—that he wasn't either remote or emotionally closed down, that as much as she needed him, he needed her.

He lifted his mouth and she could breathe again, but it wasn't oxygen she wanted. This time there was no thunder and lightning, no thick darkness pressing down, hiding motives and intentions. Her fingers slid into his wet hair and pulled his mouth back to hers. The passion was white-hot and instant.

She found the buttons of his shirt and tore them open. Seconds later, she felt the rush of cool air as he slid her wet, clinging shirt off her shoulders. A sharp tug and her bra was gone. He pulled her close, the skin-on-skin contact searing. The uncomplicated relief of being held by the man she loved spiraled through her as she lifted up on her toes and deepened the kiss.

His fingers pulled gently at the pins in her hair, destroying the remnants of her chignon so that wet strands tumbled around her shoulders. She found the fastening of his jeans and tugged, then they were on the ground. For long minutes, between heart-stopping kisses, she was consumed with buttons and zippers and the breathless humor of constructing a makeshift bed with discarded clothing.

Another drugging kiss and her arms coiled around Constantine's neck, pulling until he ended up on top of her, and suddenly the humor was gone. Despite being in the water for longer than she had been, heat radiated from him, swamping her. The rumpled, wet clothing beneath was rough against her bare skin, but the discomfort slid away as her hands found the satiny muscles of Constantine's back and she stretched out against the smooth, sleek length of him.

His gaze locked with hers as with infinite gentleness their bodies melded, the fit perfect. For long moments they simply stayed that way, soaking in what they hadn't had time for in Sydney, the slow intimacy, the hitched breaths and knowing glances.

Warm, melting pleasure shimmered through her as they finally began to move together, their breath intermingled, their bodies entwined. Past and present dissolved as the burning intensity finally peaked and the afternoon spun away.

Long minutes later, Constantine rolled onto his back, pulling her with him so she lay sprawled over his chest.

Sienna cuddled close, ran her palm absently over one bicep, stroking the pliant swell of muscle. He moved slightly, shifting his weight. She adjusted her position, making herself more comfortable.

In that moment she faced a small detail that, caught in the maelstrom of emotion and urgency, they had both chosen to ignore. This time they hadn't used a condom.

The moment had been primal and extreme, but the fact that Constantine could have made her pregnant didn't terrify her. She had wanted him inside her, touching that innermost part of her.

His eyes flickered, his gaze found hers. She bent down and kissed him, her hair a damp tangled curtain enclosing them. His hands slid up her back, tightened on her waist and she was lost again.

The rising breeze roused Constantine. He hadn't gone to sleep, and neither had Sienna. Like him, she had been content to lie quietly, her breathing settling into an even rhythm.

"We're going to have to move." His skin was darkly tanned and used to the hot sun, but Sienna with her creamy skin and honey-gold tan would burn.

Regret pulled at him as she eased out of the curve of his arm and snatched up an armload of wet clothing. The skittish alacrity with which she draped their clothing over warm boulders then walked into the river informed him that her thoughts were running parallel to his. They had made love without a condom, twice.

It wasn't something he had planned, nor would he ever force this situation on any woman, but now that it had happened he had to reassess and act.

A child. He went still inside at the image of Sienna round and pregnant. Sienna with his baby at her breast.

Raw emotion grabbed at his stomach, his chest. Until that moment he hadn't realized how powerful lovemaking could be, or how imperative it was to him that Sienna was the mother of his children.

Sienna had always been attractive to him, almost to the point of obsession.

Almost, but not quite.

Two years ago he had been able to control his involvement. To a degree, he admitted grimly. When he had discovered that Sienna had known her father was using their engagement to leverage a loan, he had been able to step back. But at some point between their lovemaking in Sydney and now he had crossed a line.

That shift had happened when Sienna had walked into his hotel ballroom wearing what he had thought were Medinian bridal jewels. In that moment he had wanted every promise inherent in the intricate weave of the bridal jewels: purity, passion and commitment.

Rising to his feet, he followed Sienna into the water. Despite the possessive urge to keep her close, he was careful to allow her space and not push any further than he already had.

Ducking down, he rinsed his hair. Water streamed down his shoulders as he surfaced just in time to see Sienna wading to shore.

By the time he walked out of the water, she was wearing her shirt, which had already dried in patches. With swift movements, he dried off with his shirt and pulled on his underwear and jeans, then replaced his shirt on its rock to dry some more, along with his socks and boots. The jeans were still damp, but the weather was so hot they would dry almost as quickly while he was wearing them.

Sienna, who had already finger-combed her hair and tied it in a neat knot, unlaced her sneakers. "That can't happen again. Making love without a condom is crazy."

"I didn't exactly plan to have unprotected sex."

His gaze narrowed when she calmly ignored him in favor of turning her jeans and socks over and aligning everything with military precision. She selected a rock, sat down and started brushing grit off her sneakers. He could feel his temper slipping then he finally got it. Sienna was a perfectionist; it had always been one of the things he had liked about her. He had even thought it was cute on occasion, although it periodically drove him crazy. Like now.

But suddenly the reason she fussed and tidied was clear. It was her way of coping when she was stressed or worried. She had done it in the office this afternoon and she was doing it now, which meant the cool distance wasn't a brush-off; it was simply a means of protecting herself.

Relief dissipated some of his tension as he walked over to Sienna. Crouching down, he cupped her face and gently kissed her. "I'm sorry I didn't use a condom, but given the way things were and the fact that I didn't have one, there was no avoiding it this time. Next time we make love I'll take care of the protection. There are condoms at the house. They were delivered along with the food."

Her gaze flashed. "You really did plan this."

"You knew as well as I did the minute you climbed in that truck what was going to happen. I asked, you agreed. I didn't make you do anything you didn't want to."

This time she avoided his gaze altogether, but he didn't need the eye contact to know exactly what was going through her mind.

Frowning, he straightened. Any woman would worry about an unplanned pregnancy. But if Sienna was pregnant, as far as Constantine was concerned, the situation was cut-and-dried. They would be married within a month.

Fifteen

Sienna studiously avoided Constantine's gaze as she finished cleaning her shoes. Heat and silence shimmered
around them, broken by the cooling sound of river water
sliding over rocks.

She was lacing one sneaker, when Constantine crouched
down in front of her and picked up the other one.

His hand encircled her ankle and something snapped.
Images flickered in her memory: the way she'd melted
the first night they'd met when Constantine had crouched
down and fitted her missing shoe to her foot. Not a glass
slipper exactly, just a black pump with black beads, but the
moment had been incredibly, mind-bendingly romantic.

She swiped the shoe out of his hand. "Don't."

She sucked in air, tried to breathe. Maybe she was being
stubborn and picky, but she didn't want those kinds of gestures unless he really did love her. Pulling at the laces, she
loosened them off enough to put the sneaker back on her foot.

Constantine frowned as his gaze skimmed critically over her. "You're bleeding. You should have told me."

She touched her scalp. There must be a cut because there was dried blood, but it was so small she had difficulty finding it. "It's nothing, a scratch."

He unfastened the pack and tipped the contents out on the ground, one of which happened to be a pack of emergency supplies. Standard issue, she guessed, for anyone who worked out at the construction site. The other was a first aid kit.

While he was sorting through the supplies Sienna went down to the river to rinse the blood out of her hair.

When she returned, Constantine appeared to be busy, tinkering with the portable radio. Dragging her gaze from the powerful line of his back, Sienna finished dressing except for the still-damp bra, which she folded and slipped into her jeans pocket. She strolled a few steps down the rocky beach, staring at the wild beauty of the landscape. With every moment that passed the commitment she had made in making love to Constantine without protection seemed more and more foolhardy in light of his glaring lack of any kind of emotional declaration.

A flicker of movement caught her eye. Constantine was by her briefcase.

Her brows jerked together as he picked it up and sneakily carried it up the bank. Out of sight.

Her temper shredding, she stormed up the bank and retrieved the briefcase. She didn't know what it was with Constantine and her things. He wasn't just satisfied with taking her company and her job; now he didn't want her to have her briefcase.

He frowned. "You don't need that. You'll only have to carry it."

"I do need it, and it's no problem carrying it." And if he

wanted to take it off her now, he would have to pry it out of her cold, dead hands.

His gaze narrowed, glittering with an edgy frustration that sent a zingy sensation down her spine. "Jewelry samples and order forms are the last thing you need out here."

She felt herself blushing at the confirmation that he had recognized her sample case back in her hotel suite. She stared at his muscled chest and a small, red mark on his shoulder she could remember making. She felt herself grow warmer. "It's not a sample case. For your information it's a portable office."

"The same thing in my book."

For a taut moment she thought he was going to say something further then he turned back to the assortment of tools he had assembled on the ground.

Still tingling with the heady knowledge that Constantine wasn't as distant and controlled as he seemed, she took the briefcase back to her rock, sat down and unlatched it. Water had seeped in, wetting the order forms but, because her laptop was zipped into a soft case inside the briefcase, it was still bone-dry.

She set the damp forms down on the ground to dry, extracted the laptop, powered it up then closed it down. She packed it away, and tidied her appointments diary and the jumbled mess of pens and pamphlets then placed the damp order forms on top. They were no longer any use, but since there wasn't a trash can out here, she would have to keep them until she could find one.

When she had finished restoring order to the briefcase, she slipped her cell phone out of her pocket and tried that, without much hope. As she'd thought, it was as dead as a doornail.

Constantine strolled over with a first aid kit. He sat down on a rock in front of her and leaned close, sandwiching her between his thighs. She was suddenly overwhelmingly aware of the broad expanse of his chest and just how physically large he was.

He tilted her head and she found herself looking directly into his eyes. His face was close enough that she could study to her heart's content the intriguing dark flecks in his irises, the red welt on his cheekbone that was rapidly discoloring into a bruise.

He cupped her face, his hold seducingly gentle. "If you get pregnant, we'll talk about it. Until then, we'll go back to using protection."

Sienna edged the briefcase away from his booted foot, ignoring his irritated frown. "Assuming there is going to be more sex."

"How likely are you to get pregnant?"

She drew in an impeded breath, suddenly floored by the thought that she could be pregnant, right this second. It was documented history that Ambrosi women got pregnant at the drop of a hat. They were psychotic power freaks when it happened, but certifiably fertile.

She did a quick count. "There's a possibility."

More than a possibility.

His thumb brushed across her mouth sending a hot little dart of sensation through her. "I'll leave you alone for now, if that's what you want. Now stay still while I take a look at that scratch on the side of your head."

Obediently, she tilted her head so he could examine the area. He took his time smoothing her hair out of the way then used some antiseptic wipes from the first aid kit.

"Ouch."

His mouth quirked at one corner. "Don't be a sissy."

"That's easy for you to say. You're not the one who's bleeding."

"The cut is small. It's hardly life-threatening."

"Then I don't know why you're bothering with the first aid routine."

He didn't reply, just angled her head again, pinched the wound together with his thumb and forefinger, which made it throb and sting, and smoothed on a small butterfly strip.

She stared at the welt on his cheekbone as he packed the first aid kit away. The bruise, which had started to turn a purplish color, made him look faintly piratical. "How did you get that?"

His gaze was slitted against the sun making him look even more dangerous. "The same way you got that cut on your head—from that damn briefcase."

She purred inside and inched the briefcase closer to her leg. She almost felt like patting it. Good briefcase, it had never meant to hurt her; it had been after Constantine.

He pushed to his feet. "The house isn't far, but we need to get moving. I checked the radio, and it still works, but we're out of the transmission area so we'll have to wait for the helicopter, which will be out to pick us up first thing in the morning."

Sienna watched as Constantine repacked the supplies and finished dressing.

He passed her a water bottle. Wordlessly, she drank. With the risk of giardia and other contaminants she hadn't drunk any of the river water, as tempting as the notion had been.

Constantine stored the bottle in the pack and held out his hand. "I'll take the briefcase."

"No. I'll carry it."

There was an explosive silence, but when she stole a sideways glance at Constantine she was certain his mouth was twitching.

The beach house, which had been less than two miles

away from where the truck had overturned, was not a cottage so much as a multilevel statement in design.

Decks merged into the side of a striated cliff and overlooked a windswept beach. Inside, the floors were glossy, the ceilings high. Huge plate-glass windows provided an unimpeded view of the sea.

Constantine pointed out the large adjacent bay, which held the old pearl facility, but by then the light was fading. Sienna could make out the tumbled remains of a building and little else.

Constantine touched a switch and air-conditioning hummed to life, instantly cool against her overheated skin.

Feeling dusty and tired, Sienna did a quick tour of the kitchen. Stainless-steel appliances were hidden behind lacquered cabinets, and a state-of-the-art oven, large enough to cater for a crowd, took pride of place. She opened a cabinet door and found a gleaming microwave and, on a shelf beneath it, an array of small appliances. "This place is fabulous. It doesn't look like it's ever used."

"It's a family retreat, but since we have to spend so much time overseas, it isn't used often. There are bedrooms upstairs and on this floor."

Constantine crossed the broad expanse of the living area, which was tastefully decorated with comfortable leather couches, and pushed open a door.

She followed him into the broad hall, which had several rooms opening off it. After a quick walk through, she chose a room with floaty white silk draperies.

Constantine showed her the bathroom, which was fully stocked with an array of products, including toothbrushes and toothpaste. "There's fresh underwear and clothing in the dresser if you want it. Freshen up, I'll go and organize some food."

After showering and changing into fresh underwear

and a thin cotton robe she'd found hooked on the back of the bathroom door, Sienna gathered up her soiled clothes and carried them through to the living area.

The aroma of a spicy casserole, which evidently had been prepared and left in the fridge, drew her to the kitchen. Constantine must also have showered, because his hair was damp and slicked back. He had also changed, pulling on a pair of clean cotton pants and a thin, gauzy white shirt.

He showed her where the laundry room was. She put her clothes and his in to wash, then walked back to the kitchen.

They sat out on the deck, a casual option that appealed more than the formality of the dining room, and ate the traditional Medinian dish followed by slices of juicy mango. The sun sank slowly, throwing shadows and investing the ocean with a soft, mystical quality that caught and held her gaze for long minutes.

When the sun finally slid below the horizon, the air temperature dropped like a stone. After the burning heat of the day, cold seemed to seep out of the rocks, raising gooseflesh on her skin. The night sky was unbelievably clear, the stars huge and bright and almost close enough to touch.

Sienna offered to clean up and make coffee, abruptly glad to escape the romantic setting and the growing tension. She stiffened when Constantine put on soft music and sat beside her on the couch but, when he didn't do anything more than drape his arm along the back of the couch, she finally relaxed.

After what had happened that afternoon, she had been prepared for a passionate interlude she wasn't sure she could resist. Instead he seemed to be doing exactly what she had asked: backing off and giving her some time.

Exhaustion pulled at her as she listened to a Beethoven adagio. But she could not forget what had happened that afternoon. She had to wonder if she was pregnant.

Her hand moved, cupping her belly. Constantine's gaze followed the movement as if he was entertaining the exact same thought.

She was suddenly acutely aware of her body.

The first shock of the idea had passed. Having a child would definitely narrow her options, but the notion of having a baby had taken firm root.

As if he had read her mind his hand smoothed down one arm, his thumb absently stroking her. The touch was pleasant rather than sexual, as if he was aware of her turmoil and wanted to soothe her.

Gradually, she relaxed against him. She was dropping into a delicious dark well of contentment when his voice rumbled softly in her ear.

"If there's a likelihood that you're pregnant, then we should get married soon."

Her eyes popped open. Suddenly she was wide-awake.

He hadn't proposed, either back at the resort or here.

Maybe there was no need for an actual proposal. Strictly speaking, that formality had been taken care of by the contract, but that didn't change the fact that she would have liked one. Although demanding that would let him know exactly how vulnerable she was about their relationship. "When did you have in mind?"

"A week. Two at the most."

"I'll talk to Mom and give you some dates." It was a surrender. The only thing left to extract from her was an admission that she loved him, but she would hold back on that for as long as she could.

Maybe denying Constantine that final victory was childish, but she was afraid that if she surrendered emotionally he would no longer feel he had to fight for her. If Constantine deemed his battle won, she could lose any chance that he would eventually love her.

He wouldn't walk away this time, so the outcome would be much worse—they could end up locked together in a loveless marriage. She may have given up on the romantic fantasy of having him fall in love with her, but gaining a measure of love, however small, was vitally important.

"That's settled then," he said quietly. "I'll take care of the arrangements as soon as we get back."

Shortly after daybreak the *chop-chop* of a helicopter split the air as it set down on a concrete pad a short distance away.

Fifteen minutes after boarding the helicopter, they set down at Medinos's airport. Less than an hour later a car, driven by Tomas, deposited them at the *castello*.

Constantine had arranged to have her things delivered to the *castello* from the resort, so as soon as they arrived she was able to change into fresh clothes.

When she was dressed in a cool, ice-blue summer shift that ended midthigh, she slipped on sandals and strolled through broad, echoing hallways and vaulted rooms, looking for Constantine. When she didn't find him, she checked the ultramodern kitchen.

Classical music had been playing, but in the lull between CDs she heard voices. She walked down a hallway, which led to the front entryway and a series of reception rooms.

As she padded closer, she noticed a door that had been left slightly ajar. The conversation, originating from that room and naturally channeled by the acoustics of the hall, became clearer. She recognized the distinctive American accent of Constantine's legal advisor, Ben Vitalis.

"…good work getting the water rights transferred so quickly…"

Her fingers, which had closed around the brass door-knob, froze as Vitalis's voice registered more clearly. "…if Sienna had contested the estuarine lease, the marina project would have stalled indefinitely. We would have lost millions in contractor's kill fees."

There was a pause, the creak of a chair as if Vitalis had just sat down. "…Clever move, inserting the marriage clause. Even if she tries to contest the transfer of the lease, under Medinian law the rights will revert to you. Where are we with the loan?"

"The loan agreement is cut-and-dried."

The deep, incisive tones of Constantine's voice hit Sienna like a kick in the chest.

She went hot then cold. The reason Constantine had proposed a marriage of convenience in the same contract that settled her father's fraudulent debt was suddenly glaringly obvious. Somehow her father had messed up Constantine's development plans. Constantine had wanted to ensure that his marina went ahead unchecked and she had succumbed to his tactics with ridiculous ease.

A painful flood of memories swamped her—the clipped conversation that had ended their first engagement two years ago, Constantine's detachment after their lovemaking in Sydney.

She could forgive the way he had gone about seducing her. Even knowing she was being maneuvered, she had been helpless to resist because she had known with every cell of her body that the desire was heart-poundingly real. But this level of calculation was not acceptable. She would have to be willfully blind, deaf and dumb not to understand that a third, even more profound rejection, was in the works.

"Okay, then..." There was a click as if a briefcase had been opened, the slap of a document landing on either a table or a desktop. "Cast your eye over the child custody clause."

Feeling like an automaton, Sienna pushed the door wide and stepped into the room just as Vitalis flicked his briefcase closed and rose to his feet. Constantine's gaze connected with hers and her heart squeezed tight. She had wanted to be proved wrong, to discover that she'd gotten the conversation wildly out of context, but in that moment she knew she hadn't.

Nerves humming, she stepped around Vitalis, picked up the document lying on the desk and skimmed it.

Seconds later she literally felt the blood drain from her face. She didn't care about land or money. She cared that Constantine had manipulated her over the water rights. It was a betrayal of a very private kind that cut to the bone because it emphasized that he didn't simply want her; she was part of a business agenda. Even knowing that, she would have gone through with the marriage. But the children she might have were a different matter.

She didn't know what it was like to bear a child, but even without the physical reality of a child in her arms, she knew how fiercely she would care about her babies.

Vitalis had prepared an amendment to the marriage deal, granting Constantine custody and rights for any children. If she walked out on the marriage, she would be granted limited access to her children, but she could never take them with her.

Before he even knew she was pregnant, should she decide to leave the marriage, Constantine had arranged to take her babies from her as coolly and methodically as he had taken Ambrosi Pearls and her career.

She transferred her gaze to Constantine. "Did you actually think that I would sign this?"

Constantine pushed to his feet. Vitalis had already retreated, melting out of a side door she hadn't noticed.

"It's a draft Ben put together. You weren't supposed to see it yet. I intended to discuss options with you next week."

Options.

She could feel herself closing up, the warmth seeping from her skin. She had known she would have a struggle breaking through the protective armor of Constantine's business process. He thought she was tied to Ambrosi Pearls, but her focus on the family business was nothing compared to his. It was possible that she was even partly responsible for the way he was handling their relationship—as if it was a business merger—because of what had happened two years ago. "But this is the deal you want?"

His expression was guarded. "Not…exactly."

Not the answer she needed.

Blankly she struggled to readjust her internal lens. "I've spent two years beating myself up because I agreed to marry you knowing that my father had organized a finance deal with yours. That was such a crime."

She replaced the pages on his desk. She was toweringly angry and utterly miserable. Marriage was personal, intimate. When she had said she would marry Constantine, she had done so imagining that he could feel something real and special for her, that if it wasn't love right now it would grow to be one day. She had been operating on hope.

The exact opposite of this cold agreement.

Constantine pushed to his feet. "I want a wife who is committed to marriage and family."

She registered that he was still dressed casually in the

jeans and loose shirt he had been wearing when they had left Ambrus. The reminder of the hours they had spent together on the island was the last thing she needed. "So you drew up a contract."

"It wasn't as cold-blooded as that. We're sexually compatible. We share a lot in common."

With the bright glare of the sun behind him throwing his face into shadow, she was unable to discern emotion either way, and in that moment she desperately needed to see something. "From where I'm standing, the only true bond we share is a seven figure debt."

In a blinding flash, being part of Ambrosi Pearls ceased to be important. For years she had been consumed with saving the company. The struggle had taken every waking moment, but with the safety of the company employees and her family assured, she didn't have to continue fighting. None of them did. Constantine would fight the battle for them. She could let go, step back, because Constantine was more able to manage her family's company than she would ever be.

But the last thing she wanted was to step into a relationship that was defined by a maze of legal traps. "And to think, I let myself fall for you all over again."

Secure in the glimpses of the old Constantine, with whom she had fallen in love. Secure in the illusion that she had some womanly power and a measure of control.

Something shifted in his gaze. "Sienna…I didn't mean to hurt—"

"No. Just control, because that's what works for you. Control me, control any children, control your emotions." There would be no messy divorce or outrageous property settlements, because the bottom line was clear-cut. "You told me that you usually get exactly what you want. I guess that really is a marriage of convenience and two—"

Blindly, she flipped pages and checked the fine print, but couldn't distinguish individual words because her eyes were filmed with tears. "Or is that three children?"

Constantine speed-dialed Tomas as Sienna walked out of his office and bit out orders, sheer, blind panic making him break out in a cold sweat. Sienna was leaving the *castello* and the island. As much as he needed to keep her with him, he knew that if he tried to physically detain her, he would lose her forever.

The fact that he had considered holding her in the *castello*—in effect, perpetrating the kidnapping she had accused him of when he had taken her to the beach house on Ambrus—demonstrated his desperation.

When Sienna had registered the contents of the child custody clause he had understood the mistake he had made, that no amount of financial or legal pressure would make him first in Sienna's life, or bind her to him the way he needed her to be if she didn't want to be there.

In that moment he had recognized her; he had seen the steady fire and strength that had always unconsciously drawn him. He had seen flashes before—in Sydney after they had made love, in the walled garden of the hotel when she had thrown his blundering attempt to make her choose between Ambrosi Pearls and him back in his face.

She had said she had fallen for him and in that instant he had known that was the reason she had agreed to marriage, not the financial breaks.

That moment had stunned him. He realized he had been first in her life all along. It was his approach that had been flawed. He had been the one who was focused on business.

His only break was that she hadn't mentioned the marriage clause. They were still engaged, on paper at least.

Tossing the agreement in his briefcase, he strode upstairs to his suite and threw clothes into an overnight bag. Tomas would make sure Sienna couldn't get on a regular flight out of Medinos even if that meant he had to buy every empty seat on the outgoing flights.

Bleakly, he recognized that when it came to Sienna, the bottom line had never mattered. The first time he had laid eyes on her he had tumbled. He had known who she was, had recognized her instantly, and he had been entranced. The problem was he hadn't believed she would simply want him. In his own mind he could still remember what it was like to have nothing, and how lacking in popularity he had been then.

Money had changed their lives. Maybe he was overly sensitive, but he knew that when women looked at him now they saw his wealth. Like it had for his father, money had been the dominant factor in almost every relationship. He had made the mistake of assuming that because Sienna needed money, that she would need him.

He had been wrong.

Now, somehow, he had to make up for his mistake, to convince her that they still had a chance.

He didn't care what it took. He just wanted her back.

Tomas rang back. The private jet was fueled; there were no longer any available flights out of Medinos. If Sienna wanted to leave today, it would have to be on the Atraeus jet.

Constantine hung up and returned downstairs to collect the keys to the Maserati. She wouldn't like it. That was an understatement. Sienna would hate the forced proximity, but he knew with gut-wrenching clarity that he couldn't afford to let her go completely. Every second she was away from him would widen the gulf he had created between them.

Thirty minutes later, Constantine parked the Maserati at

the airport, completed the exit details and walked through to his private hangar. Tomas had informed him that Sienna was already on board.

During the flight Sienna barely acknowledged him, choosing to either sleep, or feign sleep, most of the way.

Constantine forced himself to remain calm. This was damage control. If he didn't fix the mistakes he had made they were finished, and he had made a number of serious errors.

Given the choice, he wouldn't have used a marriage deal. The document had filled him with distaste, but when it had come to dealing with Sienna and her attachment to Ambrosi Pearls, shock tactics had made sense.

She had cared about Ambrosi Pearls like most women cared about their child. From a teenager, she had literally had responsibility shoved at her. She had been so focused on sacrificing herself to make up for the damage her father had done, it was a wonder he had managed to get close to her at all.

He hadn't known every one of those facts when he had walked away from their first engagement, or understood the emotional battering she had taken. He had been so used to seeing her as in charge and ultraorganized that he had overlooked the fact that Sienna, herself, was a victim of her father's gambling problem.

Two years ago he had been coldly angry that Sienna hadn't told him about her father's losses or the loan Roberto had leveraged with his father. He hadn't wanted to address the reason he had reacted so strongly, but he did now.

What he felt for Sienna was different from anything else he had ever experienced.

The thought that she was pregnant, that there would be

FIONA BRAND   179

a baby, had expanded that feeling out to a second person he could possibly lose.

The constricted emotion in his chest tightened into actual pain. He had always known what that feeling was and the reason why he had been so furious at what he had perceived as Sienna's betrayal.

She was right. He had tried to control her and any children they might have and, in the process, his own emotions. But the legal clauses he had used to bind any children, and thus ensure that Sienna stayed with him, had achieved the exact opposite.

He had ensured that what he needed most, he would lose.

Sixteen

When The Atraeus Group's private jet landed in Sydney it was after eight in the evening and it was raining. After the heat of Medinos, the chill was close to wintry.

Numbly, Sienna refused a ride with Constantine. "I can take a taxi. All I need to do is pick up my car from my mother's house, then I'm driving back to my apartment."

Constantine's expression was grim as he skimmed the airport lounge. "I'll drop you at Pier Point. She'll be expecting it. But if you're not coming home with me—"

"I am not staying with you."

He cupped her elbow and steered her around a baggage cart. "Then stay out at Pier Point." He released her before she could shake free.

Sienna's stomach tightened at the brief, tingling heat of his hold. "If that's an order—"

He massaged the muscles at his nape, the first sign of frustration he'd shown since he had boarded the jet. Up until that moment, he had been frustratingly cool and remote.

"It's not an order, it's a...suggestion." He nodded his head in the direction of the press waiting in the arrival's lounge. Almost immediately the cameras started whirring and the questions started. "And that's why."

Thirty minutes of tense silence later, Constantine parked his Audi in her mother's driveway. He carried her luggage and the briefcase in, then stayed to talk with her mother and Carla for a few minutes. His gaze captured hers while he listened to her mother's stilted congratulations and for a moment she saw past the remote mask he'd maintained to a raw throb of emotion that made her heart pound.

Just before he left, he handed her an envelope. She checked the contents and saw the child custody agreement Vitalis had drawn up torn in two. When she glanced up, Constantine was already gone.

When the sound of the Audi receded, her mother fixed her with a steely glare. "Don't you dare sacrifice yourself for the business, or for us."

Her fingers shaking, she shoved the agreement and the envelope into her purse. "Don't worry, I'm not. If you don't mind, I need a cup of tea." Despite the comfortable flight, the fact that she had faked sleeping meant she had barely eaten or had anything to drink.

Carla frowned and motioned her onto one of the kitchen stools at the counter. "Sit. Talk. I'll make the tea."

Sienna sat and, in between sips of hot tea, concentrated on giving a factual account without the emotional highs and lows. When she'd finished, her mother set a sandwich down in front of her and insisted that she eat.

"To think, I used to like that boy."

Boy? Sienna almost choked on the sandwich. Constantine was six feet four inches of testosterone-laden muscle who could quite possibly have made her pregnant. *Boy* was the last descriptive she would have used.

Margaret Ambrosi lifted an elegant brow. "So did you agree to marry Constantine to save the business?"

"No." She took a bite of the sandwich, forcing it past the tightness in her throat. It was a fact that she wouldn't have agreed to marriage if she didn't love Constantine. "It's complicated."

"You're in love with him. Have been for years."

Sienna's cheeks burned. "Just whose side are you on?"

"Yours. Marry him or don't marry him, but stop worrying about us. If Ambrosi Pearls and this house have to go, so be it, it's your decision. You know Ambrosi Pearls was never my passion."

Sienna stared at the rest of her sandwich, her appetite gone. Constantine had hurt her, deeply enough that she had done nothing but consider refusing to go through with the marriage. After the long, silent flight, and the glimpse of raw loss she had seen in Constantine's gaze, she was almost certain that he would let her go. An ache rose up in her at the thought.

Her mother, with her usual clarity, had cut to the chase. They could survive without Atraeus money. When it came to the crunch, the only question was could she survive without Constantine?

She had told him point-blank on the ride out to Pier Point that she needed time to think things through. He hadn't liked it, but he had accepted her need for space.

That, and the fact that he had surrendered unconditionally on the child custody agreement, constituted progress. She didn't know how long it would take her to heal, but those two things at least signaled a painful step forward.

Her decision settled into place as she slowly sipped her

tea. She could go ahead with the marriage for one simple reason: as hurt as she was she couldn't contemplate not having Constantine in her life.

Two weeks later, the morning of the wedding in Medinos was balmy and relentlessly clear. Although, judging by the pandemonium that had broken out in the last half hour, with cousins, aunts and the hairdresser and makeup team descending en masse, it sounded more like a street riot than a wedding in progress.

Margaret Ambrosi had insisted that if she was getting married in Medinos they needed a house for her to be married from, so Constantine had arranged for a private villa to be made available. It was an old-fashioned idea, but Sienna hadn't minded. The extra fuss and bother had at least taken her mind off the risk she was taking.

Her mother, in combination with Tomas, had pulled all the elements of the wedding together with formidable efficiency, ruthlessly calling in favors to get everything done on time and using Constantine's name to smooth the way. They had organized the dress, the flowers, live music and a church choir, plus a full-scale reception at the *castello*.

Carla poked her head around the door and handed her an envelope. "This arrived for you. Thirty minutes to go. How are you feeling?"

Sienna's heart thumped in her chest as she took the envelope and checked her wristwatch. "Great."

Skittish and unhappy, because she had barely seen him after their stilted conversation the day after arriving in Sydney, when she had agreed to go through with the wedding. When she had, they had never been alone. She was beginning to believe that the loss she had glimpsed in his eyes had been another mirage.

The limousine was booked for eleven; it was ten-thirty.

So far everything had gone without a hitch. Her hair and makeup were done, her jewelry was on and her nails had finally dried.

Her dress was an elegant, sleeveless gown with a scoop neck, simply cut but made of layers of floaty white chiffon that swirled around her ankles as she walked. The petal-soft fabric was a perfect match for the pearl and diamond necklace and earrings her great-aunt had given her as a wedding gift. They were rare, original Ambrosi Pearls pieces.

When Carla shut the door behind her Sienna studied the envelope, her heart thumping hard in her chest when she recognized Constantine's handwriting. When she ripped the envelope open, she found all three copies of the marriage deal she'd signed along with a scribbled note. Constantine hadn't activated the deal or filed any of the paperwork. No shares had changed hands. Ambrosi Pearls was still registered as belonging to her family. The water rights were also enclosed.

In short, he had frozen the entire deal. With the paperwork in her hands she was free to destroy it all if she pleased. To all intents and purposes, it was as if there had never been a deal.

Her legs feeling distinctly wobbly, she sat on the edge of the bed. Constantine had chosen to walk away from exacting any kind of reparations for her father's scam. He now risked financial disaster with his new resort development. She should feel relieved, but all she could think about was, did this mean the wedding was off?

There was a second knock at the door. Carla again, this time with a telephone in one hand. "It's de Vries."

Not Northcliffe as she had expected but Hammond de Vries himself, the CEO of the large European retail conglomerate. The conversation was crisp and to the point.

They had reconsidered, and now wanted to place the order. The sum he offered was staggering. After a short conversation, Sienna hung up and set the phone down just as her mother stepped into the room.

In a lavender suit her mother looked elegant but frazzled. "Sienna—"

The door was pushed wide. Constantine, darkly handsome in a morning suit, stepped past Margaret Ambrosi. "If you'll excuse me, Mrs. Ambrosi, I need to speak to Sienna. Alone."

There was a startled exclamation when Constantine ushered her mother out of the door. "Five minutes," he said smoothly.

Sienna rose to her feet, her heart pounding, because Constantine was dressed for the wedding and because she suddenly knew, beyond doubt, the only fact she needed to know. "I turned de Vries down," she said calmly. "I know you're behind the offer, and I know why you made it."

His gaze was wary. "How did you know it was me?"

"Hammond de Vries doesn't normally call us. One of his buyers does. Besides, they've had my number for months. It was too much of a coincidence that he called today with an offer that would cover the loan. Plus…" She let out a breath. "I happen to know that The Atraeus Group recently bought a percentage of de Vries."

Constantine leaned against the door, his gaze narrowed. "Who told you?"

"An industry contact."

"That would be your mother."

"Who just happened to have a conversation with Tomas—"

His mouth twitched. "—who is putty in her hands."

"Most people are. So…the game's up. You gave me an

out. Or…" She was suddenly afraid to be so ridiculously, luminously happy. "Did you want the out?"

He pushed away from the door, his hands settled at her waist. "By now you have to know what I want. Marriage. But this time it has to be your choice, not just mine."

Sienna wound her arms around Constantine's neck and met his kiss halfway. Long seconds later, he loosened his hold and reached into his pocket. "Just one more thing."

Emotion shimmered through her as he went down on one knee and opened a small, black velvet box. He extracted the ring, a princess-cut white diamond that glowed with an intense, pure fire. "Sienna Ambrosi, will you marry me and be my love?"

Her throat closed on a raw throb, her eyes misted. "Yes."

Constantine slid the ring onto the third finger of her left hand.

"You do love me." Giddy delight spread through her as he rose to his feet and pulled her close. She wound her arms around his neck and held on tight.

He rested his forehead against hers. "I've loved you since the first time I saw you. I can still remember the moment."

"Before the shoe incident?"

"About five seconds before my clumsy attempt at Prince Charming." His mouth curved in a slow smile. "I just had some growing up to do. Make that a lot of growing up."

He bent his head and touched his mouth to hers, and for long seconds she seemed to float. Although the moments of dizziness she had begun to experience in the mornings had an entirely different source.

When he lifted his head and she could breathe again, he ran his hands down her back, molding her against him. The touch was reassuring. She was vulnerable, but so was he; it had just taken him longer to know it.

There was a sharp rap. Margaret Ambrosi's head popped around the side of the door. She wanted to know what was going on, and she wanted to know now.

"It's all right, Mom. The wedding's on."

"Oh, good. I'll inform the limousine driver. I'm sure he'll be delighted, since he's waiting out front."

The door snapped closed, Constantine kissed her again.

Another sharp rap on the door had Sienna pinning on her veil and reaching for her bouquet. She glanced at Constantine, who was showing no signs of moving.

He twined his fingers with hers and gave her another sweet kiss, this time through the veil.

She pushed at his chest. "You need to leave. We'll be late."

"I'm not leaving," he said simply. He tugged her toward the door, a smile in his eyes.

"This time we go together."

* * * * *